PENGUIN BOOKS

The
PRINCESS
of
POTENTIAL

About the Author

Delemhach is the Canadian author of the popular series The House Witch and is already hard at work on the sequel series, The Burning Witch. When they aren't following the whims of their unfortunately intelligent cats, Kraken and Pina Colada, they are teaching music privately to their students. In their spare time outside of writing and work, they enjoy cooking, reading, hiking, spending time with family, and trying not to remember their socially awkward moments.

The
PRINCESS
of
POTENTIAL

Delemhach
Emilie Nikota

PENGUIN BOOKS

PENGUIN BOOKS

UK | USA | Canada | Ireland | Australia
India | New Zealand | South Africa

Penguin Books is part of the Penguin Random House group of companies
whose addresses can be found at global.penguinrandomhouse.com

Penguin
Random House
UK

First published by Podium Publishing ULC, 2023
First published in Penguin Books, 2024
001

Copyright © Emilie Nikota, 2023

The moral right of the author has been asserted

Printed and bound in Great Britain by Clays Ltd, Elcograf S.p.A.

The authorized representative in the EEA is Penguin Random House Ireland,
Morrison Chambers, 32 Nassau Street, Dublin D02 YH68

A CIP catalogue record for this book is available from the British Library

ISBN: 978-1-405-96705-1

www.greenpenguin.co.uk

MIX
Paper | Supporting
responsible forestry
FSC® C018179

Penguin Random House is committed to a
sustainable future for our business, our readers
and our planet. This book is made from Forest
Stewardship Council® certified paper.

To Sophie and Léa,
the princesses of potential in our family.

Chapter 1

TAKE A BREATH

A discordant chord rang out into the king's forest outside the city of Austice in the kingdom of Daxaria, followed by the dulcet tones of a young woman.

"There once was a cook in our castle,
My father said he was quite a . . . Hassle.
He saved my mother and I,
Then fought a dragon and . . .
Bloody hell, I should juust die."

Letting out a long breath, the young woman dropped her pale forehead to her hand and let her other hand fall away from the lute in her lap.

"Gods, why in the world my father thought singing in the woods would help, I'll never know. Bunch of moss and ferns aren't going to make me a better singer or fix my ruddy lungs," she muttered while slowly standing.

A loud fly whirred by her ear, making her slap its dark body against her neck and dirty blond hair.

"Muggy . . . Buggy forest . . . who in the world would—"

A rustle in the trees off in the distance startled her from her mumblings, making her go still. A surge of fear sent her heart racing.

"I . . . better . . . go . . . back . . . to the castle . . . as quickly . . . as . . . I can . . ." The young woman felt sweat prickle the back of her neck as she began walking. Another small rustle sounded behind her, making her jump.

"WHATTHEHELLARETHEREBEARSINHERE?!" Breaking into a sprint the young woman barreled through the final line of trees, and immediately clutched her chest as her gasps rattled her lungs.

"Oh Gods . . . not now." Sinking to her knees, Alina tried over and over again to take in a full breath that refused to come. To make matters worse, the sound of footfalls neared her, making her stress triple. Luckily, despite her struggles, she managed to rest her lute gently in the grass at her side.

"—Ina! Princess Alina! Are you having one of your attacks?! I'll send for the physician! Peter, stay with Her Highness!"

The young royal of Daxaria looked up, with tears streaming from her eyes as a result of her efforts to draw in any of the heavy air, and found herself staring up at a servant she hadn't seen since she was very young . . . Hannah, was it?

The elder aide by her side was a tall, lean fellow, with a kind, caring expression, his cheeks dashed with scars that were clearly from having pox in his youth. His hair was gray, but there were touches of brown in places that showed his original hair color.

"Princess! Hannah has gone for help; shall I carry you to the kitchen for a drink of water?"

Alina was unable to communicate past nodding her head as the ache in her chest grew worse, and she struggled once more to regain her breath. Though was it perhaps now starting to come back just a little?

It felt like an hour, but perhaps was less than one before the new Royal Court Physician, Harold Mudge, arrived in the kitchen.

"Here, Princess, I have the vapors in my bag. You there, please help open the princess's stays so that I might rub the ointment on her chest," the physician ordered the maid Hannah while Peter politely excused himself.

Alina could feel her cheeks burn with embarrassment.

Stupid bear in the woods . . . I can't believe this is happening the very first day I arrive in Austice.

The moment she regained an ounce of breath, the first words out of the princess's mouth were, "Please . . . please don't tell my father. There's . . . really . . . no . . . need."

Entering the banquet hall wearing a forest green dress covered with a long vest with a golden pattern that draped down into her train, the princess could feel all eyes turn to her.

Her father sat at his place at the head of the banquet table, while her brother's chair sat empty, as did her mother's.

As usual.

"Presenting Her Royal Highness, the Crown Princess of Daxaria!"

The familiar voice of her father's assistant, Mr. Kevin Howard, rang out into the hall, and as was the norm at events like this, everyone bowed or curtsied before her.

Alina's hazel eyes scanned the many familiar heads of courtiers who had remained by her father's side for many years, even in Rollom, but there were some new ones amongst them.

After all, this wasn't a normal visit to Austice.

As Alina walked, she did her best not to think about her breath; otherwise, even *that* could bring on an attack. The thought of having a physician rub salve on her in the midst of all the guests was the furthest thing from appealing to her in that moment. Especially with her father there.

He always overreacted when anything was wrong with her . . . and it had gotten much worse since her mother had died three years earlier.

Alina sat down in her chair and gave her father her best reassuring smile, which he returned with his own warm grin. Though as usual, there was a bit of a sadness to it. The next few months were sure to be riddled with these melancholy moments . . .

Turning back to the guests, the king raised a goblet. "Lords and ladies, I thank you for joining us here in our fair Austice. It has been a great many years since we have returned to this city, and it feels like a homecoming to return to my cherished daughter's birthplace. I hope you all enjoy the rose maze, as well as the glass tower with Mr. Jelani's spectacular gardens and trees with some exotic blooms I doubt many could have otherwise laid eyes upon. The library on the third floor is welcome to all, and feel free to enjoy a leisurely walk in the woods; though please resist hunting until our expedition next week."

Everyone present shared knowing smiles. All Daxarians knew that the castle of Austice was riddled with fantastical nooks and crannies . . . not the least of which was the mysterious skeleton of the dragon that was rumored to be hidden somewhere in Austice. It had become a long-running tradition of the nobles and visitors to try and discover where the bones were kept after they had been returned from the Isle of Wittica.

Some guessed that they were buried on the castle grounds. Others speculated that each bone lay in the former queen's beloved rosebushes. Some thought it a made-up story . . . Regardless of the particular theory, the allure of intrigue and magic was too difficult to ignore, even for the most stern of souls.

Dinner was served.

Alina stared down at her plate and began cutting and chewing in her usual methodical way while also wondering if different musical scores were kept in the library there in Austice or if—

"Oh Gods." The princess regarded her plate with renewed interest. It was just chicken, yet there was . . . a sauce? A white creamy sauce unlike any she'd ever tried before coated the breast while its interior was stuffed with gooey white cheese and a different sort of tomato. How did it taste so . . . perfect?

"Ah, I wanted you to be surprised," Norman murmured, pleased by his daughter's reaction.

"Father?" Alina asked, bewildered as she tentatively reached for a golden dinner roll, still steaming hot.

"A certain . . . *cook* . . . decided to lend a hand in preparing tonight's dinner." Norman's eyes twinkled jovially.

"Lord Ashowan cooked this?!" Alina burst out, only managing to remember to cover her mouth at the last moment to make sure no one overheard.

"He did indeed. I don't think you've seen him since you were a little girl after we went to Rollom to get the city back on its feet. He has two children near your age."

"Wait, are they . . . they're witches?" Alina whispered excitedly. She had heard countless stories and heard multiple ballads about the house witch, but her own memory of him was vague. A pair of knees. A few kind words. Mostly how thrilled her brother was about seeing him . . .

Despite him being a diplomat for the Coven of Wittica, Finlay Ashowan rarely left Austice and, unless the situation was truly dire, only communicated with her father via messenger. Whenever his duties brought him to the city, Fin ended up checking on his own estates and the schools he was working with the Coven of Wittica to establish.

"Fin's children? I am not certain, my dear one. He believes that when and or if his children feel like sharing about their abilities, it should be on their own terms. Though . . . back before his mother passed she did seem to believe one of them was a fire witch."

Alina straightened in her chair. Perhaps this was the perfect moment to find inspiration to write a song.

Craning her neck to look through the crowd, she was disappointed to find that she couldn't see anyone who looked extraordinary or mystical.

Norman chuckled beside her.

"They're eating in the kitchen, but they will come greet us after dessert is served."

Alina frowned. She was about to ask why nobility would be eating in the kitchen, when two men clad in black entered the banquet hall, causing everyone to fall silent.

"His Majesty, the King of Troivack, Brendan Devark, and Prince Henry Devark," Mr. Howard announced, a slight hesitancy in his voice.

The king of Troivack was a giant amongst men, broad, tall, and yet his steps were silent. Surprisingly, he was clean-shaven, unlike most Troivackian men, with straight black hair. His brother, Henry, while equally broad, was several inches shorter. His features were softer, his eyes kinder, and even his hair was an inch or two shorter than his brother's with small curls remaining close to his scalp.

Norman stood, as did Alina. When the Troivackian royalty reached the table, there was a long tense moment when neither side moved. Then, Henry bowed, Alina followed with her curtsy, followed by Brendan's bow, and finally, Norman.

A proper greeting that could have set a very hostile tone if the Troivackian prince had ignored it.

"We thank you for welcoming us to Daxaria, Your Majesty," Brendan declared loudly after straightening from his stiff bow. His eyes conveyed a dark abyss of nothing, which was deeply disconcerting.

Norman's gaze remained steady. "I thank you for traveling with the requested arrangements. May your stay be enjoyable."

The Troivackians gave barely discernible bows of their chins. Most of the courtiers in the room were sharing judgmental glances with one another that Alina couldn't help but notice.

"You are welcome to join me at my table. Royal Mage Keith Lee will make some room for you down there." Norman looked to a man in his early forties sporting an impressively bushy sandy brown beard, round glasses, and an overly eager smile.

The foreign nobility nodded their understanding; however, Prince Henry shot Alina a quick conspiratorial wink as he turned away, which took the princess aback immensely.

I thought they weren't friendly or expressive . . .

The princess did her best to ignore the odd exchange and instead immersed herself in the fantastical flavors of her food that were blowing away every expectation she had of her meals going forward in her life.

By the time she was polishing off her plate, however, she found that it was rather easy not to worry about trivial matters such as tensions with a foreign king when her meal sated something far deeper in her soul than hunger.

Settling into her ornate high-back chair, Alina felt a deep contentment settle over herself as she neared the full feeling that brought her to the threshold of intoxicating drowsiness.

"Presenting Viscount Finlay Ashowan, Viscountess Lady Annika Ashowan, Lady Katarina, and Lord Tamlin Ashowan of House Jenoure."

Mr. Howard's voice had a strange choked sound to it when the doors opened to reveal . . .

A tall redhead with a touch of white at his temples, escorting a woman whose hair was streaked with gray but who was, despite her age, still remarkably beautiful.

Behind them strode in their children.

The young lady was uncharacteristically tall for a woman, but slender. Her long gleaming red hair caught every stray ray of light, and what her hair missed, her unworldly golden eyes picked up. Never in her life had Alina seen eyes so animalistic or interesting, surveying the room as they would a forest full of prey. Lady Katarina wore a midnight blue gown with a silvery long vest, while her brother was clad in black from head to toe save for the coat around his shoulders that was gray and made of a fine silk.

Speaking of Lady Katarina's brother, for all the brilliant color in his sister's striking face, he was her antithesis. With his black hair that was long enough to touch his shoulders, the scraggly ends hung like curtains hiding the details of his face—including his dark brown eyes that matched his mother's.

The only similarities the two siblings shared was their remarkable height, high cheekbones, and catlike slanted eyes.

The young man seemed desperate to focus on the point nearest to his feet rather than his surroundings, while his sister's stare in contrast seemed determined to sear through anyone who dared to meet her glowing eyes.

The viscount and viscountess approached the king's table, and both bowed and curtsied with the epitome of grace.

"Your Majesty, it has been far too long." The viscount greeted King Norman with a warm smile that sent many fans fluttering in the hall.

Despite being in his midforties, Finlay Ashowan looked remarkably young . . . as though he had only aged perhaps a decade instead of nearly two.

The viscountess rose from her curtsy and addressed the king demurely. "I've prayed for your family's health every day."

There was a note of pain in her tone that was not lost on Alina.

She had met the viscountess far more often than she had the viscount and their children.

Annika Ashowan had been her mother's best friend, and she had seen her quite often until the queen's passing three years prior . . . though not since then.

Norman bowed his head in thanks, his eyes warm with genuine affection.

"Thank you, Viscountess. Your children have grown well. Lady Katarina, Lord Tamlin, you are the princess's age, are you not?"

The willowy redhead curtsied and rose with an odd half smile that was far too mischievous to be ladylike. "I believe my brother and I are just under a year younger, Your Majesty."

With another pleased smile and nod, Norman's eyes moved to the viscount's, and it was in that moment that a peculiar emotion crossed the king's face that pricked Alina's curiosity.

There was happiness . . . genuine happiness, but also . . . apprehension. It was as though the viscount's presence with his family meant something entirely unique to her father.

Seeing this made the princess all the more eager to learn as much as possible about the mysterious house witch and his kin as soon as possible.

Chapter 2

MEETING THE ASHOWANS

Norman eyed his daughter's uncharacteristic stillness out of the corner of his eye with a rare smile of amusement. In the privacy of his personal library with its comfortable plush ruby red couches in front of the hearth, the quiet tomes around them insulating the space against the faint summer breeze ebbing in from the tall peaked windows, it brought back fond memories of Ainsley.

Back when the former queen was still alive, after dinner sitting in front of the fire, reading well into the night once the children had been put to bed . . .

It had been one of her favorite spaces in Austice. One that Ainsley never got to share with their daughter.

"Did you say the viscount's family was going to join us?" Alina interrupted her father's thoughts, her eyes glued on the shadowed doorway.

Norman's lighthearted mindset seeped back as he watched his daughter struggle to maintain her normally quiet gracefulness. Amongst nobility she seemed meek. Quiet, but always gracious and performing her duties well.

Alone with her family, however, she had the most endearing quirks and infectious smile.

"Yes, I believe Lord Ashowan is merely seeing that the kitchen aides are fine for the evening before bringing his family up to join us."

"He still seems very interested in the kitchen. It's surprising given that he really doesn't have to bother with that anymore —"

The princess's words were cut short when the brattle of the latch interrupted her, making her spine straighten once more, her hands folded in her lap eagerly.

The first to step through the doorway was the viscountess. Her silky long black-and-gray hair was swept back in an elegant hairstyle that showed off the ruby jewels glittering in her ears.

The moment her dark eyes rested on Alina, she gave a heart-melting smile that made the younger woman blush self-consciously. The look in Annika Ashowan's eyes made the princess feel as though she knew every part of her soul, and the depth of the viscountess's knowledge and affection took the princess aback.

After Annika came her daughter, Lady Katarina Ashowan. She had a friendly smile on her face, but there was a glint of cleverness in her golden eyes that Alina already suspected meant she could be a bit of the impish sort.

The future viscount, Lord Tamlin Ashowan, stepped in next. His dark hair still blocked a clear view of his expression as he kept his head lowered.

Then, at long last, in swept the viscount. His startling blue eyes shimmered in the candlelight of the room as he cast a handsome smile at the king before he and his entire family bowed and curtsied to the royals.

"Enough with the formalities, Fin, it's just us," Norman said with a chuckle, and Alina felt her heart tingle.

Her father hadn't laughed so readily in years . . . nor had he spoken so casually to anyone other than Mr. Howard and Lord Fuks for just as long.

The viscount grinned, allowing his shoulders to relax as he removed his elegant black-and-gold coat to reveal a plain black tunic, immediately making him look more approachable.

"Thank the Gods. These formal coats are going to smother me to death, I swear."

"You should try wearing the royal mantle sometimes. Wonderful for the winter, but in the summer I feel as though I need to change every hour due to the sweat," the king said with a sympathetic smile while he, too, leaned back comfortably in his seat.

Both the viscount and viscountess were already moving around the couches to take a seat, leaving their children to dawdle behind them.

Lady Katarina nudged her brother and whispered, "It's fine. It's a library."

Alina's eyebrow twitched in curiosity. Watching carefully, she witnessed the young man gradually straighten his shoulders, though it was clear that it was not easy for him. He then set to tying back half of his hair from his face, and Alina had to admit she was more than a little surprised by how handsome he was. Even with his eyes never quite fully lifting from the floor, she realized then that the young man had taken more after the viscount in the shapes and angles of his features than she had originally realized.

Norman observed the exchange and turned to Fin with a questioning eyebrow raised, but the redhead only gave his head a slight shake to discourage anything being asked aloud about his son's obvious trepidations.

What is wrong with him? the princess couldn't help but wonder while thinking Tamlin Ashowan looked able-bodied enough as he moved to take a seat next to his sister. *Perhaps he is partly blind?*

"How have you been, Princess? Despite watching my own children grow up, I must say it is quite alarming to see you as a young adult!" The viscount turned to Alina, his smile genuine and his eyes twinkling as though looking upon a favorite niece.

"I didn't realize we had been familiar with each other when I was young, my lord, forgive me," she replied with a graceful nod of her chin.

It was the viscountess who let out a beautiful laugh then. "Goodness! Such poise and elegance; Ainsley would be proud."

Alina turned her gaze nervously to her father, her heart falling with a splash into her stomach, drenching her with worry.

Sure enough, the recurring look of pain crossed the king's face, tearing her apart. Everyone knew that they should never bring up—

"Alina, love, did I ever tell you that it was actually the viscount here who delivered you?" Norman looked to Fin, his saddened smile at least still tinged with gladness.

The princess turned her startled and somewhat mortified gaze to the redhead, who looked appropriately bashful.

"I-I thought it was your mother, Katelyn Ashowan, who had done that, Viscount Ashowan?"

"Er . . . well . . . she was doing many things surgically at the time for the queen, but I was the one who pulled you free and held you first. In fact, we had an excellent chat shortly afterward," the viscount recounted modestly with his ears turning red.

Alina felt her previous embarrassment dissipate. "Well, I thank you for pulling me into the world and having what I hope to be a thrilling first conversation."

The viscount shrugged with a small devious smile stowed away in the corner of his mouth. "You were the quiet type . . . a little lippy at the end of it, but I understand people can get agitated when hungry."

Norman snorted and began laughing a little more heartily.

Alina stared at her father, stunned for a moment, then felt relief wash over her, only remembering to respond to the noble's jest belatedly. "I promise you, I've improved greatly as a conversationalist, my lord."

"Oh Gods . . . please call me Fin. It's weird to hear that title in present company." The redhead shook his head, making Alina smile again. He really was an affable man. It was clear why anyone would like him.

"So, Princess, are you excited to meet the young men here to ask you for your hand?" the viscountess spoke up then.

Funny enough, for all her beauty and formidable appearance, and even after her initial tender look at Alina, Viscountess Ashowan had somehow managed to sink into the periphery of the group . . . something about her presence had withdrawn, though Alina couldn't fathom how.

"It is . . . somewhat nerve-wracking," the princess replied with strained politeness.

"Mum, who asks that kind of question? She barely even knows you!" Lady Katarina burst out while looking at her mother incredulously.

The viscountess gave a small wince as she turned and gave her daughter a firm look.

"I wasn't going to ask anything more. I just wanted to see how much interference I should run on Her Highness's behalf. Also, please call me Annika." The viscountess had placed a hand subconsciously over her daughter's while giving a small bow toward Alina.

"I'm not sure I understand what you mean about running interference, Viscountess—I mean, Annika."

"Well, if the idea of choosing a groom was truly abhorrent to you, I would've made you a very difficult young woman to find." Annika shrugged innocently, earning a suspicious and accusatory side glance from the king.

"Oh, while . . . while that is . . . considerate, of you, Viscountess—er, Annika—I know it is my duty. Besides, it has been delayed for three years at my behest. My father has been most considerate of it and he—"

"Alina, truly. You do not need to talk to these people as you do most." Norman issued his daughter a reassuring smile before turning back to the noble couple. "After Ainsley's death, we could've pushed ahead with the marriage season, but I was not ready as you know. Alina wanted to wait the following years as well, so we did. I'm not in any great hurry to send her off, so I was happy to let the matter rest for a time."

Fin nodded in understanding. "I'm fortunate that my daughter terrifies most suitors."

"Oh, please, it was you who began beheading a pig in front of the last man to come looking for me." Katarina snorted before rolling her eyes.

Fin stroked his clean-shaven face thoughtfully. "Herbert *was* a squeamish fellow . . . Ah well. I'm just grateful it wasn't anything I fed him that wound up being vomited and splattered all over the—"

"My dear, how about we allow the young adults to visit amongst themselves. Children, would you perhaps like to go see the rose maze, or the courtyard if your father doesn't mind, Princess?" Annika interrupted, her voice only slightly louder than before, yet still commanding the room.

Norman smiled. "A grand idea. Off you three go. Get to know one another. I'm sure you three will have a healthy store of horror stories to share about your parents. Enjoy. You're in good company together."

The young adults glanced at one another uncertainly, save for Tamlin, whose eyes hadn't left the floor and who frowned in acknowledgment of the king's words.

"I vote for the rose maze. The courtyard has a lot of nosy maids that see my hair and immediately ask about Da for some reason," Katarina grumbled while standing and stretching in a most unladylike way before stepping toward the door.

Alina said nothing, only trailed after the tall redheaded woman while waiting for Tam to move over to join them.

As the trio exited the room and strode quietly through the corridors, they at long last greeted the cool night at the east wing exit.

Katarina threw her arms in the air and let out a loud moan mixed with a sigh. "Oh, thank the Gods. It was stifling in there. Sorry, Tam, I held on for as long as I could."

"It's fine."

Alina looked up at the lord, startled. It was the first time she had heard him speak, and she hadn't expected his voice to be so velvety and low.

Stepping down carefully, Alina worried briefly about missing a step as her eyes adjusted to the darkness, only to then find that Tam was offering her his arm.

"Oh, thank you, but shouldn't you also help your sister?" Alina observed lightly while also accepting his sleeve and safely stepping down on the soft grass.

"She doesn't need help. She can see just fine," he replied before quickly releasing the royal's hand.

"O-Oh . . ." Hundreds of questions burned Alina's throat as she concentrated on the back of Katarina Ashowan, who was swinging her arms back and forth gaily as she walked toward the maze.

"You're wondering if it's because I'm a witch, aren't you?" Katarina whirled around, and Alina was startled to see her golden eyes were glowing in the dark.

It would've been an absolutely terrifying sight in the inky night if she hadn't known who they belonged to . . .

"I'm sorry. I'm sure you don't want any unwanted questions," the princess began despite desperately wanting the answer.

Katarina waved her hand dismissively as Alina joined her side with Tam trailing behind them.

"No, no, you're the nice sort. That is one thing my parents are always great at knowing pretty quickly. They know good people when they meet them. We don't mind you knowing a bit about us. I'm a mutated witch. My strength is aligned with fire, though while my magic is incredibly weak, I do have handy little skills. Seeing in the dark is one. Not needing much sleep, if any, is another. Hm . . . what am I forgetting Tam?"

"You're the skinniest pig that's ever walked the earth," her brother replied without missing a beat.

"Ah, yes. I can, at times, be endlessly hungry. I've outeaten all my family members combined when I've been doing a lot of walking, or riding, or . . . other activities. I burn through it all. Oh! I also am always warm. It doesn't matter if the ground is covered in ice and snow, I will be a human coal pan. It's one reason I dislike being in stuffy rooms. It's also one of the reasons it is very difficult for me to get sick. Which is nice . . . though when I do, it's bloody murder."

Alina drank in the information as though it were the water from the Goddess's sacred pool before turning to look over her shoulder. "Tam . . . mind if . . . if I ask what . . . ?" Somehow, she knew the answer wouldn't be quite as forthcoming from the other Ashowan twin.

"Oh, uh . . . well," Katarina flashed her brother a quick glance over her shoulder, locking eyes with him for a brief moment, before he flitted his eyes back down to the ground.

"He is technically also a mutated witch, but . . . ah . . . no one knows what he can do."

"I see . . . do you have problems with your eyes?" Alina faced the young man as she walked, unable to contain her curiosity any longer.

Only, Katarina tapped her shoulder and drew her gaze back. "He doesn't, but he doesn't like big open rooms and spaces. It's one reason we won't be attending many banquets or balls unless necessary."

Alina nodded in understanding, her earlier guess confirmed: that while the one Ashowan was an open book, the other was firmly shut.

"Now, we've already shared some pretty juicy details; how about you tell us what you know about our father and your brother getting into a fight and not speaking to each other? Where is your brother, Prince Eric, anyway? Isn't he supposed to be here to help judge the suitors?"

Alina felt her mouth clamp shut.

She was beginning to understand her father's complicated expression from earlier that day.

While the Ashowan family was undoubtedly likable, and seemed genuinely kind, there was something about how they could cut through with ease to the heart of anyone and reveal all the wounds and secrets one had ... and yet still make you feel drawn to them.

Taking a deep breath, the princess braced herself. She could already tell that she was doomed to be horrifically good friends with the Ashowan family.

Chapter 3

SPILLING THE TEA

Norman sank even farther into his chair, the fire crackling happily beside him as he gave his friends a weary half smile.

Annika and Fin offered similar expressions in return, before sharing knowing looks with each other. Leaning forward so that his elbows would rest on his knees, the witch looked to his king sympathetically.

"Alina seems great, though a bit . . . on edge," he observed while lightly clasping his hands together.

"She's the light of our lives. Truly. I'm deeply saddened that we are looking to wed her off already; if I could have even one more year . . ." Sighing and shaking his head, the monarch straightened his shoulders. "No. It'll always be the same. Just wanting one more year, one extra day, or one extra second where she is my daughter, and my daughter only. Not someone's wife, or . . . Gods . . . someone's mother . . ."

Closing his eyes, Norman dropped his forehead to his hand.

"I can't imagine how tough this is." Fin's quiet voice and Annika's sorrowful stare were beginning to make the king feel choked up as he wished he could be sharing their company with Ainsley.

"Well, one day you will know. Your daughter, Katarina, is incredibly striking. You've made a daughter with the bearing of a queen, and the beauty to match — perhaps a little quick to be informal. Though I don't have to speculate who she got that trait from," Norman mused fondly as Fin laughed and Annika let out a very telling sigh that bore a hint of exasperation.

"So if you do not mind sharing, what is the story behind your son, Tam?" The king's eyes moved to Annika, but when he recognized the impenetrable stony wall of emotion, they returned to Fin, whose expression of deep guilt and pain alarmed Norman greatly.

"We don't . . . exactly know. Tam was, until the age of five, a normal child. Incredibly quiet, and always observing, but he would laugh and play with other children, often trying to talk Katarina out of trouble or apologizing for her when he failed." Fin's eyes with their ethereal glimmering shone a little brighter.

"What happened to him?" Norman asked, his concern for the heir to the viscount house deepening.

"One day, he was terrified. Terrified beyond anything a child his age should feel. I-I felt it. I could feel his heart-stopping fear . . . but I couldn't see where he was or what caused it. You know if members of my direct family feel endangered or scared that I see visions of where they are, but I couldn't that day. All I know is, Katarina returned half carrying him as he cried uncontrollably from the lawn at the back of the castle."

Norman's frown grew even more worried as Annika looked as though she were fighting off her own despair and sadness.

"Kat didn't know what had happened. She said she had run off to play with one of the boys, and that she couldn't find Tam for hours . . ."

"Did someone take him?" Norman asked seriously, while sitting tall in his seat once more.

"We have no idea. She says she found him near the cottages on the castle grounds crying and unable to speak. He refused after that to receive any magic training despite us not even knowing what magical power he possesses in any capacity. Tam did agree to the usual tests to determine his power, but they were inconclusive. All we know is that he becomes agitated in big rooms or spaces and doesn't like looking up much. It's like he's scared all the time. Sometimes it's as though he thinks, if he looks up, he will see the devil himself smiling at him.

Fin shook his head and rubbed his eyes wearily. "Whatever or whoever did this to Tam, I want to break with my own hands. However, he won't talk about it. I don't even know if Kat knows what happened, and she normally knows everything about him."

Norman's frown was starting to strain his forehead. The entire situation was alarming, and he couldn't deny that it had affected a small plan of his . . . "I won't lie to you, Ashowan, I strongly considered your son as a candidate for Alina's hand. She'd be in a family I trusted, and with ties to the coven, but . . ."

"Tam is troubled. I am genuinely worried about the day that he is meant to take over as viscount, let alone marry," Annika interrupted while giving the king a very firm look.

"I can see that now. Don't worry, I won't bring it up again." Norman held up his hands easily. "Besides, everyone is hoping for her to marry a duke at the very least."

Fin nodded. "A few unpleasant nobles already gossip about my commoner background as is. Alina doesn't need to have those insults hurled her way. Nor do you need any more headaches."

Norman smiled. "Since when do you care a whit about my headaches?"

The redhead grinned mischievously. "I'm competitive, you see, I have to be the biggest one."

Laughing, the king settled back into his seat. "Don't worry, you place in a very firm second. Right after that cat of yours. Tell me . . . how much longer is it that familiars normally live compared with other animals of their species?"

"Hard to say . . . Kraken is already twenty and says he feels fantastic. He might die only ten years before I do if he's affected by my mother's curse."

Norman's eyes narrowed and even Annika couldn't stop herself from chuckling.

"You haven't had to live with him in years, Your Majesty. I promise Kraken has calmed down a bit," Fin said, attempting to soothe the ruler's obvious agitation.

The low grumble that emitted from the king made Fin laugh.

"Well, don't worry, we are living in our estate in Austice, so there shouldn't be any pressing matters that require him to be here."

The king looked at the witch warily for a moment, before his expression faded to one of a more serious nature.

"Are you ever going to tell me what happened between you and Eric?"

Fin froze. "What have you heard?"

"Nothing. Nothing from either of you, which makes this whole silence strange . . . I have a hard enough time hearing from my son. Ever since Ainsley's death he has spent all his time in Sorlia and is always conveniently busy. I'm lucky if I see a letter from him for the Winter Solstice these days." Norman sighed and cast his eyes to the fire. He failed to notice the hard expression on the redhead's face, or the spark of anger in his eyes.

"I'm hoping he at least comes back in time for Alina's engagement ceremony, though he did indicate it might not be until the wedding . . . I'm beginning to worry I shouldn't even hope for that."

Annika gently rested her hand on her husband's shoulder. "Your Majesty, would you like to hear what the workers under Elizabeth Nonata have been able to gather from the Troivackian king's entourage?"

Giving his head a shake, Norman returned his attention to the viscountess. "Of course. Are his men respectful? Violent? What news have they brought of Troivack?"

The rest of the evening's discussions carried on between the trio without further mention of the children; however, that did not mean they were far from their parents' minds. In fact, the information that had been shared definitely required more consideration.

For one, Norman hadn't been completely honest about giving up on the notion that Tamlin Ashowan could be a favorable husband for his daughter.

Wincing as she cranked the lute's peg, Alina continued plucking the poor string until it succumbed to her will.

"There you are. No funny business today, you understand, Beau? I get you all to myself for exactly an hour. So there better be no trickery with the tuning," the princess muttered as she strummed a couple of chords to warm up her hands.

"Now, where did I leave off? . . . Let's see . . . I tried singing about the house witch last time but that was a failure . . . his daughter is incredibly striking. She seems so . . . intense!" Alina closed her eyes, her knee beginning to bounce frantically as she searched her mind for inspiration.

"Then his son, Tam, is . . . not right. Something is strange about him. Is it because of magic? Or is he just mentally ill?" the princess speculated aloud to her empty chamber as the quiet morning outside her window failed to offer any sort of explanation.

"Well, I suppose the mystery around him could make for an intriguing ballad." Switching to a minor chord, Alina hummed experimentally, when a loud knock interrupted her.

"Of course," she lamented under her breath. "Enter."

In strode her handmaidens and the elderly Head of Housekeeping, Ruby.

"Your Highness, it is time to prepare for your courting time with the king of Troivack."

It took all of Alina's etiquette training to stop herself from groaning.

"That isn't for at least three hours, why in the world do I—"

"Forgive me, Princess. We won't be so fastidious for all your courting dates, but this is for the most esteemed guest present. He is the monarch of another kingdom and is the highest ranking—"

"I understand; pardon my exasperation," Alina managed with a sigh, even though she wanted to kick them out to enjoy her morning in peace.

Ruby smiled warmly down at her. "We shall go as quickly as possible, Your Highness. I must say, I was delighted to hear that you have developed such a lovely singing voice! We were all terrified about your lungs when we heard—"

"Oh my, is that the gown I'll be wearing today! How lovely! Pardon my interrupting you, Ruby." Alina swiftly stood and leaned her lute against the wall, before smiling beautifully at the Head of Housekeeping and strolling over to where the servants were pulling out a white gown with a long, pale-blue satin vest that would run into its train. Truthfully, if the dress was comfortable, Alina didn't care what she wore on her courting dates, but she hated people bringing up her breathing affliction and always changed the subject as quickly as possible.

"Yes, Your Highness. This is the best of the dresses your father ordered for you. Given that the second courting date is normally an afternoon spent riding, we determined this would be the best chance to show off your beauty!" The maid who was answering her was young, probably about four years younger than Alina, but it was clear as day that she was the honest, earnest type.

"I see, what wonderful strategic thinking! What is your name?"

The young woman blushed. "Paula, Your Highness."

"Wonderful. Now, what all did you have planned to prepare me for my date with the Troivackian king?"

"Oh, nothing too special, just a bath and massage with special oils, then we would comb your hair until it shines. Once dry, we will fashion it into the latest style amongst nobility. Then, dress you, and spend the final forty minutes deciding on jewelry!"

The words left Alina's mouth before she could stop herself. "Gods, really?"

Everyone in the room froze.

Noting the stunned faces that surrounded her, Alina forced a pleasant expression on her face as Paula began to step backward.

"That all sounds so exciting! Shall we start?"

Alina sat in the center of the castle courtyard beside the glittering greenhouse tower. The day was hot, but in the shadows, it was quite pleasant.

She regarded the snowy linen of the table in front of herself, which was laden with fine pastries and delicate sandwiches, and found she couldn't imagine a giant brute like the Troivackian king enjoying the spread. He seemed more the type to enjoy an entire boar leg with a barrel of mead . . .

"Announcing His Majesty, King Brendan Devark of Troivack."

Alina lifted her gaze while simultaneously taking a tired breath, only to nearly go into a gasping episode.

The Troivackian king was standing beside the table directly in front of her. She hadn't sensed him draw near or heard anything!

"Princess, I did not mean to startle you." The Troivackian gave a brief short bow before straightening. The cold expression on his face was not helping his intimidating presence.

"Ah, I must have been in deeper thought than I realized. Please have a seat." Alina did her best to hide her shuddering breath as she gestured to the white wrought-iron chair across from herself.

The Troivackian noble bowed again and then swiftly moved his large form to the seat across from her that made Alina feel like a child playing tea party with a true adult.

No. Even if I were a great and accomplished person, this table would still be set this way . . . The princess found herself trying to remind herself of common sense as the king, who wore all black from tunic to trousers, sat across from her with black eyes, betraying nothing.

"I was told that our meeting was for the luncheon hour, was I mistaken?" Brendan's voice was stiff but commanding.

"No, you aren't, I just arrived early. Would you like some tea, Your Majesty?" the princess asked while reaching for the pot in the middle of the table

"If you must."

Alina hesitated and instead drew her hand back into her lap. "Do you not like tea?"

"Not particularly."

"What drink do you like then?"

"Water, or Troivackian moonshine." The Troivackian king's tone was neither rude nor condescending. It was merely . . . toneless. Somehow this was even more agitating to Alina.

"There are a number of drinks in between those," the princess pointed out while attempting a small smile.

"None have made an impression thus far," Brendan replied while his eyes for the briefest of moments flitted to the glass tower behind Alina.

"Ah, well . . . we could try to find another one during our courtship. How about that? It'd save us from mindless chatter."

The king's intense stare moved back to her and bore into her eyes relentlessly.

"Is that what these courting meetings are to you? Mindless chatter?"

Alina felt her insides quake, then solidify as her annoyance grew. "I was trying to say we don't need to make meaningless conversation if we so choose. However, you have butchered that nuanced approach." The princess paused to take a steadying breath knowing fully well that she was risking an attack on her lungs by becoming emotional.

"I do not do 'nuanced' in discussions as serious as marriage. I am here because it would be beneficial to both our kingdoms to form this alliance. Though I doubt you would be able to survive Troivack as you are now."

Without thinking, Alina stood, her cheeks flaming in embarrassment.

"Then I suppose we have ruled me out as a candidate as your future queen. Good day, Your Majesty. I hope the rest of your stay in my kingdom is enjoyable."

Giving a small curtsy Alina stormed away from the table, leaving Brendan Devark staring after her, only unlike before, his emotionless expression was broken by the smallest of frowns etched between his thick brows.

Chapter 4

SURPRISE ATTACKS

Aliina had barely managed to keep the ire from her voice when she had ordered the maids from her chamber, insisting she was feeling weary from her luncheon date with the king and wanted to rest alone.

Of course, once the room was cleared, she set to doing what she always did when angry.

Pacing and chattering to herself under her breath.

"That gigantic arse of a king! Thinks he knows all about me just because we had half a conversation . . . not even half! More like a quarter. What an arrogant, self-important—"

Alina dropped her forehead to her hand and forced herself to take a calming breath to once again stop the threat of another episode.

"Oh, well. At least that rules him out as a possible husband nice and quick. Let's see, tomorrow I have the luncheon with his brother, and the Zinferans didn't send any suitors this year . . ."

Ambling over to where her lute had been set down that morning, Alina picked up the instrument and nestled gratefully back down into her seat.

"I just wish . . . I wish I hadn't lost my composure. I wish he didn't have to poke at the one thing I . . ." Feeling a swell of emotion in her throat, the princess shook her head free of the thoughts and began strumming away on her instrument instead.

"Let's see, I think I'd prefer to sing a—"

A loud rigorous knock cracked out.

"Godsdamnit."

"Enter," Alina called while once again forcing her annoyed expression into a neutral one.

When the door opened, instead of a maid or Ruby, it was Katarina Ashowan who appeared.

Her long red hair was twisted behind her head, and her dress was despairingly frumpy as a brown sheath with only a single golden cord settled around her hips. Wait . . . was that dirt on her hands?

"Ah, good! You're here! I bet my mother your court date this afternoon wouldn't last an hour." Kat grinned triumphantly. "Now that you're finished with that unpleasant business, would you mind helping me with something?"

Alina's brow furrowed. "Help you with what exactly? Your brother warned me to always say no when you ask me that."

Kat rolled her eyes and allowed her left hip to jut out. "Oh, please. He embellished a lot of those stories."

"The one about the donkey and the wine barrels really couldn't have been embellished that much; I even heard about it in Rollom. I just didn't know it was you who was responsible for it."

"Alright, I'll have you know Harold the Ass had the best day of his life, and since then our relationship has improved drastically. So come on now, I'll even let you rant about your terrible date if it means you'll come along."

"It wasn't terrible, it was—"

"Yes, yes, things that could be told to me while walking, let's go!" Katarina clapped her hands, and for some reason, Alina found herself obeying as she hastily put the instrument down and joined the tall redhead.

"Wait, do you have anything else to wear that isn't . . . princess-y? You know what, it doesn't matter, I'll steal one of my mother's dresses."

The princess was growing both more alarmed and intrigued by the second. "Just *what* are we doing?!"

"It's better to show you; I promise you will like it."

Next thing Alina knew, she was being pulled by the hand out of her chamber by the whirlwind that was Lady Katarina Ashowan.

"Okay . . . I admit it . . . this is quite wonderful. Are you certain your mother won't mind me wearing this dress, though?"

Katarina grinned at the princess. "Don't worry, I'll have it washed and back in her wardrobe before she notices a thing."

Alina sighed and looked down at the gaggle of tiny adorable kittens all mewing about the loft of the stables. "How old do you suppose they all are?"

"Six weeks. I remember their mother looking particularly round about that time."

The princess picked up one tabby kitten with bright, intelligent eyes. "These little beasties are just what I needed today, thank you." Turning her sunny smile to the redhead, Alina was surprised to see that the young woman across from her was frowning.

"Well, guess it's none of them. Come on, there's another litter in the abandoned house down the road. My father's familiar manages it, so we'll be welcome, but just be prepared for . . . strong smells."

Then, without allowing for a breath to pass, Katarina vaulted her body gracefully over the edge of the loft onto the ladder and was already halfway down before Alina managed to place the kitten in her hands down.

"W-Wait, what do you mean? More? Why are we looking at more kittens? Also, what do you mean your father's familiar manages a house?"

"I'm looking for my own familiar," Katarina replied while leaping off the ladder before the last two steps and turning with her hands braced on her hips to look up at Alina.

"The spiritual friend witches find when they are where they are supposed to be?" the princess asked earnestly as she slowly and carefully finished her climb back down without realizing her question about a cat managing a house had been discreetly overlooked.

The redhead laughed. "Glad to hear education on our kind was introduced into your curriculum."

Alina blushed. "Ah, my apologies . . . I'm just keen to know . . . For some reason, my father is always so hesitant to talk about your father and I . . . I have many questions."

Katarina clapped the royal on the back and let out a loud charming chuckle. "Don't worry, my da tries to tell me stories, but my mum always makes him shut it because, and I quote, 'Kat doesn't need any more ideas.'"

Alina laughed, only when she did so, the hay dust in the air was sucked in and . . . she began coughing.

Oh Gods . . . Oh Gods no . . . Coughing over and over, tears began spilling over her eyes as she tried to regain her breath.

"Oh, oh no. What do I do? Do you need a physician? Or a drink of water?" Katarina rested her hand on Alina's shoulder and looked around to see if anyone was within shouting distance as the princess slowly melted to her knees while attempting to draw breath.

"HEY! HEY, YOU TWO! YES, PLEASE! PHYSICIAN! NO, DON'T COME RUNNING HERE— Oh good Gods. I'm so sorry. I swear I didn't know it was them." Katarina's frantic whisper while clasping Alina's upper arms only made her dread double.

Why is she apologizing? She wouldn't do that unless . . .

"Princess! Here, Brendan, let's take her outside. Perhaps the fresh air will help!" Through her blurred vision, Alina could make out the friendly and concerned face of Henry Devark, the prince of Troivack, and standing behind him looking as calm and unconcerned as ever, his older brother the king.

"It's alright. Your Majesty, how about you summon a physician while the prince and I carry her out. She doesn't weigh much, I can manage this much," Katarina was not releasing Alina's right arm, and thankfully, Henry seemed happy to listen.

The king on the other hand remained rooted to the spot.

"Princess, do you think you need a physician?" his deep voice asked without any inflection in his tone.

Alina managed to shake her head, but she was unable to see what everyone's reaction was as she was then hauled out of the barn, her feet barely touching the ground.

She could feel Katarina's burning touch and was amazed at her strength . . . Truly she wasn't a normal woman.

Soon, the lush green grass was within her sights, and sure enough her raspy breath began to come out a little smoother.

After a few moments, her throat ragged from her coughs, Alina dashed the last of the tears from her cheeks and turned her face away from the prince and king toward Katarina, her red eyes pleading.

Kat, whose worried expression still marred her face, turned to the king unabashedly. "Why are you just standing there staring? You could get her a cup of water, you know."

"I don't perform useless tasks. She didn't signal she needed water."

"So you're too damn dense to figure it out yourself, is that what you're saying?" Kat was on her feet, her hands on her waist. "Even if she didn't need the water, it would've been about ten times more productive than what you did by just standing watching your brother and me."

"What if you hadn't been able to carry her, or the princess had needed a physician after all? It was a wiser decision for me to stay put," came the equally calm reply. "You're being incredibly uncouth toward a king, are you aware of that, or is that normal for a Daxarian?"

Kat let out a scoff while rolling her eyes. "King or not, if I see someone being an idio—"

Alina reached out and grasped Kat's hand; the woman's unbridled words were too shocking to go unchecked.

"L-Let's go," the princess managed weakly.

Kat shot another withering stare at the king before helping up the princess, then bowing her head to Henry, who was watching the entire scenario play out with an astonished smile.

"Thank you for your *assistance*, Prince Henry. It was greatly appreciated. We will be leaving now."

Katarina was beginning to stride away, when she noticed Alina wasn't at her side.

Instead, the royal stood with her blushing face turned to the ground. "I . . . apologize . . . for my friend's discourtesy, Your Majesty."

"Don't apologize for me, I'm not a child," Katarina said irascibly before rounding back and walking over. "I just don't think people should ever be in a rank where they can't be called out for being arseholes."

Heavy silence followed the redhead's words, until Prince Henry burst out in hysterical laughter.

Dumbfounded by his reaction, Alina turned and looked at him.

"She's . . . your . . . worst . . . nightmare!" Henry wheezed toward Brendan while he clutched his sides and made zero attempt to quell his merriment.

Alina glanced nervously at the king, who was staring at his brother with obvious disapproval.

It was the first expression she had ever seen on the man.

"A-Anyway, Your Majesty, if you could please not repeat any of this. Especially in front of my father, I—"

Henry's laughter petered out then, as Brendan turned his frown to the princess.

"That's strange"—the prince began while gently rubbing his sore abdomen—"you said the same thing yesterday."

"Yes, well, I don't like— Wait. Yesterday?" Alina redirected her confused stare to Henry, completely missing Brendan's look of alarm.

"Ah . . . right. I was taking a stroll through the woods to loosen up my joints after arriving yesterday and I . . . er . . . I believe I startled you." The Troivackian prince smiled sheepishly.

"You . . . I thought you were a bear!" Alina burst out, a smile of her own beginning to form as she recalled the rustling foliage that had frightened her into fleeing the woods.

"I know, it was actually somewhat funny until you started having another breathing issue . . . You're a wonderful singer by the way!" Henry complimented her quickly while taking a careful step closer. "In my opinion, I don't think nature and you are close friends."

Alina laughed easily and found her lightened mood lingering as an undeniable wave of comfort swept over her due to the prince tactfully shifting the topic from her ailment.

"Well, I suppose we will have to hear you sing sometime, Princess! Now, shall we go look at the other litter?" Katarina's interruption brought Alina's attention back around, though her smile dimmed slightly when she noticed the Troivackian king's cold expression had returned.

"Yes, but we must hurry before dinner tonight."

Smiling, the redhead winked down at the princess. "Don't worry, we will be down there and back up before anyone even notices you're missing."

Norman stared at his daughter's appearance flatly.

Her brown hem was caked in mud, her hair was frizzing out in multiple directions, and there was a strange odor lingering about her that he didn't care for in the least.

"You missed dinner, and come back just before we send out knights to look for you. I expect a full explanation."

Alina clasped her hands in front of her skirts and bowed her head. "You see, Father . . . I, well, went into Austice . . ."

"Without any escorts?! Alina, it isn't like you to be so careless! You know with all the suitors here you need to be especially cautious. What if one of them proves to be horribly unfavorable and attempts to harm you?!" the king burst out instantly.

"I-I wasn't alone! It really was fine, I was dressed like this so no one knew who I was, and we just went to—"

"We? Who is 'we'?" Norman asked while rounding his chair with a strange glint in his eyes that Alina wasn't sure was a good thing.

"Oh, um, Katarina Ashowan, Father. You like the Ashowans, though! You wanted us to be friends!" Alina exclaimed, also desperate.

The king rested his forearms on the back of his chair by the fire and dropped his head while letting out a loud moan. "Oh Gods. It's happening again . . . Kevin was right . . . I should've been more cautious."

"What does Mr. Kevin Howard have to do with Katarina?!" the princess demanded in confusion as she strained her mind to recall why the assistant could possibly have said anything bad about the infamous noble family.

Norman sighed and lifted his head to look defeatedly at his daughter. "I think I may have censored my stories about Finlay a little too much."

"What do you mean? What's wrong with the Ashowan family? You said you trust them completely!"

"And I do. They just tend to . . . cause trouble before setting things right again." Sighing deeply Norman rounded the chair and laid his hands on his daughter's shoulders. "As long as you are safe, that is all that matters. Now, how was your luncheon with the Troivackian king?"

Alina openly grimaced. "Father, if I never ask you to tell your stories about your time with Finlay Ashowan, will you never ask me about my dates with the Troivackian king, and trust me when I say they are inconsequential?"

Norman studied his daughter for a long moment, his identical hazel eyes searching her own.

"Very well. As long as he hasn't offended or hurt you, I will leave it be. I trust you."

Letting out the breath she had been holding, Alina allowed her shoulders to slump forward. "Thank you. I'll go to bed now."

Leaning forward and planting a kiss on her father's cheek, Alina then lightly stepped to leave the library. Right before she reached the door, however, she cast a cheeky smile over her shoulder and said, "I must admit though, Katarina Ashowan has already told me that there is a certain mystery surrounding the nine fountains on the castle grounds. Apparently there is a tenth and she wants us to go look for it tomorrow."

Closing the door behind herself, the young princess couldn't help but giggle when she heard her father loudly exclaim, "Son of a *mage*! GUARDS, SUMMON VISCOUNT ASHOWAN THIS INSTANT!"

Chapter 5

MEDDLESOME MEN

Norman quirked an eyebrow at his assistant, his stern features remaining firmly in place.

"Oh Gods . . . where to even begin with how much I disagree with this . . ."

The king leaned back in his chair and clasped his hands together. "Enlighten me, Kevin. You've given me sound advice in all my decisions as a ruler."

The assistant placed the wine goblet back on the table before resting his elbows on either side of the beverage and rubbing his wizened face furiously.

After a moment, his formerly neat hair was sticking up at odd angles and his eyebrows looked slightly demented.

"You want the princess to marry the son of a mere *viscount* for some reason, and not just any viscount. The *Ashowans*! Do you know the stories I have heard about them all the way in Rollom?! They are infamous for their oddities!"

"Also for saving the kingdom and advancing our technologies with the Coven of Wittica's help far beyond anything we ever dreamed. Our economy is booming, and we are well underway to having a publicly funded education system that could further these revolutions. We are even in discussion with a group of earth witches that could not just build us roads of stone in our cities but connect them! This is all headed by Finlay, Annika, and the coven. You know I've tried to make him a duke time and time again, and he refuses. His accomplishments are all thanks to his oddities."

"Did you not hear the story about his daughter and the donkey? Or about the barn fire and his daughter? Or the time she ran off and—"

"I have. She was a few years younger then. Not to mention all those stories are about Katarina, not her brother—"

"Fin's son is not right in the head, Your Majesty! I am sorry, I know we all don't wish to insult the poor lad, but he is not well."

"Finlay had his own issues when he first arrived here, and he overcame them with flying colors. I believe Alina is more than capable of helping Tamlin Ashowan on that journey," Norman reasoned.

"You're the only parent I know who wishes hardship on their daughter. You want her to heal him?" Mr. Howard snapped before grabbing his wine goblet and chugging down its contents in one go.

"No. I believe that he will do that himself, and having a kind companion can be a blessing during those times."

"Alright . . . I didn't want to have to resort to this, but . . ." The assistant fixed his deep blue eyes on the ruler and took a fortifying breath. "If Alina marries Lord Ashowan's son, whenever you go to visit her estate, you will have to see Kraken, his familiar."

The king's face paled.

Silence rested over the pair for several long moments.

"Perhaps I was hasty in the planning of this arrangement. Or maybe I can insist that they live here instead . . ." Norman murmured to himself with a deep frown.

Mr. Howard let out a very long frustrated sigh. "In my opinion, Your Majesty, we should wait and see what the princess thinks about the suitors herself; she is a young woman of sound judgment. Sire, I know you want her to marry Fin's son because you are afraid she will choose one of the Troivackian men, but I doubt she would consider them as a viable option."

Norman's expression saddened as his eyes fell to the council room table in front of himself. Sunlight the color of honey poured in through the windows, illuminating the lazy dust drifting through the air.

It was a peaceful afternoon that didn't have any business being as wonderful as it was.

"I can't lose both my children. Eric, I . . . I don't know if he will ever return, or if he will ever be ready to be king. If something should happen to him or myself . . . Alina and her husband would need to be able to take care of this land. They would also need to win support so that the four dukes don't go to war to inherit the crown, and the only house I can think of that could face those odds would be the Ashowan family."

Mr. Howard said nothing. He knew the prince's absence had only added to the grief of losing Queen Ainsley, and what made it even more difficult and worrisome was that Eric was incredibly adept at hiding his activities.

Despite this, Norman believed that, if he just gave his son time and privacy, he would one day return.

Only Finlay Ashowan had ever found out the details of Eric's whereabouts, and ever since that day, the two had not spoken. Nor would the redhead relay anything other than that the prince was alive.

If Kevin Howard were entirely honest with himself . . .

It was something he could never forgive the house witch for.

As he stared at the king, his employer, his leader, his friend, and saw the intense pain in his eyes of not knowing the well-being of his own child, the assistant wished for the thousandth time he was capable of getting the information out of Finlay Ashowan once and for all—and could punish him properly for his silence.

Despite remaining unwed and childless, Kevin Howard didn't have to have either to know that no parent should have to worry about their children disappearing off the face of the earth.

Alina stared at her reflection grimly, despite the flurry of excitement behind her being of a more happy, robust nature.

Maids gushed to one another and exchanged endless ideas about her hair and jewels that made her gut rot with anxiety.

For some reason, they were all beside themselves anticipating her date with Prince Henry.

After her unpleasant encounter with the Troivackian prince's older brother, the king, she didn't have high expectations for the date.

"Princess Alina! We heard that at least half a dozen young maidens are completely smitten with Prince Henry, and another half dozen of married women are the same! Yet he shows no interest. He is just so friendly, and warm . . . his voice is beautiful too." The maids continued on regardless of Alina's listless response, leaving the young woman to speculate on how best to avoid their bombardment of questions after the courting date.

A knock on the door interrupted the maids, and Alina found herself grateful for the brief hush the visitor had instilled.

One of the maids opened the door a crack, and after a few words the servant turned back to the princess looking disconcerted. "It seems we got carried away— It . . . it's time to go meet the prince!"

Nodding with the severity of a prisoner on their way to the chopping block, Alina turned and exited her chamber, only to walk directly into a very firm chest.

"Oh — Ah . . . yes, I know it isn't normal that I come to escort you myself, but I had a request to make of you, and it was best that I make it before you got too far."

Alina froze when she realized that she had accidentally walked straight into none other than Prince Henry, and he was gazing down at her with a friendly, good-natured smile.

"W-What re-request?"

"Your singing really was beautiful that day in the forest, and I was wondering if you might bring your lute with you! I quite enjoy singing myself, but it is murderously hard to find someone here who will do so with me."

Alina blinked up at the prince for a moment before realizing that she was still standing pressed into him. Taking a hasty step back, she bumped her head against her open chamber door. Just inside the room stood her gaggle of maids, who were all so enthralled with the scene that they openly gaped, unable to move.

After another beat of awkward silence, one of them had the presence of mind to grab the forgotten instrument and slowly hand it off to the princess before backing away while bowing.

"Th-Thank you," Alina croaked over her shoulder.

"Wonderful, shall we go now?" Henry grinned down at her, oblivious to the tension of the moment. Offering his arm to the stunned royal, he waited patiently as she accepted his escort.

Then, they set off to their luncheon in the courtyard.

Alina could feel her face burning as she attempted to tune the instrument in her hands. The Troivackian prince was sitting contently, gazing up at the glass tower with a curious expression, as though thinking of wondrous things that he'd like to know more about.

"Pardon me, Your Highness, but —"

"Please, call me Henry. Let's save our breaths for more important things," he interrupted happily.

"Right . . . Henry . . . forgive me for saying this, but you aren't anything like the other Troivackians I've met."

The prince chuckled. "I know. I've heard that my whole life, especially from my brother."

"I'm sorry to bring up such a . . . a painful —"

"I'm used to these things." Henry waved off her apology. "It's one of the reasons I actually submitted my application to join my brother as a candidate

for being your fiancé. I wanted to come to your country to see if perhaps I'd
fit in better here."

Alina stilled as a sorrowful expression moved across Henry's face.

"I already can tell I am far better suited to your land than my home, but
. . ." An emotion shone in the prince's eyes that made Alina lean forward.
Her heart thudded against her chest.

Somehow, in that moment, she understood perfectly.

"You . . . are worried about your brother."

Henry's gaze snapped up to hers; it was clear he was stunned.

"How did you know?"

For some annoying reason, Alina felt tears threatening to ruin her composure. "I . . . I'm worried about my loved ones too."

In the moment of quiet understanding that passed between the two royals, a gentle breeze passed over the exquisitely set table.

"Princess, would you like to sing a song together?"

Alina found herself unable to stop herself from smiling at the prince.
Someone who could finally understand the pain, heartache, and endless
worrying that came with having troubled family members who meant the
world to them sat across from her, asking her to do one of her favorite
things . . .

"I would love to."

Strolling back to her chamber with her lute in hand, Alina couldn't keep the
smile from her face.

To think she had been able to spend almost her entire luncheon with
the Troivackian prince singing, and learning new songs from his home,
was beyond her wildest expectations of the date. He really was charming,
kind . . .

"Your Highness! What a joy to see you in such high spirits!"

Turning with her smile still intact and her cheeks rosy, Alina faltered for
a moment when she realized that she was faced with none other than Lord
Richard Fuks.

The man was . . . beyond elderly. He had always been thought of as a tad
mad, yet as his age advanced into his nineties, the earl seemed to become
more and more ludicrous with each passing year.

Currently, the infamous noble was clad in a crimson robe, under which
his long sleepshirt was visible. Clutching the head of his cane with trembling wrinkled hands that were missing a good number of fingers, the earl
attempted to bow to her.

"Good day, Lord Fuks. I pray to the Goddess that this day finds you in good health?"

"Yes, yes. Nothing wrong with me. Tell me, did you have a good date with that Troivackian?"

Alina blinked at the elder's bald-faced question.

"I . . . er . . . Yes, I did."

"Excellent! You know I worried about that child becoming king at such a young age. Can't imagine what nonsense he had to put up with." Lord Fuks shook his head sadly.

"Oh, I actually had my luncheon with the king's brother, Prince Henry."

"That pup?! Forgive me, but that man is abysmally directionless and unambitious, who would do nothing but lounge around and play music all day if allowed to."

"There is nothing wrong with music!" Alina burst out before realizing her show of emotion was making a passing steward turn to stare at the two nobles curiously.

Lord Fuks sighed. "Of course not, but . . . ah, well. Ignore my ramblings. Tell me, have you seen my grandson anywhere? I was just coming out here to see if the lad might be interested in taking a carriage ride with me into Austice."

Alina managed to resume her polite smile after a brief moment of forcing her face into a plain expression. "I haven't. My apologies, Lord Fuks, I was unaware your son, Les, had had a child!"

"Ah, no need to apologize. He's a fine young lad, only four years old now! He's named—"

"FATHER!"

Alina turned startled as Les Fuks himself rounded the castle corridor and charged down to them with impressive speed.

"You can't just disappear like that because you don't want a physical examination!" Les panted, his white hair still slicked back despite his sprint.

"Nonsense! I don't need yet another examination! I had one not even a fortnight ago. Now, stop hiding my grandson from me, I want to treat him to a carriage ride and perhaps some strawberry tarts from one of the shops in Austice!"

Les Fuks straightened slowly while still breathing heavily and pinching the bridge of his nose.

"Father, you— Oh! Your Highness! I am sorry I didn't greet you properly!" Les dipped into a deep bow before Alina, who gripped her lute closer to herself reflexively.

"No . . . it is not a problem! Lord Fuks was just asking if I had seen your son. I was apologizing in truth, because I don't even know your child's name!"

At this, Les Fuks stiffened and shot his father an accusatory glare, which was met with the most innocent expression imaginable.

"My son's name . . . is . . . Aster."

"Oh, what a wonderful name, Lord Fuks!" Alina smiled while attempting to ignore the glow of pride from the earl himself. It was clear something was somewhat amiss.

"Yes. A wonderful boy—takes after myself quite a bit!" Lord Richard Fuks managed to straighten his spine ever so slightly as both his hands rested atop his cane. "Though, Princess, please feel free to call him by his nickname. Ass."

Alina was so shocked that she barely remembered not to laugh. She had been warned by her father about Earl Fuks's tendency to try and garnish favors from people who might find his name funny.

"I . . . I beg your pardon?" she asked while blinking several times in a row.

"Father, we are not calling him . . . Ass . . . as a nickname. Please, you are offending the princess!" Les Fuks begged his father, but the elder was ignoring his son's pleas wholeheartedly, his eyes shining with pride.

"Nonsense, what is there to be offended about? I am allowing Her Highness to feel comfortable with one of her loyal subjects. My dear grandson, Ass Fuks, will be a loving and devoted noble in her brother's court one day!"

Alina bit down on her lip hard enough to draw blood, and yet when Les Fuks dropped his forehead to his hand, she couldn't help but burst out in hysterical laughter.

Ah well, she was only human.

Chapter 6

TROUBLING TONES

I t was a peaceful day for Fin. Tam was sitting at the kitchen table reading, Annika was in Austice checking on Elizabeth Nonata's report, and he was in the middle of baking fresh herb bread for the king's pork roast dinner. Even though Fin wasn't the official Royal Cook anymore, whenever he had the time, he would give his replacement, his former kitchen aide Peter, a day off.

The viscount had just finished magically floating the bowl of mixed herbs he had prepared beforehand onto the table, when the castle door was thrown open, and in stumbled the princess and his daughter holding each other up as they roared with laughter.

"I-I owe him a favor now, but I couldn't resist!" Alina clutched her abdomen as the tall redhead supporting her wiped tears of humor from her cheeks.

"Oh Gods—I thought everyone had heard about it! You should've seen my da when he found out! He had to be locked away in his chamber for hours!"

"When I found out what now?" Fin asked while turning curiously to his daughter and her new friend.

"Lord Fuks's grandson's name," Katarina explained with a devilish grin that had Fin smiling back at her.

"Ah, yes. How is little Asster doing?"

"I've heard he's cute, but a little shit disturber," Tam cited casually, earning a look of glowing pride from his father.

Alina was unable to take it and was once again doubled over laughing.

Fin was chuckling to himself as Katarina helped heft the princess onto one of the three tall chairs while patting her back. Tam glanced at the young royal with a half smile before returning to his book.

"Easy there, Princess. If you have another one of those attacks, my father might not be as calm." Katarina plunked herself down in the center seat and reached over to grab an apple from the fruit bowl in front of her brother.

"Viscount, you . . . you know about the incident yesterday?" Alina asked, dropping her eyes to her lap as she tried not to show him the disappointed and anxious expression she knew she was growing in place of laughter.

"Kat told us, yes. She made me promise not to tell your father, but, Alina, if your condition is getting worse—"

"Wait, you already knew about my condition?!" the princess demanded, her eyes flying to Fin's calm blue ones.

"I do, yes. When you had your first incident, your father reached out to me to see if I knew of any cure that my mother may have made a note of in one of her notebooks. Sadly, there wasn't one that she knew of. However, the vapors and ointment the Royal Physician has been administering for you are based on one of my mother's creations. She did make a note that some people grow out of the condition, though for children born early it was more likely to last for the duration of their life."

The princess felt her teeth clench and her hands grip her skirts as she recoiled from the pitying gazes of both the Ashowan children.

It was in that moment that an impressively large amount of fluff suddenly leapt into her lap.

"Oh, what—"

Alina blinked, stunned, down into two green eyes belonging to a handsome cat, whose puffy chest with its dash of white at the throat made him look rather distinguished.

"Ah, that there is Kraken."

"*The* Kraken?! The animal responsible for taking down a dragon?!"

The feline in her lap chirped before circling her lap several times and beginning to knead his paws against her thighs.

"He says he is pleased to make your acquaintance," Fin remarked while a small flicker of another emotion crossed his face. He was the only one who could understand the feline with their strong bond as familiar and witch. However, he was more than happy to relay messages from the fluffy cat.

"Is that really all Kraken said, Da?" Katarina asked while she glanced playfully at her father.

"That is all he said that is worth being repeated," the viscount retorted while leaning his hands on the cooking table and fixing his daughter with a familiar warning look.

Katarina grinned back before continuing to munch on her apple. "So how was your second date?"

Alina smiled prettily down at Kraken as she reached up and scratched his cheeks. "It was wonderful. Prince Henry is a very kind man; I had a lovely afternoon with him."

There was a beat of silence that finally made the young monarch raise her gaze to the Ashowan family, which in turn made her bashful.

Fin took one look at her face and shook his head. "Gods . . . your father is going to be heartbroken."

"N-No! It doesn't have to be like that! Henry says he prefers Daxaria and wants to live here," Alina began desperately, unable to stop her burning cheeks.

"Calling him Henry already?" Katarina observed while her jovial expression began to fade from her face.

"Princess, you do know that it isn't for Prince Henry to decide if he can live here with you. It'd be up to his brother, King Brendan. While I agree, given the Troivackian nobility's propensity for backstabbing, this could seem like a tempting option for him, there are many variables to this," Fin began, his tone apologetic as the young woman before him visibly shrank.

"W-Well, I can try to talk to him. The Troivackian king, that is."

"Alina, he is here for your hand in marriage as well; that might not be something that he would be pleased about," Fin remarked, unaware that he was already addressing the young noble as he would his own daughter.

"Da, are you really someone who can say something like this is impossible? You were a Godsdamn cook when you met Mum!" Katarina burst out vehemently.

"Language," Fin warned before straightening and crossing his arms over his chest.

"Sorry, but you know I'm right!" Katarina was on her feet in an instant.

"The princess hasn't even had all her courting dates; maybe you all are overreacting to an event that isn't a certainty," Tam cut in, his quiet voice carrying little emotion as he proceeded to turn the page of his book.

Alina glanced at the heir to the viscount's house but discovered that he remained fully immersed in the text before him, as though nothing of consequence was happening.

"Actually, Tam . . . That is something I wanted to talk to you about, but I'm also going to mention it with Her Highness here." Fin turned his shimmering gaze to his son, who finally looked up at his father.

The house witch then faced Alina, looking more than a mite awkward.

"Your father, the king, is interested in a pairing between the two of you. I know he doesn't want you or Tam to know his intentions, but this is not something I think should be kept from either of you."

Tam's expression was one of great alarm and distress as he shook his head and held up both of his arms in an X while at the same time the princess exclaimed, "Oh, Gods, no."

Momentarily taken aback by both of their strong reactions to the news, Fin took a dazed moment to process the information before chuckling. "I suppose that should be a relief to me."

Katarina turned to Alina with her arms folded over her chest frowning. "What's wrong with my brother?"

"Kat, you really don't need to—" Tam began to interject before his sister adjusted her position so that the full of her back was facing him, which effectively cut him off.

"Oh . . . I'm sorry . . . I mean no offense to . . . to either of you—sorry, Tam!" Alina added hastily.

"None taken," the young noble responded while poking his sister's shoulder.

"It's just that I already . . . I already see you more as a brother than a romantic partner." Alina was inching away from the blazing stare of Tam's sister, when Kraken's paw suddenly shot out and rested on the redheaded woman's lap.

Snapping out of her frown, Katarina turned her attention to the familiar and stared into his sleepy green eyes, which then slowly blinked up at her.

Letting out a long sigh, the redhead's shoulders slumped forward. "Damnit. I really wanted to have a sister-in-law that I like."

"Kat, language!" Fin chided again, though he laughed a bit as he did so.

"Why? You and Mum swear all the time at home! Besides, no one here cares—"

It was then the garden door opened a crack, drawing everyone's gazes up in time to see a small boy with a mop of soft brown hair and dark blue eyes stare up at them uncertainly.

"Why, hello, Aster!" Katarina greeted with a warm smile that had the child scuffling quickly into the room and closing the door behind himself. Kraken leapt down from the princess's lap and sauntered over to the nearest patch of sunlight.

"Katty, it's Ass, remember?" the small boy half whined, half pouted as he ran over to the cooking table.

"Oh, are you Aster?" Alina asked while smiling down at the small boy.

"Yeah, but my friends call me Ass. Who're you?" he asked while accepting a pear that Fin was handing him.

The princess didn't get the chance to answer when the garden door burst open with great force, and standing in its frame was none other than Brendan Devark, the Troivackian king.

"There he is, my lady. I believe that is your son?"

Everyone was too stunned to move until a slight woman in her early forties stepped around the giant of a man. "Y-Yes, thank you, Your Majesty."

Aster didn't run away when his mother rushed over to him and picked him up, though it was most likely due to the fact the lad appeared petrified to the bone of the foreigner in front of him.

"Good day, Viscount." Lady Fuks dipped into a shaky curtsy to Fin.

"Morning, Cheryl. Take care, Aster!" Fin waved with a friendly smile that had the boy waving back, and then shouting as his mother carried him through the castle doorway. "I told you! Call me Ass!"

"I cannot have heard that child right."

Alina nearly leapt out of her skin when she turned in her seat to find the giant Troivackian man had moved stealthily up behind her again and was staring at the closed door the child and his mother had just exited through.

"Ah, it is a family tradition of the Fuks heirs," Fin explained while directing his bright smile to the newcomer.

He then executed a perfect bow and straightened once more. While his smile remained friendly and warm, Fin had a shimmer in his eyes that only his children recognized.

"I am Viscount Ashowan, Your Majesty. Welcome to the castle kitchen."

The king stared at him stonily for a moment. "So you're the infamous house witch."

Katarina was in the process of rolling her eyes, which the Troivackian caught when his gaze cut to her sharply.

The lady didn't bother looking cowed. "Pardon my lack of curtsy, sire. You are crowding the exact spot where I would be paying my respects."

"Kat!" Fin snapped, his eyes flashing angrily.

At the reminder of proper greetings, the three youths stood. While Kat's curtsy was lackluster, Alina's and Tam's greetings were flawless.

"A Troivackian." Brendan's voice was raised in curiosity when he locked eyes with Tam, who swallowed.

"Your Majesty, this is my son, Tamlin Ashowan," Fin explained, his voice calm, but his expression no longer friendly.

"I see . . ." Brendan tilted his head as he studied the young man before him scrupulously.

"Viscountess Ashowan was born in Troivack, Your Majesty," Alina interrupted, drawing the king's gaze back over and down to the shortest person in the room.

"Annika Piereva, then Annika Jenoure, and now Annika Ashowan, of Viscount House Jenoure, correct?" the monarch asked, his intense attention fixing itself onto Alina, immediately flustering her.

"Th-That's—"

"That is my wife, yes," Fin interjected coolly.

The king turned back to the viscount. "I look forward to formally meeting the viscountess."

"She is a wonderful member of our court!" Alina interrupted, once more claiming the king's attention. "She was my late mother's best friend, in fact."

Brendan's facial expression didn't shift at all as he continued staring down at the princess.

"I am sorry for your loss."

Alina could feel her hands begin to tremble, and so she clutched them together to make it less obvious.

"S-She passed a while ago. I'm sorry you lost your father as well."

"He died honorably. There is nothing to be sad about."

The silence that followed was deafening.

"Aside from locating Ass Fuks, was there a reason you came to the kitchen?" Katarina asked through a smile of gritted teeth.

Fin stiffened behind the table at his daughter's use of the noble's name in front of the king.

Brendan's face darkened fractionally when he addressed her. "I happened upon Lady Fuks while I was perusing the castle grounds and offered my assistance in locating her son. Though I did want to come and see the viscount later this evening."

Fin frowned at the man's militaristic speech and responded with similar formality. "What is it you would like to speak to me about, sire?"

"Your daughter. Lady Katarina Ashowan."

At this the room fell completely silent, though the lady in question was balling her fists against her skirts and her eyes gleamed dangerously.

"Kat, Tam, please step outside. Princess, please pardon us." Fin dismissed the young adults without moving his gaze from the bear of a man. The edge in his tone left no room for any objections.

Once the trio had exited through the garden door and closed it, Alina half collapsed against the nearest garden post, her legs feeling like they had turned to jelly.

"Gods, what does that pain in the—"

"Kat?" Tam stood in front of his sister. "Kat, what did you do?"

"Nothing! I swear, this time I . . ." The redhead's defiant expression faltered, though, and a small hint of guilt appeared as she tucked an errant strand of long, red hair behind her ear.

"Kat! Did you really do something to the king of a foreign country?!" Tam burst out seriously, his dark eyes wide with fury and fear.

"I was just . . . a little . . . *terse* with him the other day, but he was being a complete arse!"

"Oh, Gods." Tam pinched the bridge of his nose, and in that moment, he looked identical to his father. "Did you *tell* him he was being an arse?"

"Of course I did! You know I can't help it!" she announced desperately as her brother began rubbing his face.

"Kat, this is bad! If Mum finds out—"

"If Mum finds out what?"

All three nobles froze and turned to stare at none other than Viscountess Annika Ashowan herself, with her maid, Clara, by her side. Both of their expressions were unreadable for a moment before Annika stepped forward, her dark eyes smoldering.

"Katarina Ashowan, what in the Goddess's name did you do now?"

Chapter 7

CLAWS OUT

Fin folded his arms across his chest as he regarded the Troivackian king in front of him emotionlessly. "What is it about my daughter you would like to discuss, Your Majesty?"

"Today's greeting aside, your daughter has exhibited unacceptable behavior. Her rude disposition and lack of discipline is abhorrent and needs to be addressed. Not only today, but yesterday as well. I take this matter to you and not your king for now. Should it continue, I will not let it end with a discussion," Brendan informed the cook, his deadened gaze unwavering and his hand casually resting on the hilt of his sword.

The viscount failed to have the expected response, however, when he replied with, "I see. I would like to corroborate this incident with my daughter in the room to decide on the best course of action, Your Majesty."

Raising a black eyebrow, the Troivackian king studied the viscount, who was currently wearing peasant garb, with a glint of curiosity.

"I will allow it."

There was the shadow of a twitch in the redhead's left eye, when the garden door magically opened on its own. Outside, Alina remained slumped against the garden post, unaware that her unbecoming position was on display. Katarina had her back to them and was speaking to someone, while Tam stood off to the side with his hand covering his mouth in obvious dread.

"Kat," Fin called, making his daughter turn and reveal that the person she was speaking with was his wife.

Without addressing the viscountess, the witch's gaze settled on his daughter. "Come here, we need to have a talk."

Annika stepped forward then as Clara stepped backward. "I will join the discussion."

The couple locked eyes for a moment, and a wordless conversation took place before the viscount gave a nod of affirmation and, then waited as both mother and daughter strode forward to the kitchen. While the viscount and viscountess remained stoic and unreadable, their daughter failed to mask her irritation and hesitancy.

Fin closed the door and magically sealed all sound from leaving the room as he faced his daughter squarely.

"His Majesty has just informed me that you have been disrespectful to him not only today, but yesterday as well, and is asking that you be rightly punished. I want to hear your side of things. Now."

The young woman's stricken face lasted all of a second before she turned a furious gaze to the monarch.

"Katarina," Annika's tone was low, and deadly.

The monarch tilted his head and the corners of his eyes tightened as he stared around the tall redheaded woman to her mother.

"Da, Alin— The *princess* was having an episode of her affliction, and the king here stood by and didn't think to get her a drink of water, or help. I pointed out that it was not appropriate that he respond so carelessly."

"I believe your words were, 'If I see someone acting like an arse, I will call them an arse,'" Brendan Devark cited disapprovingly.

Both the viscount and viscountess shared yet another silent exchange with a lengthy glance.

"Katarina, did you say that?" Annika demanded, the ire in her tone bringing the tension in the room to the precipice of snapping.

The redheaded noblewoman balked for half a moment before rounding quickly toward her mother, her voice rising defensively. "I told him he could have been more helpful when the princess was choking to death! She couldn't even speak and he just stood there!"

"Did it occur to you that the princess in her state could have expressed her needs for herself?" the Troivackian king asked. "It has already happened before where she did not wish her father to be alerted, indicating she prefers fewer people reacting to her episodes of breathlessness." The faint anger in Brendan's voice added even more weight to the confrontation.

It was then Annika's eyes flitted to the young ruler, and a look of intensity passed between them, followed by an understanding that made both Fin and his daughter feel oddly out of place . . .

"Katarina, the king was showing the princess the utmost respect as a possible ruler. You aren't aware of this as it is a Troivackian custom, but sickness or fault is considered a weakness—a potentially deadly one in court. He was allowing the princess to keep her position safe. You owe His Majesty an apology. Even if it wasn't a gross misunderstanding, you should *never* treat a foreign leader like that."

Katarina's cheeks flushed crimson, and it was clear she was beginning to stave off tears as she stared at her mother's composed face that remained fixed on the Troivackian king instead of her daughter.

"Mum, didn't you always teach me that—"

"Katarina, apologize this instant." Annika's countenance was cold, her tone commanding.

Her daughter visibly recoiled as though a blow had struck her chest.

Slowly, her eyes drifted down, and she turned to the Troivackian king, who bore witness to the exchange passively.

"I . . . I apologize for my rudeness. Your Majesty." Katarina curtsied laboriously. She didn't want to break down in front of the monarch. She didn't want to feel powerless and childish.

The shame, pain, and anger she felt collapsed upon itself as she somehow managed to stay rooted to the spot when all she wanted to do was scream and fight.

"Kat, I know you thought you were defending your friend," the viscount's soft voice broke through the charged silence. "I know you meant to be helpful, not hurtful."

Turning abruptly toward Fin, Katarina dipped into another curtsy, her next words biting. "I understand, *Father*. I misread his intention."

The young noblewoman didn't wait to hear any additional chastisement before she strode toward the garden door, tears choking her as she moved swiftly despite her hands shaking.

"Kat," Fin called out, clearly distressed.

His daughter failed to respond, however, as she gently closed the door behind herself, leaving the viscount, viscountess, and king alone.

Shooting a frustrated glower at his wife, Fin pressed his fists into the cooking table's surface. "There was a better way to handle that. You know she didn't mean to—"

"It doesn't matter if it isn't intentional, she can't just spout off like that!" Annika snapped, rounding on her husband.

"So we teach her to curb it with reason and calm! Not make her feel ashamed!"

"Viscount, your daughter needs discipline. Were I a quarter more of a man like my father, she would be exiled from Daxarian court. There are serious consequences to her outbursts," Brendan Devark informed the witch calmly.

"Discipline and domination are two very different things, Your Majesty. I don't give a cat's fluffy ass if she speaks up against someone being unkind. I agree that she should evaluate the situation and address the opposing person more tactfully, but I don't believe that was the lesson she took from this!" Fin exclaimed, his blue eyes brightening until they appeared unnatural.

"Katarina is old enough to know better! You've given her too much leeway!" Annika interrupted forcefully.

"To a point, yes! But you are always condemning her. You don't acknowledge her side nearly enough," Fin fired back, his hands moving to his hips as items in the kitchen began to float back to their magical duties.

"We are not discussing this here! There is the Troivackian—"

"Yes, the Troivackian king." Fin turned to Brendan, a strange knowingness in his eyes making the king suspicious. "Tell me, sire, what is your take on our daughter?"

Brendan sensed that he needed to choose his wording carefully. Something about the couple was oddly intimidating yet also . . . engaging when it came to speaking one's thoughts freely. Perhaps because they were unabashed about arguing so openly in front of him.

"My perception of your daughter is that she is immature. Passionate, and perhaps her intentions are well placed; however, she has never learned to control her emotions or her tongue. She is all impulse and no thought."

Fin's gaze became deadly. "No thought?"

"She acts before she thinks matters through. Something we forgive in children under the age at ten, but never . . . what is it . . . nineteen?"

"I will speak to my daughter, Your Majesty," Annika interrupted evenly once again, before her husband could continue arguing with the foreign leader.

Brendan's gaze cut to the viscountess, and the two once again shared a brief moment of strained understanding before he bowed to her and she curtsied to him.

The man swept out of the room through the castle door, leaving Annika and Fin entirely alone in the kitchen.

Turning to his wife, his brows lowered, the witch was clearly infuriated.

"What the hell was that? In front of a monarch?! You shamed your daughter in front of the leader of an entire kingdom."

"I did not shame her! I showed her consequences—and better here than a banquet hall full of nobles! Fin, this was immensely generous of him. He didn't take it to the king, and he didn't demand a public apology; do you know how merciful that is?!" Annika insisted while placing her fingertips on the cooking table.

"I know we need to help Kat mind her manners, but we didn't need to treat her like that in front of the Troivackian king!"

"Yes, we did! She isn't learning, Fin. She is reckless and has faced no repercussions because of you and me saving her. We need her to start accepting consequences to be a better person. Aside from the donkey incident, there was also the time she released three different herds of cows. Or the time we found her drunk on her sixteenth birthday under Elizabeth Nonata's watch, and don't get me started on the fire!" Annika waved her hand exasperatedly, her desperation and aggravation blurred together.

The redhead stilled. "Yes, she needs to rein in some of her impulses, but she should always know we are here for her. Also the donkey incident was *during* that escapade on her sixteenth birthday, remember?"

"I don't want to remember," Annika grumbled quietly before returning to the greater problem at hand. "She needs to know we are there for her, yes, but only to a point."

"What does that mean?"

"Fin, you and I both learned how to be independent because we didn't have anyone else to count on. We learned to survive and grow on our own. Katarina needs that now."

Neither the viscount nor viscountess moved.

"She will tell us when she is ready for that," Fin began, his voice growing hoarse.

"What if she doesn't? What if she thinks she can live life mouthing off to whomever she chooses? We have a tough enough time with our son! Tam can't even handle standing in a large room for an hour! Why don't we focus on the child we can handle?!"

"Our children"—the viscount rounded the cooking table, his eyes beginning to glow brighter as he moved—"are not beings we have to 'handle.' Tam will be fine. He will—"

"Fin! I don't want to think of the worst of our children any more than you do, but you have to admit, there is a chance we could destroy them if we don't act rationally now!"

Silence stretched on between the couple as they stared at each other. Both hearts raced, both experienced the same dread of knowing the risk they took of releasing their children into society without their protection.

"Katarina isn't like other noblewomen. She is a witch to some capacity and she —" Fin began, only for his wife to cut him off.

"That has nothing to do with basic manners and you know it. I knew, of all people, you'd be blinded by love for your children, but you can't let it be at a detriment to everyone!" Annika finished firmly.

For a few tense breaths, Fin said nothing, only focused on wading through the haze of anger in his mind to see the situation objectively.

"We will discuss this more tonight. I have to finish making dinner," the viscount managed to say, though his voice was hoarse.

Annika let out a small sigh and turned to take her own leave. She knew that the redheaded members of the family tended to need time to calm down after a fight.

Once the door had closed behind his wife, the witch felt his eyes close while he took a fortifying breath.

"*I know that look. Your eldest kitten giving you troubles again?*" Kraken's low purr rumbled up from the floor where he lounged in the sunshine.

"Yes," Fin murmured as he halfheartedly began covering the bread bowl with a tea towel to let the herbed dough rise.

"*Hm, well, nothing new there. Though that large strange human . . . he was interesting. Even I had trouble hearing his footsteps.*"

"That's the king of Troivack."

"*Oho! Another leader who will need to greet me with the proper respect! It took me ages to get your king to do so; hopefully, this new one is a little smarter.*"

Fin decided he wasn't in the mood to chide his familiar's insult to his friend, the Daxarian king, and he was just about to end the conversation when an idea occurred to him.

"Kraken, would you be able to keep an eye on the Troivackian king and his brother, Prince Henry? Not spying *per say*, but he isn't a forthcoming man and I'm wary about him now that he's made Kat his enemy."

"*Our eldest kitten has declared him her enemy?! I will take him down myself. He will grovel at her feet and only be allowed to act as her slave to breed the finest giant grandkittens known to the world —*"

"No, don't you dare. Leave him be. Besides, if you ask me, he almost seemed more drawn to the princess . . . but maybe that's just wishful thinking on my part. I'd rather he be more interested in romance with her than a battle with my own child. I know it is selfish of me . . ." the viscount admonished while shaking his head with a frown.

"*Very. However, fear not. I will have my spies keep an eye out, and I will alert you if I see anything suspicious.*"

Fin nodded in thanks and then returned to the cooking table. He decided he wouldn't mention the arrangement with his familiar to Annika just yet; after all, there was a chance nothing would happen anyway.

Chapter 8

NUANCED NAÏVETY

"Haaah . . . I did not know the viscountess could be so terrifying . . ." Alina breathed as she and Tam strode around the side of the castle near the rose maze.

"She normally is composed, but, well, Kat always manages to bring *that* side out of her," the Ashowan heir explained, his stare once again directed at the ground, but when the princess turned to peer at him, she noticed the worry in his eyes.

"So they don't get along?" she ventured hesitantly.

"It's better than it was a few years ago, but their temperaments are just too different. Kat is more like Da in that she has trouble hiding what she's thinking or feeling, but it's more extreme . . . meaning she always winds up in trouble—even if she had the best intentions. She also doesn't have his uncanny luck to get *out* of trouble."

"So you're more like your mum?"

Tam frowned, and Alina immediately grew fearful she had crossed some kind of line. "I . . . I guess."

"Ah! Your Highness, Lord Tamlin!"

Both the nobles looked at the same time to see Mr. Howard striding toward them holding scrolls under his arm as his long, burnt-orange satin vest with its gold designs swished behind him. The man was smiling as he approached them, but he seemed nervous as he looked between Tam and Alina.

"Out for a leisurely stroll . . . alone?" the assistant asked, while attempting to keep his tone light.

The princess opened her mouth to reply, but surprisingly, Tam beat her to it. "Yes. We are talking about how wonderful family is, aren't we, Alina?"

Tam turned his dark stare to her, making her mind turn blank at the sudden hint of warmth in his tone. Finlay Ashowan's words echoed in her mind.

The king is thinking of marrying the two of you.

That, paired with Alina's knowledge that some kind of romantic history existed between the viscount and her father's assistant, she could guess what to do.

A beautiful smile lit up the princess's face, her eyes twinkling with mischief as she addressed Kevin Howard. "Yes, Mr. Howard. You know, Tam and I really do have similar views on the importance of family and duty. Not to mention we both agree how wonderful cats can be for a healthy home dynamic."

Mr. Howard visibly paled and swallowed with what appeared to be great difficulty.

"I-I see. You know . . . Lord . . . Lord Tamlin, you really shouldn't be strolling with the princess when she doesn't have a chaperone. Given . . . given the guests here who seek to . . . to . . ." The poor man almost looked as though he were having a stroke.

"Ah, quite right. Especially given my *heartfelt* intentions regarding the princess that I *sincerely* expressed earlier. I hope this oversight doesn't color your opinion of me, Your Highness." Tam turned fully to Alina and bowed, and it took her entire might not to laugh.

His sincere statement earlier had been that he had no interest in her becoming his wife . . .

He was clever! He was simply serious and dry in his humor.

A small, choked garble erupted from the assistant, who was beginning to brighten in color once more, only he was crossing the threshold of a healthy flush into that of a fevered panic.

"Please . . . uh, please don't apologize, Tam. Excuse us, Mr. Howard, we will head inside now." Alina knew she needed to leave the situation; she wasn't as smooth in her lying as Tam was.

The assistant managed to stumble away, muttering something about, "The nightmare that never ends."

Once out of earshot, Alina turned and playfully smacked Tam's upper arm, though she was already chuckling. Even the normally serious man had a handsome smile brightening his features despite his eyes once again being focused on the ground.

"Here I was naïvely thinking it was just your sister who goes around causing trouble! You're just as bad, aren't you?"

Tam continued smiling as they veered toward the castle. "Not quite as bad. My fun tends to just be more subtle, and less physically demanding." Then after a beat of silence, his smile faded ever so slightly as he slipped his hands into his pockets, a move that made him look like his father. "You don't seem like you've had a lot of fun in your life, though. Which is strange, because I thought young princesses and princes would have the most opportunity to enjoy themselves. But you appear very . . . serious. At least until my sister's around."

Alina felt the weight in her chest return as her thoughts drifted to the disappointing reality of her life; her time with the Ashowans seemed more like a dream than reality.

"You'd be surprised how much responsibility there is from a young age. But I'm not completely boring! I don't think so anyway. I-I like music."

"I didn't mean any offense, sorry," Tam added hastily, his features returning to their usual neutral mask.

"I didn't take any offense . . ." Alina began to panic that she had lost the small fun side of Tam already. She hadn't meant to be so depressing. "Besides, I think what surprised me the most was how easy flirting was to you. You sounded like a real lover just now!"

A small humorous spark returned to Tam's eyes as the pair mounted the castle steps and returned to its cool shadows. "If you'd dragged it on, you would have quickly found out I have very little romantic skill. So don't be fooled."

"Still, it doesn't help that you tied some of your hair back today. I mean your looks are—"

Tam stared at her incredulously.

"—Dangerous. When, uh, when you actually look . . . look and smile at people." Alina was starting to wish there was a hole she could leap into to avoid her embarrassment. "I'm not interested in you, I swear."

Clearing his throat and turning away from her shy gaze, Tam shook his head. "At least I know another girl other than my mother finds me attractive. Pity I'm as attracted to you as I would be toward a—"

"Please, for my own pride, don't finish that sentence." Alina laughed easily, and then walked straight into something very solid.

Strong hands clasped her upper arms, holding her steady on her feet, and then after a moment gently pressed her back.

Alina looked up, and then up some more, into the troubled gaze of the Troivackian king.

"They should put a bell on you," she blurted out.

Tam let out an astonished laugh before hastily bowing. "So sorry, Your Majesty, she just caught me off guard."

The Troivackian king's attention toward Tam was honed, and deadly. Fortunately, Tam missed it as he bowed to the monarch.

Alina was gingerly touching her index knuckle to her aching nose. "S-Sorry, Your Majesty, you just . . . keep surprising me."

"It's fine. You wouldn't be the first person to comment on my walk, though you are the first to insult it," Brendan replied flatly.

Alina winced. "Ah, well, sorry again. I just was surprised."

"Yes, you said that," Brendan observed, tilting his head to stare at her with a small frown.

It was as though there was something annoying about her that he couldn't quite place, but before Alina could grow to be uncomfortable, he looked to Tam, who shifted back in response.

"You should go tend to your sister. She is upset."

Tam straightened, his expression sobering. "What happened?"

"That is up to your parents to inform you. Good day, Lord Tamlin."

The future viscount's eyes met the king's, and Alina couldn't help but be caught off guard by how brazen he was being. In fact, the coldness in his gaze shocked her deeply. She didn't know he was capable of looking so fearsome.

"Princess, please show me to the castle falcons so that I might send a missive to Troivack." Brendan turned abruptly back to Alina, his broad shoulders partially blocking the younger lord from her view.

"Are you asking or telling?" Tam's icy voice made the king look back at him.

"I beg your pardon, Lord Ashowan?"

"Your tone toward Her Highness was disrespectful."

Brendan squared off with the younger noble, and Alina's heart leapt to her throat.

"I'd be happy to take you, Your Majesty! It's in the opposite end of the castle, near the barracks. Shall we?" she called out desperately.

The king returned his attention to her slowly, as though he was struggling with the urge to pummel Tam repeatedly.

However, he eventually disengaged from the strange standoff and began walking ahead with Alina at his side. Though she did glance over her shoulder to Tam and mouth, *What were you thinking?!*

Tam lifted an eyebrow and gave a mystifying half smile and shrug before letting out a visible breath and continuing on his way back toward the kitchen.

The Troivackian king and princess then proceeded to stride down the castle corridor in silence, though servants who passed them hurried their steps and hunched their shoulders protectively.

I wish I could run away too, Alina thought to herself pityingly.

"You seem quite close with the Ashowan family, despite only having met them the other day," the king observed as he walked.

"How did you know I met them just the other day?" the princess asked blankly without bothering to glance at him.

"You have lived in Rollom for the majority of your life and haven't traveled much. The Ashowans have stayed in Austice, and the viscount rarely was in audience with his king after the war."

For some reason, the depth of the man's knowledge made Alina unconsciously shift away from him.

"It is hard to ignore the Ashowan family. A commoner witch was knighted and ennobled. A war hero who turned down the position of duke multiple times. A Troivackian wife . . . there are a great many things that are strange about them," the king expounded while trying to sound casual.

"That's what makes them wonderful," Alina responded tensely.

Brendan stared at the princess. "Why do you believe so?"

"It isn't hard to figure out. I'm sure you know what people say—"

"I want to know what *you* think."

Alina balked. Then she looked at the ground. Somehow, though, even thinking about the viscount's family was enough to bolster her mood and courage.

"The viscount came from nothing and only wanted enough power to marry his wife. He refused any more. In fact, the rumors say if it were up to him, he would've happily remained a cook here his entire life, but because of her, he worked until he was able to be by her side."

"There was a great deal of suspicious politics about the whole ordeal," the king recounted tonelessly.

"I agree that there are some mysterious parts of the story that I don't think I know everything about . . ."

"Especially pertaining to the viscountess's involvement in the war and persuading the king to have the house witch elevated in status."

Alina's gaze snapped to Brendan's face as she halted in her tracks. "Your Majesty, it feels as though you are trying to get information from me about the Ashowan family."

The king regarded her calmly. "They are an interesting topic. Why not try to learn more about them? I learn about you in the process. It's efficient."

"Why do you want to know more about them and me?" she asked testily, unable to stop herself, though she was once again trembling under his calm reaction, and she hated it.

"Them, because I don't like powerful families who have so much and yet hide their dealings. You, because I'm here to learn more about you."

"They aren't hiding anything! They are always trying to help people, and you already made it clear you don't believe I'd survive in Troivack, so why—"

"I said you wouldn't survive as you are now. Not that you couldn't ever," Brendan explained as though surprised she had missed such a small detail in his previous statement.

Alina felt her cheeks burning. She wanted to leave. She wanted to kick him in his ruddy shins and hide in her bedroom for the rest of the day. What the hell was wrong with him?!

"Sire, you have offended me and insulted a family I care deeply about. Excuse me, I would like to be alone now." Alina turned to begin to stalk off, only to find that the king was still keeping pace beside her.

When she rounded on him again, he held up his hands and even dared to show her an innocent expression.

"I have no idea where the falconry is. I assumed I just had to keep going in this direction. Is that the fastest you can walk, Princess?"

There was the faintest note of humor in his voice, and Alina found that she was closer than she had ever been in her life to screaming her lungs out at a noble.

A king, no less.

Without deigning to respond, Alina stormed past him going the opposite direction, sending a very clear message that she didn't want him to follow.

Letting out a long sigh, Brendan decided the falconry could wait. Perhaps there was a thing or two he needed to rethink . . .

"You . . . You told her she was unfit for Troivack?" Henry stared blankly at his brother.

"As she is now, yes."

The prince barely managed to swallow a hearty gulp of moonshine from his goblet before setting down the drink on the round table between them and bursting out laughing.

"Stop that," Brendan snapped while staring into the evening fire.

"You've always had a way of understating things, but with women, especially Daxarian women, you need to speak plainly, brother," Henry managed to say while sinking into his seat and folding his hands atop his belly.

"Since when are you an expert on women?" Brendan remarked acidly while taking a drink from his own goblet.

"I'm not, but they like me, which qualifies me as a master compared to you."

Brendan shot Henry a warning glance. "She will be a good queen. She just needs to be more assured and learn to be less emotional."

"So you plan on being the most irritating man alive so that she becomes immune to anything bothering her?" Henry wondered dryly.

"Is that a good plan?" the king asked seriously.

"I wish I could speak the old tongue like you do so that I'd have another way to say no. Absolutely not."

"Hardly anyone in Troivack still speaks it, don't worry."

"That was not . . . the point." Henry dropped his chin to his chest exasperatedly. "Don't laugh at her when she gets angry. It will make it worse. Also, don't interrogate her. Try to have a real conversation."

"You told me to ask about her life and to find mutual interests. The Ashowans are an interesting part of her life that I have many curiosities about. A mutual interest, and that went horribly."

"Let's go back to my point about *not* making it an interrogation."

Brendan grumbled deeply while finishing the contents of his cup.

"Did she actually make you laugh?" Henry asked wearily.

After a moment of recalling the way the princess had furiously tried to storm off, a softer look entered the king's eyes. "Almost. Watching her try to move quickly was like watching a mouse run across a frozen lake."

"Right. Never. And I mean *never* say that to her."

As he rose, Brendan turned to stare at his younger brother seriously. "I'm beginning to think choosing her to be my wife is more trouble than it's worth. She's too young."

The king then set about grabbing his coat off the back of his chair and heading toward the door joining their two rooms to retire for the evening without a second glance back.

As he watched his giant of a brother retreat, Henry's jovial expression faded. Turning back to his goblet and refilling it to the brim, he couldn't help but murmur aloud his true thoughts, "Actually . . . she might be what saves you."

Chapter 9

RISING RESERVATIONS

Alina was experiencing a rare peaceful morning as she played her lute and sang experimentally with her blank leather journal propped open by her side, ready for any words of inspiration that may strike her.

As the hours flitted past lazily, a knock eventually signaled the end of her solitude, and with a small sigh, even the princess had to admit she had had more than enough time to enjoy her hobby.

Her chamber door opened to reveal her personal handmaiden, Lady Marianne Dobbs, who was in charge of keeping track of the princess's schedule. Marianne had straight dark chestnut brown hair and a small delicate face, with a sprinkling of freckles across her nose. Despite her pretty appearance, however, she tended to be judgmental and reticent.

"Your Highness, Prince Henry has requested your presence in the rose maze center this afternoon. Afterward you will have your first courting date with Duke Rhodes's son from Xava. Tomorrow morning will be your second courting date with the Troivackian king. Your luncheon with Earl Lamont's son will follow. After that you will have to prepare with your maids for the ball that is to take place in a week's time—"

"In other words, I'm busy until the men all leave for the hunt at the end of the week."

"Yes. Precisely," Marianne recited dutifully, her stare both bored and appraising.

Secretly, the princess wished that Marianne would simply leave her position to focus on her own wedding, which was to take place the following year, and save Alina the awkwardness of having to handle her passive-aggressive nature. Sadly, she knew it would be unlikely, as the prestige of the position of handmaiden to the princess of Daxaria was highly sought after.

No, it was almost a certainty Marianne would be with Alina until her own royal wedding, at which point, depending on whom she ended up marrying, the princess would have to rely on her future spouse to arrange for her serving staff.

"You accepted the prince's invitation without asking me?" Alina asked after a moment when she recalled the very first piece of information Marianne had recounted.

"Forgive me, Your Highness, you were speaking highly of him last evening so I assumed it'd be acceptable." Marianne curtsied and subsequently hid her eye roll as she bowed her chin.

Alina could already guess that she was making such an expression, but she didn't feel it was a battle worth picking.

"It is fine. In the future, please check with me though."

In truth, it wasn't the first time the Lady Marianne Dobbs had taken it upon herself to control the princess's schedule but despite previous warnings Alina had given, the woman continued to do as she saw fit. Whenever the princess began to consider doing something about it, though, she found the churning in her stomach deterring.

I only have to put up with her for a few months at most . . . why get someone else when everything is so stressful and busy? It isn't worth it.

After getting ready for her impromptu meeting with the Troivackian prince, Alina left her chamber and made her way down to the rose maze where Henry stood, his arms crossed as he stared up at the sky.

Feeling herself smile instantly, Alina approached him with a slight skip in her step.

"Good day, Your Highness." She curtsied, and by the time she had straightened Henry was looking at her with his familiar warm grin.

"Thank you for joining me on such short notice, Princess." The Troivackian bowed dutifully.

"Happy to oblige." Alina's eyes twinkled happily.

"Wonderful; you see . . . I have an even bigger favor to ask of you," he began while gesturing to the entrance of the maze for them to enter with Alina's ladies-in-waiting falling behind out of earshot.

"Oh? What is that?"

"Well, you see, a lot of people have a very harsh opinion of Troivack because of the war, but we are just another country of humans. We have our own culture, with its own beauty."

Alina listened thoughtfully and nodded along.

"Which is why I was hoping that during the ball . . . would you mind singing some of the Troivackian songs with me as a duet? I think it'd help the general opinion of my kingdom."

The princess's jovial expression faltered then grew strained, and her steps slowed ever so slightly. "Ah. I . . . I sympathize with your dilemma, and agree that it isn't right to condemn an entire nation of people due to the past, but my father has never been fond of me performing."

Henry cocked an eyebrow and turned a quizzical stare to her. He looked incredibly similar to his brother in that moment save for the gentleness in his eyes.

"You see when I perform, my heart beats faster and I . . . sometimes I experience one of my attacks," Alina finished awkwardly, shifting her gaze to the side of the path to avoid meeting the prince's eyes.

"Ah, I understand completely; please feel no pressure. I merely thought it'd be a nice show of our kingdoms uniting harmoniously." Alina risked a small side glance at the prince, to see if he realized the pun and found he was grinning politely with sincere humor touching his eyes.

"You know what I . . . I . . . want to. So let's do it!" Alina burst out.

"Princess, I don't want to cause you any troubles. If your father would prefer you don't, there's no need to—"

"No, I think that this is a great opportunity to improve our relationship!"

Realizing the implications of what she had just blurted, Alina paused for a breath before she was able to speak to Henry, her face entirely red. "The relationship between our kingdoms, I mean."

The Troivackian noble laughed happily. "Well . . . if you're certain, I'd be happy to. By the way, don't think I haven't noticed you no longer calling me by my first name," he teased, while Alina dropped her eyes awkwardly. "Don't worry, I understand that you might feel the need to be more careful. Shall we discuss the song list for our performance instead?"

Alina smiled gratefully and happily changed the subject under the prince's gentle encouragement. It was turning into the most splendid day . . .

And who knew, perhaps it would be her first time successfully performing!

Norman stared at the document in front of himself with deepening concern. The room was deathly quiet despite there being six other people present.

"You are certain that these eyewitnesses hadn't met before to corroborate the story?" the Daxarian king asked gravely.

"Yes. The first was from a mining group, the second from a small town that is isolated from most of Troivack," Brendan Devark explained evenly.

Leaning forward in his seat and resting his forearms on the long table before him, Finlay Ashowan spoke. "A dragon and golems with moss growing on them?"

"Yes," Brendan replied without batting an eye.

"Were they hostile?" Captain Taylor of Daxaria asked while frowning.

"The dragon allegedly consumed a herd of cattle. The golems that the miners spotted were unaware of their presence, and they did not engage with them."

"Aside from the loss of livestock, it doesn't sound overtly harmful, but I agree this is alarming," Norman added while setting the report down on the table before himself and leaning back in his chair. "I take it you would like military aid?"

"No, Your Majesty. Troivack's forces are well equipped for the dangers. There is a civil war brewing, but this might be what unites us again," the Troivackian king replied calmly.

"Then why alert us of this potential threat?" Lord Fuks leaned forward shakily. Despite his impressive age, there was the undeniable note of rigorous interest in his voice.

"I want as much information as possible about these beasts. I was hoping to submit a formal request to the Coven of Wittica via your diplomat, Viscount Ashowan." Brendan turned his dark stare to the witch, who had raised an eyebrow while listening.

"I will submit the request today. Your Majesty, will you allow me to explain the sightings to the coven? Or would you prefer to keep that confidential for the time being?" Fin asked while looking to Norman.

"Request the information and see if the new coven leader will allow it without further explanation. If they press you, we will revisit this topic," Norman explained wisely while nodding to himself.

"There is another matter I wanted to discuss with both Your Majesty and Viscount Ashowan." Brendan Devark glanced at his own assistant, a silent reedy man who was clean-shaven and wore round spectacles. His brown eyes, however, were as sharp and deadly as any strong Troivackian soldier's should be. "Mr. Levin."

At hearing his name, the assistant unfurled a blank scroll and dipped his quill in the nearest inkpot.

"What is this matter?" Mr. Howard asked while eyeing the Troivackian assistant with skepticism.

"I want to discuss the day my father died, and the day my father's former chief of military, Aidan Helmer, was executed as well."

The room fell into a shocked silence.

"For what reason would you want to discuss this?" Mr. Howard demanded, his face paling as Norman straightened his shoulders, a frown moving over his features.

"I would like to know the true story of how my father died. The account reported to me was that it was you, King Norman Reyes, who slayed him in battle. Yet another report I received implied that it was an archer who struck him down. I ask for my peace of mind." Brendan gave a respectful bow of his head to Norman, but the glint in his eyes resembled a mountain cat surveying a potential threat.

Mr. Howard opened his mouth to presumably object, but Norman held up his hand and stopped him.

"Your father was charging toward the castle, leading his men. He deflected a rain of arrows with his shield, but once he reached our front lines, he discarded it as our archers ceased to preserve our men's safety. However, one particularly skilled archer felt confident enough to take the shot when your father and I were about to clash swords."

"What is the name of this archer?" Brendan asked while clearly trying to keep his tone light, but failing.

"For the sake of their safety, I will not share their name," Norman replied, eyeing the young king sternly.

Closing his eyes for a brief moment, Brendan leaned back in his chair and let out a breath.

"I do not ask for the purpose of vengeance. You may be misunderstanding my anger right now. War brings death, and Troivack was the first to attack. I know my father's death occurred where he would've preferred it, on the battlefield. I'm asking because I don't like disloyal subjects, or duplicitous dealings."

"How does your father's death contribute to duplicitous dealings?" Norman queried while regarding the youth with feigned passivity.

"I have reason to believe that a master spy has been working under you, Your Majesty, for some time. I want all informants removed from my court."

The stillness in the room was as fragile as cracked glass.

"What has this to do with your father's death?" Captain Taylor demanded, his voice loud in the mounting tension.

"It was a loose end that answered my question. Your spy who killed my father has great power here and can even reach my own castle walls. While there was some speculation about who it was back during my father's day, it was never properly addressed. I will reveal their identity and further details of this individual if these spies are not removed from my court."

"If you know who these spies are, why not remove them yourself?" Norman asked, tilting his head curiously.

"Because I don't know who all their informants are. I know by how I am treated here, however, that someone has been reporting my military moves. I take it that while your spy is powerful, they were unaware of the civil war I mentioned before. I am not preparing to attack Daxaria." Brendan's gaze never wavered from Norman, but the Daxarian king remained almost entirely at ease, save for a slight narrowing of his eyes.

"Why do you wish to know about my father's death?" Fin interrupted, though unbeknownst to him, his eyes were glowing a little too brightly.

"Your father warned you all of an old power returning to this world, and he himself had a dragon as a familiar. I want to know exactly what was said as it pertains to me defending my people."

"There aren't any more details other than he spoke of the death of our children, and that the old power was rising once more," the witch informed Brendan bluntly.

"I see. Thank you." The Troivackian king nodded to his assistant, who began scribbling down notes. "I suppose I will leave these two matters to rest for today. What is the next item on today's agenda?"

While the topics shifted to the upcoming hunt, no one could deny the unease that permeated the air, making everyone feel uncomfortable with the news of the strange creatures that had been spotted in Troivack, and the Troivackian king's suspicion regarding a master spy.

Fin, however, was already filled with worry over his wife. For some reason he couldn't put his finger on, he didn't think the young ruler was bluffing about knowing who the mastermind was behind the curtain.

As the viscount pondered this more deeply, the Troivackian king's gaze cut to him, and behind the deceptively still depths in Brendan's eyes, Fin saw the dislike and mistrust the man bore for him.

This could prove troublesome . . .

Alina swished into the library happily and glided over to the shelves where a handful of music books had been stored. She wanted to find a song that would best rouse the Daxarian courts to put them in good spirits, even if she didn't execute the performance as well as she'd like.

Humming as she moved, the princess failed to notice her father sitting in the armchair by the cold hearth with a book in his hand.

"Did you have a pleasant luncheon?" Norman asked with a small chuckle at his daughter's good mood.

Jumping and clutching her chest, Alina spun around to face her father. "Gods, I-I didn't see you there!"

Closing his book slowly, Norman leaned his head onto his fingers and regarded his daughter's flushed face and overall glow. "Were you spending time with Kat and Tam this morning?"

Alina clasped her hands together and shifted her gaze ever so slightly. "Actually, I . . . I was with Prince Henry in the rose maze."

There was a pregnant pause before Norman leaned back in his chair and visibly schooled his features. The princess felt her stomach twist with anxiety over the response.

"He isn't like the other Troivackians I've met. He's kind, and he laughs a lot. He likes music like I do, and—"

"So you are . . . interested in him?"

Blushing fiercely, Alina dropped her gaze. "A little."

"I see. How do you feel about Tamlin Ashowan?"

The princess's eyes jumped back up to her father, a kind smile in them. "He's a lovely man. A little . . . I don't know . . . I know something isn't quite right, but he isn't touched in the mind. It just seems as though he sees or hears . . . or *fears* something if he is left in a vulnerable position."

Norman nodded sagely, but it was hard to miss the hopeful light in his features. "Then last but not least, tell me your feelings regarding the king of Troivack, Brendan Devark?"

Alina couldn't explain the surge she felt in her chest or the strange flip in her stomach. Nor did she realize what kind of face she was making that startled her father.

"My dear one, I don't think I've ever seen you make an expression like that before. Mind if I ask you to explain?"

"It . . . He's just . . . he keeps popping up! I don't hear him coming, and he keeps surprising me! Then he'll say something that sounds like an insult, but turns out it isn't, and then I keep misunderstanding. He's entirely too forthright, and yet I don't know exactly what he's thinking and . . . and . . ."

"And?" Norman asked, completely taken aback by how befuddled his normally composed and sweet daughter was becoming.

Gripping her hands firmly, Alina frowned while trying to find the precise words to use about Brendan Devark. "He's the most vexing person I've ever met, but I don't think I hate him. Yet."

Staring in awe, and not saying a word, the Daxarian king wondered why that response was the one that filled him with the most concern of all three. Perhaps it was because his daughter rarely ever became so emotional.

Regardless, he began to hope more fervidly that Tam Ashowan would start to show signs of overcoming whatever it was that plagued him. Otherwise, there was the slight chance that his daughter may be asking to move far away from him, and . . .

He wasn't sure his heart could take it.

Chapter 10

SILENT STRUGGLES

Gleaming plates loaded with scrumptious steaming food sat before them. Wine goblets had been filled, the candles lit, but aside from the crash of the waves more than a hundred feet beneath them, the occupants of the dining hall sat in silence.

Tamlin Ashowan leaned forward and was the first to pluck up his fork, pointedly focusing on the food instead of his family members.

"Kat, would you be able to pass me the dinner rolls?" he ventured, hoping to get the conversation started between them all again.

The brown wicker basket was slid across the table with great force, and when Tam lifted his face fractionally, he noted that his sister's arms were once again crossed over her chest.

She doesn't even know she looks like Mum when she does that.

"You can stop looking so dour, Katarina. You were in the wrong. It could have been much worse if he had pursued the matter," their mother began. Without needing to look, Tam could tell that the viscountess was eyeing her daughter with the knowledge that she was emotionally volatile in that moment. They could all tell by the slow steady movements Kat made while cutting her emerald green beans, her cutlery glinting in the firelight.

"I was right to tell him he was being an arse. He just left her there—"

"I already explained this. In Troivack that is the most courteous thing to do. If Alina was still conscious and able to communicate, it was up to her whether or not she needed a physician."

"There were other ways he could have helped!"

"No, there weren't. She didn't signal for water, and both you and Prince Henry were hauling her out of the barn," Tam casually interrupted while taking a large bite out of his dinner roll.

The room fell silent as Tam continued eating without even bothering to look up from his plate.

Kat huffed loudly, "You weren't even there, so why are you—"

"Alina told me what happened. She felt terribly about you landing in trouble as a result, but—"

"Thanks for the backup, brother," Kat snapped angrily.

"—But I have more of an issue with how the Troivackian king spoke to her this afternoon," Tam finished while entirely ignoring his sister's interruption.

"What do you mean, Tam?" Fin asked. The viscount had been oddly quiet that evening.

"When I was walking with Alina into the castle yesterday, he intercepted us and dismissed me, then more or less ordered her to show him where the falconry was."

There was a prolonged moment where no one spoke, until Kat burst out again.

"See?! I knew it! *He* says I need to learn my manners? What about *him*? Who the hell is telling this Troivackian king what a pretentious, rude lug he is being?!"

Annika set down her fork and fixed her daughter with a steady gaze. "His bad behavior doesn't excuse yours. It doesn't mean either one is tolerable."

Glaring at her mother, Kat managed to tear her gaze off the viscountess to turn to her father. "Da, you know what I mean, don't you? He needs to be taught a lesson."

Fin let out a long, breath before easing back into his chair and fixing his daughter with a sympathetic, but slightly weary stare. "He needs to learn to be more gentle in his speech, and more patient, yes. However, after my meeting with him today . . . I believe he has had no choice but to become who he is."

Kat frowned, and Annika was swift to turn to her husband. "What do you mean by that?"

"The Troivackian king was very clear in stating that he hated deceit and hidden motives. I think his time growing up as a child king has worn away any patience or mercy in him, and instead we have someone who has had to learn to be strong or else be destroyed. I think he is . . . struggling with nuanced politics, and that he hasn't had a real chance to be human in a very long time."

The weight of his words settled on Fin's family, making a grim mood emerge amongst them.

"Any Troivackian has to be strong or else be destroyed," Annika pointed out, though there wasn't the edge in her voice that had been there earlier.

"None with the constant weight of their country on their head. Or ones who have had to be subjected to betrayal and elaborate assassination attempts from the time of childhood," Fin expounded, his eyes lost in thought.

In the quiet that followed his insight, the witch then raised his face to his family.

"Kat, Tam, we'll send up your dinners with you, but I need time alone with your mother."

Kat stiffened in her seat, and Tam, without bothering to glance at his family members, shoveled the final bite of his dinner into his mouth and stood. He was the first to exit the room, leaving Kat to follow suit at a far slower pace.

Shoving his hands into his pockets, Tam focused on the familiar stones of his childhood home one step at a time. He just wanted to be alone in his room. Or even the library . . . Perhaps some of the new books he had ordered had arrived . . . then he could get away from the unpleasant air that had settled over the evening.

Don't think about that now . . . it's tough enough keeping "it" from happening, he recited to himself out of habit.

"Tam! Wait up!" The sound of his sister's unmistakable long steps caught up to him easily.

"Don't you care what all that is about?" Kat asked while matching her walking speed to her brother's.

"Not particularly. Mum and Da will figure it out. You know they don't like to talk about politics with us."

Tam was forced to stop in his tracks as he noticed his sister's familiar cream-colored skirts in his way.

"You're going to be the next viscount. You should care about this stuff, too."

The youngest Ashowan didn't have to look to know his sister's arms were once again folded over her chest as she stared at him. He risked lifting his gaze to hers. It was dangerous to engage in such a topic when he already wanted to flee . . .

"Not for a long time. Thanks to Grandma Kate's curse he is aging at half the normal speed. If you look at Lord Fuks still leading the earldom in his nineties, I might die before ever having to be viscount." Tam shrugged while sidestepping his sister and moving onto the stones before the grand staircase that would carry him closer to his desired destination.

"Don't you give a shit about anything?!" Kat shouted at her brother's back, her hands falling to her sides and balling into fists.

Turning around once again, Tam risked meeting his sister's golden gaze, which was glowing fiercely in the day's dying light.

"Not all of us have to scream and make a scene to show we care, Kat."

The angry flush in her face almost made him regret his words.

"So how do you show *you* care, hm? Enlighten me! Because as far as I can tell, you sit and observe and judge everyone around you, but very little actual effort goes into caring for the people who love you. You just run away or avoid any conflict!"

Tam stared at his sister for a long moment, the rising anxiety in his chest growing unbearable, but even so, he waited until her angry breaths slowed. A trick the late Captain Antonio had taught him . . .

"I show people I care by being around them. For me, that's all I can manage without risking anything."

"Risking what?! You're always spouting off bullshit like that! What risk is there? What are you so damn scared of that you're letting it reduce you to being a scared child who would be dead or nothing without his parents!"

It was Tam's turn to feel a wave of emotion cross his face, and he could see a flicker of remorse appear in his sister's features. It was rare that he let anything bother him.

Even so, he knew it needed to be said . . .

"Kat, don't pretend like I'm the only one who is given extra privilege and accommodation thanks to our parents. I think yesterday with the king was more than enough of an example of that."

Pivoting away from Kat's stricken reaction, Tam swiftly climbed the stairs, eager to put as much distance between himself and his twin as possible. He was especially relieved when he didn't hear her scurrying up after him. It was taking every ounce of strength in him not to run the rest of the way to his chamber, and all because her words had definitely made more of an impact than he liked.

With one of his new books in his lap, Tam sat comfortably in the shadows by the barracks.

Normally the noise and rowdiness of the knights was a deterrent for him, but having to fight off the distraction was helping him occupy his mind instead of dwelling on his fight with his sister the previous night.

Most of the time the men knew better than to try and bother Tam, but an unfortunate coincidence was already brewing . . .

"Your Majesty! What brings you to our humble training ring!" Captain

Taylor's voice boomed out over the men, silencing the clangs and grunts instantly.

Tam lifted his face toward the commotion to find himself staring at not only the king of Troivack, but also his younger brother, Prince Henry. Both wore armor and had broadswords strapped across their backs and short swords on their right hips. The captain strode through the crowd of knights, who all immediately cleared a path for him.

"We have come hoping to train. Is this a good time?" Brendan asked after the captain had given a respectful bow. Sir Taylor's beard only had a few patches of black left, and his thin hair atop his head was almost entirely gray.

"We are happy to accommodate you; in fact, would you mind giving us a demonstration of the Troivackian method of fighting? This could be a great chance for our men to learn."

"A wonderful suggestion." Brendan Devark's eyebrows were raised, but he was clearly pleased with the subtle compliment the captain was paying him.

Tam slowly closed his book and found himself drawn to the sidelines of the spectacle as the knights all filed out of the ring to observe, while chortling amongst themselves about the demonstration and jesting with one another.

However, upon approaching the ring, Tam realized that even with his height, he wasn't able to get a clear glimpse over the heads of all the men. So he casually rounded their backs and made his way over to the captain's watch chair that stood several feet in the air. Its base was always kept clear should their military leader need to descend and instruct, but Tam knew Captain Taylor wouldn't mind if it was him leaning against one of the front legs.

Sure enough, when he locked eyes with the military leader, the two shared a nod of understanding before Tam pressed his shoulder against the leg and observed the Troivackian men circling each other.

Only the king wasn't facing his brother. He was staring directly at the future viscount over his shoulder, his blade glinting in the sunlight.

For a moment, everything faded away from Tam's senses. All sound disappeared, and it was as though everyone had suddenly vanished.

It was no longer the early summer day under a warm sun surrounded by lush grass and trees, but instead Tam felt as cold as the deepest blue winter. If he had seen the Troivackian king's breath, he wouldn't have been surprised. Colors were beginning to fade, and all at once the familiar tug in Tam's gut pulled at him, only it was stronger as emotion swirled in his chest.

He wanted to shout in the king's face.

He wanted to yell at Brendan Devark to stop staring, and to stop making everyone in the castle stressed and hostile . . . that he should leave and let things stay as they were.

Yes, to Tam, the moment he had heard of the Troivackian king coming, something in him knew that it meant change. It meant something far bigger was coming, and he couldn't shake the feeling. It had started in his bones and had grown and continued to grow even in that moment.

Tam tried to break the eye contact, tried to fight the overwhelming instinct of the magical thing in his being that terrified him every waking moment . . . but it was making him want to vomit.

Then, the king smiled. It was a knowing, calculating smile that told Tam the Troivackian nobility had seen his true feelings, and that he had him figured out . . .

Only, he *didn't* know.

Brendan Devark couldn't possibly imagine what would happen if Tam kept staring. Bitterness, mixed with mind-numbing fear, began to fill the future viscount.

As Tam tried to take slow calming breaths to silence the screaming in his mind, a different look passed through the king's eyes. One of apprehension.

Perhaps while he didn't know everything, he had seen a shadow of what Tam was restraining . . .

Then, Prince Henry's blade swung down, and Brendan's rose to meet it, letting out a loud clang that broke the momentary spell.

"Thought I had you there for a moment, brother. It isn't like you to be distracted," Henry chortled happily, unaware of the intense moment that had just passed.

"I wasn't distracted. I merely thought I glimpsed something interesting," Brendan replied loudly enough to be heard by the onlookers.

Henry attempted two more strikes, and with a flip of his wrist he almost landed a blow on his third, only Brendan Devark moved faster than the men could see and had the sword out of his brother's hand and on the ground in the blink of an eye.

For a Daxarian knight, that would've been the end, but Henry's second sword was already in hand and in motion. "So . . . what is it . . . you thought you saw?"

Brendan parried, and then, for the first time, attacked. It was a close-range blow that Henry blocked, but while he had been putting all his strength into defending against the broadsword, his brother's short sword appeared and the hilt dropped into his knee, immediately bringing the prince to a heap on the ground.

"That was dirty play!" one of the Daxarian knights shouted out angrily.

Though in fairness, Henry's fighting style toed the line of "clean" sparring as well.

Brendan turned toward the knight who had shouted and stared emotionlessly at him, which made the man take a hard swallow. "In a true fight, it doesn't matter if you fight dirty, it matters if you come out alive. Fair play is for children so we don't murder them while they learn."

His words brought about deathly silence before he once again faced his brother and offered him his hand to help him stand. "The strength of your hold in the third attack has greatly improved. You nearly had me."

"No, I didn't, but it is kind of you to say so." Henry laughed, still ignoring the wave of distrust that had rippled out amongst the Daxarian men. "So what was this thing you thought you saw?"

The prince mistakenly thought the answer would bring the conversation back to a lighter topic, but instead, Brendan glanced briefly again toward Tam. The future viscount stood rooted to the spot, his face pale as he worked with all his might to calm himself.

"Oh. I thought I saw a monster, but it must have already gone back into hiding."

Chapter 11

DEFT DUELS

Alina was on her way back from an unpleasant courting date with the heir to the Lamont earldom, when she heard the fervent whispers of the servants regarding the Troivackian king and prince training by the barracks.

As much as she wanted to screech to a halt and demand the details, she had her attendants with her.

Even so, she couldn't just ignore a chance to see the infamous Troivackian techniques . . .

"Shall we see what all the fuss is about at the training ring?" Alina asked aloud while managing to make herself sound disinterested.

"Your Highness is too ladylike to handle the brutality," Marianne, her personal handmaiden, replied dutifully.

Alina felt herself grow awkward and embarrassed.

"I . . . I suppose you are ri—"

"ALINA! Thank Gods I found you, we *have* to see this!" Katarina Ashowan came barreling down the corridor while nimbly dodging the princess's entourage and Marianne, who tried unsuccessfully to subtly get between the two women.

Grabbing Alina's arm, Katarina turned her devious grin to her new friend. "I hear Captain Taylor has allowed the king of Troivack and the prince to train in the ring as a learning experience! There is no way we are missing it!"

Marianne stepped forward, her disapproving frown still somehow appearing elegant. Though her face was tilted down, her stiffened features were easy to discern.

"Dueling, particularly Troivackian dueling, is a rough and unseemly activity. It is not ladylike for Her Highness to attend."

"Doesn't the princess get to decide what is proper or not as the highest-ranking one of us here?" Kat asked, straightening her shoulders to her full height, and raising a sardonic eyebrow toward the handmaiden.

"Speaking of *rank*, Lady Katarina, you have not greeted me properly," Marianne reminded sharply.

The redhead's right eye twitched as she belatedly lowered into a curtsy, though it was done laboriously.

The assistant had a smug smile on her face, but she was caught off guard when Katarina once again grabbed Alina, who was standing rooted to the spot unable to make a move as indecision on how best to respond vacillated in her heart.

"Good day, Lady Marianne."

Katarina took off, pulling Alina along with her. The two were setting off on a jog, and the princess was beginning to feel an unconscious smile appear, when they rounded the corner, and she felt the familiar shudder of her lungs. Skidding to a halt, Alina closed her eyes and did her best to take very slow, long breaths to stave off the rattle of coughs that threatened her lungs.

"Ah, sorry about that. Forgot you can't really do much running." Katarina, who had stopped a few feet ahead, rounded back with an apologetic smile.

Alina gave a small dismissive wave. "It's alright. We can walk quickly if you prefer?"

The redhead turned back to face the western side of the castle with a delighted gleam in her features while offering her arm to her friend. "Shall we, Princess?"

Alina laughed while hooking her elbow with Katarina's. "I'd love to."

Sword in hand, Brendan faced Tamlin Ashowan, who was standing rigid by the base of the captain's watch chair.

"I'd like to train with you, Lord Tamlin. I presume as the future heir to the viscount house you have received some basic degree of instruction."

Captain Taylor leaned forward, his previously studious expression turning strained. "Your Majesty, the young lord has never trained in front of a crowd. There is no need to put him on the spot."

"With all due respect, Captain, I will see what the young lord thinks of my request." Brendan bowed his head to the military leader before once again fixing Tam with his unwavering gaze.

"Brother, it's a scratch. I'm fine to continue training with you," Henry called over from his place on the sidelines where the Royal Physician was in the process of stitching shut a small yet deep gash on his upper arm.

Tam met Brendan's gaze, and surprising everyone, he seized the captain's sword that was leaning against the base of the chair, while also placing his book down. Without hesitating for a moment, he strode forward, his sights never wavering from the king.

"This will be light training," Tam directed the statement to Brendan in lowered tones. "For instructional purposes."

One of Brendan's dark eyebrows rose upward. "Tell me, is it that you think you can best me, or is it that you fear I can see that you are more than you appear?"

Tam didn't say a word as he struck a beginning position and waited, though there was a slight trembling in his hand.

Addressing the crowd of knights around the ring, Brendan raised his voice. "Lord Ashowan's feet are not far enough apart, if I strike him as he is now, he will lose his footing like so." Swinging his sword from the side faster than anyone had been expecting, the king struck near Tam's ribs.

Only instead of countering the swing, Tam darted out of its arc.

Brendan smiled. "Avoiding a blow when you suspect your opponent to be stronger than yourself isn't a bad move, though it is entirely dependent on you maintaining your speed and awareness of your surroundings."

The monarch then executed four quick jabs that backed Tam into the wooden railing of the training ring.

"As you can see, if you fail to do one of those two things, it makes it easy for an opponent to corner you."

Tam held up his hands in surrender. He had intended for it to end as soon as possible, but he had been surprised at just how talented the Troivackian king was. Tam pried himself away from the fence and began following behind the monarch toward the ring's exit.

Just as well. He needed Brendan Devark to lose interest in him. It was becoming dangerous . . .

As the king reached for the gate, a sudden cry rang out.

"TAM, WATCH OUT!"

The Troivackian king had stealthily begun to withdraw his short sword while making it appear as though he was moving for the gate latch, and he was swinging the sword right for Tam's middle.

Reacting on instinct without thought, Tam deflected the blow, then proceeded to step closer to the king intending to kick his groin. Only Brendan was drawing out his broadsword again and blocked the kick while bringing the other sword in his hand down in an arch over Tam's head.

Ducking under the Troivackian's arm easily due to his close proximity, Tam whirled around to face the king's back, his own sword rising upward for a strike, only despite his size, Brendan moved remarkably nimbly as he twisted and blocked the attack with his short sword.

Facing each other once again in a dueler's stance, Tam was about to announce the end of the fight, when Brendan rushed him.

Forced to step closer to the Troivackian to defend one sword and avoid the other blade, Tam managed to instep the king's foot and ram his elbow back into Brendan's nose, momentarily stunning him, and allowing Tam to knock the short sword out of the king's grasp into his own before twisting out of reach again.

"Enough," Tam panted, feeling the familiar tug in his gut begin to grow stronger. He just wanted the fight to end before he lost control.

Brendan Devark, wearing a hungry smile, wiped the blood from his nose with the back of his hand.

"I knew your Troivackian blood would come out sooner or later."

Tam's face turned stony and for a moment, he remained perfectly still as the spectators shifted awkwardly and whispered amongst themselves. After a dark look in the king's direction, Tam began to move, striding past Brendan with his shoulders tensed. Sheathing the captain's sword, Tam left it by the base of the chair where he had first found it. He then proceeded to stick the king's short sword into the ground, and picking his book up where it had laid on one of the watch chair's beams, he continued walking without looking back.

"Your Majesty . . ."

Everyone's eyes turned from Tam's retreating back to Katarina Ashowan and Alina. Katarina's expression was murderous. However, it had been Alina's meek voice that had spoken out.

The king's eyes softened when he noticed her tentatively entering the training ring, clearly uncomfortable with all the attention being placed on her.

"Yes, Princess?" Brendan returned politely with a bow.

"I would like to have a private word with you . . . over . . . over there." Alina nodded over to the wide expanse of green lawn just south of the training ring where not a single soul stood. "We will be within sight of the captain," she added suddenly.

Brendan was puzzled about why that mattered, before recalling he hadn't officially made her his betrothed yet. In his mind it was as good as done.

Sheathing his sword and exiting the ring, he stopped in front of the princess, and appreciated that for once she didn't flinch under his pointed attention. Offering her his arm, he noted the look of surprise on her face, which then quickly resumed its previous uncertain expression while they strode away from the ring.

As soon as the knights thought the royal pair were out of earshot on the castle lawn, they began murmuring amongst themselves.

Once she was certain they would not be overheard, Alina released her hold on Brendan's arm and faced him, her cheeks pink.

"That was a poor choice of words to describe Tam— I mean, Lord Tamlin. Y-You should apologize."

Brendan blinked in astonishment, unable to speak for a moment. "I don't understand."

Alina flushed more deeply, and her hands gripped together in front of her skirts, but still she managed to form a reply. "After the war, Troivackians were not treated kindly here in Daxaria. Even if Lord Tamlin is the son of the great house witch, his mother and he faced a lot of prejudice from some of the nobles and civilians."

Brendan's hand idly rested on the hilt of his sword, and his head lowered slightly to the princess. "I noted his Troivackian heritage as a compliment."

"I-I recognize that you see it that way, but announcing that in front of the knights is going to have repercussions for him," she managed to say while finally breaking free from his overwhelming gaze.

"Then as an heir to a viscount title he should be strong enough to handle it. Though admittedly I'm surprised that you are the one speaking to me and not the lord's sister," Brendan observed, changing the subject swiftly.

He wasn't sure why there needed to be such a discussion to begin with. Everyone could be an enemy; it was up to the individual to be strong enough on their own.

"I'm speaking to you because it is my duty as your host here in Daxaria. You need to be mindful that there is bad blood between the nations, and Tamlin Ashowan, no matter how strong he may or may not be, cannot take on an entire country's wrath. Nor should he." Alina found it far easier saying what she needed to with her frown directed at the lush green grass rather than whatever expression the Troivackian king was making toward her at that moment.

"You expect me to believe Lord Tamlin is the only mixed-race Troivackian on your shores? Is his sister not half Troivackian as well?"

"Don't be obstinate," Alina burst out before she could stop herself. She risked looking at Brendan but found his hard obsidian eyes all the more terrifying. Even so, she forced herself to keep speaking. She knew if she didn't, Katarina would intervene and the well-intentioned redhead would once again land in a world of trouble.

"Tam is one of five nobles here in Daxaria who are Troivackian or share Troivackian heritage; he is grossly outnumbered. Following the war, there were numerous innocent citizens of Troivackian backgrounds who were murdered in the streets out of fear and hatred. While things have improved here gradually, you have damaged how our men-at-arms see him. Katarina bears little to no resemblance to her mother and so people have been more lenient toward her if the rumors I've heard are true."

Brendan straightened and then folded his thick forearms with their coarse black hair across his chest.

"You seem determined to be the defender of the Ashowans. Though I have to wonder what they have done to earn such loyalty from you. Their wealth is great, yet they have ties with criminals and questionable establishments. The viscount has the power to defend thousands of people alone, and the viscountess . . . there is more I wish to say, but won't. My point is that they have much to hide, and I do not believe it wrong to be wary of them. Especially when they seem perfectly capable of defending themselves."

"The Ashowan family is—! Never mind." Alina cut herself off; her eyes were watering and she hated it. Even so, she needed to drive her point home. "The viscount and viscountess have nothing to do with Tam right now. You are in the wrong, Your Majesty."

Tears had begun to slip out against her will, and the princess was doing her best to dash them with the back of her wrist to avoid causing a scene.

The Troivackian monarch said nothing for a moment, as though he were giving her time to compose herself . . . or was he waiting to express his displeasure over her request?

"For referencing Lord Tamlin's Troivackian blood, I will offer my . . . regrets. However, I will not apologize for my skepticism of 'the great' Ashowan family. Though I do believe Tamlin Ashowan hides a different nature rather than illicit dealings. I can see the shadows he is capable of ruling and his ease with death's carriage driver. If you favor him, Princess, be careful."

Alina raised her gaze sharply to Brendan's, her hazel eyes bright as the tears seemed determined to keep falling. "He is a good man, and he has done nothing wrong. If your dislike of Tam stems from talks of he and I becoming betrothed, I thought it was clear that there is no future between—"

"You and the viscount's son becoming betrothed?" Brendan's casual puzzlement in turn made Alina frown.

Then blinking his eyes wide and giving his head a shake, the king dropped his arms so that his hand rested on the hilt of his sword. "Ah, I keep forgetting to say that the matter has been settled already. I believe with some training you will make an acceptable queen for Troivack. I was supposed to inform you of this later today."

All color drained from Alina's face. "I . . . I beg your pardon?"

"I was told it was customary here in Daxaria to discuss it with the prospective bride before her father, so I was going to do so this afternoon. However, I will tell you now; I have decided it is a good union so there is no need for your other courting dates to continue."

As Alina's mouth opened and closed without a sound coming out, Brendan briefly wondered if the princess had another affliction aside from her breathing difficulties.

"I . . . am not . . . going to marry you. How *dare* you try to take my choice from me!" Despite her best efforts, Alina's throat was closing from the swell of her emotions. It grew so tight, in fact, that she worried yet again that a breathing attack would beset her . . .

"I have not agreed or expressed *any* interest in marrying you. I do not wish to speak to you ever again about this. Goodbye, Your Majesty." She turned on her heel, striding away hurriedly, and Brendan stared after her, completely stunned.

What had he said that was wrong?

Also, why in the world was she crying? What was the customary thing to do when a Daxarian woman cried?!

Looking back toward the training ring, Brendan found himself staring at a sea of matching frozen faces.

Save for two that bordered on bloodthirsty . . .

One belonged to Lady Katarina Ashowan, and the other to King Norman Reyes of Daxaria, Alina's father.

Chapter 12

COUNSELING A KING

Norman stood in his council room staring out the window with his back to his sole visitor. The large Troivackian king stood rigid, his hand gently clasping the hilt of his sword. Should anyone have looked upon the man, they'd have thought he were about to engage in a casual conversation about the weather.

If Prince Henry, Brendan Devark's brother, had peered in, however, he would be most amused to see his brother looking ever so slightly . . . scared? Nervous?

"We will speak candidly, Brendan. As this pertains to my daughter, and we are alone, you are not a king right now. You are a man courting my child, and less than an hour ago, you said something to her that made her cry. I want an explanation. Now."

Norman turned and finally faced the Troivackian who silently admitted the hardness in the Daxarian king's eyes nearly made him avert his own gaze and shift the weight in his feet.

"Your daughter, Princess Alina, was drawing my attention to a comment I said in the training ring pertaining to Viscount Ashowan's heir. It had not been said with any insult intended, but apparently it was interpreted badly," Brendan finished while noting that his heart rate had increased for some strange reason.

"Why was she crying?" the elder demanded imperiously.

Brendan balked.

A moment of weakness.

He hadn't had one of those in years . . .

"I . . . do not know. She sounded more angry than saddened. I think." Brendan's hand at his side began to clench.

"You 'think'? Were you not present for the exchange?" Norman asked angrily.

"I was, but I can't understand what was said that would cause the princess to become emotional. I hear some women during their monthly courses—"

"If you finish that sentence, I will have you thrown into a cell for the rest of the night."

Brendan frowned, completely taken aback. "Your Majesty, I do not understand. What have I said to cause such hostility?"

With a murderous glare, Norman studied the Troivackian king for several moments. "I cannot tell if you are being willfully ignorant, or if you truly do not know what you have said."

Growing irritated, Brendan's stunned expression changed to a very flat exasperated scowl. "I'm beginning to think we are speaking a different language. I haven't the slightest idea what has everyone so upset."

"Alright . . . I sincerely hope you mean what you say. Otherwise the next few hours will be painful for no reason."

Brendan let out a disgruntled sigh. "As long as some clarification is— Wait, hours?"

"Guards, please summon Lord Ashowan, Captain Taylor, Lord Fuks, and, Gods help us, Mage Keith Lee."

"Sire, what about Mr. Howard?" one of the guards called back through the door, a note of excitement in his voice.

"Ah yes, of course!" Norman replied with a slightly manic glint in his eyes as he turned to face the younger man once more. "Prepare yourself, Brendan Devark, king of Troivack. It is time you learned a few things."

"So . . . I . . . am confused about what is happening," Prince Henry announced, glancing across the table at the row of Daxarian men all in civilian garb.

Wine bottles and one lone bottle of Troivackian moonshine were floating around the table filling goblets. Meanwhile, trays of cold meats, cheese, and fruit were laid in the middle of the table.

Norman remained standing at the head of the table, a lively glow around him that no one had seen since before Ainsley's death. "Men, I have asked you all here to help understand and explain what the king of Troivack has done to upset the princess, and how he insulted Lord Tamlin Ashowan. I myself do not know all the details, but given what I've already heard from the king, I knew this would be necessary."

"You insulted Tam?" Fin interjected, his attention swiftly moving to the Troivackian king, who sat across from him with Henry.

"I thought I was offering him a compliment," Brendan growled, not liking the magical glow in the viscount's eyes.

"Ah, I understand," Henry interrupted, his good-natured smile returning. "Brother, did you summon me to translate?"

"Translate?! Have I finally gone senile? I thought we were all speaking the same language! Godsdamnit, Les might've been right—" Lord Fuks exclaimed with great alarm. The unexpected interruption caught the men off guard, but once all had recovered, they noted that it had markedly lessened the tension in the room.

"Ah, pardon me, Earl Fuks— Great name by the way," Henry added on with a roguish smile.

"You have good taste." Lord Fuks settled back down and grinned peacefully.

"I thank you for the compliment. What I meant about translating, however, is that, well, the Troivackian king is straightforward to a fault, but . . . he is often misunderstood. He also doesn't understand when people interpret things in a way he can't empathize with."

"Henry, you will mind your tongue," Brendan warned darkly.

"That means he might hit me over the back of the head if I keep talking about him as though he—"

The Troivackian king's giant hand snaked out and cuffed his brother's head roughly.

"I believe I understand. Prince Henry is here as someone with a deep understanding of both yourself and those with a more . . . sensitive nature," Mr. Howard volunteered while tucking into a plate of food and a goblet filled to the brim with wine.

"I don't understand anything," Keith Lee informed everyone while blinking in confusion.

There was a beat of silence before Norman resumed control of the conversation. "Your Majesty, would you please recount what you said to both Lord Tamlin Ashowan and my daughter, verbatim."

Looking as though he would much rather be on a battlefield bathed in blood and surrounded by corpses in that moment, the Troivackian king slowly, and painfully, informed them all of his exchange with the young lord and princess. Though he left the details about his suspicions surrounding the Ashowan family out of it.

By the end of the tale, all men around the table were a tableau of extreme reactions.

Norman stood frozen, clearly trying not to launch himself at the younger king to throttle him. Keith Lee was frowning, still trying to understand, Mr. Howard had his face covered with both hands, Captain Taylor was cringing and trying to hide the expression by rubbing his forehead vigorously. Lord Fuks was laughing hysterically, and Finlay Ashowan looked both appalled and flabbergasted at the same time.

Feeling his rage rise over his embarrassment, Brendan turned to his brother, only to find that he, too, was staring at him with his mouth hung open and his eyes wide in mortification.

"AaaaAAAUUGHHH!" Mr. Howard let out a loud moan mixed with a shout before he dropped his hands from his face to address the Troivackian king again. "You *genuinely* don't know that it is considered beyond rude, and—"

"Bullyish," Captain Taylor added before being able to stop himself.

"Yes, bullyish. To *tell* a princess that she will marry you and that is the end of the discussion? Without you having talked with her father? Without allowing her to attend all her courting dates?"

"Before the ball?!" Keith Lee interrupted, having finally caught up and then becoming equally incensed.

"Right! Before the bloody ball!" Mr. Howard added, his hysteria mounting.

"Brother, that was . . . not your finest moment." Henry's voice was quieter than the others, but his was the one that made Brendan turn, and a shadow of pain passed through his eyes.

"Our union would be beneficial for both kingdoms. I thought that if it were an acceptable match, it made the most sense," Brendan explained, his voice unexpectedly hoarse.

"Your Majesty," Finlay Ashowan's calm voice passed over the table, making Brendan visibly tense and his expression grow shuttered once more as he looked back to the viscount. "The princess is an intelligent young woman. You attempted to undermine her judgment and take any power she has in this situation. Do you understand?"

As much as Brendan wanted to dismiss or question anything the witch had to say, the man wasn't being condescending. He was explaining patiently, without any derision in his tone.

"In Troivack, our women have no say in these matters. Their judgments are saved for managing the education of children until they are six years old.

Then they split their arranged lessons with the father's education path for them. Our women manage the household, and even some of the financial accounts; however, pertaining to large-scale decisions such as marriage and business, they are seldom a part of them," Henry explained, his face blank as he subtly defended his brother's behavior.

"I'm aware of your customs. Which is what brings me to ask, why is it *you* know differently?" Norman turned to the prince, his voice deceptively calm.

"Ah . . . I am not what is considered normal in Troivack. If it weren't for my brother being the king, I would most likely be exiled as a radical. However, that is why—"

"—That is why I believe Princess Alina will one day be a good fit for Troivack," Brendan interrupted, his shoulders beginning to straighten once more.

"What do you mean, sire?" Mr. Howard asked, leaning forward with his hands clasped tightly together.

"She composes herself with dignity and can express herself well when she overcomes her fears. I believe once she becomes more self-assured, she can help me bring change to Troivack's attitude toward women garnering more say in our courts and laws."

To say everyone was stunned would be an understatement.

"You . . . You wish to break Troivackian tradition?" Keith Lee spluttered in awe.

"Troivack's tradition is to be strong. I believe we can be stronger this way," Brendan replied tonelessly. It was clear the whole ordeal was wearing on him greatly.

"What is it that brought about this opinion? It is quite different from the beliefs your father held," Norman asked seriously.

At this, an iciness settled in the Troivackian king's stare. "That is a private matter. Now, aside from chastising me like an errant child, is there any use to this meeting?"

"You need to apologize to Alina, and to Tam," Fin answered firmly, once again drawing Brendan's stare to his own.

"Troivackians do not apologize."

"But a man does," Captain Taylor interjected wisely. "Man, or woman. A person of strength and honor can grow and regret their follies. Have you grown and regretted the offenses you've committed, Your Majesty?"

Brendan's gaze moved over to the military leader, and it was clear he didn't wish to answer.

"If you still want a chance with the princess, I recommend it, sire!" Lord Fuks added with a wry grin.

"I will not compete with lesser men for her hand," Brendan replied ambiguously with the corners of his eyes tightening.

"Your opinion on who is the greater and who is the lesser is not relevant." Fin's hardened tone made everyone in the room once again grow tense. "It is who she prefers or deems worthy. What makes a man greater or lesser is relative, Your Majesty."

There was a breath of silence, in which everyone present could clearly glean the viscount's wish to verbally strip down the ruler's arrogant and stubborn attitude.

Standing abruptly, Brendan regarded the men, the air about him beastly. He then turned and left the chamber without another word. He was not going to tolerate being ganged up on in a hostile room.

When the door slammed shut, the walls of the castle shook.

Henry smiled nervously at the Daxarian men. "I swear, he is a decent person. He's loyal to a fault, it just . . . takes him a little longer to change than others."

Picking up their goblets, most of the men drained their beverages in a single gulp.

"Who knows, perhaps the princess already has a possible husband in mind," Fin casually mentioned while locking eyes with the prince.

Henry looked slightly uncomfortable and taken aback by the statement, but he dissolved the awkwardness by smiling and reaching for the bottle of moonshine on the table and topping up his beverage.

"This is a nice little gathering; do you all do this often?" Henry asked lightly, while leaning back into his chair and pointedly changing the topic.

His tentative relaxation halted when he noticed the glances between everyone but Captain Taylor and Mage Keith Lee.

"Back during the war. This was my inner council," Norman explained, a sadness filling and darkening his hazel eyes. "The summer before the war . . . Alina was born, and we had the best of men here. Sadly, Captain Antonio passed away six years ago now, my Ainsley three, and Keith's father two . . . May the Gods rest their souls peacefully."

Fin's gaze dropped to his chalice as the somber mood moved over the group.

"AND I'LL BE NEXT!" Lord Fuks declared with a roar that felt too big for the shriveled old man.

"Oh Gods, Dick, you know saying things like that makes people uncomfortable—" Norman began to say despite his lips twitching.

"NO! Don't brush this off! Those other arses stole the full glory my funeral was supposed to have by dying first! Now you're all always just a little bit sad all the ruddy time! It's not the same! I *will* be the next to die, and you all *will* show up drunk with your wives or so help me Gods— I WILL CRAWL OUT OF MY GRAVE AND MAKE YOU DO IT RIGHT!" The senile old man had risen from his chair and shook his shriveled fist to the heavens, his eyes ablaze with righteous fury.

"You want the women drunk, too, my lord?" Prince Henry asked, unable to stop himself even though he had been warned about the man's antics. In truth, he was finding it rather difficult not to break down into hysterics . . . then again he was not alone in that struggle from the looks of the other men's faces.

Then of course, Lord Fuks drove the final nail home.

"OF COURSE! I WANT AT LEAST FIVE BABES CONCEIVED THANKS TO MY DEATH!"

Sir Taylor and Fin were the first to succumb to their uncontrollable laughter and snorts, closely followed by the king himself, whose shoulders were quivering right before he let out the loudest boom of a HA! anyone had ever heard from him. Soon afterward Keith Lee joined, though more so because the laughs were contagious.

Leaning over to Mr. Howard, who was the last one not laughing, Prince Henry couldn't help but ask, "Is Lord Fuks senile? Or . . . ?"

"Believe it or not he has mellowed over the years," Kevin Howard replied seriously before he proceeded to drain his cup yet again. Even the perpetual grumpy assistant had a hard time hiding his smile, however, as the room erupted in much needed fun.

It truly had been too long.

Chapter 13

REGENT REGROUPING

Alina sat furiously wiping the tears from her face as Katarina paced angrily several feet in front of her on the castle lawn by the servants' cottages. Alina was facing the trees, and hoping that no one else would pass by and gape at her blotchy face . . .

"So he wants to marry you. Maybe you should tell your father that you'd rather set your skirts on fire than agree to it!" the redhead exclaimed suddenly, flinging her hands in the air.

"It . . . It'd be good for our kingdoms. I had just assumed he . . . he didn't want to marry me because I'm . . . weak." The words choked Alina, her deepest insecurity coming forth from the dark shadows of her heart.

Yet Katarina didn't hear the quiet declaration over her fuming. "Plus, he forced my brother to fight?! I'm shocked Tam even managed it without throwing up! Normally, as soon as things get too stressful, he starts going pale and stumbles away . . ." Turning swiftly and plopping herself down beside the dejected princess, Kat let out a very loud groan. "I wish I could've jumped into the ring and gotten a few swings myself at that giant lu—"

"What's this about taking a few swings?"

The two young noblewomen jumped at the voice behind them. As they turned around swiftly, both Alina and Katarina found themselves staring up into a pair of deep blue eyes framed by golden wisps.

"Ah, Hannah! It's just you." Kat flopped down onto the grass in relief.

"Glad to see you, too, Kitty Kat. Your Highness." The blonde aide curtsied dutifully to Alina, who bobbed her head awkwardly. "So, ladies, what is all this excitement about?"

"Well, the Troivackian king made my brother duel him in the training ring, then brought up his Troivackian blood. After that, he told Alina he decided to marry her and that she should stop attending her courting dates."

Hannah blinked several times. She then dropped her ear toward her shoulder thoughtfully and rested her hand on her hip while a small frown creased her forehead.

"Huh."

"Is that it?! 'Huh'?! The infamous kitchen aide who nearly killed a man with my dad's frying pan?! Where's the thirst for blood?!" Kat demanded, sitting back up with bits of grass still caught in her red hair, which was quickly growing more and more disheveled despite being pinned to the back of her head.

"I'm getting old, give me a break," the blonde replied dryly. "Besides, Kitty Kat, I love you, but you tend to get fired up before gathering all the information. So I take what you say into consideration, but I'd like to hear—"

"Alina was there! She can vouch for me! The Troivackian king really did all that!" Katarina insisted while reaching over and tugging on the princess's sleeve.

Rubbing the remaining tears away best she could, Alina looked up at Hannah shyly. She hadn't spoken much to the maid, and Hannah hadn't refuted nearly clubbing a man to death, which made her a mite more fearsome than her slight physique suggested.

"It is true . . ." Alina managed to confirm her friend's tale.

Hannah's mouth stretched to the side as she slowly crouched down to be eye level with the nobles. "So do you want to marry the king?"

"Of course she doesn't! He's an arse! A bully!"

"Kat, I was asking the princess, let her answer." Hannah shot the redhead a patient yet warm glance before returning her attention to Alina. "Go on."

"I . . . I don't think so. Honestly, I feel more comfortable around his brother, but if I married the Troivackian ruler, our marriage would do really wonderful things for the kingdoms. I can't ignore that this could change the future relationship for Daxaria and Troivack for the better," Alina's voice croaked as she gripped her sleeves a little more tightly.

"Wouldn't marrying Prince Henry have similar results?" Hannah asked gently.

"Maybe, but if King Brendan wants me as his wife, it could cause an even greater divide . . ." It was then the overwhelming hollow ache in Alina's belly began.

It was familiar, and painful . . .

She wanted to talk to her mom.

Her mom would know what to say; she could help her daughter figure out what to do and she . . . she would hug her like when she was little and—

"Perhaps try talking about this with His Majesty, your father. Our king is a fair man, and a wise one. He might have insight that could be helpful." Hannah's kind voice had interrupted the usual spiral of grief the princess found herself in when she started thinking of her mother. Gradually, she was able to bring her mind back to the present, moving away from the usual fog of sadness she could become lost in for days.

"My father *is* a great ruler but when it comes to me . . ." Alina blushed. "He's a little biased at times."

"Lucky." Kat sighed while blowing an errant wave of red hair out of her face.

"Kat, your parents give you plenty of leeway. You just don't appreciate how hard they're trying to make sure you don't—"

"Turn out like an arsehead?"

"I was going to say alienate everyone around you, but sure, that works, too. Look how persnickety Mr. Howard is, for instance!"

Kat's deflated expression suddenly livened with a mischievous smile. "What a great idea, Hannah! Bothering him always cheers me up! Alina, do you want to come and help me find some new prank to play on him? One time I stole every left shoe he owned and he went bonkers for a day."

"That was you?! We all thought he had a spontaneous mental break-down for a week for no reason!" Alina's jaw dropped and her eyes rounded.

"Well, I mean . . . he *did*, I just was an unknowing catalyst to it is all."

"You're playing with that word 'unknowing' as though you don't know what it means," Hannah remarked with narrowed eyes.

"Look, I honestly didn't expect him to be bedbound from the incident. How could I have known that he was going through bad insomnia at the time?"

"Everyone knew," the maid replied drolly.

"Well, I thought it'd get him to loosen up a bit is all. He was only visiting Austice for a month, and everyone was saying he needed to find a distraction from all the work he was trying to handle with interviewing mages."

Hannah sighed; she knew a losing argument with Kat was better con-ceded early on. "Listen you, I admit, you can be funny." The maid tapped her index finger to Kat's nose, making her golden eyes cross for a moment. "Sometimes, though, you need to rein yourself in. Otherwise you're going to stress your parents and whoever you end up marrying into an early grave."

"I don't even want to get married. I wanted to try and be a knight, but Mum and Da were unanimously against it."

"Given how seldom they seem to agree on anything pertaining to you and your brother, you should take it to heart," Hannah pointed out before standing with her knees cracking in several different places. "Now, I best return to see what Ruby wants me to do. And, Princess?"

Alina looked up at Hannah, her throat still feeling raw from emotion despite enjoying the banter between Kat and the maid.

"Don't worry, these things have a way of working out. Just do what you believe to be right, and don't lie."

Hannah gave a small reassuring smile and turned back to the castle, leaving the two young noblewomen to their plights.

"Don't let her relaxed appearance fool you; when she gets riled up, she scares most of the knights. Of course it doesn't help that she is close friends with Captain Taylor," Kat explained while stretching back onto the grass and closing her eyes.

"Wait . . . is she the Blonde Kitchen Lass?!" Alina burst out excitedly.

Kat smiled. Five years after the Daxarian and Troivackian war, a scholar penned a work called *The Great Mysteries of Austice*. The author had listed the beautiful Blonde Kitchen Lass, who remained unwed, as one of the smaller mysteries of the infamous city, set behind the mystery of whether or not the king's assistant would ever love again after having his heart broken by the Viscount Ashowan.

Unsurprisingly, the assistant had not handled his sudden rise to fame well.

Hannah, on the other hand, had used the extra attention to shine in her duties, and shortly thereafter moved from the kitchen to be the right-hand woman to Ruby, with the intention of taking over her position as Head of Housekeeping once she retired. However, the author had lovingly noted a good deal about the Blonde Kitchen Lass, stating she wielded an iron skillet with ferocious tenacity when properly enraged.

"She nearly broke that poor man's toes when he kept pestering her for the reasons she never got married," Kat recounted fondly. "Or so my da says. So you read that book, did you?"

"Of course I did! Everyone was talking about it back in Rollom . . . I'm still curious where the body of the dragon wound up!" Alina smiled, her worries momentarily forgotten as she and Kat began diving into another fun, yet frivolous topic that would consume the rest of their day.

It was certainly a nice thing to have a friend, even if they weren't able to solve any problems.

* * *

"Henry, as much as your energy was . . . appreciated . . . uh, you—"

"I was flat and it was terrible, I know. No need to mince words." The Troivackian prince laughed while reaching for the goblet of water that was set on the wrought-iron table in the rose maze for him. Alina's handmaidens sat under the sunny sky working on their embroidering, while she and Henry enjoyed the cool shade of the gazebo, practicing their song list for their planned performance.

It was the day after the training ring incident, and Alina was determined to try and find a solution regarding the Troivackian king's abysmal proposal before her father left with the suitors for the hunt.

"What if we didn't use the lutes for this song? There is something raw and genuine about just a vocal duet sometimes," Henry suggested as Alina stretched her arms above her head with her lute resting in her lap.

The princess visibly hesitated. "Are you . . . are you sure you can stay in tune?"

The prince chortled. "Yes, I am. Perhaps, Your Highness, it is your barbaric hammering of the strings that is throwing me off my normally perfect performance," he teased.

Alina couldn't stop the blush or the chuckle that left her mouth. "I see your pride isn't willing to let you take anything lying down."

"While I am not like a Troivackian in many ways, my frayed pride is indeed still holding fast." Henry smiled boyishly before his lips relaxed slightly and his forehead stiffened. "By the way my . . . my brother didn't happen to speak to you today at all, did he?"

Alina's good humor disappeared instantly. "No, he hasn't."

"Ah . . . alright then. Well, shall we try this song without the lute and see if we fare any better?" The prince swiftly returned to the safer topic and put down his flute.

"Very well," Alina agreed, though she couldn't disguise the worry Henry's question had sparked. Brendan Devark wasn't going to try to talk to her again about their marriage, was he?

No . . . she had been very clear about not wanting to hear from him again. There is no way he would try to bring it up.

Unless of course he had talked to her father about it . . .

Giving her dirty blond waves a small shake, the princess tried to free her mind of worries she could do nothing about and instead focus on matching Henry's impressive volume.

Little did Alina know however, that near the entrance to the center of the maze, the Troivackian king had been standing bearing witness to her rehearsal with Henry for quite some time. He remained rooted to the spot, his gaze fixed on her, yet his presence went entirely unnoticed as his assistant stood equally as still by his side.

"Your Majesty, we never did get to send that missive to the Troivackian Court Physician; perhaps we should try to do so now?" Mr. Levin remarked softly.

Turning from the sight of his brother and the Daxarian princess spending a perfect afternoon together, Brendan strolled purposefully back into the maze with the intention of finding the exit as quickly as possible.

"She has a lovely voice. It's almost a pity she can't sing louder. I imagine it is because of her breathing difficulties," the assistant noted idly with his eyes remaining focused ahead.

"Yes. It is . . . unfortunate." The king said nothing more, but even so, his response warranted the briefest of pauses in Mr. Levin's calculated steps.

Once they had finally cleared the infamous maze and were striding back toward the east wing entrance, Brendan addressed his assistant over his shoulder once more.

"When they have concluded, please send my brother to my chambers. I wish to have a word with him."

The assistant bowed his head despite the monarch being unable to see. "Yes, sire."

Henry greeted several servants that passed him in the hallway with a smile before finally reaching his destination. Despite his usual charismatic outward appearance, the prince was uneasy about Brendan summoning him. It was rare that his older brother sought him out for a private audience; it was normally Henry who kept popping up and forcing his company on Brendan.

Once he had opened and closed the door behind himself, the prince took stock of the room before him.

In less than a week, his brother had managed to turn the entire chamber into a sty much like his one at home. He had official documents spread out on the desk with little to no organization. His bed was unmade because he refused to allow any maids in the room while he worked — which was nearly always, and when he wasn't he never bothered notifying the serving staff.

"Brother, you sum— Ah!" Henry tripped over one of Brendan's boots that lay strewn on the floor. "You summoned me?" he finally managed after regaining his balance.

The Troivackian king looked up from the papers in front of him. He wore only a loose black tunic and tan trousers without anything on his feet . . . a sign that he had truly made himself comfortable.

"Yes. I have a question for you." Brendan slowly stood.

Even without his black leather or armor, he was still a giant who could dwarf anyone. Henry resisted the urge as he had for most of his life to take a step backward, and instead smiled up at his sibling.

"Ask away, it was a pleasant surprise to hear you called for me in your—"

"I think the princess is interested in you."

Henry froze, then clamped his mouth shut.

"You aren't an idiot despite what my advisers think, so I know you are aware of this fact," the king pointed out in his usual neutral tone. Only there was something different in his face . . . something more hesitant.

The prince didn't say anything, only shifted his weight on his feet awkwardly.

"Does she know of your . . . sickness?" Brendan asked carefully.

"Brother, I fell in love with a nomadic fortune teller, that is hardly—"

"You fell in love with a commoner who swindled you, and you still pine after her. I'd call that a sickness of the mind."

Henry momentarily clenched his teeth.

After taking a long steadying breath, he said, "Is that what you wanted to ask me about? If I had told the princess about Kezia?"

"No, what I wanted to ask . . ." Brendan cleared his throat.

Henry's face once again split into a grin. For his brother to become tongue-tied? It had to be good.

"What I wanted to ask was . . . how did you make the princess like you?"

Chapter 14

TOSS A COIN TO YOUR DEVIANT

T am sat reading in the castle's library, tucked away in a shadowed corner, safe from the summer heat that was steadily rising under the fierce sun's rays shining through the window. He had just managed to get comfortable and was about to begin the second book that he had ordered and had arrived at his estate in Austice, when he heard the unmistakable scuffling of shoes and giggles of a couple slipping away from prying eyes.

Letting out a silent, weary sigh, Tam momentarily regretted leaving his chamber for the day. Admittedly, he had done so with the hopes of avoiding his sister, even if it meant potentially running into the Troivackian king. After Kat and Tam's argument, Brendan Devark was undoubtedly the preferred evil . . .

However, not wanting to be a spectator in whatever sordid love affair was taking place, Tam began to map out the best route for him to leave the library. That is, until the shelf nearest the one and only exit from his spot rustled softly, as though a body had been pressed against the leathery tomes.

Gods . . . could this week get any worse . . . the young lord thought to himself blithely while closing his eyes and pinching the bridge of his nose.

"Mm, no . . . not right now! We have meetings and . . ." the woman whispered, though one could hear the smile in her voice.

Tam froze. *Oh Gods. Oh no. Please. Gods no.*

"Not for a little while, and we are pretty efficient . . ." came the languid reply from her partner.

The dawning horror of the youngest Ashowan was worsening.

"Fin! We came in here to talk about Tam and Kat! We really should — Oh . . ." Annika's voice trailed off when a suspicious kissing sound interrupted her.

Unable to take another moment of listening to his parents grow more amorous with each other, the future viscount stood up abruptly and walked loudly around the bookshelves. Though he kept his eyes fixed on the floor, it was for an entirely different reason than normal . . .

"Tam! Wh– How long have you been here?!" The voice of his mother spluttered with the obvious ruffling of clothes reaching his ears.

"As impressive as it is that I don't have seventeen younger siblings, this is the fourth time this week!" Tam snapped, finally turning to face his parents knowing they would be back to rights once more.

"We're sorry! It's just, er, . . ." Fin trailed off, his ears scarlet as he rubbed the back of his neck self-consciously. "You and your sister aren't usually out and about quite so much and so . . ."

"Da—"

"Fin—"

Both mother and son started at the same time. Both Annika and Tam were pinching the bridge of their noses in an identical fashion.

"Right, well, you get the picture," the redhead finished while looking anywhere but at his son.

"I really don't want to picture it. Or *hear* anything like it. Ever again. Ever." Tam shuddered then quickly took his leave.

Annika and Fin found themselves unable to make eye contact with each other for a beat of silence as they waited for the sound of the library door to open and close.

"How is it you didn't know he was in here?!" the viscountess demanded while turning on her husband, her voice breathy with embarrassment.

"Oh, I don't know; maybe someone trained him how to be inconspicuous and to blend with the shadows," Fin pointed out dryly.

Annika let out a small chuckle despite herself. "Because that was a compliment on my teaching, I'll let it slide."

The viscount let out a long breath while moving his hands to his hips. "So, we were going to discuss our children?"

Annika folded her arms over her chest and felt her previous good mood fade ever so slightly as the familiar worries of parenthood once again overtook her mind.

"Yes, I think Tam and Kat had a fight. They are avoiding each other like the plague. Even yesterday after the whole training ring debacle, normally Kat would be following him around swearing revenge on Tam's behalf. Instead, she's off with Hannah saying that there's a surprise guest coming today that they are preparing for."

"A surprise guest?" Fin frowned. "Whose surprise is it? Kat's, or our king's?"

Annika balked. ". . . Godsdamnit."

The couple were off in motion once again, already wondering just what their daughter may or may not have plotted this time.

Fin stood with his arms crossed and his expression flat.

Annika wore her usual mask when faced with the general public, of polite indifference, but even that was telling.

"Come on! It's a great idea for a birthday gift for the princess, wouldn't you say, Da!"

"Kat, who else knows you summoned . . . *him* here?" the viscount asked pointedly while not taking his eyes off the surprise guest.

"Come now, Viscount, you tall drink of water! Is that any way to greet an old friend! Viscountess, you're keeping up with our slow-aging Lord of Looks. Good job!" The latter half of the man's compliment was far less enthusiastic.

"Kat, how did you even know how to find . . . *him*?" Annika managed with a beautiful smile that only her family knew to fear.

Katarina cleared her throat and did her best to feign confidence under her mother's obvious irritation.

"Well, I was talking with some of the merchants last time you and Da took me down to the docks, and I heard he was coming to town!"

"Now, now, Viscountess, it almost sounds as though you aren't happy to see me! Viscount, you must be glad at the very least! I mean, I haven't seen you two since I finished my contract with the castle here. Your twins were often lulled by my dulcet tones, don't you recall?"

Reese Flint, the former bard of the court, stood before the Ashowan family in the castle's solar. He then turned to Katarina and plucked up her hand in his own. He planted a smooth kiss on the back of her knuckles, which caused a guttural growl to echo in Fin's chest.

The musician was what many noblewomen tended to call "a silver fox." He had aged incredibly gracefully. Gray touched his temples, the edges of his face had become more angular, and his eyes appeared wiser.

To the parents of a young woman, neither Fin nor Annika liked the changes at all.

"So you see, I thought we could gift Alina with singing lessons from a professional bard! I asked her, and she only ever got to study with her tutors who *liked* singing as a hobby! He could teach her even more songs! She especially loves folk music."

Reese Flint smiled charmingly at Katarina Ashowan as he listened to her chatter innocently about her friend.

"Whose idea was it to take Katarina down to the docks?" Annika murmured through strained lips to her husband.

"Yours, actually," Fin reminded her, his foreboding stare never leaving the bard.

"Remind me why I did such a thing?"

"To stop her from getting into trouble."

"How is it that even when keeping her out of trouble she finds it?" Annika asked rhetorically before stepping forward, her hands clasped in front of her purple skirts. "Mr. Flint? It is a pleasure to see you; however, I believe I would like to take my daughter home for her afternoon lessons now. I apologize that she dragged you all the way here for nothing."

Reese Flint laughed, a very pleasant sound that was certain to make many unsuspecting men's and women's hearts skip a beat or two. "Dear Viscountess, of course it wasn't for nothing! For one, I got a chance to see the beautiful young woman your daughter has grown into. For another, I will be accepting the job with pay and board graciously."

The bard bowed, and Annika's spine stiffened. "Why is it that you believe—"

"—After all, Lord Ashowan here owes me a favor, doesn't he?" Reese's eyes glinted, and Fin felt all the color drain from his face.

"Son of a mage," he muttered.

How could he have forgotten he owed the bard a favor?

A pretty damn big one at that.

"Viscount? What is . . . Mr. Flint referring to?" Annika's voice had raised a pitch and Fin winced.

"My dear, perhaps you and Kat should go home, and I will sort out the details with the bard."

There was a tense pause, but eventually, Annika acquiesced to her husband's suggestion. The viscountess and their daughter left the room, though not before Annika shot her husband a murderous stare that communicated a great many things she wanted to ask and say.

Once the two men were alone in the solar, Fin's tentatively polite expression dropped to one of annoyance.

"Are you honestly calling upon your favor for a teaching job?" the redhead demanded exasperatedly.

"The teacher for the princess of Daxaria? Of course! Your daughter said her singing is already quite lovely, and if I can make her an even more accomplished virtuoso, I will be heavy in the pockets again!" Reese explained while perusing the solar and examining a particularly expensive-looking vase.

"I remember you being . . . *moderately* well liked, so it doesn't make sense that financially you'd be strapped. You were even the court musician in Zinfera; you should have the wealth akin to a respectable merchant. How could you lose it all? Is it gambling? Addiction?"

Reese turned to face the viscount and leaned his forearm above his head comfortably against the window.

"Nothing like that. I can see you've found some darker corners of the world since I last saw you if that's where your mind first goes."

Fin said nothing, only continued studying the man. His tunic was perhaps a little faded, his figure a little leaner . . .

"If I'm going to vouch for you to the king, I need to know precisely what has drained your funds," the viscount began tentatively, and he watched as a hopeful spark brightened Reese's smile.

"Nothing . . . *truly* terrible. I just . . . felt like donating it. Only I was in too much of a giving mood and didn't save enough for myself. Ah well."

Fin frowned, his eyes glimmering. "Reese, this isn't something I can just let pass. I'm putting you directly beside the royal family. A private teacher for the princess is not something that anyone in a tavern can just waltz in and do. If anything comes out after I've recommended you for this position? I'd not only be more or less disgraced from court, but so would my children and wife."

"A wife and children who wouldn't exist if not for me?" Reese pointed out with a flirtatious waggle of his eyebrows.

Fin was not amused. "I need the whole truth."

Letting out a long sigh, the bard's jovial expression faded, and suddenly he appeared his true age . . . and he looked tired.

"Everything was going splendidly until about a year and a half ago. I had just picked up with a new traveling troupe, and we were going to try to sweet-talk our way into the kingdom of Lobahl. Everyone in the past five years has heard about it, but unless you are from there, no one has seen it. It was to be my next great adventure . . . only I stumbled across . . . something . . . on my way."

The bard cleared his throat as a swell of emotions passed through his handsome features.

"I came across a mother and daughter, and I . . . knew them. Or, her, rather. Lorelai. It'd been fifteen years, but I remembered her well. Only, her daughter was fourteen."

The realization of where the story was going washed over Fin, making him close his eyes and let out a long breath while shaking his head silently in understanding.

"Except things were a little more complicated than just that. You see, my Lorelai, with her beautiful auburn hair and big brown eyes, happened to find a few other of my paramours through the years and, erm, well, it turns out I . . . have a small horde with my spectacular looks and vocal range."

Fin's eyes shot open as he looked at the bard in great alarm.

Reese rightfully looked a bit sheepish.

"How many children?" the redhead heard himself ask raggedly, already fearing the answer.

"Was it . . . twelve? Twenty-six?"

"HOW DO YOU NOT KNOW EXACTLY?! THOSE NUMBERS ARE NOT CLOSE TO EACH OTHER!" Fin exploded, his aggravation making him feel more than a little unhinged.

The bard held up his hands defensively. "Alright, alright, you noble stud, easy. You're really making me say it?"

Fin waited wordlessly while folding his arms across his chest.

"Thirty-two."

"Godsdamnit." Fin dropped his forehead to his hand.

"Who knew so many women had a propensity for so many babes?! I have *two* sets of triplets, Finlay! *That's six children from two women alone!"*

"This is why you shouldn't sleep around with everything that settles for you!" Fin threw his hands in the air, feeling as though he were taking part in some strange outrageous play.

"Hey now! No need to fling more dung my way! I did the right thing when I found out!"

Fin's expression morphed into one of horror. "Gods, man, even you must know you cannot marry multiple women!"

Reese waved him off. "I'm a whore not an idiot. No, I divided my wealth amongst them all so that each child would have the funds for schooling and for dowries."

"So all these women found each other and are now all living in the same town?" Fin asked while already mentally planning to drink heavily that evening.

"Not exactly; they all convened within an hour of the rest to support one another. Help one another out with the children, which goes to show the quality, caring type of women I find myself drawn to—"

"Reese, finish the damn story before I decide to castrate you right here and now."

The bard remained unflappable despite the threat, leaning against the castle wall and folding his arms casually. "Well, not all of my former paramours are unwed. Many found good husbands, and some found husbands, but unfortunately not good ones. I can't do much about that, however, aside from ensuring that those men can't access the funds I've left to my beautiful brats. Only, one of the men isn't exactly fond of this new arrangement. Lorelai's husband. He was saying I owe him money for raising my bastard daughter, but my covering her dowry and current expenses exceeds what meager coins he's thrown their way."

Reese's eyes grew shadowed, which was a very different look for the annoyingly peppy man.

"He's been trying to find me ever since I stole Lorelai and my daughter from him one night and hid them with a dear friend of mine whom I can trust to keep them safe. I can't perform without drawing him to me, or the people around me. Teaching, though . . . he wouldn't dare approach nobles. I can live off my trade, and everyone remains safe. So, imagine the divine Goddess's timing when I received your daughter's missive!"

The man turned on his foppish smile to the viscount once more. "So what do you say, Lord Ashowan?"

Dropping his chin to his chest, Fin thought about the bard's story.

It was absolutely insane, but . . . knowing Reese . . . it made sense.

Not only that, but Reese had never been a liar. Quite the opposite, in fact; he had been grossly honest the entire time Fin had known him. Even during the present interaction, the witch hadn't detected any hint of deception while he told his tale.

"Alright, Reese, here's the deal. You get ten lessons with the princess to last until the end of the summer. That's it, and I will do this with fair pay and board in the servants' quarters, but on one condition." Fin held up a single finger and fixed his electrifying blue eyes on the bard.

Reese's burgeoning delight faltered.

"You will tell me the name of the man who is chasing you down, and everything you know about him."

Chapter 15

CLEARING SOME COBWEBS

Alina let the final chord of the ballad ring out in the rose maze, the blooms happy for the performance as Henry's voice faded perfectly into the quiet, earning polite but pleased applause from the princess's handmaidens.

"I think we're ready!" The Troivackian prince turned a beaming smile to Alina, making her blush prettily; her demure smile was adorable enough to make everyone share knowing looks.

"Do you think people will dance, or will they just listen?" Alina asked, unable to fully hide the growing bubble of happiness in her chest.

Henry grinned fondly at the princess and leaned back in his chair, unable to take his eyes off of her. "I think they'd be too frightened to ignore either of us, so they'll probably all stop and listen."

"Oh no . . . my palms are already sweating! Everyone staring on top of that?" Alina lifted her pale hand and stared at her clammy palm with her heart skipping several beats.

"I thought you were being modest when you said you had never performed," Henry remarked as his smile faded and his warm brown gaze grew concerned.

Fortunately, Alina didn't see the appearance of his trepidation, as she still found herself unable to muster the courage to face the prince just yet knowing that she was probably the color of a tomato.

"No, I tried to sing for my father and a few of his closest council members, but I had a horrible attack. Mom had me stay in bed the rest of the day . . . we tried again a few years later, and I managed to get through the whole performance for Duke Rhodes and his wife, but . . . I was trembling so much I played horribly. Since then I've been far too nervous to try again." Alina took a deep steadying breath and forced herself to sit a little straighter.

Finally, she faced Henry, but his expression took her aback instantly.

He looked uneasy, and his lips were pursed as though about to start suggesting canceling the whole arrangement.

Alina had seen that look hundreds of times in her life, and it made her stomach drop unpleasantly.

"Princess, I . . . I am worried that you might—"

"I can do this! It's for our kingdoms! If I can't do this much, I mean . . ." Alina began defensively, her hand instinctively gripping the neck of her lute.

"Don't think like that. You are more than just your singing, Your Highness. You are kind, and fair. You are . . . an exemplary noble. Soft-spoken, but a calming presence to be sure."

Alina didn't know why his compliments hurt her so deeply or how to properly explain it. Well, she did know why they did, but she had a sense that she would only sound like she was being difficult if she complained about the nature of Henry's words.

When described like that I feel like I'm just a . . . a . . . a cherry on top of a dessert. More decoration than substance like any good noblewoman should be. Not strong, or . . . or of any importance aside from my ability to give children, and who knows if I can even do that?

"Princess, if I've said something to upset you, I offer my deepest regrets. I merely meant that you have more strengths than just your musical tal—"

"It's fine, Your Highness. I'm sure it's just my nerves," Alina heard herself say the words.

She could always keep up her friendly and affable appearance even without thinking.

Still, Henry knew well enough not to be fully convinced. "Don't worry, we will still try to perform tomorrow at the ball and—"

"Ah, pardon me, Your Highness, I think I need to retire to the castle. It's . . . it's getting quite warm out here." Alina stood swiftly, and setting down her lute a little too roughly, turned and began hurriedly striding down the stone pathway.

Her maids were unable to pack up their sewing and skirts quickly enough, and realizing this, Alina sped up her pace even if it meant risking another attack.

"Princess, please wait for me, I am just about—" Marianne called, the note of irritation heard by everyone within earshot.

Without daring to look at the group of pitying gazes, Alina called over her shoulder, only stopping for a moment. "Marianne, please return my lute to my room with the women and wait for me there."

"Your Highness, it is not wise for you to be left unattended with —"

"Do as I say!" Alina shouted angrily before her small hands curled into fists as she resumed fleeing.

Striding out of the maze as quickly as her legs would carry her, Alina began to think where she could possibly go to be left alone.

Her chamber or the kitchens were out of the question.

Tam was probably in the library, and she knew if she asked him not to say anything he would listen, but she didn't want him to see her like that.

She didn't like the woods . . .

Turning toward the castle's eastern entrance, she finally decided to go to the one room she knew would have to be empty no matter what, even if it might make her feel even worse.

Brendan was making his way down the western corridor toward the main staircase along the north side of the castle, in his hand a list of hastily scrawled points. He was moving his mouth as he read through them over and over, his brow furrowed, his concentration undivided as he was relatively certain that he was alone in the immediate vicinity, when he heard a strange sound in the room to his left. It was like a gasp followed by a shuffle . . .

His instincts sharpening, the Troivackian recalled that the last three chambers of the hall were supposed to be empty and left untouched — the Head of Housekeeping had been adamant about it.

Knowing he risked another dispute with the Daxarian king, Brendan turned to the door directly to his left and wrapped his hand around the handle, pressing his thumb down onto the latch.

I can just say I heard something and wanted to make sure an animal hadn't broken in . . .

When he opened the chamber door and peered in, he wasn't sure what he was going to see, but he hadn't been anticipating a spacious bed chamber, with the furniture covered in sheets.

A layer of dust coated the stone floor, and the hearth sported several wispy cobwebs, yet on the mantel above it stood the only item that looked to be regularly cared for.

A portrait.

Stepping farther into the room before considering whether or not it was a wise decision, the king quietly closed the door behind himself, his curiosity over the gilded frame getting the better of him.

Slowly, he moved to stand before the picture, and once positioned beneath, he found himself staring into the faces of the Daxarian king, and queen, with their two children, but it was clearly painted many years ago . . .

In the picture, the queen was smiling with an adorable blond curly-haired girl in her arms staring at the painter seriously. The king had his hand resting on the shoulder of a little boy with dark blond waves, his mouth in a serious line, but his eyes that matched both his father and sister seemed mischievous somehow.

A happy royal family in their throne room.

The slight rustle against the stone floor reached Brendan's ears, drawing his attention back to the presence in the room he had sensed the moment he had entered, but deemed unthreatening.

"Is there a reason you are hiding, Princess?" The Troivackian king turned, his hands clasped behind his back to gaze upon the tearstained face of Alina, a fully grown young woman, no longer a babe in her mother's arms. She was crouched on the floor with her back against the same wall of the door, her knees drawn up to her chest.

She stared at him with a frown. It was obvious that he was intruding, yet he didn't budge.

"I wanted to be alone. No one comes in here."

"Hm." Brendan regarded the painting again and then noticed two other smaller portraits in oval wooden frames on the mantel that were not as well maintained as the larger painting.

On the left was the Crown Prince Eric Reyes, perhaps sixteen years old, looking young and proud beside his sister, who sat demurely on a satin-covered chair. His hand was clutching its back, and something about the way they were angled indicated their closeness. The second picture was of the king and queen in the center of the rose maze. The royal couple were seated in their finery in front of the ruby blooms, their smiles warm and eyes bright . . .

"Could you please leave?" Alina's throat was hoarse from crying, and she really didn't want *him* of all people making her feel worse.

Brendan returned his attention to her, his eyes unreadable before they surveyed the rest of the room and he noted the three swords above the bed. One a wooden training sword, the other a child's first blade—usually gifted when they were twelve—and the last in the center, a sword master's gilded handle. A fine blade left to gather dust, which somehow made the room feel even more melancholy . . .

"This is Prince Eric's bedroom, is it not?" Brendan's brows were lowered and his head tilted thoughtfully over his shoulder.

"It is, and no one but myself, my father, or my brother are allowed in here, so if you could—"

"Where is the crown prince, Princess? No one has heard of him, or seen him in any official capacity, in three years."

Alina's hands trembled as she slowly, and with stiff movements, pushed herself to a standing position from the floor. Dusting off her golden skirts, she fixed her red-rimmed eyes on the king, hoping that she wouldn't start crying again.

"That is private business. Now, I will not—"

"The well-being of the crown prince of Daxaria is not private business, Princess. Pardon my interruption, but the leader of the continent is supposed to be as transparent as possible with his people. It is his duty to be active in all political ventures to prepare for his inheritance of the throne."

"Well, what if I'm going to inherit the throne?!" Alina snapped, her hands clutching her skirts tightly as she felt the stupid tears come to her eyes again.

"Is that what you want?" Brendan asked, completely unmoved by her watery gaze, which was both unnerving to her, yet also oddly refreshing.

Alina could feel her thumbnail digging into her curled fist at her side to stop her lips from quivering. "Maybe it is. Do you think that is ridiculous?"

The Troivackian king thought for a long moment, his eyes moving to the floor with a serious expression for several moments more.

"No, I do not. Though you would need to start attending council meetings and being more active in the court starting as soon as possible. However, if you wish to take the throne while unmarried in the next five years at the soonest? Perhaps consider training with a weapon. With your current physical well-being, I'd recommend a small bow or crossbow. I've heard musical training is wonderful for hand-eye coordination development, which is a useful skill."

Alina found herself taking a subconscious step back from the shock she received and hitting the stone wall behind her.

"You, as the king of Troivack, would acknowledge me as the queen regnant of Daxaria, and take no exception or look down upon me?"

"As long as you performed your duties well, why would I?" The man once again showed no emotion, yet his words sounded genuine.

"Don't you believe women are to be in the background? Be kind, calm, and dutiful? Bear children?"

"I believe those are strengths they can have; however, some are predisposed to other callings," he explained thoughtfully.

If Brendan were being honest with himself, he was moderately pleased the princess seemed so interested in talking with him. Not to mention she had stopped crying for whatever reason . . .

"Why? Isn't that against what the rest of your people believe?" Alina asked, not caring if the question was personal or untoward. She was too interested in the answer.

"Most, yes. The reason I think it is time for change, however, stems from the powerlessness my mother experienced when my father died. If she'd been allowed to act as a monarch, I could have transitioned into my role as the next king seamlessly, and my people wouldn't have had a literal child as their sole leader."

There was the barest hitch in the king's voice, and Alina felt her curiosity double. "I can't imagine how . . . difficult it would have been to be king at that age. Surely you had advisers who—"

"Princess, are you aware of the political nature in Troivack?" Brendan's voice took on a hardness she then realized hadn't been in his voice before, despite always thinking it was.

"I know it is a merciless place where a successful backstabbing is treated with great reverence."

Brendan's smile didn't reach his eyes at her reply. "Correct. It is rare that an adviser to a king doesn't have his own hidden agenda. Which is why I want to change things. To be cunning is good, but if we are constantly testing each other we slow down progress. It's this belief that has kept Henry alive."

Alina frowned. "What do you mean?"

"Most kings make sure their siblings are slaughtered once crowned. It ensures no rebellious factions form in the court. If they are a woman, banishment is carried out if they express interest in ruling."

"Like Princess Nora, who betrayed Daxaria to regain a title during the war?"

This time Brendan nodded his approval. "Very good, yes. Exactly like that. Princess Nora Devark is a prime example."

Alina gave a small conspiratorial smile at him then, feeling a little proud of herself.

Until a new thought occurred to her . . .

"Your Highness, if you are in support of me ruling Daxaria, does that mean you no longer think we should marry?" Her heart thudded against her chest.

Brendan Devark's face grew pensive once more, and he didn't speak for several moments. He didn't look angry, and it was then Alina noticed that he often was very careful in expressing his opinions; and given his straightforward nature, it meant that he always believed his words completely.

"Well, I would propose the idea that we rule both countries, Troivack and Daxaria, as a wedded couple, with you being the queen regnant of Daxaria and me the king of Troivack."

Alina blinked. "You would allow me to rule Daxaria without interference?"

"Here in Daxaria, yes. I would be a king consort here, or a prince consort, depending how your court prefers to title things; however, in Troivack, I would be king, and you would be the queen consort."

"What of children?"

"We'd better have two then." Brendan straightened his shoulders, his face assured as though he had figured out all the answers.

"And you . . . you wouldn't betray me? You're not plotting to take my kingdom in some elaborate ruse?"

Brendan's bout of expressiveness came to a sudden halt. "Do you think you'd even be able to tell if I were lying to you?"

At this, Alina allowed a slow grin to lift her features. "What I think . . . is that you have built yourself to be the type of man that doesn't rely on lies to strengthen himself. Rather you know, without any duplicity, that you are strong. So I have a feeling you will answer my questions honorably."

He couldn't help it.

For the first time in a long time, Brendan smiled out of genuine gladness, and it made him so shockingly handsome that Alina felt her heart flutter in her chest.

"Princess, I think you can see how pleased your reply has made me. So I will answer you, as you predicted: truthfully. I want to form strong ties with Daxaria, but I do not believe now is the time for our two kingdoms to become one. Therefore, I have no designs on conquering the country through political or brutal means."

Alina gnawed on her lower lip in an effort to stop smiling before her expression froze, and the smile slowly melted away.

The sight of which made Brendan's brow furrow.

"Well, I am happy to hear that, Your Majesty. Though it doesn't really matter, because no matter what, my brother *will* become king. But . . ." The princess's face regained a fraction of her happy glow from before. "I . . . I thank you for your support and advice. It is far more than I've ever received. Now, if you'll excuse me, I will go before my maids start looking for me."

With a small curtsy, Alina swept out of the chamber, leaving the king of Troivack with more questions than answers, which he didn't like one bit.

The first and most troubling of which being . . .

Where in the world was the crown prince of Daxaria?

The secondmost pressing question was whether or not Crown Prince Eric was really fit to be king.

The third, and strangely the one that made Brendan's chest begin to tighten . . .

If the princess wanted to rule, why did someone who couldn't bother to show his face to his people get to walk right into the position?

Chapter 16

NO TIPTOEING ALLOWED

F in was speaking in hushed tones to Annika's closest maid, Clara, in the castle's north corridor. Servants passed by them without sparing a glance at the familiar sight, and with the viscount's black tunic and the maid's navy blue gown, both blended easily into the shadows despite it being a little after midday.

Brendan saw them as he walked back to his chamber and noted the seriousness in the redhead's face, and the maid's usual cold expression.

After another few brief words, the head of the Ashowan family straightened and glanced around them casually, which was when his shimmering blue eyes met the Troivackian king's.

A moment of stillness passed between the two men, before Fin turned, and began to move toward the west wing exit to the barracks.

Slowly, and without making a sound, Brendan followed him.

He didn't try to hide his presence, but he also didn't draw unnecessary attention either.

When the king ambled outside to the knights' barracks, he noticed the viscount speaking to Captain Taylor, once again using lowered tones. The captain frowned darkly and nodded, then appeared to be asking a question.

Brendan watched the back of the viscount's neck remain straight, until it suddenly swiveled so that his profile looked over his shoulder and his ethereal gaze landed on the monarch once again.

There was a sharpness in his look that appeared threatening, and there wasn't a hint of the infamous kindness or warmth that people spoke of anywhere around his person.

The captain noticed the king, and asked the witch something else, making the viscount look back to him to answer before he turned and began to walk away from the barracks. His hands were buried in his pockets.

Brendan shared a shallow nod with Captain Taylor before continuing to follow Finlay, but he missed the worried look the military leader donned after the exchange.

The viscount had disappeared around the southwest turret, and so Brendan picked up his pace. However, when he rounded the same turret, his hand instinctively went to the dagger on his hip.

Finlay Ashowan stood leaning against the stone wall, his arms crossed, his expression clouded, and his eyes glowing brighter than before.

"Your Majesty, is there something I can help you with?"

"I see you've already forsaken the appropriate greeting for a monarch," Brendan observed, the edge in his voice impossible to miss.

Fin stepped away from the castle wall and bowed, then locked eyes again with the Troivackian, his aura no less frightening.

"Have I done something to anger you, Viscount?"

Fin tilted his head to the side. "I don't particularly like being followed and spied upon."

"We have that much in common at least." Brendan's gaze was steady and cold.

The viscount stiffened, but his expression remained the same. "Is there something special about today that has you tailing me?"

Brendan dropped his hand from his dagger and clasped his hands behind his back, his head tilting ever so slightly over his left shoulder. "I had an interesting discussion with the princess recently."

Fin's eyebrows twitched in surprise, but he said nothing as he waited for the king to continue.

"The conversation made me realize just how strange it is that no one seems to have seen or heard of the crown prince's whereabouts or well-being in three years. No one knows what city he is in, let alone if he is in good health. He hasn't attended a single meeting or been a part of any diplomatic envoys since before the queen's death. He was supposed to be present during the princess's courting season, yet no word has been sent to confirm or deny his attendance."

The viscount waited, knowing exactly the question that was bubbling closer to the surface.

"No one, not even the king, seems to know very much. Not that I've asked him yet . . . but of all the people in this castle, the one and only name I keep hearing about this situation is yours, Lord Ashowan. You were the last one to have seen the prince, but you haven't relayed any information. To anyone."

Still not moving a single muscle, the redhead stood patiently as the Troivackian king spoke.

"Then imagine how strange it is that I hear your son is one of the partners courting the princess. A son of a viscount amongst heirs to dukedoms and foreign royalty. It seems rather . . . suspicious."

"Is there something you would like to ask me, Your Majesty?" Fin's voice was even, but it was clear one aggressive move would propel him into action. Brendan could see it in the man's eyes.

"Yes. Where is the prince? Is he alive? And are you plotting to put your son on the throne to rule all of Daxaria?" Brendan waited, his dark expression conveying the latent threat of his questions.

Fin caught him off guard then, by relaxing and answering him flatly.

"Eric is alive; he is in Sorlia, last I heard. My son will never be a king. It is not what he wishes to be." Fin withdrew his hands from his pockets and folded his arms. "Any further questions regarding the prince should be addressed to His Majesty, King Norman."

Brendan nodded. A loyal answer. Short and to the point, and nothing indicated the viscount had lied. Though it was interesting that he was on a first name basis with the Daxarian prince. The way the witch had said it had been natural, as though he hadn't even thought about it either.

Even so. With everything he knew about the viscount's family, Brendan took the exchange with a grain of salt.

"I see. Thank you for your frankness, Lord Ashowan."

Fin gave a slight bow, his eyes no longer glowing quite as brightly as before.

"Has your wife sent word to her spies to withdraw from my court?"

Finlay straightened, a small smile touching the corners of his mouth.

Brendan didn't like it one bit.

"Your Majesty, are you telling me you believe my wife to be the one in charge of the leaks in Troivack?"

The king widened his stance. "It is only us here, Viscount. Not to mention I imagine with your abilities, you've already seen to ensuring this conversation is private. Annika Piereva was the sole surviving grandchild of the great spymaster Georgio Piereva. While men of the older generations chose not to suspect her because of gender, I am not nearly so closed-minded."

Fin's smile faded, but his features became . . . unreadable. Brendan couldn't tell if the witch was laughing at him, curious, or angry.

"Your wife killed my father, and countless others. Some in self-defense, I'm sure; it goes with the territory of her work. However, we are not at war anymore, and she needs to realize that if things are to remain peaceful, there needs to be trust. I am no more like my father than you are like yours, Lord Ashowan."

Fin's smile returned, only his eyes were calculating. "You don't like me much, do you?"

"Your entire family has built wealth and power based on deception and secrets. While the citizens of your kingdom see you as the champion of their home, I see something very different."

"What if we built our house off good intentions, my wife's brains, and I am not jesting when I say this, a frightening amount of luck? Especially with your father stabbing me to death."

"That would be easier to believe if your wife withdrew her spies and your son wasn't courting the princess who could be the next heir to the throne." Brendan pointedly ignored the legend of the viscount's two-way trip with death's carriage driver.

A strange knowingness rose in his features. "Tam and the princess have no interest in marrying each other, but you seem quite fixated on that point."

Brendan didn't know why but something in him suddenly felt . . . uncomfortable. What was the witch getting at?

"Why is he bothering to attend the courting dates with Her Highness if there isn't the possibility?" Brendan countered before realizing that the man had sidestepped yet again the matter of his wife's spies.

"My daughter is usually with them on the courting dates, sire. They're friends." Fin was having an absolute ball of a time as he watched the hint of panic in the younger man's face. "You may want to mind your possessive nature, Your Majesty. Alina won't like it."

"Since when did the princess say you could call her—"

"Viscount! Is everything alright?" Clara, the viscountess's maid, approached the men, her eyes briefly sweeping over the Troivackian king before giving a graceful curtsy.

"Yes, Clara. By the way, I want to apologize for telling you to stop teasing Annika about our relationship."

Brendan and Clara both looked to the redhead, who had dropped his hands to his hips.

"You were right. It *is* fun watching it happen to someone else."

Letting out a long sigh with his mischievous smile still in place, Fin shook his head and patted the king on the shoulder before continuing to walk toward the castle kitchen.

"Viscount! What are you trying to say? When did the princess tell you to use her first name?!" Brendan called after the house witch, who had a small spring in his step as he strolled away.

"I'm a king, he can't just walk away like that whenever he—" the Troivackian was beginning to grumble before he realized the maid Clara was staring up at him blankly for a brief moment before she, too, began smiling.

"Try not to let on too much to the viscount that he's gotten to you, or you might end up like Mr. Howard."

Brendan frowned. "What did the viscount do to the king's assistant?"

The maid's grin turned every bit as devious as her master's. "I suggest you ask Mr. Howard yourself. Though perhaps have some moonshine ready when you do."

Then, with another proper curtsy, the woman turned and followed Fin; however, Brendan found himself wondering if he had heard a small giggle from the infamously icy maid of the Ashowan house.

At long last it was the night of the ball.

Alina stared at herself in the mirror and smiled nervously. Her maids really had outdone themselves.

She wore a white dress as tradition dictated, though a triangle of pale green began at the golden rope that settled around her hips and flared out into the crisp white of her skirts. Her sleeves were wide and loose, the neckline square, and the veil pinned to her shining locks sported golden flowers embroidered along its edge. Her crown held it in place as it ran back into her train, and when she turned back from staring at herself, her hands clasped together in an effort to hide her nervousness, every single one of her attendants was smiling.

Even Marianne looked slightly less sour than usual.

"Your Highness, you look exquisite!" the younger girls gushed excitedly.

Alina blushed, but accepted the maid's hand to step down off the stool she had been on while the seamstress finished sewing the back shut.

"Thank you all for your assistance. I couldn't ever have done it without you all." Alina nodded her chin regally to them and received curtsied responses.

It was then there was the knock on her chamber door.

"Your Highness, His Majesty is here to escort you," Mr. Howard's voice rang out into the room, and Alina felt her face break out into a nervous smile as her attendants opened the chamber door, and her father dressed in his finest clothes, and clad in his emerald mantle, appeared. His golden crown with its emeralds and lone diamond glinting in the glow of the setting sun.

"Princess, you look . . . beautiful." Mr. Howard smiled, an uncommon shine of pride in his eyes.

Alina turned to her father, already feeling horribly embarrassed by the extra attention. However, she was distracted from the fact by the sight of tears welling up in her father's eyes.

"Your mother would . . . she'd be so proud." Norman's voice cracked as more than one errant tear escaped and dripped onto his cheek.

Stepping forward hurriedly, Alina reached out and brushed the falling tears from her father's face, a lump of her own appearing in her throat, threatening to choke her.

But she couldn't succumb to her own feelings just then. Her father needed her.

"I'm sure she's still watching over us," Alina whispered, while pretending not to see Mr. Howard's own misty eyes searching around the chamber desperately for a distraction.

"She . . . she was so happy that you didn't get her massive feet . . ."

"Father, Mom's feet weren't—"

"They were huge. Trundled on every toe I have thousands of times."

Alina couldn't help but laugh while for some reason her father cried a little harder.

"I inherited your small feet, but if you'd like I can try to stomp on your toes a few times when we give the opening dance," she offered, her voice beginning to croak.

"I'd like that," Norman managed to say while Alina used the sleeves of her dress to dry her father's face before accepting the handkerchief Mr. Howard offered her.

Her heart ached seeing her father's grief resurface anew . . .

"Then brace yourself, Father. These shoes have heels so that I don't break my neck trying to stare up and dance with the Troivackians. So your beloved toes will be bleeding through your stockings."

At her final jest, Norman finally took a deep breath and stood tall again. He then reached out and grasped the back of his daughter's head; drawing her forehead to his lips, he planted a fatherly kiss that nearly had Alina breaking down in tears then and there.

"Well, shall we face those good-for-nothings who don't deserve you?" the king asked, offering his daughter his arm with a smile, despite his eyes still being bright with pain.

"Might as well indulge them, hm?" Alina wrapped her hands gently around her father's arm, and it was then for the first time since the entire courting season began that it occurred to her that the days where she could comfort her father and have him be her partner to the balls were dwindling.

Swallowing with great difficulty, she started to question whether the surprise performance was really something she wanted to do when the cherished moments with her father were coming to a close.

As the royal pair left the princess's chamber, Alina's stomach in knots, and Norman's cheeks still damp, both couldn't help but feel the excitement of the night fade into sad reluctance.

Chapter 17

PERFORMANCE PLIGHTS

Alina had completely forgotten that the entire purpose of the ball was for her to meet and dance with the lower nobles who may be interested in courting her.

She was rudely reminded, however, when she stepped into the banquet hall and found at least a dozen heads with vulture-esque stares swiveling to gawk at her at the same time.

"Oh Gods," Alina blurted out in a mutter through her smile.

Norman tightened his hold on his daughter's arm. "You don't happen to see Tam anywhere, do you? Perhaps if you two chat for a while the others may get the hint."

"What hint, Father?"

"The hint that they don't stand a chance." The king's voice had turned to a rumble as he beheld the numerous hungry-looking young men all eyeing his daughter beneath their lashes as they bowed to him. It wasn't hard to tell that they all recalled how Norman had once been a lesser noble just like them.

After the entire room had bowed and given the royalty their greetings, Norman sought out Fin and Annika. He found the couple lingering near a far-off corner of the room, as was their habit during large events. The three shared a look and nods of understanding that had the viscount and viscountess moving through the crowd of people toward their king.

"Tonight, Alina, if you ever are in a situation with a lord or knight who is making you uncomfortable and I am otherwise occupied, I want you to look for Lord or Lady Ashowan. They will intervene in such a way that is discreet."

The princess wanted to laugh her father's grim concern off, but she found herself becoming a mite fearful instead.

Despite this, she didn't want to make her father even more worried or stressed than he already was, and so, she gave a polite nod of her head, her mouth curved in a pleasant smile.

"Don't worry. I'm sure everyone will be on their best behavior. If I do experience any . . . unpleasant advances, however, I will be sure to signal the Ashowans for help," Alina reassured her father when he began to turn to her to object to her faith in their fellow nobility.

The king and princess had officially reached the dais, and as they stepped up before the thrones, Norman took his daughter's hand and turned to address the guests. The room had fallen into the customary silence, but as Alina's hazel gaze swept over the crowd, she found Henry several rows of people away watching her with his usual bright warm smile.

Smiling back at him, she began to move her sights to the back of the room, when she noticed Brendan Devark leaning against the farthest wall from her, his arms crossed and a goblet in hand as his piercing dark eyes held hers. Something about his stare made a faint tremor run through Alina, as it became very apparent that in the room of crowded nobles, she was the one, and only one, he was paying any attention to.

"Ladies and lords, it is with a heavy heart . . . we gather this evening," Norman began his greeting, snapping his daughter out of the strange hypnotic moment she had been experiencing with the Troivackian king.

"It is a father's saddest moment to have to send his beloved daughter into the arms of a husband, but thus is life. The only possibility of comfort is the knowledge that she goes to a *good* man. One of integrity and loyalty that I can be proud to call a son-in-law."

Many of the young men who had been staring at Alina with obvious thoughts of impurity shifted uncomfortably, though there were a select few who smirked.

"I trust you all to behave with the utmost respect toward the princess. Particularly with the knowledge that anyone who may become blinded by his own desires will face consequences of *unimaginable* strife."

The few young lords who had dared to flippantly disregard the first half of the king's speech grew still then. There was a cold, yet heavy meaning to the monarch's threat, which was only aided by Lord Ashowan's magical blue eyes as he glanced sharply at the men nearest himself, and Captain Taylor, whose thick brows lowered when he locked eyes with his own knights from his corner of the room.

"Now, a toast." Norman held out his hand and Mr. Howard appeared from the shadows to place a goblet in his hand while Marianne appeared and handed one to Alina, who was still a little stunned to see the murderous side of her beloved father.

"To my beautiful daughter, the light of my life. While no father ever thinks any man is good enough for his daughter, I hope that you find one who treats you as the treasure you are."

Alina blushed deeply as everyone around the room chanted: "To the princess!"

Taking a sip from her goblet, Alina smiled shyly at the nobles, unable to meet anyone's direct stare, which had the profound effect of melting many brooding and indifferent hearts.

"Enjoy the festivities everyone!" Norman clapped his hands, and the ball officially began.

While seated in her throne, Alina couldn't resist nervously picking at her nails as the time for her surprise performance with Henry drew nearer. Initially she had been worried that she would be flooded with invitations to dance, but her position beside her glowering father and just behind Finlay Ashowan, who had conveniently chosen to stand directly at the base of the dais, seemed to be a good deterrent.

However, it also meant any move she made was noticed immediately, making her plan of slipping away discreetly to grab her lute significantly more difficult than she had initially planned.

Well, that only left the tried and true excuse.

"Father, I will go freshen myself before beginning to dance with some suitors." Alina leaned toward Norman as she attempted to smile innocently. In actuality, she felt as though the tension was going to crack the very skin on her face as it stretched to accommodate the expression.

Norman rounded abruptly toward his daughter, his face already creased with concern. "Are you feeling ill? Do you need to go to bed?"

"N-No, Father! I just need to go r-relieve myself." The princess dropped her voice to a whisper as she fidgeted uncomfortably, which in turn soothed the king.

"Of course. Sorry for being overbearing tonight . . . I thought I could be a little more dignified on such a night. I just worry for you."

Alina felt her heart break at her father's openly loving and vulnerable expression.

"It's alright. I love you, but I . . . I'm stronger than you think!" Alina announced, attempting to sound confident, her eyes eager to convince him.

Smiling warmly in response, Norman reached over and covered her hand with his own. "My darling daughter, I wish . . . I wish your brother . . . Ah. Never mind."

Alina's expression froze.

Had he been about to wish my brother was here to protect me?

Standing swiftly so that her father wouldn't see her true feelings, the princess kept her gaze cast to the ground.

"Excuse me. I'll be right back."

Moving nimbly through the crowd, Alina did her best to avoid all eye contact and curious glances from the nobility around her. She had grown up knowing many of them, and there was no need to fear them . . . even if some of their smiles suddenly became predatory at the possibility of a plump dowry.

"Ah! Excuse me, Princess!"

"Princess, here is some wine if you—"

"Your Highness, I noticed you have not yet danced, would you—"

Alina ducked past many of her suitors with a demure smile and vague bob of her head as she moved toward the hall doors.

How am I supposed to get back in here when everyone is sticking to me like fruit flies on a ripe strawberry?

Alina was beginning to worry that the elements of discretion and surprise would be completely eradicated from her plan, when she ran headlong into a sharp shoulder.

"Gods, I feel sorry for the maids who have to mop up the drool from all these men."

Alina looked up with joyous relief into the face of Katarina Ashowan.

The redhead had donned an emerald dress and a cream vest with gold embroidery that ran long into her train. Gold studs glinted in her earlobes and matching rings sparkled on her hands, but her wild wavy thick hair remained unadorned flowing down her back.

Her golden eyes flitted around the room in their usual disconcerting manner, but there was a smile on her lips that put Alina at ease.

"Don't worry, I can see my da and the captain already dispersing the truly . . . *sticky* pursuers."

Alina laughed. "Well, with that taken care of, I have a small favor to ask of you."

Katarina dropped her expectant gaze to her friend.

"Can you help me get out of here and return without anyone noticing? The guards will probably try to follow me."

Kat smiled wolfishly before once again casting her sights to their surroundings. "Gladly. Though I'm going to have to make a temporary peace with my brother for perfect results."

Alina drew back in surprise. "Temporary peace? I thought you and Tam got along wonderfully?"

Kat waved her hand dismissively while still searching the room. "We had a fight. It happens with siblings; you know how it is."

Her brother's smiling face sprang into Alina's mind. Her right hand gripped into a fist at her side as she pushed the image hastily back from the forefront of her thoughts.

There is no point in thinking about him . . . I just need to wait, and one day he'll return . . . and then everything will go back to how it should be.

Eyeing the fist Alina made, Kat could tell her friend was recalling something troublesome. "Easy there, Princess. I often want to punch my brother in the face these days, but I still love him . . . mostly." Kat clasped her hands on Alina's shoulders, her impish yet warm smile lighting her ethereal features.

She doesn't even seem human . . . Alina observed dumbly for a moment before giving her head a shake.

"So you need to get out of here? Leave it to me. Getting you back in will be Tam's job." Kat grasped the princess's arm and hauled her along toward the great doors where four guards were stationed. Two in the corridor, two within the room.

As they approached, the two guards within the ball bowed to the princess. "Your Highness, we shall escort you to your destination—"

"OH *my*! The heat!" Kat slapped the back of her hand to her forehead and collapsed to the floor making several nobles around her clear a small space for her.

Alina couldn't help but feel embarrassed for her friend as many elderly nobles rolled their eyes and several young noblewomen laughed at Kat's theatrics.

"My lady, are you alright?!" One of the guards from the door stepped forward.

"My *word*, does no one feel this stifling air?! Goodness. You there . . . fan me." Kat waved to the other guards dramatically, all of them looking completely torn between complying and wanting to make someone else deal with her.

"Gods, I might *faint* if a great wind doesn't cool me." Kat grasped the hand of the nearest guard, her breathy desperate plea captivating his attention completely. To add an extra layer of drama, Kat closed her eyes and willed her expression to turn grim.

All eyes became glued on her performance, allowing Alina the perfect moment to slip out unnoticed.

"My lords and ladies!" Henry's voice called out, his tone already laughing in good fun.

Everyone in the banquet hall ceased their conversations; the bardic group had already paused their performance to rehydrate.

"I am incredibly appreciative of the Daxarian king for welcoming my brother and me so graciously to your shores. I know given our history, it is hard for us all to share good tidings, but Princess Alina Reyes and I have prepared a special performance to help you all enjoy the beautiful side of our kingdoms! We hope you enjoy our collaboration!"

Norman's eyes rounded as he scooted closer to the edge of his seat, fully intending to interrupt, when a path cleared from the doors to the hall revealing Alina shyly clutching her lute to her chest.

No one dared to whisper as she nervously strode down the path toward the dais where Prince Henry stood with an encouraging smile and apprehensiveness in his eyes.

Alina tried not to worry over the hesitancy in his expression, though she couldn't deny the intensification of the trembling in her hands.

The Daxarian king clearly wished to speak out to break the expectant silence, but a pleading glance from his daughter had him frozen to his seat as she finally reached the dais and then seated herself down on its step, her lute automatically fitting into her grasp without a second thought.

"This first song is a Daxarian sailor song that I'm sure more than a few merchants have heard before!" Henry's easy nature was settling a few of the haughtier members of their audience, but a great deal of interest was still being cast toward the Daxarian princess.

Clearing her throat, and giving Henry a shy glance, Alina began tapping the wooden base of her instrument, setting a steady beat.

Then, they sang.

It was a familiar song, and while at first everyone was too stunned at the charming duet the pair executed beautifully, soon pleased smiles began to spread through the crowd as the prince kept his open friendly expression and smiled warmly at the princess, who was glowing with pleasure.

The song concluded, and the applause that came was not out of mere politeness as shouts for an encore began. Laughing, Alina turned to Henry, who was grinning and waving to the crowd as though he were a natural-born performer.

Looking up toward the crowd from under her lashes, Alina noticed a good many young noblewomen eyeing Henry and whispering to their closest companions. Feeling small next to the prince and his captivating aura, it was then she noticed the Troivackian king staring at her with an expression that stole her breath.

He looked . . . crestfallen. As though he had just lost something.

"Princess?"

Alina blinked and turned back to Henry, who was watching her expectantly.

"Yes, sorry . . . the next song?"

"Would you like to announce what it is?" the prince asked while dropping his voice to a whisper.

Alina was going to say yes, until she faced the crowd and felt the unpleasant tickle of fear in her chest.

"N-No, that's okay."

Nodding without missing a beat, Henry turned to the group of nobles. "This next song is a traditional Troivackian folk song. If I had my instrument from home, it'd be a little bit closer to how it was originally written, but we hope you won't mind the princess's expert lute playing instead."

The nobility chittered, and something about it made Alina wince.

Even so, she struck the first chord, its discordant haunting tones ringing out purely into the crowd. When its melody switched to the soft fluttering of notes, she noticed that the room had once again fallen dead silent.

As she played, Henry joined in seamlessly, helping Alina become more and more engrossed in the song; she didn't even raise her gaze from her left hand until it was her time to join in to sing. When she lifted her face to look at Henry, however, she found his eyes were lost to a far-off memory.

Her voice was too quiet compared to his. Taking in a bit more air, Alina managed to match his volume; that is, until she looked out into the crowd. She saw the infatuated stares at Henry, and a few of the young men staring straight at herself . . . their expressions either bored or studious as they listened.

It was then the horrible rattle in her chest began.

No! Please . . . Gods—

She coughed.

Dropping off, Alina continued playing the lute, though her tempo was picking up speed thanks to her panic, and Henry was finally snapped out of his trance. He looked to her and stopped singing.

Alina felt her face flare red, which only amplified her embarrassment when she opened her mouth to talk and began choking.

"A cup of water! Please, someone!" Henry called out to the crowd.

No! Stop making this worse! Alina could feel the tears beginning to roll down her face as she coughed.

Out of the corner of her eye she noticed her father rising from his chair and moving toward her. Despite barely being able to breathe or see through her tears, Alina thrust her lute into Henry's arms and launched herself into the crowd.

They scattered from her as she continued gasping her way toward the doors as though she were contagious.

"ALINA!" Norman's voice boomed over the crowd making her feel even more like a small child running from their parent.

As she was beginning to wonder if she were trapped in a nightmare, Tam and Kat Ashowan appeared in front of her.

"Move as quickly as you can to the left of the corridor. We'll redirect them," Kat whispered hurriedly while giving her friend a small shove that had Alina stumbling free of the crowded room as the twins faced off against the herd of nobility all stuck in inaction as the king dismounted the dais and followed his daughter's trail. The anxiousness in his face was impossible to miss.

"Right," Tam murmured under his breath to his twin. "Any idea how we're going to buy her time?"

"You're the brains, I'm the brawn." Kat answered through her teeth.

Tam swore colorfully under his breath before he stepped forward; his long dark hair was once again unbound in front of his gaze as he kept his face turned toward the floor.

"Sire, the princess said she is going to her chamber. Can we perhaps send for the Court Physician?" Tam asked the king, who had finally reached them.

"Mr. Howard has already sent for him. I can—" Norman tried to move around Tam, only to find the man had stepped to block him . . . supposedly by accident.

"Oh, pardon me, Your Majesty. I'll just . . . oh dear." Tam shuffled awkwardly, still blocking the king until he could no longer make it look like natural clumsiness.

Norman stopped his strange dance and shot the younger man a sharp look that made Tam flinch.

Stepping slowly around Tam, who was already bowing in apology, Norman finally moved into the dark corridor, only to find that his daughter had vanished into thin air.

Chapter 18

NIGHTTIME AMUSEMENTS

With her knees pulled to her chest and her gasps ragged and wet from her tears, Alina sat at the bottom of the stairs of the castle's east exit, a violet bruise forming on her thigh and arm from where she had fallen down the steps moments before. Her crown was clasped loosely in her hands. Her veil was lying in the dewy lawn a few steps away, already forgotten . . .

She was finally calmed, and the summer air was beginning to take on a slight chill, yet she couldn't bring herself to move. Even as goosebumps pricked her skin and her limbs grew stiff.

Gods, how childish can I get? Running away? Alina thumped her head against her knees. *I even choked after only singing two songs because I got so worked up. How weak can a person be?*

A heavy weight suddenly enveloped her shoulders, bringing with it blissful and enticing warmth. It smelled of the outdoors, and leather . . . with the faint hint of some other intoxicating wood. Henry smelled like it from time to time.

Looking up expecting to see the very prince she had run from nearly an hour earlier, Alina was surprised to find that no one stood or sat beside her. Puzzled, she turned back toward her knees and then realized a pair of legs was standing in *front* of her.

Lifting her chin, Alina found her gaze continuously traveling upward until it rested upon Brendan Devark's face.

He didn't say anything, only stared with his usual dark unfathomable gaze.

"I-I'm not in the mood to fight with you." Alina looked away, already feeling fresh tears springing to her eyes.

"Why do you presume I'm here to start a fight?" Brendan's deep voice was still intimidating, but at least he didn't sound condescending.

"You think I should go inside and face everyone, and I'm not going to do that."

"I'll make you a promise, Princess. I won't try to assume your thoughts if you don't mine." Brendan's flat tone had a note of irritation, making Alina wince.

Feeling even worse, she let out a small breath of defeat and hung her head. "Sorry. Please just leave me be . . ."

"I'm out here to ask if you'd like to be stronger."

Alina's eyes flew up to Brendan's once more, her shock making her heart skip a beat.

"W-What do you mean?" she managed to ask once regaining the ability to speak.

"You aren't a child. You know how to manage your anger and look after others. The only time you falter is when your weakness is exposed. So that means we need to make you stronger. Perhaps then you will have faith in your own abilities and be less prone to similar events in the future."

Alina felt desperation well up inside of herself.

Yes. She wanted to be stronger. She wanted to no longer have everyone worrying about how they could take care of her or help her. She wanted to no longer be treated delicately by those around her.

"How . . . and . . . why?" the princess managed to ask, her voice croaking.

"To begin, I believe you need more physical exercise in your daily life. You aren't ever pushing to grow your breath capacity, and so it remains the same no matter what."

Alina resisted the urge to grimace. Physical exercise never sounded appealing to her . . .

"You still haven't said why," she pointed out softly.

Brendan's eyes warmed then, and to say it took Alina aback would be putting it lightly. There was a spark of caring in his eyes that was making her stomach somersault.

"I see myself in you."

Alina blinked. Whatever answer she had been anticipating, it hadn't been that one. The summer breeze rustled the grass, and made the torches outside the castle exit flicker, and in their light, Alina saw an entirely new expression on the king's face. One of pain, determination, but also . . . assurance.

"How do you see yourself—"

"Are all Daxarian women so talkative?" Brendan interrupted, his impenetrable mask falling back into place as he folded his arms over his chest.

Alina's eyes narrowed as she inadvertently pulled his cloak tighter around herself.

"I am not chatty, and you know it."

After a small huff, the princess slowly brought herself to her feet using the stone railing. She found that despite standing on the steps while he was on the ground, she still wasn't quite as tall as the Troivackian in front of her.

"Are you offering to help me to try and convince me to marry you?" Alina asked seriously.

Brendan tilted his head, as he often did when thinking about his answer thoroughly.

"I don't need to convince you. I am as you see me, and I cannot change. If that isn't what you want, so be it."

"More like you won't change," Alina said before she could stop herself.

The king took a step closer to her, and in the stillness of the night, his proximity made her momentarily forget to breathe as he stood mere inches from her.

"I am alive today because of how I am, Princess."

Alina couldn't move her gaze from his. She didn't know why, but giddiness was spreading through her being.

"Are you happy?"

Brendan's eyebrows twitched to a small frown. "I am a king. My duty is to my people, and not to self-serve my own desires."

He expected her to look hurt, or angry even, and was preparing himself for when she would inevitably flee to cry again. Only she once again reacted to him in a way that gave him pause.

She looked at him with tender worry.

"You must've gone through a great deal of pain to not even be able to consider having both."

All at once, Brendan felt his air grow ominous, and he watched the young woman grow wary at the sight.

"I am not a being in need of caring and love, Princess."

Instead of growing quiet or apologetic, Alina felt a strange indignation at his words, and a glare of her own shifted across her features.

"King Brendan Devark, a good ruler *should* need that. Without it, you will never be able to properly understand or care for your citizens."

"A romantic notion," Brendan replied coolly.

"One that comes with a perfect example," Alina fired back hotly, her mother and father appearing in her mind's eye.

"Your parents were the exception not the rule, Your Highness," Brendan replied as though having read her thoughts.

Despite her devout beliefs, Alina couldn't deny she was starting to feel like a child for arguing something so idyllic to such an impenetrable, worldly man . . . Even so. She would not back down.

"So tell me, Your Majesty, for my own edification, what should I expect from our marriage then? A business venture without an ounce of care or compassion?" she queried with feigned casualness.

Brendan knew he should feel defensive at her question, but he was a little too surprised and pleased at her referencing their marriage to be truly irritated.

"A relationship based on respect and a common goal of making our kingdom a better place."

"That sounds exactly like a business partner. Do you expect bedding each other to be equally formal?"

So flummoxed was he by the innocent lamb of a princess discussing bedding, that Brendan's jaw dropped and he failed to hide his emotions for a few moments.

"That isn't . . . Bedding is . . . it is not appropriate for unmarried . . . persons . . . to . . . to discuss," the king managed though Alina was beyond thrilled to see the effect her words had on the normally unshakable ruler. His cheeks had deepened in color, and his gaze had become shifty as even his hands twitched at his sides.

"Why not? It is best to know who I'm getting in bed with as a business partner, isn't it?" Alina couldn't help it. She knew she was being wildly inappropriate, but his reaction was so refreshingly fun.

"Who . . . who has discussed such things with you that you can speak of it so easily?" Brendan's breath was coming out a little faster than normal, and the princess thought she might laugh aloud.

"My mother, of course. She taught me that there is nothing untoward about enjoying intimate times with a husband." Alina's smile was a rather vexing mix of radiant and devilish.

Brendan felt a strange emotion seize his chest then as he stared at her, his face still burning from her words, but there was something else powerful building in him.

Leaning forward, his eyes dark with intensity, he could hear the princess take in a small breath of air at his sudden move.

"As long as you know, Princess, that now you've said such things to me, you cannot ever say such things to another man again."

Alina swallowed with great difficulty, and her cheeks pinkened again. "I-I will say whatever I like to whomever I please."

"I don't think you know what kind of invitation such comments make. Especially if I'm the first one you have said such things to. So I am trying to give you—"

"—A lesson on chastity?" Alina wanted to sound angry, but instead her voice rasped. Why was her heart beating so quickly?! So what if he was only a few inches from her face!

"No. I'm pointing out that you said that such enjoyments were reserved for husbands, and you seemed to be taking great *enjoyment* in sharing such an intimate topic with me."

"I was not! I was only—"

Brendan's hand came up then, cupping her face and drawing her closer to him so that her breath could be felt on his lips while his thumb brushed her skin, warm but slightly damp from her tears.

Alina had fallen still and her eyes had closed briefly.

Brendan felt his blood roar with the demand to kiss her right then and there. To show her *exactly* the nature of things she was toying with.

Instead, he took a steadying breath. "Men tend to get the wrong idea when you speak so lightly of marriage and bedding, Princess."

He gradually withdrew and dropped his hand to his side. The princess's flushed face and shallow breaths, with the glow of firelight behind her casting her hair aflame, was making her all too alluring.

"I . . . I see. Well, thank you for your . . . insight," Alina managed, trying to collect herself.

Gods, what was I hoping for? Did I really want to kiss him? she wondered dazedly.

"I shall leave you for now, though I recommend returning soon. The humidity on a night like tonight isn't going to help your breathing." Brendan had resumed his normal composure as he moved toward the castle.

When he stepped onto the stair beside her, however, he turned and caught her eyes with his own. "I'll see you in the morning, Princess. We'll go for a long walk before I leave for the hunt with your father."

Alina didn't say anything as the king then continued moving up the stairs and into the dark recess of the castle walls, leaving her to catch her breath and calm down alone.

As the void of the night once again engulfed her, the young royal found herself staring distractedly off into the darkness feeling a little too out of sorts for her liking . . . though unlike when she had fled the ball, this time the sensation was rather . . . thrilling.

Brendan rounded the corner of the east entrance to the castle, and without even bothering to turn, addressed the shadowy figure who stood leaning against the doorway with his arms crossed.

"You're rather adept at hiding in the dark."

Tamlin Ashowan peeled himself away from the wall and regarded the king somberly without saying a word.

"I'll let it go because I know you couldn't hear anything, but it'd be best not to take to *spying* on others."

Tam continued to say nothing as he watched the Troivackian king silently disappear down the corridor. Gritting his teeth for a moment, the young noble forced himself to relax again before turning and walking out the door and down the steps to where Alina stood staring out into the night, completely unaware of her surroundings.

"Shall we go back inside?" he offered quietly.

"Tam! When did you . . . wait . . . you didn't happen to-to see anything did you?" Alina asked with a stricken expression that made Tam frown.

"I saw the Troivackian king just leave," he answered evasively. "Your father is more than a little concerned, so perhaps you should go speak with him."

Alina swallowed guiltily while nodding but looking away. She knew her father was more than likely beside himself after her dramatic exit.

"Perhaps I should take His Majesty's cloak. People might start getting the wrong idea," Tam pointed out as the princess turned toward the castle door.

Alina blinked and straightened her shoulders as the realization sunk in that the heavy cloak keeping her warm was in fact Brendan's.

"Oh . . . a-alright." Handing the garment to Tam, she then accepted his arm as they headed back into the castle. Though Brendan's woody smell still clung to her neck, and something about it made her face hot as the memory of his rough hand on her cheek made a burst of electricity rush from her stomach through to her fingertips . . .

"Are you feeling better?" Tam asked as they finally reached the top of the steps and he noted the slight limp in her gait.

Alina opened her mouth to ask why would she not be feeling fine, but then she remembered her embarrassing performance just over an hour earlier.

Oddly, when arguing with the king, she had completely forgotten about it.

He's so annoying that he distracts me from my problems, Alina thought amusedly to herself and gave her head a shake.

"Yes, I'm fine. I'm ready to face them."

Alina fixed her attention ahead of herself, for some reason completely untroubled by what could be an emotionally draining conversation with her father. As she prepared herself mentally for what was to come, she totally missed Tam's worried glance. Though even if she had seen it, somehow, she felt far surer of herself than she had in a while.

Chapter 19

AN EYE-OPENING ENGAGEMENT

As Alina approached her chamber, she could feel the stares and whispers of the servants and guards around her. Despite not being able to make out what exactly was being said, she couldn't help but be grateful that Tam was there with her.

Then again, perhaps his presence was part of the kindling to the spark of gossip that was igniting around her.

Once in front of her chamber door, Alina could hear her father speaking to someone, most likely either Mr. Howard or Marianne, her handmaiden.

With a deep steadying breath, she opened the door.

Only it wasn't Marianne or her father's assistant the king was having a serious conversation with; it was Lady Annika Ashowan.

The two turned and looked at Alina in unison, and Norman hastily rushed to his daughter and hugged her.

"Are you alright?" the king asked, his voice hoarse.

Alina wrapped her arms around her father and gingerly patted him on the back.

"Yes, Father. I'm sorry for worrying you."

"Why would you try to sing for everyone when you knew what would happen?" Norman asked as he refused to end the embrace.

"Prince Henry and I thought it'd be a wonderful way to share the beauty of both our kingdoms." Alina pulled back from her father despite feeling his resistance. She was surprised to see that they were already alone. She hadn't even noticed Lady Ashowan or Tam leave.

"Father, I did it because I wanted to. I can't just hide forever. Look, I truly am fine." Alina held out her arms to show herself unscathed—though she was grateful the bruises on her arm and leg from falling down the stairs were hidden.

"Even if you were going to be fine, running out of the ball and disappearing when suitors are in the castle is not safe for you."

"Didn't you once tell me that with Lord Ashowan within the walls, if someone was actually terrified or in danger, he would be able to sense it?" Alina countered while trying to remain rational.

Norman fell quiet.

It was true that Fin's powers had sharpened over the years so that whenever he was in one particular structure of his "home," he could sense anyone within the walls and no one outside of them—unless they were his wife and children. In their case, he could sense them anywhere when endangered.

"Regardless, Alina, what if he hadn't been here? Would you have allowed your guards to follow—"

"Father! Can I please just . . . be alone every now and then?! I'm not trying to be reckless or, or do outlandish things! I just wanted a moment alone, and to do the performance as something that would benefit our kingdoms wasn't crossing any political lines—"

"Performing with the Troivackian prince *was* a political statement, Alina. Did you not realize that when you planned this?" Norman's question wasn't accusatory so much as genuine concern that his daughter had missed something so important.

The princess grew still. "What do you mean?"

"Your performance with Prince Henry was a message to every suitor present that you had made him your choice to be your husband. It indicated you two had spent significant time together and even worked to signify a unifying of the kingdoms. That is what everyone has taken from this evening; was this not your intent?"

Alina felt all color drain from her face.

"No. It wasn't."

Norman read the shock in his daughter's face, and with a long sigh, he leaned forward and kissed her forehead.

"We can talk about how we will handle this tomorrow morning. Get some sleep, dearest."

Alina squeezed her father's hand as he passed her toward her chamber door, stopping him in his tracks when she spoke.

"What if I did want to marry Prince Henry? Then what?"

Norman regarded his daughter closely for a moment, his hazel eyes warming as unspoken memories flashed through his mind.

"If you truly wanted to . . . that would be something we could discuss more seriously. However, the idea has clearly filled you with dread. Perhaps you should think about why that is."

Alina balked as she realized the truth in her father's words.

"The two of you really did sound wonderful together," Norman called softly over his shoulder, casting one final loving smile at his daughter, who managed to smile back slightly in thanks before he took his leave for the night.

Once alone, Alina turned her sights to her window. She hadn't meant things to go so horribly awry . . . and why *did* she feel reticent about marrying Henry? Hadn't he been the one she'd liked the most?

Maybe it's because he treats me like everyone else, and I'm tired of feeling like . . . like all I am is amiable company to him. It's easy to be kind and polite to Henry, but it feels like that's all I'd ever be. I'd forever feel weak and useless like I do now.

Shaking her head and stepping closer to the window, where a pleasant but cool night breeze drifted in and touched her cheek, Alina began to think about the Troivackian king's offer to make her stronger.

He certainly didn't treat her like everyone else. Nor did he draw out her people-pleasing tendencies. Though that wasn't necessarily a good thing . . .

Alina glimpsed the sight of her troubled reflection in the glass and immediately realized two unfortunate undeniable truths.

The first was that, any moment her maids would come to help her undress for bed, and the second . . . she would be up most of the night thinking about what she should do about the new dilemma.

The heat of the morning following the ball was transforming the morning dew to a muggy haze. Bugs whizzed by lazily and cicadas in the trees heralded the future scorching temperatures of the day.

Alina was already in a poor mood to begin with when she had officially been summoned by the king of Troivack's assistant to accompany His Majesty on a lengthy walk.

Marianne had been apoplectic over the abrupt invitation and change in schedule. Were it not for Mr. Levin's stony expression and adamant insistence that it had been an arrangement agreed upon by both parties, the meeting would not have happened.

Standing at the west exit, Alina surveyed the outdoors grimly.

She would not be surprised if she had an attack just by setting foot outside from the soupy humidity and pollen.

"Apologies for making you wait, Princess."

Alina turned to face the king, who strode toward her, wearing a cream muslin tunic, black leather vest, and only one dagger clipped at his side. She had never seen him in anything other than black, and it was a startling change on him.

"You look tired. Did you not sleep restfully?" Brendan observed as he noted the dark bags under the princess's eyes and the lack of effort in her appearance. Her hair had been pinned sloppily into a bun atop her head, and her periwinkle dress appeared to be a few inches too short . . . as though it had fit her years ago.

"I did not. How long is this walk going to be?" Alina asked flatly as Mr. Levin bowed and took his leave of them.

Marianne and two of her maids stood several feet back waiting quietly.

"We will see how you fare," Brendan answered ambiguously.

Alina openly scowled, and for some reason, this made the king struggle to keep his expression neutral.

Why did he find the princess being grumpy so . . . amusing?

"Well, come on. Let's get this over with. I'm sure you're looking forward to the hunt." Alina stalked out of the castle, and once again seeing her furious little walk had Brendan straining muscles in his chest to stop himself from chuckling.

As he quickly caught up to Alina, the king glanced around at the quiet scenery and felt his mood rise. It was nice to be free of the confining castle walls.

"Did your meeting with your father go well?" he asked good-naturedly.

"No. Apparently everyone thinks Prince Henry and I are going to be engaged shortly." The princess's glib reply was followed by her slapping a fly on her cheek.

"Were you not aware of that beforehand?" The faint incredulous note in Brendan's voice earned a look of irritation from his companion.

"Is that why your brother asked me to perform?"

"No. He did it because he genuinely thought it'd be a nice gesture between the kingdoms," the king replied.

"So he didn't know that's what it meant either!" Alina brightened at the thought that she wasn't the only person who had missed the implications of their singing.

"He didn't know until the ball, but he couldn't really tell you to cancel it at the time. The reason people assume that you've made him your choice, Princess, is that you have actively avoided every single suitor except him, and performing together sent a very clear final message. He wasn't aware of this until he realized you did not dance with a single person, and as the night continued, that's what he heard from your suitors."

Alina's mood blackened. "So . . . did you think I was choosing him as well?"

"Yes. Until the second song."

Turning to stare at the giant beside her, Alina noticed Brendan kept glancing at their surroundings, as though watching for an attack.

"What about the second song made you think otherwise?"

"When Henry didn't look back at you, you didn't seem bothered about it. The only thing he did that upset you was not take your restrictions with breath into account when he sang a little louder."

"That's a bold assumption to make on very little information."

"Then, should I be preparing to sign the papers issuing my blessing for your coming engagement?" Brendan asked calmly, though the princess wondered if she heard a little bit of tension in his voice.

Alina stopped walking and turned to face Brendan. She took a slow steadying breath and cast a single glance at Marianne and gave a single nod. The maids fell back several more feet, placing them completely out of earshot.

She hadn't anticipated having this conversation with the Troivackian king until after speaking with her father, but . . . well . . . he'd brought it up first.

"No. You shouldn't be drafting an engagement contract between me and your brother."

The ruler squared himself in front of the princess; several small muscles in his face suddenly relaxed, and Alina knew then that she had been right that he had been worried about her answer.

"Your Majesty, I believe that I would instead like to marry . . . you."

Brendan blinked, and for some mystifying reason, he forgot to breathe for a moment.

"You see, last night when my father told me he would proceed with preparing for my engagement to Henry, I realized I hated the idea. Not because he isn't a lovely person, and I . . . I will admit I like him a great deal, but . . ." Alina closed her eyes briefly, trying to ignore the heat rising in her cheeks. She wasn't used to being so open about her feelings.

"I don't want to give up what I want most in the world for him."

Brendan waited as he stared down into the princess's eyes that burned with a determination he hadn't seen before.

"What is it you want, Princess?"

"I want to be stronger, and . . . I believe I'd like to be queen."

The Troivackian's eyebrows shot upward.

"I want to lead people and bring about good changes. When I realized last night that this was the most important thing to me, more than anything . . . ? I understood it didn't matter if I didn't marry for love or affection. You seem an honest, honorable person, and you care deeply for your people, and that is something I believe we will share. So, Your Majesty, your idea of our union was a wise one after all."

It wasn't often that the Troivackian king was struck speechless or emotional, but he had to admit hearing the princess's words was one of those times.

She had acquiesced to their marriage faster than he thought she would, and seeing the iron in her begin to solidify made him want to smile.

However . . . one other feeling twinged in his gut unpleasantly. It was when she had said that it no longer mattered if there was love in her marriage, and it wasn't because he thought she was wrong, but rather . . . he wished she were.

"Well then, Princess. Shall we finish our walk and tell your father the news?" Brendan asked, unsure of whether or not it was polite to start walking again. He was also finding it increasingly difficult to keep emotions from his face.

Alina sighed, already dreading having to explain herself to her father. She could already envision his displeasure over her marriage being decided for political reasons.

"Yes, though if you would like to skip the walking part, I won't complain . . ."

"Come, Princess. We need to make you stronger—especially if you are going to be the next queen of Troivack."

With her stomach actively fluttering and her breaths threatening to quicken at his referring to her as his future queen, Alina had to admit she felt a little excited. She had just gotten engaged.

She glanced at Brendan then and felt a small smile tug at the corner of her mouth.

The moment hadn't been grand or sweet with a love so powerful that it rendered her speechless, but . . . knowing that she was closer to being something more than she was made her brighten from the inside out.

When Alina entered the council room with Brendan at her side, she had anticipated her father and Mr. Howard waiting for her; however, she was surprised to see every man of the inner council seated around the table with the addition of Lady Ashowan.

"Princess, thank you for joining us, and . . . Your Majesty." Norman eyed the Troivackian king beside his daughter with newfound wariness.

Alina glanced to Brendan to see if he was going to speak first but was surprised to see he was staring at her expectantly.

In that moment, he gave her a single bow of his head, and she immediately knew that he was giving her the power to make the announcement on her own with his consent.

Something about the gesture made her feel even more assured in her decision.

"Father, and esteemed council members, I understand we are gathered to discuss the implications of my performance with Prince Henry last night. I apologize for the confusion and stress. I did not know my actions would bear these results, and I am formally denying any wish to become engaged to the Troivackian prince."

Norman let out a long breath and smiled happily at his daughter.

His expression of relief nearly choked the next words in Alina's throat.

It was going to be harder than she thought.

"Rather, the Troivackian king and I have . . . have agreed we are the better match. We are officially requesting to be engaged to be married."

The room fell into a deathly silence.

All color drained from Norman's face as he stared in open dread at his daughter's eyes and saw that she was serious.

No one dared to breathe for several long moments as Alina clasped her hands in front of herself and began to feel more than a little terrified of the next words that would be spoken.

"HA! PAY UP!" Lord Fuks suddenly exploded from his chair cackling gleefully while pointing his finger around the table.

Both Brendan and Alina stood stunned, uncertain of what to say or do as everyone present wore their emotions on their sleeves, and not all of them were pleasant save for the infamously mad Lord Dick Fuks.

Their morning was going to be a lengthy one indeed.

Chapter 20

THE KIDS AREN'T ALRIGHT

"Alina . . . saying such a thing—" Norman began, his voice hoarse.

"Father, this is what I want, I promise," the princess interrupted despite her trembling hands.

"Everyone but Her Highness leave the room, now." The king's dark tone set everyone in motion instantly.

Everyone except Brendan Devark, who turned to Alina and locked eyes with hers.

Despite there not being a hint of emotion in his face . . . she could see the question in his eyes.

She nodded, and he turned to leave.

The exchange was only noticed by Annika Ashowan, and the viscountess grew anxious for the near future.

Once they had all filed out, and the door closed behind them, Brendan found the entire inner council all turned to face him, save for Annika Ashowan, who was already far down the corridor, her presence once again dissipating easily.

The most joyous—by a large margin—of the men who remained behind was Lord Fuks.

"Open your coin purses, Captain, Mr. Howard, and you, Keith! I told you she'd pick the king!" the old man cackled happily.

Brendan frowned at the men as they all reached into their pockets and drew out their coins with looks of disappointment.

"What is this about?" Brendan asked coldly.

"Isn't it obvious? We had bets, Your Majesty. I bet on you and so I am three gold pieces richer for it!" Lord Fuks replied while snatching the money from his fellow council members and stowing it in his leather pouch attached to his cane.

"Who all did you bet on?" Finlay Ashowan asked dryly. Evidently, he had not been included in the gamble.

"I bet on Prince Henry," Mr. Howard grumbled while folding his arms across his chest.

"I had my money on your boy, Viscount." Sir Taylor nodded to the red-head apologetically.

Everyone turned to Keith Lee expectantly.

Sighing, the man leaned on his staff wearily. "I bet on the viscount's daughter, Lady Katarina Ashowan."

"I . . . beg your pardon?" Fin began slowly.

Brendan had had enough of the madness of the Daxarian king's inner council. He just wanted to wait in peace to learn how the meeting would be handled and had intended to stand outside until the princess had finished speaking with her father and . . .

Why do I need to wait around? The king will summon me once the agreement is drawn up. Brendan then realized he was doing something out of character and useless.

Alina's nervous eyes when she had looked at him flashed in his mind.

Shaking his head, the Troivackian king turned and began striding away from the council room.

Their marriage would be between two strong and capable individuals. He didn't need to hold her hand like a child when difficult times arose.

A strange resistance in his chest made it a little harder to leave, but . . .

Mr. Levin was waiting with news from Brendan's court. He needed to handle that so he would have time to review the engagement contract later. Besides, if he could avoid spending time with the Ashowan family members as the council loitered outside the room, that was an added bonus.

With his thoughts and beliefs once again firmly set in place, Brendan continued on his way back to his chamber, and he didn't spare a second glance over his shoulder as he did so. Though annoyingly enough a small tightening in his gut did not seem to want to release him just yet.

"Alina, has he forced this decision upon you somehow?" Norman demanded while staring at his daughter, who had seated herself on his right-hand side.

"No, Father. I want to marry him. I want to be the queen of Troivack and help the kingdom evolve into something better."

"You sound as though you are marrying him just to *be* queen," Norman observed, his voice hard.

Alina felt a firm lump grow in her throat. "I-I am. I want to lead people and become stronger. That matters more to me."

"Then the betterment of the citizens isn't your priority, your ambition is," Norman countered coldly.

"No, it isn't! I-I just think I can help. I can bring what has worked for Daxaria to them, and try to—"

"It won't work in Troivack. Their nation is barely ready to allow women having a voice, let alone one changing their traditional laws. You are choosing a life of hardship away from your friends and family, and a husband who will only see you as a means to an end. When the dust settles, all you will have is the title, but none of the power to make a difference."

"I can still try! I'll learn more before going! I can start to attend council meetings, and—"

"No. Alina, this marriage will have you dead in a year."

Standing up abruptly, Alina's heart was aching, and her tears falling. "I'd rather die with a title and the knowledge I did everything I could to make a kingdom better than die here weak and alone as a coward. I can no longer stand always being coddled with no purpose other than as a piece of fluff meant for comforting people who are greater."

Norman felt his anger, fear, and sadness ebb away at the sight of his daughter's tears.

He saw she meant her words. Saw the desperation in her eyes to never live a life as anything other than a monarch . . .

And it broke his heart.

"Alina."

His daughter didn't wait to hear what he would say next, however, as she stormed out of the room and slammed the door behind herself.

Sinking back into his chair, Norman looked to the ceiling before swallowing with great difficulty.

He had handled that horribly, but how could he let his daughter risk everything she was—her safety, her happiness, her family—for such a union?

"Ainsley, what do I do? Our girl wants to leave and . . . I'm scared. I'm scared I can't protect her anymore. I've lost so much already . . . first you . . . and I don't even know if Eric will ever return. Gods, my love. It's been a mess ever since you left. I don't know what to do," Norman's anguished voice croaked into the silence as a coldness settled over him despite the summer heat.

Dropping his head to his hands, the Daxarian king felt dread and grief fill his heart.

Soon, he would be alone, and when that happened? What point was there to living?

Alina hesitated in front of her chamber door, her hand raised over the handle.

She knew the moment she entered, her maids would descend upon her disheveled state and would begin trying to fix her appearance. They didn't care what could have made her upset. Their primary duties lay in maintaining her pure, flawless image.

She didn't want to deal with them. Turning toward Eric's room she began to stride to the comforting sanctuary.

"OY!"

Halting, Alina glanced over her shoulder reluctantly, only to see the familiar grin of Katarina Ashowan.

"W-What is it?" the princess managed to ask while wiping her nose with the back of her wrist.

"I see you've had a rough go of it since the ball . . . do you maybe want to go on an adventure with me?" Kat looped her arm around Alina's and was already pulling her away from her chamber.

"I-I just want to be alone."

"To do what?" Kat asked with a raised eyebrow before carrying on in a philosophical tone. "Look, you can dwell on the misfortune that is clearly bothering you, or you can push it to the back of the shelf and take a look at more interesting activities available to use up your time!"

Katarina waggled her eyebrows down at the princess, and like a moth to a flame, Alina felt herself be drawn in.

"W-What kind of adventure?"

"That's the spirit! Come on! You've tried wearing trousers before, right? How do you feel about dying your hair? Ever held a knife?" Kat proceeded down the corridor, happily dragging along the princess at her side into her next grand plan for her day.

Tam stared at his mother serenely.

"How long have you known?" Annika asked her son tentatively.

"Since I overheard your meeting with Clara six years ago. I was in the solar hiding from Kat and heard the entire thing."

She nodded thoughtfully.

"Though if I'm honest, you secretly teaching us evasive moves, how to survive in the wilderness, plus dagger handling and throwing was a bit of a tip-off that you might be involved in more than just regular noble duties."

Annika smiled slightly at her son's words. "I knew it was a matter of time before one of you figured out that it wasn't the norm for Troivackian women."

"Mum, why are you sending so many messages with our family hawks lately?" Tam asked seriously. "Is something wrong with the Troivackian king?"

The viscountess's features fell to an expression of neutrality. "Don't worry about it, love. Your father and I can take care of it."

Tam shifted in his seat. "You heard the news today; His Majesty Brendan Devark and Alina are going to be engaged. The princess deserves to know if there is something suspicious, or at the very least tell me so that I—"

"So that you can do what, Tam?" Annika asked calmly. "There is nothing that you would be able to change. What I know cannot be revealed to Alina, or else we risk exposure."

"When are you going to start trusting me as an adult? I just want to help protect people like you and Da do."

Annika's expression softened as she leaned forward in her seat. "Love, the day you say you want to start taking over as viscount for your father, we will talk. That to me is what indicates you are ready to start joining our political activities. Until then, don't worry. We will handle things."

"Mum, I can't even be in a large room without trouble. That isn't exactly an ideal trait of a viscount. I shouldn't ever be—"

"Tam. Whatever it is you are so scared of, you need to either seek help to conquer it, or learn to face it alone. You haven't told anyone whatever could be so terrifying, but—"

"Stop." Tam stood up and stared down at his mother, who sat primly at the edge of the sofa in the solar. "There are some things worth being scared of, and there is a reason. You don't know what facing it means."

"Then try to tell us!" Annika rose, her eyes filled with worry and desperation. "We've had this discussion for years, Tam, but you keep shutting your father and me out. How can we— Tam!"

The young noble had already begun leaving the room, his gaze fixed downward as he wrenched open the door and slammed it behind himself with enough force to shake the stone floor.

Sighing, Annika seated herself back down and pinched the bridge of her nose.

"Is this a bad time, mistress?"

Slowly opening her eyes, the viscountess turned to see her pupil, who had just entered through the window. His gray cloak was drawn over his features.

"No, Likon. It's fine."

The young man silently dropped to a single knee and bowed his head before Annika.

"We received word from the last of our informants. Lord Miller doesn't know how anyone found out who you were. We have looked into all the nobles, but nobody—"

"Mr. Levin, the king's assistant, he is not a noble. You asked about him, didn't you?"

"I did, mistress. He is an orphan. He inherited a substantial amount of wealth from his family after they died aboard one of their merchant ships. He was six years old at the time, but after their passing he dedicated himself to his studies. He married two years ago, and his wife found out she was expecting their first child only a week ago. Mr. Levin is unaware of this just yet."

Annika frowned.

Even more dead ends.

"What of the Coven of Aguas? Is there perhaps anyone there with connections here in Daxaria?"

"I have not checked yet."

"Please do. They have been quiet since the war and I am not sure if it is because they fear the new king, or if they are plotting something."

"Yes, mistress."

"Did Lord Miller have any idea about the king's threats to remove my people?"

"He said the guards had been doubled around the castle, but that wasn't uncommon when the prince and king were gone together."

Annika nodded slowly. That didn't sound too strange.

"Oh, Lord Miller also said to inform you that the final madam agreed to your most recent offer. You now own more than twenty-five percent of the brothels in Troivack."

The viscountess smiled wearily. "Tell him to retreat from the court along with the others. I can renegotiate their return with the king shortly."

The young man's back stiffened. "As you wish, mistress."

"Likon, I won't send you to offer my terms, don't worry."

Raising his brown eyes to the viscountess, the man in his early twenties lifted a quizzical eyebrow. "Are you intending to go yourself?"

Sighing, Annika shook her head. "No. I'll send Tam once we know for certain that the Troivackian king has evidence that I am the Dragon."

Likon straightened immediately and grave concern sprouted on his face. "My lady, Tam has no training and—"

"He needs to start taking on responsibility sometime, and he seems to already dislike the king. It should be the best motivation possible for him to start thinking more seriously about taking over as viscount."

"Mistress, what about Katarina?"

Annika stared flatly at her protégé. "I adore my daughter with all my heart, but you know as well as I do she is not going to hold her tongue if she is angered. It could make the situation worse."

"I know, my lady, but perhaps giving her some responsibility would—" Likon stopped talking then and leapt to his feet in time for Annika to turn to the door. They both knew someone was coming.

With a small rustle of his cloak, the young man had disappeared back through the window just in time.

The solar door was thrown open with great force. Both Fin and Clara stumbled into the room out of breath.

"Annika, have you seen Kat anywhere?!" Fin burst out, his eyes already glowing, meaning he was already searching for their daughter using his magicks.

"Not since early this morning. Aren't you supposed to already be at the hunting grounds? It's going to be nighttime soon!" Annika glanced at the blazing pink sky outside the window.

"I was, but I ended up waiting for Lord Harris to show up; he's running late. Clara and the princess's maids came and found me and said they haven't seen either Kat or Alina in hours."

Annika pinched the bridge of her nose. "Oh good Gods."

"You know where they are, don't you?" Tam's voice echoed out from behind his father and Clara.

The three elders gazed at Tam's angry expression, his focus fixed solely on his father, his hands deep in his pockets.

"Where is Kat banned from going but would love to be?" Tam asked with a subtle note of exasperation.

"Oh shit." Fin turned to his wife, who had the same expression of horror mixed with anxiety.

"She went on the Godsdamn hunt, didn't she?" Annika uttered in faint disbelief.

Tam didn't look at his mother but nodded. "And she dragged the princess along with her by the sounds of it."

Chapter 21

CAMPING CONCERNS

"Kat . . . ?" Alina asked while eyeing the dimming light of the woods warily.

"Yes?"

"What exactly are we doing for this grand adventure?"

The lithe redheaded woman turned in her saddle and smiled innocently, her golden eyes already beginning to glow in the nearing dusk.

Alina shifted her aching backside in the saddle to face her friend better. "Kat, you said we could be back by nightfall."

"And we can! . . . Well, if we run these horses to the ground," the redhead finally admitted before clearing her throat and attempting to stifle her smile.

"Kat, are you serious?! My father will be terrified! They will send out a search party! What if there are bears, or . . . or . . . bandits?!" Alina spluttered while nearly dropping her reins. She was still getting used to riding the horse astride like a man . . . though she had to admit she feared falling off the beast significantly less.

"I left a note! I just said we are going on a small outing; completely safe! They know I won't actually get you harmed or anything," Katarina defended her actions while beginning to look apologetic at her friend's incredulous expression.

"Where are we even going?!" the princess demanded as she felt anger rise in her chest.

"We're going to camp outside! Don't worry, we are actually within an hour of the hunting party, so your father is nearby."

Alina's jaw dropped. "You . . . took us to the hunting grounds?! Kat, that party is for the men!"

"Precisely! So we're having our own party! I'm sorry I didn't really tell you, I am! But you've been so tense lately, I thought maybe having a night away from all your maids and expectations, and just joking around with a brilliantly fun friend might help." Kat glanced at Alina with a small smile, instantly lessening the princess's anger.

"This was still too reckless, and we are going back tomorrow morning."

Kat's face lit up then as she finally pulled on the reins to her chestnut mare and swung off the mount with great ease. "Excellent! I will set the camp up; you don't have to worry about a thing!"

"I'm not lazy, I'll help. You just have to— Oof!" Alina, while attempting to dismount her own steed, stumbled and would have crashed to the ground were it not for Kat swiftly catching her.

"Ahh, sorry. You got Patches here for a reason." Once Alina had steadied herself on her aching legs, Kat patted the horse's rump. "He's got a fat arse but is a sturdy horse that doesn't scare easily and takes directions well. I figured if you aren't used to riding like a man, he'd be the best one for you."

Alina barely had the energy to nod as all at once her eventful day caught up to her, despite there being a few more hours of daylight.

Sensing this, Kat gave her friend's shoulders a reassuring squeeze and turned to her own horse that carried their supplies.

"Wait . . . do you not have a tent or a covering? What if it rains?" Alina slowly realized the majority of the redhead's provisions seemed to be food.

"It isn't supposed to rain, and if it does, we have our cloaks . . . I think . . . but we'll be fine!" Kat replied happily as she clicked her tongue and took both horses over to a grassy patch by a nearby tree where she tied them and allowed them to graze.

"How can you predict if it will rain?" Alina asked suspiciously.

"I'm a witch," Kat replied teasingly.

When she received the princess's less than enthused response, she let out a small sigh then answered more seriously. "There isn't a cloud in the sky! My bet is it may rain tomorrow afternoon, but by then we'll be back."

The princess did not look convinced, but she was too tired to argue further, so she walked over to where Katarina was pulling out a loaf of bread, seven apples, seven sandwiches, sausages, a hunk of cheese, two flagons of water or ale—Alina couldn't tell which—and then even more food seemed to spill out of the bags.

"Did you rob your father's entire pantry for a particular reason?" the princess asked faintly as she stared at the items that Kat was in the process of setting on a blanket.

"Oh, you've never really seen me at mealtimes, have you?" the redhead asked brightly.

Alina grew alarmed. "You eat this much?!"

"Well, my brother did tell you I'm the skinniest pig you will ever meet. It's part of my magic; my body burns through the food. It's even worse if I'm being really physically active like today. After most of this, I'll still be pretty hungry and will probably go hunting." Kat shrugged and then straightened.

"Right, do you want to join me and help me find firewood, or would you like to rest for a while?"

Alina blinked dazedly up at her friend, who was retrieving a hatchet from one of the horse's saddles before walking across the clearing toward a wider gap between the maple trees. "You're . . . You're going to hunt? It's almost dark! Even if you can see at night, isn't that dangerous? Also, how do you know how to hunt?!"

Kat chuckled while brushing a stray strand of flaming hair behind her ear. "Ah, my mother always said people should know how to take care of themselves, and so we often went camping as a family. Da hated the hunting part, but Kraken could never get enough of it. One time he caught a rabbit and ate its head, then the rest of the body was strewn—"

Alina held up her hand, cutting off the rest of the story. "I can't believe your mother, the viscountess, would go out into the wilderness with her children like that! She is a pillar of elegance in our kingdom."

At the description of her mother, Kat rolled her eyes. "Ah, yes. Most people see her that way. She may be an overbearingly strict teacher, but even I have to admit that the truth is she can take care of herself really damn well. She says it's because she grew up in Troivack that she's not afraid to get her hands dirty."

Alina frowned. "Troivackian women are treated like valuable items in that country. Amongst the kingdom's many flaws, their devout commitment to their wives and protecting them is one of their lesser evils."

"I think you mean protecting their breeding stock." Kat snorted while shaking her head. "Honestly, the women are expected to keep quiet and stay in control at all times. It sounds like their marriages are so horribly serious and dull."

At this, the princess's cheeks flamed, and she felt herself growing rather irritated. "Well, you haven't ever left Daxaria so you can't know that for certain. They are people just like the rest of us, so of course they love and can have fun and—"

Kat laughed. "They may look like the rest of us, but their thinking about such things is radically different. What isn't grim about a kingdom's people who pride themselves on backstabbing and slaughtering one another? I imagine everyone has to sleep with one eye open. My mother is from there, remember?"

"Well, maybe they are ready for change! Your father managed to persuade several units of Troivackian men to surrender or even help us during the war! As for your mother, she's from there, and she doesn't sound like a pushover either!" Alina was on her feet then. She didn't want to stare up at someone who was agitating her so fiercely.

A strange look crossed Kat's face then as she studied her friend. "Why is this making you so upset?"

Folding her arms across her chest, the princess narrowed her gaze and forced herself to take a steadying breath before replying.

"I'm betrothed to the Troivackian king."

The hatchet that Kat had begun to pull from her pack fell out of her hand as her eyes grew round and her jaw fell open.

"He wants women to carry a voice in the Troivackian court, and he wants to change the laws so that they can hold titles and lands without a spouse," Alina added as her heart hammered in her chest.

The redheaded woman continued staring at her and saying nothing.

"Oh, for Pete's sake! Say something! It isn't that surprising, and he is not as beastly as you think," the princess snapped exasperatedly.

"You . . . You trust him?" Kat asked slowly as she took another step closer.

"I do. Of all the poor social habits he has, dishonesty is not one of them."

"How can you know that? You only met him a few weeks ago." Katarina was visibly shaken.

"I only met *you* a few weeks ago, and you've lied to me more than he has! Dragging me out here into the woods—for your information, I hate the woods! I hate the bugs, and beasts . . ."

"Alina, if you go to Troivack he could change his mind about these 'changes,' and you won't have anyone to help you! You could be getting tricked and—"

"MAYBE I CAN PROTECT MYSELF! HAVE YOU EVER THOUGHT OF THAT?!" the princess roared as her nasty affliction of angry tears began rising to her eyes. She clenched her hands into fists so tight that her nails dug into her palms.

"This isn't about you being strong, it's about you getting trapped in a marriage where you have no means of escaping!" Kat began desperately, her eyes wide with fear.

"That won't happen! I've met countless nobles in my life, and I know Brendan Devark is not going to be dishonorable!"

The look of doubt on the redhead's face was making Alina's fury begin to bubble up once more, when her friend surprised her.

"I'll go with you then."

The princess froze, completely taken aback.

"Wh-Why? Because you think he'll bully me and that I'll sit back and do nothing?" Alina asked, her tone accusatory.

"More like I think it sometimes helps to have someone on your side and no one else's when you are faced with a whole Godsdamn kingdom biased against you," Kat replied heartfeltly. "And, yes, I admit I don't like him. However . . . If you want to try and change a bad place into something better, I know I want to try and be a part of it. You're special, Alina. You've got this light in you, and . . . I don't want to see anything happen to it."

The princess dropped her gaze bashfully. "That's a bit rich coming from you. You look like you're a mix of a Goddess, a beast, and pure magic."

Kat chuckled weakly before once again growing serious. "I'll bring it up to my da that I want to go with you. At least for a little while— I don't know that I want to live there permanently. My parents might even agree easily if it means delaying me getting married."

Alina nodded then shifted on her feet awkwardly. Despite her earlier ire, the princess had to admit that the idea of having a friend with her when facing a room full of men as terrifying as her affianced felt like the greatest gift in the world.

"Will your brother come, do you think?" Alina asked, a little quieter.

"Probably not. Tam on a boat with wide open space isn't exactly a great place for him. Besides, the dummy needs to learn to stop hiding behind me to avoid his duties as the next viscount." Kat reached up and rubbed the back of her neck thoughtfully.

"Are you certain that they will let you go to an entirely different continent?" Alina asked as she felt the danger of the joyous spark of hope for her future begin to blaze.

"They'll fight with me and make me take all kinds of classes I'm sure, but . . . at the end of the day, I think so. My parents kind of started the tradition of protecting your family. I'm not exactly like them, but I promise, I will always be on your side, and I will always do everything in my power to protect you."

Alina couldn't help herself anymore, she burst out into a beautiful smile, which her friend before her matched in kind.

"Now . . . shall we get a fire built to ward off the mosquitoes?" Kat queried with a coy grin.

The princess's good mood immediately lessened as she once again remembered that she was, in fact, stuck sleeping outside, all thanks to the woman who had just sworn to be her guardian.

Brendan sat around the fire with the rest of the courtiers, who all joked and drank merrily, seemingly without a care in the world. Henry was amongst them, singing lewd ballads that had them all slapping their knees.

All of them except the Daxarian king, who was staring with a frown toward the edge of the camp. Norman sat apart from the others, and no one seemed inclined to goad him into joining their revelry.

Brendan stood, making several of the men nearest him shift out of his way hastily. Striding over to the other monarch, he slowly seated himself in the empty chair on his right.

"Is there something amiss?" the Troivackian king asked casually.

He didn't sense anything wrong about their surroundings, nor had he heard anything during their journey to the site, but the Daxarian king was alert in a way that made Brendan wary.

"Lord Ashowan and the duke of Iones, Lord Harris, were supposed to arrive by now," Norman answered, his eyes remaining lost in thought.

Brendan leaned back in his chair and considered what he knew of the two men.

"It could be that the duke arrived later than he anticipated and they decided to stay another night at the castle."

The Daxarian king shifted in his seat. "A reasonable idea, but my gut tells me otherwise. I had a similar feeling the time I was on a hunting party just like this one, and on our journey back we discovered Ainsley was in danger of losing Alina early in the pregnancy." Norman recounted more to himself than his companion, but the story made Brendan straighten in his seat all the same.

"It was a difficult birth then?"

"Yes. Even with Eric it was risky . . . I worry Alina will face similar complications in her future." The Daxarian king sighed wearily and shook his head before remembering exactly who he was talking to.

Turning to face Brendan squarely, he evaluated the man openly.

"I do not like the idea of this marriage at all. I think your kingdom's culture will be too domineering for Alina, and that she will be unhappy there, but . . . she says this is what she wants. So you better do your best to make sure my worries don't come to fruition. Understood?"

Brendan bowed his head. "You have my word. I believe she will grow to be a strong queen that my people will come to respect."

Norman grunted skeptically before shifting and turning his gaze back to the edge of the camp. "I want you both to come visit. Especially with any grandchildren."

Brendan almost smiled.

It was obvious how deeply the king loved his daughter and that he was desperate to see her well taken care of.

Such unconditional love was a rare thing amongst nobility in Brendan's estimation.

It also made him take to heart the man's uneasiness about the viscount and duke's absence.

Standing and giving Norman a bob of his head that was barely acknowledged, Brendan headed toward his horse.

I believe in trusting my gut, but the princess should be safe at the castle. The only danger she could be in is from that terror Lady Katarina Ashowan . . .

Somehow, that thought made even the king of Troivack more assured in his decision to ride back a short ways . . . just in case there was a messenger from the castle.

Chapter 22

A DAUNTING DUKE

M oving silently through the dark forest, Brendan could smell the other camp before he could see it.

The scent of burning wood . . . no cooked food, however, which could mean a number of things.

When he could make out the flickering light between the trees, the Troivackian king dismounted his steed silently, his sword already clipped at his side as he picked his way carefully through the underbrush.

He wasn't as stealthy as he usually was, but it was all because he was unfamiliar with the Daxarian terrain, particularly in the dark.

The shadowy greenery shifted beneath his feet and the occasional nocturnal creature was startled from its activities and scurried away from him.

Yet there was no movement from the campsite.

He wondered if it could be bandits. Regular nomads would never risk traveling so deeply into the king's forest. He tentatively rested his hand on his sword at his side.

As he neared the clearing, however, all he could make out was one sleeping form beside the fire, and whoever it was was quite small.

Drawing his sword carefully, he felt his senses prickle as he looked at the surroundings of the campsite.

There was a lack of any bulky provisions or weapons, suggesting they were traveling with speed in mind.

It was then Brendan noticed the horses tied across the clearing from where he stood.

He stilled at once.

There were two horses, but only one sleeping form.

That was when an arrow whizzed by his ear, making him duck reflexively into the undergrowth, his sword gripped firmly in hand as his eyes sought out the archer.

"I didn't miss because you're a dainty target. Who are you?"

The voice behind the king made his mood blacken.

He had been feeling restless cooped up in Daxaria, and he was spoiling for a good fight . . .

Instead, he let out a long sigh, resigning himself to having to speak instead.

"Lady Katarina Ashowan, I take it the one sleeping on the ground is the princess?"

Brendan heard the creak of the bow as its wood slackened.

"Oh. It's you. Your Majesty." Kat's flat tone greeted him dully. Brendan didn't have to bother trying to guess if she had curtsied or not.

Already displeased over having to face the viscount's daughter, Brendan turned around ready to start chastising her for her careless decision to bring the princess without any armed guards out in the middle of the woods, but when he turned and saw Katarina standing ten feet behind himself, he fell speechless.

Her golden eyes, glowing in the dark, were watching him as a beast watched an irritating mouse.

"Yes, yes, I know I'm not exactly normal. No need to look at me like I'm the devil."

"You can see in the dark?" The Troivackian king's astonished tone made the redhead grin wolfishly.

"Damn right I can. How can we help you, Your Majesty?"

Brendan sheathed his sword as he remembered exactly why he was out in the middle of the woods at night.

"Your king had a bad feeling when your father and Lord Harris failed to show up. I was coming back to see if there were any messengers on the way to our camp."

Kat raised a skeptical eyebrow. "You rode an hour away from your camp just to see if a messenger was hanging around?"

"I was going to ride another hour when I smelled your fire. Are you a fool?"

Kat's expression morphed in the flickering campfire through the trees. "Do I need to remind you that I could have easily shot you before you spoke?" Her voice was tight.

"Like mother like daughter," Brendan muttered darkly. "Regardless, you think you can take on a group of bandits? Or even stay awake all night?" he asked so that she could hear.

"I can stay awake for days quite easily. What was that about my mother?"

Closing his eyes briefly, Brendan chastised himself for bringing it up.

Katarina most likely had no idea that her mother was probably the one to have shot his own father. Otherwise there may have been some measure of caution in her behavior.

With his tone weary and exasperated, he finally replied. "Lady Katarina, I recommend we wake the princess and return to the king's camp."

"No."

Both the Troivackian and Katarina jumped at the sound of Alina's firm objection that came from behind the large king.

When Brendan turned to face the princess, he found she was staring calmly up at him, making his hard gaze immediately soften, not that he was aware of this. Her golden hair was in disarray from the humid night air, and there was dirt smudged on her cheek, but the way the firelight warmed her dirty blond waves made her appear . . .

Cute, the Troivackian king found himself thinking before he could stop himself. The princess just looked so disheveled and mildly irritated . . . he couldn't help it.

"It is the middle of the night. We will leave at dawn to go back to the castle, and none of us are going to breathe a word of it," the princess announced evenly.

Brendan raised an eyebrow. She seemed quite assured of herself. It was a nice change.

Even so . . .

"Why are you so certain that is the best decision?" the king asked patiently.

"She doesn't need a reason to want a night to herself," Kat snapped from behind Brendan, which set the king's teeth on edge. He didn't bother glancing at the viscount's daughter and instead waited for the princess to respond.

"It is more dangerous for me to go to a camp full of would-be suitors and my irate father than stay here. If you are truly concerned that in the next five hours someone will attack us, feel free to wait until it is safe for us to ride in the morning."

Brendan found himself smiling. "Princess, you are saying the trouble you would get in over being discovered is worse than being possibly murdered by wayward souls?"

"My murder is a guaranteed event if my father finds out about this, yes," she replied, a small smile working its way onto her face at the sight of the king's rare grin.

Staring at her pleading eyes mixed with her teasing smile, Brendan heard himself say words without even taking a moment to think! Which disconcerted him only for a brief moment . . .

"You will leave before the sun rises. I will sleep forty paces south of your site. Lady Katarina, if you try to shoot me again, you will regret it."

The redhead behind the king snorted.

He chose to ignore it.

Instead, he gave a bow to Alina and began to walk his forty paces, when the sound of two men's voices echoed through the trees.

"—Then she said I wasn't taking fatherhood seriously! Can you believe that? I swear, I didn't think it was strange that he ran around naked. I mean it's hot out this time of year, and he's only four! Or is it three . . . anyway, I mentioned how pigs keep cool, and you know what, so what if he was a little muddy?! I'll buy her a new dress and she knows it."

"What were you doing when he was in the mud?" came a familiar voice beside the original speaker.

"I was drinking with the knights, but he was within my sights . . . mostly. The dogs would've gone crazy if he was doing something actually dangerous."

"So in other words, you were relying on your dogs to ensure your son's safety, who was rolling around in the mud, in the pigs' pen." The glib response was barely hiding a laugh.

"Oh Gods," Kat groaned, her head falling back, her eyes closed in a grimace.

The king and Alina glanced at each other. They guessed exactly who was drawing closer.

"Is that my *darling, obedient, and RESPONSIBLE daughter I hear*?!"

Kat slowly opened her glowing eyes and turned to the two shadowy horses that approached them. Taking in their riders, her face stretched into a forced smile that looked moderately painful.

"Hi, Da; boy, you sure are up late!"

Finlay Ashowan emerged from the darkness into the light of the campfire, his expression livid as he fixed his attention on his daughter, completely ignoring the two monarchs in his presence.

"Godsdamn, Kat, this is too far. You risked not only your own neck, but Alina's! I can't believe you did this, and for what reason? You wanted to prove yourself to the courtiers that you could hunt better? Why did you—"

"Viscount," Alina interrupted softly, her hands clasped nervously in front of herself.

Fin turned to face her, and she winced at the magical sparks in his eyes that flashed briefly before settling once more into a peaceful look instead.

"I could have refused, but I didn't. I . . . I really did need some time away from the castle. If you could perhaps—"

"Princess Alina, the entire castle is in chaotic panic because of your absence. We should head back this instant," Fin interjected firmly before turning to the duke. "Can you please continue on to the camp to let His Majesty know I will be delayed joining the hunt."

"Da, I left a note saying we were going camping, there shouldn't be—"

"What note?! We have looked in your chamber, and every nook and cranny in our estate as well as the entire Godsdamn castle for you two! Do you know what consequences this could bring? You could be exiled, Kat!" Fin rounded on his daughter, and she visibly shrank before him.

"I-It was on my desk at home," Kat responded weakly, looking entirely unlike herself as she faced her father.

Taking a careful breath at the sight of his daughter's timidness, the viscount's features softened, his shoulders slumping forward as he raised his hands up to rub his face.

"Kat . . . do you know how scared we all were? Anything could have happened."

"We're an hour from the king's camp, it really wasn't that dangerous, I swear!" Tears glistened in Kat's eyes, and the moment they appeared Fin pulled her into an embrace.

"Kat, you're getting more and more . . ." The viscount's voice cracked as he trailed off.

"Erm . . . as . . . touching . . . or heartbreaking? One of the two, anyway. As memorable as this first meeting is with Your Majesties"—Lord Harris bowed to Alina and Brendan, his boyish smile making him appear significantly younger than his years—"perhaps we all decide what to do. In my estimation, if all of us sleep here, Viscount, you can return the princess and your daughter tomorrow morning, and whether or not the king hears of this little adventure . . . well . . ." Lord Harris shrugged, his hands turned upward.

"Do you honestly think no one will mention how his daughter went missing for an entire day?" Fin asked drolly.

"What if we say it was a miscommunication?" Alina interjected while stepping forward. "We tell the staff my father wanted to spend some quality time with my fiancé and me, which will be the first official announcement of my engagement to the Troivackian king. It'll distract everyone, and when he arrives, everyone will be too excited to bother mentioning it. Besides, even my maids would be too embarrassed to admit such an oversight in my schedule. His Majesty can just say . . . erm . . . that he left camp due to forgetting an important correspondence to respond to. Hopefully with that added, the chaos will make it much harder to discern the truth."

The only sound that followed the princess's idea was crickets.

Lord Harris was the one to smile first. "That is quite . . . devious, yet brilliant. To think everyone said you were a model of what a good, demure maiden should be."

Alina winced.

"Don't worry, this is much better!" the duke quickly added while the viscount stared at him exasperatedly.

"Harris."

"Yeah?"

"Shut up."

"Right."

The two men then faced the princess. Fin slipped his hands in his pockets as his daughter hastily wiped the remaining of her tears away with her wrist. "We will try to adhere to this plan, Alina . . . I will be the first to admit I'm agreeing to it to avoid Kat having to face exile from the court. So I thank you from the bottom of my heart."

"You forget, Lord Ashowan, I have not consented to this," Brendan interjected sharply.

But the princess whirled on him and took him by surprise.

"Oh, yes you do, because if you don't, I'm going to tell my father about the discussion we had outside the east entrance regarding what is a comfortable topic for husbands and wives."

Brendan's eyes grew round. "You . . . You were the one to bring up the topic of bed—"

Alina slapped her hand over his mouth before he could finish his sentence, her expression crazed and desperate.

Her heart thudded in her chest.

She prayed to the Green Man and Goddess that no one had heard.

Begged the kind heart of her mother up in the Forest of the Afterlife that no one would say anything . . .

"What was that about beds?" Lord Harris asked loudly while bouncing up and down on the balls of his feet.

Father always did say Mother had a cruel sense of humor . . . Alina thought to herself grimly while looking nervously over her shoulder, her hand still firmly clasped over the king's mouth. She hadn't noticed that his hand had reflexively risen to stop her from doing it but had managed to stop at the last moment.

Fin gave the duke a small shove while unable to mask his own dubious expression when eyeing the princess and king. "Knock it off, that isn't appropriate for the wome—"

"No, no! I swear I heard him just fine! He mentioned that the princess had brought up something regarding beds! Perhaps there is a *perfectly* good reason why they were having such a discussion!"

"Harris," Fin's voice carried a warning note.

"You can't silence me on this one, Fin, it's too damn interesting! Even the infamous Troivackian king looks like a deer caught in the sights of a hunter."

"I'll tell your wife about your decade-long crush for a certain maid we both know."

The duke's smile froze, his wide eyes suddenly blind to his surroundings as visions of his own gory death filled his mind.

He then gave his head a shake and held out his hand toward the young couple, who were watching the scene unfold, completely paralyzed.

"Nice to meet you, I'm Lord Harris of the Iones dukedom. Former kitchen aide to the house witch, and I have a big mouth that I occasionally remember to shut. Congratulations on your engagement!"

Chapter 23

SHOWERING OF SURPRISES

When Alina woke up the next morning exhausted, her skin dewy and littered with bug bites, she vowed that never again would she allow herself to be convinced by Katarina Ashowan to voluntarily sleep outside.

"Morning!"

The very redhead Alina was debating strangling greeted her brightly. Too brightly for her liking . . .

Kat appeared perfectly happy to sit by the morning fire sipping what smelled like tea.

The princess spied another steel pot that smelled of coffee. She had never been one to enjoy the bitter beverage, yet she was hoping it might occupy her hands and mouth to stop herself saying or doing anything violent.

Wordlessly, she reached beside Katarina's seat, stood up with a grunt, then stalked over to where the pot sat steaming. Filling up a nearby cup with the black liquid, Alina sipped it desperately before turning to face the viscount's daughter, who sat by herself watching her with a gleam of amusement in her eyes.

"Didn't sleep so well?"

The princess didn't bother answering. "Where are the men?"

"Ah, they went to water the horses by the nearby river. We're going to head back as soon as they return. Are you ready to face the courtiers?"

"I'll have a few hours to prepare myself," Alina mused aloud irritably, before taking another sip from her cup.

Kat chuckled. "So . . . I take it camping will require some getting used to for you?"

"I will *not* get used to it, because I will *never* do it again. Understood?" Alina's imperial tone stunned Kat for a brief moment before she roared laughing.

"Gods, you're always so polite and sweet! I never knew you could be such a *princess*, Princess!"

Alina scowled. "Next time I sit through a five-hour council meeting without my back touching the chair even once, I will make you join me to do the same and see how *you* feel."

Annoyingly enough, this only made Katarina laugh harder. "If the Gods were to create my own hell, they should talk to you . . ." she managed between gasps.

The men returned then leading the horses, and all looking worse for wear after the poor sleeping conditions, save for the Troivackian king, who looked like his usual self.

"What is so amusing?" Brendan asked while eyeing Alina's flattened expression warily.

"Your Majesties, we should leave now to ensure the castle doesn't send another messenger," Lord Ashowan interjected while handing off the reins of the second horse he led to Alina, who stared at them unimpressed.

Alina drained her cup of coffee and handed the tin back to Kat, who was already finishing loading up her horse while Lord Harris appeared and tossed dirt and brush onto their campfire.

"Good. The sooner I'm out of these accursed woods, the better." Alina turned with a huff toward her fiancé, who was watching her with a raised eyebrow.

"Just think, at the very least you'll have a greater appreciation for your bed!" Kat called at her friend's back, which had Alina swinging around and flipping her middle finger into the air, making her friend break out in hysterics again while the men all looked mildly taken aback that the normally mild-mannered princess was using such a rude gesture.

"Where did you learn that sign?" Brendan asked slowly, though he was relatively certain he had an idea.

"From the very woman who seems to be enjoying it the most," the princess grumbled while snatching the reins from the king and stepping away so that she might mount her horse.

The Troivackian glared daggers at Kat, until he was interrupted by Finlay Ashowan stepping between them, his own ominous expression dissuading the king from saying anything.

Shaking his head, Brendan turned away and mounted his own horse.

"Let's get moving, I smell rain coming."

"RAIN! OF COURSE!" Alina's furious shout once again stunned everyone except Kat, who was clutching her sides, unable to contain her mirth.

Brendan sighed.

It was looking like it'd be a long ride back to the Daxarian castle.

About two hours into their trek back to the castle, Alina regained some of her composure and calm as she sidled her beast up next to the duke, who was somehow managing to stay quiet that morning.

"I apologize for my outburst this morning, Your Grace."

Lord Harris shot her a bemused smirk. "Not at all, my lady, I'm well aware how irritating the Ashowans are."

Fin cleared his throat loudly behind them and the duke laughed. "Given that we are all here instead of warm under some blankets because of your kin, Viscount, I think you should cut me a bit of slack today, hm?"

There was another grumble from Fin as he rode beside his daughter, who avoided her father's gaze at all costs.

"Out of curiosity . . . did . . . did my brother say if he were coming to my engagement ceremony?" Alina's heart was in her throat as she feigned a casual posture on her steed.

It didn't work how she wanted, however, as the duke stiffened, and all humor faded from his face. With her gut twisting, Alina instantly knew things were far from right with the prince.

"He . . . He didn't say, Princess. My apologies."

No one spoke in the delicate silence that passed, and Alina wondered if she'd be able to successfully stop herself from begging the man for information right then and there.

Her emotions swelled, and she kept her eyes glued ahead of her as she tried to regain control.

"How . . ." she began after a moment, only to find that her voice rasped. She cleared her throat and blinked rapidly. "How is he doing? Is he learning all about the way the courts run in Sorlia? Or is he still training the novice knights?"

She couldn't bring herself to look at the duke, and it was a good thing too, because the pain and remorse that crossed Lord Harris's face would have made Alina more likely to break down her tentative grasp on decorum.

The one who did see the small glimpse of the duke's conflict was Brendan Devark from Lord Harris's left-hand side.

Brendan's brow lowered and his expression hardened, especially when the duke glanced over his shoulder at the viscount, who gave a small, almost imperceptible shake of his head.

Katarina Ashowan failed to notice the exchange as she stared worriedly at her friend's back.

The Troivackian king felt a black rage begin to fill him that he hadn't felt in years as he observed the entire situation and had to fight back from speaking his own thoughts.

"He . . . He is getting to know the citizens of Sorlia, and spending some time in the countryside," Lord Harris finally responded, before clearing his throat.

"Does he receive the letters my father and I send? You give them to him, right?"

The duke was saved having to answer when thunder rumbled above them.

Brendan pulled on the reins of his horse and fell back so that he could round the group's backs and instead come up on Alina's right side.

Without a word, he reached over and hauled her off her steed into his saddle.

She let out a surprised yelp as the duke grasped her horse's reins reflexively to take hold of the beast.

"Your Majesty, you forget yourself. Return the princess to her horse now." Fin's firm voice didn't garner a response from the Troivackian king. Instead, he removed his cloak from his shoulders and wrapped it around Alina as she spluttered in the saddle in front of him.

"Your daughter failed to bring a cloak or proper blanket to keep the princess dry, Viscount. With the current condition of her lungs, a cold could kill her." The acid tone in Brendan's voice made Katarina scowl, and even Lord Harris's eyebrows shot up.

"I-It's really alright, I—" Alina was cut short when the deluge of rain began to pound down from the sky, pattering against the thick foliage of the forest in a lively rush. "You'll be soaked," she observed quietly while staring up at the stoic Troivackian, who didn't bat an eye at the sudden downpour.

"I'm harder to kill," he replied shortly, ending the debate.

They rode in silence for another while until Katarina Ashowan's horse trotted up beside the king's.

It was then Brendan noticed steam rising off the woman, and she somehow appeared mostly dry . . .

"Why can't she ride in her own saddle now that she has your cloak?" the redhead asked pointedly, her golden gaze boring into him.

The Troivackian king turned his stare ahead of himself, already displeased by her presence, even if her ability to stay dry was more than a little interesting.

"She can if she asks, but I believe it is perfectly clear we are riding like this now because we want to."

Alina felt herself blush all the way up to the roots of her hair. "Gods, did you really have to—"

Brendan turned his chin down to her, his eyes softening. "Am I wrong?"

After blinking in surprise over his bluntness, the princess found herself biting her lips to ward off a smile as she struggled to meet his gaze. "N-Not . . . quite . . ."

Even Katarina looked a little befuddled as she allowed her horse to fall back in step with her father's.

"Well, that's a surprise," she muttered under her breath before turning to risk a glimpse of the viscount's profile.

However, Fin's eyes weren't anywhere near the princess and her fiancé; instead, they were lost in thought.

Kat felt her stomach grow knotted. She already knew she was in trouble, but whenever the prince was brought up, her father's mood would always turn horrid. Meaning, her mild punishment might be made significantly worse . . .

Sighing, she caught the eye of Lord Harris, who gave her a mysterious half smile and shrug, though even he still seemed downcast after the princess's questions.

Frowning, Kat wondered just what the annoying future king of Daxaria was really doing? Had he run away? Was he up to his eyeballs in prostitutes? Was he sick? Perhaps he had eloped with someone from the mysterious western kingdom of Lobahl and her father was trying to track him down.

She had constructed many interesting theories and ideas ever since her father had returned from visiting Eric Reyes years ago, yet no one, not even her mother, seemed to know what exactly had happened.

"Are you alright?" Brendan asked softly as the rain continued to swamp their efforts of getting through the forest. No one could hear their words over the downpour, and given how quietly he was speaking, it was clear he didn't want anyone but the woman in his saddle to hear.

Alina had to admit she was incredibly grateful to be beside the hulking Troivackian as she nestled closer to his warmth and remained only slightly damp, while he looked like he had been dunked in a river.

"Fine, thanks to you, though I'm looking forward to a good fire and dry bed once we get back."

"I meant about the duke's replies regarding your brother."

Alina tensed, and as Brendan instinctively hunched his shoulders farther around her, he found himself enjoying how she fit perfectly against his chest.

"He has my father's permission to release as much information as he deems necessary," she answered while feeling her throat restrict again.

"So even your father doesn't wish to know where his own son is?" The disbelief in Brendan's voice made Alina's chest tighten.

"I . . . I don't know. He might have more information than I do, and they all think they're protecting me . . ."

"Well, given how this affects you politically and otherwise, I'd say it isn't protection so much as disrespectful to you." The growl in the king's voice somehow made Alina feel a little better. As though him being angry on her behalf helped lessen the burden.

"I suppose they'll tell me when they think I'm ready."

"What of your brother then? He has a responsibility to his kingdom and family, and you said he hasn't responded to any of your letters."

Alina was grateful for the rain then as she quickly wiped a couple of tears that escaped her eyes.

"I know when my mother died it changed him . . . but I suppose I always thought it was just that he . . . he was doing something important in order to come back to us. Then he would explain everything and we could . . . we could be a family again."

Brendan was silent for a long time after that, and so Alina settled back against him and tried to stop herself from shivering as the temperature dropped around them.

"I will bring your brother back before you leave for Troivack. I promise you, on my pride and honor."

Alina felt her eyes grow round.

A Troivackian vow on their pride was the most serious one they could make. If broken, no matter who or what trivial matter the vow was regarding, they were treated as disappointments and symbols of shame to the Troivackian people.

"Y-You don't need to do that. He could be doing something important and—"

"—Then I'll help him finish up whatever important business he has, because one way or another, even if I have to gag and bind him, he is going to come see you and explain himself."

Despite the casual threat of violence, Alina was moved beyond words, and some corner of her heart couldn't help but feel a little more tender toward the massive, terrifying Troivackian king. Sitting in his saddle, his face set in its usual neutrality, his shoulders and arms protected her from the rain, as he placed his beloved pride at risk to give her the greatest wedding gift anyone could—or be shunned for trying.

Gods, if I'm not careful, I may end up liking this man a little more than I thought was possible . . .

Chapter 24

COURTLY CONFRONTATIONS

The moment their horses broke through the final line of trees, the castle exploded. Servants seemed to trickle out of every entrance, window, or crack as shouts of the princess's return filled the damp air.

Yes, the rain had stopped . . . mere moments before they arrived at the castle, but it didn't seem as though the reprieve would last long, as the skies above rumbled ominously.

"A fitting end to my first and last time sleeping outside," Alina had remarked idly while lowering her hood. Then, casting Brendan an apologetic smile, she shook her head and said, "Gods, make sure you take a hot bath the moment you step foot in the castle."

The man was completely drenched, his eyes with their usual dark unwavering calm fixed ahead at the servants rushing toward them. He was so focused on the hoard drawing nearer, however, he failed to notice Alina reach up and gently wipe away several errant raindrops from his forehead before swiping his soaked hair so that it parted to the side.

He jerked back in alarm as though she had pricked him with a needle.

"S-Sorry, I didn't mean to startle you. You just look a little drowned is all."

Brendan faltered for a moment and cleared his throat. Alina wondered if she saw a faint blush on his face . . .

"To think the man who teased me by almost kissing me would be so prudish . . ."

His face colored deeply, and his gaze dropped to his horse's mane.

The princess couldn't tell if he was angry or trying not to smile, but there wasn't time to find out before the servants had finally reached them.

"Princess! Are you alright?! We had no idea where you were! What happened?!" Ruby, the elderly Head of Housekeeping, demanded as the nobility gradually began to exit the castle—they weren't in as peak condition as the serving staff when it came to running.

Alina straightened in the saddle and began to open her mouth, when the duke of Iones stepped forward.

"The princess had been requested to spend some time with His Majesty, the Troivackian king, in light of their recent discussions," Lord Harris declared, his regal tone shutting down anyone's inclination to question the riding party unprompted.

He then turned and looked to the princess and gave the Troivackian monarch an encouraging nod of his head.

"Did you want to do the announcement now, or after warming up?" Brendan murmured to Alina while sweeping his gaze over the servants and growing number of courtiers before them, making the crowd pause their trajectories toward them.

She sighed and, for the briefest of moments, leaned back into his chest and took as much strength as she could from that touch. What surprised the king in return, however, was that he felt as though she had indeed taken some of his own fortitude, and a strange jolt of disappointment surged in his gut once she pulled back away from him.

"Us riding like this is rather telling, but even so . . . it'd be best to try and follow the court standards as closely as possible. I'll call for a formal hearing in the throne room. My father may be annoyed later that I did it without him, but I'm hoping that Lord Ashowan will be able to—"

"I will speak with your father about the circumstances."

Alina grew wary. "Are you going to have my friend exiled from court after all?" she asked softly, her hazel eyes already filled with quiet hurt.

Brendan felt his chest tighten.

He wanted to report the irritating redhead more than ever—it was clear as day that she needed discipline and to begin learning the more serious consequences to her actions—but . . . truthfully . . . Brendan had started having his own plans for his future wife's best friend.

"No, I won't. I'll think of something, but for now you should address your people." Brendan's attention moved to the sea of faces expectantly awaiting their princess's next words.

When she realized she had completely forgotten about them, Alina turned to face the people, her hands already gripping the reins nervously and sending her shoulders straight back into Brendan's solidness once more.

Yet just like before, feeling his incomparable brawn behind her had the very liberating effect of bestowing upon her an attitude that could only be called gumption.

"I will be more than happy to share what has transpired; however, I will do so after we have all bathed and dressed, and these horses are fed and watered. Before we dine tonight, I will address my father's vassals in the throne room. No one is harmed, but explanations and questions will be addressed in the proper setting."

It was short, awkward, and no one moved despite her words; that is, until Brendan stirred his horse forward and made the people blocking his path shift away and finally break the tenuous silence.

Once they were free of the curious gazes and whispers, the Troivackian drooped his head toward Alina's profile again, his breath tickling her ear. "You did well. A bit of practice and you will command them like the queen you are soon to be."

"I'll need a great deal more practice if I'm to command Troivackians, not just Daxarians."

Brendan chuckled, and because of how close he was to her ear, Alina felt herself shiver.

"Yes, it will take time, but you will bring them to their knees."

A small, pleased smile spread over the princess's face as she unconsciously straightened at his words.

Behind the royals, the viscount's studious gaze regarded the couple, and Katarina watched openly with a puzzled frown. However, Lord Harris seemed to have come to an understanding all on his own, as he set to waggling his eyebrows at Fin and gestured with his head to the couple with a knowing smile.

Alina was where she had dreamed of being the entire bug-ridden night and soggy morning . . .

In a hot bath.

As she eased the blasphemy that was the outdoors from her person, she did her best to ignore the animated whispers between her maids and the agitated remarks from Marianne.

Only, her most senior handmaiden's comments were gaining volume—and vehemence.

"Spending the night in the woods is not what a princess should have to endure," came Marianne's first audible comment.

Alina decided not to respond as the maid poured a goosebump-inducing pitcher of warm water over her hair.

"Then riding in on the Troivackian king's saddle . . . of course we all assume grave injury, but, no, the duke and viscount show their humble beginnings by thinking such behavior is acceptable to nobility."

At this, Alina's eyes opened and her lips pursed.

The handmaiden was treading on very thin ice.

One of the other maids washing Alina's hair tensed at seeing the rare sight of the princess's obvious displeasure.

"Honestly, I knew those Ashowans were troublesome. Not to mention the questionable lineage of Lord Harris . . . My father is still appalled that just because the viscount was a witch he was elevated from peasant to lord. Not to mention a bastard between a peasant and the former Duke Iones taking power . . ." Marianne fumed while shaking her head. She then noticed the maids selecting Alina's dress and was distracted. "No! Not the blue, the white! We need to remind the court that Princess Alina is a pure, simple young maiden who was merely duped by Katarina Ashowan to—"

"You are formally dismissed, Lady Marianne Dobbs."

The room stilled.

The marquis's daughter turned, a quirk of humor on her lips but calm understanding in her eyes.

"Very well, I shall retire for the evening and return for your schedule reading tomorrow morn—"

"No, you are fired." Alina stared at the woman and was grateful her hands rested on the edges of the tub, as she felt herself tremble. She had never once in her life stood up for anyone or anything in such a way—the political ramifications were always on her mind—but . . .

The response earlier that day when she'd tried to command people was itching her confidence fiercely. No one respected her enough to take her seriously, and she was damn well sick of it.

Marianne let out a long breath and smiled wearily down at Alina as though she were a child throwing a tantrum.

"Princess, I understand I may have been speaking a little freely, but you must admit the Ashowan and Iones families are not—"

"I did not ask for a defense. I said you're dismissed, now leave!"

There was a brief vacant expression on the woman's face before she curtsied and walked toward the door, her eyes rolling to the ceiling as she went.

"See you in the morning, Your Highness."

"Marianne," Alina called, her anger steadily rising.

Marianne did not turn around, pushing the princess's emotions even higher.

When the handmaiden left the room with a swish of silk skirts, her noble superiority wielded in front of her nose, Alina's inner politician drowned.

She stood up from the tub, stepped over its ledge, and moved swiftly to the door despite the gasping maids lunging for towels.

She held a hand stopping them in their place as she strode forward, naked.

For some reason, she'd never felt self-conscious of her figure, and in that moment, she used it to her advantage.

Stepping into the corridor, her guards spluttered, then turned wordlessly from her body.

"Marianne," Alina called again to the noblewoman, who was several feet ahead.

The woman's back stiffened before she turned slowly and gazed in open horror at the princess's shameless display of wet nudity.

"Good, I have your attention." Alina ignored the chill rushing over her damp skin as she strode toward the maid, her hazel eyes glinting as the suds in her hair rustled down her locks.

"Lady Marianne Dobbs, you are dismissed. Not with a kind recommendation, but because you have been openly disobedient and disrespectful. There are countless staff members who will corroborate this. If you should try to return tomorrow morning, I will have you thrown into a cell and prolong your release as long as possible so that the news of your insolent behavior reaches far and wide."

Marianne grew pale, but her jaw set as though about to threaten the princess with political consequences.

She never got to voice those threats, however.

"You disparaged Duke Iones and Viscount Ashowan, when they have saved our kingdom from utter ruin. You have undermined my judgment countless times and ignored my orders. Were I a vindictive being, I'd have you charged."

Marianne faltered back from the princess.

Despite her confident words, Alina was still trembling . . . and beginning to grow a mite cold.

Yet why in the world she felt stronger in that moment than she ever had in her life, she had no idea.

"Now, pack your trunks, Marianne, and hope your betrothed doesn't hear of this before you are to marry."

Marianne greened.

Alina held her gaze, the puddle at her feet widening with every moment.

If I'm to be a queen of Troivackians . . . I need to be stronger . . .

"Guards, please see that Lady Marianne Dobbs is removed from the castle premises before the dining hour."

For a moment Marianne opened and closed her mouth as though torn between wanting to argue, and being sick, but Alina didn't bother spending any more time waiting to find out. She only hoped no one could guess that her slight shivering was from fear, not the chilly evening air.

Turning her back on the woman who had passively bullied her for months, Alina retreated to her chamber, hoping that the tub remained as hot and comforting as it had been moments before. A strange peace and steadiness was building in her belly as she withdrew from the scene, which made her feel a little bit better despite the confrontation. She only hoped that given time to think about the impulse, she wouldn't come to regret it.

Brendan stood passively on the edge of the dais of the throne room. His hands clasped behind his back as whispers rushed by him.

He had never noticed Henry's absence so keenly as gazes he couldn't quite decipher probed his being.

The feeling of being the subject of the harshest of judgments seeped into his skin. Despite his calm expression, the king had to admonish to himself that it had been many years since he had been before such a hostile crowd that didn't openly fear him. Still, regardless of how it made his hand itch for his sword, he stood waiting for the doors to open.

The princess would come.

They were going to announce the betrothal in front of everyone, and even though there'd be hell to pay when King Norman returned, Brendan knew he'd think of some way to lessen the blow. In fact, he already had one or two ideas that could make the Daxarian ruler all too happy to overlook any recent follies.

That is . . . *if* the princess came.

Worry began to tighten Brendan's chest as he faced the room full of judgmental nobles and wondered if Alina had had another breathing episode, or if perhaps worst of all . . . she grew too afraid to speak up and follow through with the plan.

If she chooses to wait until the king arrives, I will understand, Brendan tried to convince himself while the ladies of the court began whispering amongst themselves and eyeing him in a different manner than he liked.

Still, he stood like a statue.

Until, at long last, the doors opened, and there was the princess.

Only, she looked . . . different.

Alina had donned a black dress with a long white vest with gold edging, and she strolled in smoothly, without a hint of hesitancy. Her hair was partially swept back in a style that made her appear older, and she wore her crown upon her head, a delicate piece made of gold with emeralds and diamonds fashioned into its points.

The crowd shifted as Alina proceeded into the room. Her breaths were beginning to grow rapid, and the Troivackian king noticed the quivering in her hands at her side.

Before he knew what he was doing he had moved forward a step, his eyes burning as they called her attention to him.

As soon as they locked gazes, relief filled Brendan's chest and he watched her breath come out a little slower. The hint of a smile warmed her face.

The Troivackian king's eyes softened as he nodded at her reassuringly as though they had just shared words of encouragement with each other.

Once she reached the dais, he bowed to her, offering his hand, which she accepted as she turned to face the room.

At seeing the large crowd, Alina tensed yet again, but Brendan's grip turned a little firmer around her hand, and suddenly she felt like the strongest person in the world.

"Lords and ladies, I thank you for coming on such short, informal notice. I want to apologize for worrying you all as there was a miscommunication regarding my schedule the past few days," Alina began with only a slight hitch in her voice.

"We had wanted to wait until my father had returned from the hunt to make the announcement; however, given the trouble caused, it is unavoidable."

Glancing briefly at Brendan the princess felt more than a little anxious when she noticed his gaze was remaining fixed on the nobility before them.

To everyone in the crowd, the king looked impenetrable, but to Alina . . . she could see the flicker of emotion on his face when he said the words, "I have requested marriage from Princess Alina Reyes, and she has accepted. We are betrothed to be wed."

Brendan's voice carried effortlessly as he imperially surveyed the room, daring anyone to object.

There were several gasps, and the whispering grew worse, but before Alina could try and placate the nobility's surprise, the Troivackian king had once more taken her hand, and her arm, in fact, and was guiding her back to the doors.

Smiling, Alina managed to murmur through her teeth to the man, who was walking briskly from the room.

"Shouldn't we try to answer any questions or concerns they have?"

"It isn't up for discussion with them, is it?" Brendan asked as they cleared the throne room doors, yet he didn't release her arm or slow his pace as he put even more distance between the room full of nobles and themselves.

"N-No, but I did say they could as—"

"The fewer answers they have, the more they will grow obsessed with the news and forget your absence yesterday."

"That does make sense," Alina acknowledged after a brief moment to catch her breath. Then she added, "Please stop or slow down, otherwise you'll be dragging me down the hallway."

Brendan halted immediately, his eyes still focused on the corridor ahead of them as he took a near imperceptible breath in, his heart pounding in his chest as he turned to face Alina.

"You were scared, too?" she asked quietly, her hand pressing his gently.

Brendan's jaw flexed but he said nothing. He couldn't tell her about the times he had faced crowds of people screaming at him, the times they threw things . . . the assassins he'd met after gatherings like the ones they'd just faced . . . though for a moment, he wanted to.

Then her soft voice coaxed him from his memories, his focus homing in on her at once.

"I feel better knowing that even you were a bit nervous about that meeting . . . should we go get some food that wasn't made over a campfire?"

The Troivackian king's features relaxed as he allowed himself to be comforted by the princess's nearness and soothing voice . . . though he couldn't deny his heart was still racing to a near ache in his chest.

"Very well. Your viscount did promise me the best meal of my life."

Alina's smile brightened at his reply until it blazed brilliantly, and despite the rain and mist outside, Brendan was relatively certain that in the years to come, he would remember it as a sunny, beautiful day for some strange reason . . .

Chapter 25

A CHAOTIC COLLABORATION

Alina had never eaten a meal so delicious.

A pork roast accompanied with apples, carrots, and onions all simmered together in the meat's juices.

The potatoes . . . creamy and golden . . .

She worried she would begin drooling at first, but there was one saving grace.

And that was that the most delectable meal was being paired with one of the most awkward situations of her life.

She had opted to have the viscount's meal be a more private affair, and so she found herself dining in her father's council room.

On her left sat Brendan, stoically eating without bothering to glance around himself.

On her right sat Katarina Ashowan; across from her sat her brother, Tam, who was staring at the people around the table in open bewilderment. Beside him sat Lord Harris, followed by the viscountess, Lady Ashowan, and at the head of the table, the infamous house witch himself, Finlay Ashowan.

Lady Ashowan was staring at her daughter without blinking for an unnatural amount of time.

Meanwhile, the viscount was shooting warning glances at Lord Harris, who looked as though he wanted to say something troublesome, and Katarina was . . . well . . . actively pretending not to notice the murderous aura emitting from her mother as she focused on eating the impressive heap on her plate.

Alina did her best to pull herself away from the food and attempt to ease the uncomfortable atmosphere.

"So . . . Duke Iones, do you find yourself in Austice often?" she asked, her voice pitched higher than usual.

The lord looked at her with an amused grin that for some reason made her feel shy.

"Every now and then I like to come for a few weeks and heckle the Ashowans, yes."

Alina nodded and gave a strained smile.

As the sound of nothing but cutlery on plates could be heard in the room, it prompted her to try again.

"Do your wife and children join you normally?"

The duke made a show of picking up his napkin, wiping his mouth, and leaning his forearms against the table as his eyes sparkled with mischief.

"No one wants that chaotic brood joining me unless it's unavoidable. Now, are we all going to address what exactly we're going to say to our beloved king when he returns? Your Majesty, you disappeared in the middle of the night, and suddenly are back here, with his daughter, announcing your engagement. If I know anything about our king and his protective nature toward his children, I'd say he might jump to some . . . colorful conclusions."

Alina frowned in confusion, while Brendan's fork dropped and he leaned back in his chair, glowering menacingly at the duke.

"I'm not sure I understand . . ." Alina looked at Tam to see if he understood, but he seemed to be focusing intently on shoving a rather large piece of roast in his mouth.

"Alina, dear . . ." Annika cleared her throat uncomfortably while fixing the young woman with a pained stare. "Your father might wonder . . . if you've been compromised."

The princess's face burned. "Gods, he wouldn't! He knows I would never—"

The viscountess's tone grew apologetic. "He knows you might not *intend* to, but—"

"Any further insult to my honor will be duly noted, Lady Ashowan," Brendan growled, his black stare boring into the woman.

Annika's gaze grew sharp, but her face remained calm. She was definitely a strong Troivackian woman at heart.

"This has nothing to do with honor, or what either of you have or have not actually done. It is what the king might assume when he realizes how strange it is."

"Why can't we just tell him the truth again? That Alina and I decided to go camping? I feel like the truth is significantly less troublesome than all this," Katarina remarked glibly while reaching for her goblet and taking a drink. "We could also just say we got lost and they all came to find us."

"Well, there is the matter of you whisking her off without guards, into the woods, with her breathing condition, which consequently will most likely have you exiled from court. And no one will believe that *you* got lost in the king's woods. Everyone knows you know Austice and these grounds just as well if not better than most servants," Annika reminded her daughter coolly.

"What makes it especially difficult is that His Majesty Brendan Devark disappeared in the night, for hours into the forest. A lot could be questioned by the nobles," Lord Harris said, for once looking slightly more serious. "Which brings us back, Princess, to what you are going to tell your father when he finds out that you and your betrothed announced your engagement. We sent a messenger to inform the camp of the Troivackian king's whereabouts. However, once our ruler returns there will be a great deal of questions. So . . . perhaps we organize our stories, hm?"

"Gods, Harris, sometimes I forget that you're all grown up and a duke now," Fin complimented with a wry smile directed at his friend.

Lord Harris raised his goblet to the redhead and took a drink with a cheeky grin.

"Well . . . I need a reason for my disappearance, and what we can say is that I was with Kat at your estate," Alina began slowly.

Fin nodded seriously. "That would make sense, and it is guarded. We just need a reason for you to have disappeared there."

"It should be something not too serious, but definitely something that would make sense if you asked the viscount and me to summon Brendan," the duke continued slowly.

"It needs to be something only he could help her with, and not an emergency . . . it'd be better if it was something she would feel too awkward to ask her father," Annika added while withdrawing her flask from her skirts and topping up her goblet.

She wordlessly offered some to the Troivackian king, but the man simply stared icily at her in response.

Alina worried her lower lip as she thought about what potential excuse could be so believable . . .

"What if you just said you were second-guessing the engagement?" Kat suggested while resuming her work on her dinner.

"Not a bad idea, but it could make the king grow suspicious of whether or not Alina truly wants the marriage or not," Fin noted thoughtfully.

"What about if I pretended to be worried my new fiancé would be attacked by the other men on the hunt, who may want to eliminate him as a contender for my hand?" Alina turned to Brendan but found that his eyes were still fixed on the viscountess.

She knew that the woman was still remarkably beautiful, but it was a little hurtful that he was staring so openly at her; then again he didn't appear to be looking at her in any kind of friendly way . . .

"Princess, I mean this as respectfully as possible to the both of you," Lord Harris began, pressing his hands together. "No one, not even Lord Laurent, would be dumb enough to try to attack the Troivackian king. Pardon my saying so, Your Majesty, but you look like you would get a kick out of breaking people's limbs."

Brendan nodded sternly at the duke. "Thank you."

"That was not a compliment, you giant dum—" Katarina began to mutter, before her mother and father stared at her with such fury that she resumed filling her mouth with potatoes.

The Troivackian king shot Kat a flat look of disapproval, and Alina was heartened to see that he no longer looked at her friend with obvious animosity.

Glancing across the table at Tam, the princess found herself wishing that all the Ashowans could endear themselves to Brendan. While she had only just met them, they made her feel . . . happy. She felt safe in their midst as though she had an extended family that adored her . . .

Alina froze.

"I know exactly what I can say." Her eyes grew bright as she smiled excitedly. "However, if it's going to work, we're going to need Tam's help."

The future viscount finally raised his face from his food and gave her a look of mortal dread while everyone around them shared looks of uncertainty.

Alina waited for her father nervously in their library, Lady Ashowan keeping her company at her side, quietly reading as the day passed. Katarina was sadly grounded until further notice, and since Alina had fired her highest-ranking handmaiden, she needed a chaperone around the castle.

Annika had been all too happy to help, and as the sun drifted across the sky and the princess's nerves grew more and more raw, Alina found herself growing increasingly grateful for the woman's calm, steady nature.

Then, at long last, the door burst open, and in strode Norman. Covered in mud, his face a mask of tension, his eyes flew to his daughter. Mr.

Howard was behind him, and behind the assistant was the viscount and Duke Iones.

"Alina, I have just received news that you and King Brendan Devark announced your engagement."

Alina stood and nervously clasped her hands in front of her skirt. "Y-Yes, we did, Father."

"How is it . . . that this happened when a day and a half ago, that man was in my hunting party, and not mentioning a *word* of this to me?"

Alina felt herself growing pale.

Gods, can I really do this? Lie to my father to save Katarina? Perhaps he wouldn't be as angry . . . but then again I've already come this far.

"Y-You see, Father, while you were away, something happened."

It was at that moment that Brendan Devark and his own assistant entered the library; they had both clearly hurried there after hearing that the king had wasted no time in seeking out his daughter.

"What happened? Did he do something? I thought it was strange he disappeared in the middle of the night! Also, why are people saying you were scheduled to have a meeting with him? I never condoned such a thing!" Norman stepped closer to Alina, who unconsciously flinched.

"Well, Father, I-I had to say that because I was actually at the Ashowans' estate in Austice, when I discovered from Katarina something rather important."

Norman folded his arms impatiently, his gaze furious.

"So, it was there that I . . . I discovered that Tam Ashowan was intending to propose to me in a highly public fashion while everyone was away."

The Daxarian king blinked in astonishment.

It was at that moment that the very man his daughter was talking about appeared from the shadows of the library. No one had even noticed Tam was there, save for his mother and the princess, who had already been aware of his presence.

"It-It's true, Your Majesty. I was unaware that the princess was already engaged to the Troivackian king."

Norman turned on Tam, who had his eyes fixed on the ground and his hair hanging around his face, hiding the embarrassed flush in his cheeks.

"Lord Tam . . . I thought you had made it perfectly clear that you had no intention to marry my daughter." Norman barely managed to lower his voice.

"Ah, well, that was because I . . . well . . ." The young man was rigid, and for a moment, everyone's breath was held as they wondered if he was going to crumble under the pressure.

"It's because I'm strange."

There were several beats of deadened silence.

"I'm not sure I understand what you are getting at, Lord Tam," Norman began slowly.

"I . . . said I wasn't interested because I'm strange, and I didn't think I was good enough for the princess. I thought I would bring her nothing but misery." Tam succeeded in getting the words out, though it sounded as though he were being strangled.

"So when did you change your mind?" Mr. Howard was the one to interrupt as he stared around the room at everyone's stricken expressions.

"My mother . . . told me that my da had the same fears before they got married. So I figured I would ask the princess, and see how she felt."

"What was this . . . lavish proposal going to be?" Norman asked, looking highly skeptical.

Everyone could see Tam's fists balled up in the pockets of his trousers.

"I . . . was . . . going to have her new vocal teacher sing in the center of the rose maze, where I would have placed a special custom-made lute that I'd ordered for her. I'd be nearby, and . . . would . . . propose."

Alina had to admit, the part about the handcrafted lute was a nice touch. Though what was that he had mentioned about a new vocal teacher?

Norman eyed the young man in the quiet for several long moments before turning to stare at the anxious faces around him.

Finally, his gaze moved to his daughter. "So you learned of this plan, and immediately summoned the Troivackian king? How? There wasn't any messenger."

At this, Brendan cleared his throat. "What you had said by the campfire that night bothered me. You had mentioned your gut instinct, and so I rode an hour from the camp toward the castle, when I came upon the duke and Viscount Ashowan. They said that the princess was stressed. So I decided to return, and they chose to go with me seeing as it concerned the viscount's son, and Lord Harris didn't feel safe riding alone to the camp."

Norman's eyes narrowed when he glanced at Finlay, whose expression was completely blank.

"So why were the viscount, Alina, the duke, Lady Katarina, and the Troivackian king coming out of my forest instead of from Austice if they were returning from the estate?"

"We . . . we didn't want people to know Alina had stayed the night at my estate with Tam, so we made it appear as though she had been ordered to spend supervised time with her betrothed. Katarina came to help the princess feel more comfortable," Finlay recited a little too hastily.

The Daxarian king's expression was wry as he looked around at everyone. For many moments he said nothing, until he glanced at his daughter's wide, fearful eyes.

"I don't buy that nonsense for a ruddy moment. Now, what in the world is going on, and so help me if any of you attempt to lie again!"

Chapter 26

FACING THE FACTS

For a brief moment, no one moved.

Norman waited while everyone around him sported their impressive tableau.

At long last, his assistant spoke for him.

"For the love of the king's beard! Just tell him! It's obvious you all are in cahoots to cover something up . . . wait." The man rounded on Fin, who unconsciously drew himself up to his full height, before forcing his shoulders into a more relaxed position.

"Sire, I believe I can hazard a guess about what could have possibly united all these people into attempting to deceive you . . ."

Norman turned and raised a sardonic eyebrow at Mr. Howard, who was in the process of studying each of the Ashowans present.

"I have kept tabs on you lot through the years. Even while in Rollom, I made sure to receive regular reports from anyone and everyone I could from here in Austice, Viscount. Your propensity for trouble, and driving me to the cups, is so well known that bards have compiled a lifetime of tales about you all."

Fin rolled his eyes to the ceiling before sharing a knowing look with the king. The monarch momentarily forgot that he was annoyed with the redhead.

Mr. Howard had become more theatrical in his advanced age.

"Now, isn't it strange that we have three out of the four Ashowans here?" The assistant paused for dramatic effect. "My guess . . . is that Lady Katarina did something that everyone in this room is covering for. Because the Ashowans reduce even the most disciplined of people to actions just as chaotic as their own." The assistant shot a brief glance at the princess, then the

Troivackian king, who was about to take moderate offense to the inference, but he had to acknowledge to himself there was some level of truth to the sentiment.

"So what did Lady Katarina Ashowan do, hm? What is it you all are trying to protect her from?" Mr. Howard finished folding his arms across his chest and seeking out each member of the viscount's family to gauge their reactions.

Norman's skeptical expression mellowed when no one spoke.

"Father"—Alina's quiet voice broke the silence—"I . . . I would like to speak with you privately, please."

"Princess, would you mind if I joined your meeting?" Annika Ashowan interjected while suddenly stepping forward, her face as serene as ever.

Brendan Devark glared at the woman. He didn't like being shut out of a meeting with the spy . . .

Glancing between Annika and his daughter, Norman pondered the request for a moment, then gave a slow nod.

"Everyone, please, leave us."

One by one, the remaining audience filed out without a word of complaint.

Brendan was the last to leave, but before he followed his assistant, he and Alina shared a silent moment of eye contact where he tilted his head in a silent question.

She gave a nervous half smile followed by a slower nod.

Satisfied, Brendan turned and left.

Annika watched the exchange pensively, but when the door finally latched shut, she turned her full attention to the king.

Norman, however, was already fixing his daughter with his displeased attention, completely ignoring Annika. Less out of disrespect and more out of habit, he was used to pretending the viscountess wasn't there.

"Is Mr. Howard's theory at all correct?"

Alina let out a small tentative breath. "Yes. Though Kat didn't mean any harm! All that happened was she saw that I was upset after our talk the other day, and we ended up going camping."

Norman's jaw clenched briefly and his eyes flashed. "She took you camping, without any guards or a physician?"

"Yes, but we were an hour from your camp, and nothing happened. Then the Troivackian king came and said he was going to take us to you, but I insisted we stay where we were as it was the middle of the night. Then—"

Norman had dropped his face to his hand and was pinching the bridge of his nose. "Let me guess. Lord Ashowan and Lord Harris found the three of you on their way to notify me that you were missing?"

"T-That would be correct."

Norman raised his gaze to Alina, his disappointment written over every line of his face before he turned to Annika.

"Viscountess, I think we need to have a chat with your husband present regarding your daughter."

"No, Father!" Alina burst out vehemently. "If you agree to our story, then no one has to know! Please don't send Kat away! I wanted to get away from the castle, and you need to let me make some decisions that—"

"Trust you to make decisions?! Alina, you just coerced some of the most powerful people in *two* kingdoms to go along with your lie to me!"

"Because they all knew you wouldn't be reasonable!"

Norman's anger grew more severe. "You think it unreasonable?! How easy would it have been for the king of Troivack to take advantage of you when he found you two!"

"Given that Kat almost shot him, not all that easy," Annika interrupted casually.

Norman rounded on the woman, his ire over her interruption clear.

"Your Majesty, before this discussion goes further, I need to remind you of a very specific promise your wife, Her Majesty the queen, made you swear with me on her deathbed."

The king's face paled, before he managed to find his words. "*You* dare *to call upon that promise when you have been completely absent from my daughter's life since that day until now?! No, what motherly advice could you possibly offer?!*" His voice was too hoarse to shout, but his fury was enough to make his daughter's tears fall; she was so shocked at his reaction.

Alina had no idea what promise the viscountess was even talking about.

"Your Majesty, you promised her. You will hear my input on Ainsley's behalf whether you like it or not."

"Not when the matter pertains to your own daughter, Viscountess. You are using that promise to save your own child, this has nothing to do—" Norman snapped before being promptly cut off.

"Exile Kat if that's what you feel is the fairest decision. I won't fight you on that punishment. She does need to learn consequences. As much as I love her, my daughter is growing too bold. No, what I have to say is something that has needed to be said for a long time, but without Ainsley, no one can breathe a word of it to you."

Alina was trembling over her father's ire. She had no idea how the viscountess was staying level-headed! How was she so . . . strong?

"Well, then? What?" Norman demanded, his eyes glinting dangerously.

"You need to let your daughter make her own decisions. You don't have any faith in her. Even before today . . . which is why she hides things from you. You don't trust her to know what she wants, or needs, and you continuously rob her independence because you are terrified of losing her."

Norman scoffed, but still Lady Ashowan steadily continued.

"She's getting married, Norman. Bad things might happen. There is nothing you can do to change that, and you shouldn't torture her, or yourself, because you fear it."

Norman stumbled back a step.

"Do you think Alina is a good person?" Annika asked, moving forward to remain close, her dark eyes never leaving the king's, as though hypnotizing him.

"Of course I do! She just—" Norman took another step back.

"Would she ever try to hurt someone?" Annika continued stepping after him.

"No! You aren't seeing what—"

"Is she smart?"

The king finally stopped his backward retreat from the viscountess. "Of course she is. She's Ainsley's girl."

Alina felt her tears begin to flow like rivers down her cheeks as her mother's kind smiling face and her mischievous eyes looking at her father flashed into her memory.

"Then you need to give her more say and freedom. There is a reason she hides things from you and is making these reckless decisions. It's because you lose your mind whenever she does things outside of your control."

Norman steadied slightly under that accusation. "You're telling me going camping with just your daughter, without anyone's knowledge, was a great idea?"

"Not at all. I'm furious with my own daughter for that. However, the princess made that decision after feeling stifled and as though she couldn't get a moment to herself. Also . . . Norman . . . let's be honest. Of the absurd acts of rebellion our girls could make, is camping really what we need to respond so drastically to? Camping?"

Norman's shoulders sagged forward at Annika's call to common sense. "With her breathing issues it could have been serious!"

"If Alina felt endangered she would have said something," Annika reminded. "Furthermore . . . I'd like to give credit to the Troivackian king.

Despite his traditional upbringing, he has been giving your daughter a world of leniency and respect."

For several moments, the viscountess and king stared at each other. Eventually, Norman's breath returned to its normal rhythm, and his frown disappeared.

"I need some time to think. Alina, Lady Ashowan, you are excused." Norman waved his hand as he slowly turned from the women and, already lost in thought, stared at a particular bookcase.

The women left silently, with Annika offering a supportive hand to Alina, whose one arm was wrapped protectively around her middle and the other silencing the small gasps that came with her cries.

Norman needed to be alone without his daughter's pain present . . . He couldn't think straight otherwise.

However, the day was not yet through with the Daxarian king. Not an hour had passed before there was yet another knock on the library door.

"Alina, I'm not ready to see you," Norman called out, his head still lost to the memory of the first night he'd even met Ainsley in the library stealing books . . . because her father wouldn't allow her to read.

"Your Majesty, it is the king of Troivack."

It was unmistakably Brendan Devark's voice, and Norman found himself already dreading whatever stress the foreign king was about to pile on him.

"Enter."

The younger man stepped into the room, looked around cautiously as though to make sure no one was hiding in wait to attack, then closed the door behind himself.

"I understand intruding on your time is not ideal. However, I wanted to speak with you before you settled on a punishment for Lady Katarina."

Norman faced the foreign ruler listlessly. He didn't even bother asking the man to speak, knowing that everyone seemed rather happy to say their piece regardless of his own thoughts on recent events.

"Your Majesty, were you aware that Katarina Ashowan can see in the dark?"

Whatever Norman had been expecting, it wasn't that.

"I beg your pardon?"

"I'm given to understand she doesn't get cold, or sleep much. Rain doesn't even bother her—it steams off her." Brendan prattled on, his face earnest. "She can eat more than three men combined and not bat an eye."

"I did not know this, but what is it you are getting at?" Norman clasped his hands behind his back as he regarded the Troivackian with caution.

"She has incredible potential, if trained properly. She could be a useful scout or even a knight with her abilities. She would be an asset to your military, only—"

"She is a lady with parents who do not wish her to be involved in dangerous activities," the Daxarian king said, his regal tone growing sharp.

Brendan paused, weighing his next words carefully. "I was going to say, only she needs *discipline*. I think she should come with the princess to Troivack after we marry for a year . . . maybe more . . . as her handmaiden. We could train her. If it's to be with your daughter, the Ashowans would agree in a heartbeat."

A chill entered Norman's eyes. "You want me to lie to the Ashowans in order for you to train her."

"Weren't they lying to you not even an hour ago?"

"More for my own daughter's sake than their own."

Brendan frowned. He didn't understand . . . Hadn't the entire façade been for the princess's best friend?

After another moment of silent thought, the Daxarian king drew himself up to his full height. "Here is my counterproposal, Your Majesty; I am happy to sign off on that punishment for Lady Katarina, but only if she and her parents agree. The Gods know I would prefer to have some kind of power behind Alina when she leaves. However, you will not lie to the Ashowans when you make this suggestion to them."

"Pardon me . . . did you just say that *I'd* be making the suggestion?" The Troivackian's eyes widened fractionally.

"Well, why not? You are going to be in charge of watching out for their daughter with this idea. Not to mention you are making the decision with your future *wife* in mind, right?" Norman's eyebrow raised imperially.

Brendan felt his gut harden. "I cannot command your citizens."

"No, but you can ask Alina if this is an idea she is comfortable with. She would have the authority to ask."

"You mean . . ." The Troivackian king felt the situation sliding further and further outside of his control.

"Yes. I mean you will have to tell Alina exactly what you told me, and then she will have to speak with the Ashowans. A good test as a couple, wouldn't you agree? Unless of course you would like me to decide for myself what should happen to the viscount's daughter."

Brendan felt his black brows furrow. "What punishment would you decide?"

"Exile from the court for three to five years. Or perhaps she will be sent to the Isle of Wittica to study and work for the kingdom for that time. A more dignified absence without a doubt . . . perhaps there she could learn the 'discipline' you say she is so desperately in need of."

Brendan growled. "It is a gamble with the princess's mental well-being you take when banishing her friend. Removing one of the few people she seems to be close to seems to be more of a punishment for your daughter."

"*My* daughter understands there are consequences to decisions. Are you saying you are the expert regarding the princess due to your engagement?" Norman asked, his voice rising.

"I am saying that you are taking a great risk when you have already lost a son."

Norman felt all color drain from his face, then he opened his mouth and . . . he wasn't exactly certain what came out, or what happened after, because his mind went rather black in that moment after being pushed too far for one day. All he knew was that his anger, grief, and pain brewed itself into a formless force that sought destruction, and the Gods themselves, should they appear, wouldn't be entirely safe from it.

Chapter 27

FINDING THEIR FEET

For some reason, the castle residents all seemed to be in a flurry of activity, but whenever Alina would get closer to question what was happening, they'd scurry off.

Even her guards seemed . . . reticent. They kept avoiding her gaze, and their replies weren't entirely forthcoming.

After Alina's confrontation with her father, she had retired to her chamber to think about what she could do to lessen his anger and convince him not to send Katarina away, but when she had come out for the dining hour . . . there had been a strange stillness, as though something had happened that she knew nothing about.

Upon entering the banquet hall, the murmurs filling the room fell silent.

A sea of eyes looked at their princess with expressions mixed with pity, disappointment . . . some even fascination, making Alina grow incredibly worried.

Then when both her father and Brendan failed to arrive and the servants began carrying in the meal, she panicked.

Peering around the room, Alina sought out Mr. Howard, only he wasn't looking at her, and his expression was grim.

Captain Taylor was the only one who risked giving her a nod of respect, though he appeared uncomfortable as he did so.

Checking the room once more, she found then that the Ashowans and Prince Henry were also missing!

The uneasiness in her gut churned twofold, and as her desperation settled in, she decided to do the only thing possible in that moment . . .

Pretend nothing was amiss until she could ask her father's assistant just what in the world had happened.

* * *

Mr. Howard tried to avoid Alina by darting out of the banquet room, but little did he know, her nerves were frayed, and so she did not hesitate or think of the embarrassment of shouting over the heads of nobles.

"Mr. Howard, a word if you please."

The courtiers hurried their pace flowing past the assistant, who was stuck to the stones beneath his feet, his back still turned to the young monarch.

Once the doors of the banquet room had closed, Alina leaned back in her chair and crossed her legs as she waited for Mr. Kevin Howard to turn around and approach her.

After several breaths, he finally did so. His face was pale as he took painstakingly slow steps toward the young woman, whose patience was dwindling rapidly.

"For the love of the Gods, what is going on?" Alina demanded, not liking how shrill her voice sounded.

Mr. Howard flinched as he folded his hands at his front.

"You see, Princess . . . there was . . . an altercation between the . . . the two kings earlier today."

Alina felt the blood drain from her face.

"What . . . what do you mean?"

"The details are a little tough to follow, but I believe your betrothed was trying to convince the Daxarian king to not exile Lady Katarina, and then from there he somehow mentioned your brother. Your father, His Majesty . . . said some things . . . threw some things . . . The Troivackian king had to get stitches when a candlestick hit him. Then there were threats. Your father is trying to end the engagement, but the Troivackian king refuses . . . and now Lord Ashowan is trying to appease your father, and Prince Henry is doing the same for the Troivackian king."

Mr. Howard cleared his throat awkwardly as the princess's eyes bulged and her mouth hung open.

"My father . . . the king . . . *attacked* His Majesty Brendan Devark verbally and physically?"

"Yes, Your Highness."

"Did His Majesty Brendan Devark physically harm my father?" In Alina's mind she could just see the bear of a man breaking her father's skull and every tooth he had from one punch.

"No, no. He merely deflected and eventually detained the king, your father . . ."

Closing her eyes for a moment, Alina took a deep, soothing breath.

It was happening again.

Her father was known as a wise, fair, and kind ruler. He had led the land tremendously for decades, only, after losing Ainsley and her brother disappearing . . .

Norman Reyes had begun to unravel more and more, and if someone pulled at one of those threads . . . ?

It was one of her deepest fears that her father would become completely unhinged and allow his grief to consume his former self.

It's why she wrote to her brother every month, begging him to come back to them.

Their father needed Eric, as the weight of the crown was beginning to be too heavy for him to bear without his queen.

Alina was on her feet in an instant. "I take it my father doesn't want to see me."

Mr. Howard shook his head.

"I can't go to the Troivackian king as that would cause rumors to circulate, but please let me know what the Royal Physician has to say about his injuries. As soon as Lord Ashowan has finished with my father, I would like to speak with the viscount."

The assistant eyed the princess warily, and she could almost hear his thoughts as he did so.

I'm not sure how involved in this you should be. This might best be left to the adults.

Gritting her teeth, Alina locked eyes with him and stared pointedly until he finally bowed and turned to leave her.

Now's not the time for this. Come hell or high water, I will get to the bottom of this. It's time we all stopped pussyfooting around this family drama.

Sitting in the council room in her father's chair, Alina looked at Lord Ashowan grimly, which was difficult because of his caring expression.

Mr. Howard sat on her left and appeared incredibly interested in his wine's exact shade of burgundy.

Alina desperately wanted to fidget, to hide and be comforted, but with her father being as he was, no one was there for such a trifling matter as comforting her.

"Lord Ashowan, where is my brother?"

Finlay leaned back in his seat, clearly taken aback by the direct question, and when an answer didn't immediately leave his lips, the princess knew she had to push even more.

"My father is losing himself little by little every year, as though the hope of my brother's return is fading away. It's as if my father is grieving him when I've been assured time and time again the prince still lives. How much longer can my father rule like this, Viscount? He attacked a foreign king today. Personal relationship aside, politically he made a grave error."

Fin didn't say anything as he regarded the young monarch with an interested tilt of his head.

"Princess, what are your feelings on your camping adventure with my daughter?"

Alina's cheeks turned bright red. "Are you being insolent, Viscount?"

Smiling apologetically, Fin held up his hands. "I'm just trying to glean your character . . . it helps me understand your motivations."

"My character is not what needs examining, Lord Ashowan. You and Lord Harris insist that my brother is in Sorlia. Is this true?"

The viscount continued to stare at her nonplussed, as though he were trying to figure something out, and Alina didn't like it one bit.

"I dislike camping and the outdoors. It agitates my breathing, and I dislike bears and bugs. What I enjoyed was the freedom of not standing on ceremony with someone I consider a friend. Now, I've answered your question, you answer mine. My brother needs to come back and help my father. Why hasn't he done this? He should be preparing to take over the throne and be ready to do so at any moment."

The viscount folded his arms over his chest. "The prince is not able to take on his responsibilities at this time."

With her anger and agitation becoming borderline maddening, Alina tried again, ignoring the tears that always came when she got enraged.

"Will he ever be able to take over as king, because if not I—"

"You what, Your Highness?" Fin asked, leaning forward and resting his forearms on the table. He didn't sound as though he were mocking her, and his tone was gentle. The glint in his eyes indicated he genuinely wanted to know . . .

"I need to know if I should consider taking over the responsibility."

Mr. Howard choked on his wine while Fin's eyebrows shot up in shock.

"You would abandon your betrothal with the Troivackian king to rule Daxaria?" the viscount asked carefully.

"That, or we discussed my being queen regnant here, and he, the king consort. Roles would be reversed when it came to Troivack, of course."

"Was this something the Troivackian king suggested?!" Mr. Howard managed, his eyes still watering from his choking.

"He did, yes."

Fin's face grew shuttered. "Alina, that is incredibly suspicious."

"A lot less suspicious than your evasive answers pertaining to the prince. I don't want to take what is meant to be his, but where the hell is my brother?! Why do only you know, and not even our father?!"

Pain flashed through the viscount's eyes, and when his shoulders hunched, Alina was stricken by how worn down the infamous Daxarian hero suddenly seemed . . . as though the burden of his knowledge was already heavy enough.

"Your father doesn't want to know. He asked me to keep it secret, and when the prince returns . . . *if* he returns, it is up to him to share the details." Finlay's voice was raised, and firm, and despite Alina having to dash the tears from her cheeks, she appreciated that he didn't try to console her.

"So, in other words, Lord Ashowan . . . I *should* be more active in taking over some of my father's duties."

"If you were planning on being the ruling queen without the Troivackian king, I could see it being a wise and bold move."

Alina felt her chest tighten.

Cut off her engagement to Brendan?

Why did that idea fill her with dread?

She knew the Troivackian king would be angry, but he wouldn't hurt her or retaliate . . .

He'd probably just try to explain that it was ridiculous that they not marry for that reason.

"I see. Why do you think so, Viscount?"

Fin cast an uncertain glance at Mr. Howard, who was in the process of once again topping up his goblet.

"The Daxarian people will be uneasy about you ruling here if married to King Brendan because it could be interpreted as him manipulating you in order to control our land." Alina opened her mouth to interrupt and argue but the viscount held up his hands, stopping her. "I'm not saying that is how it is. I'm saying why the people could feel skeptical, and consequently, less supportive of the union."

Despite hating the reason, she had to admit Finlay Ashowan had a point. "Are there any other problems with it?"

"Yes, an important one . . ." Fin sighed and slumped back in his chair before giving her a tired smile. "Marriage is hard enough when you live together. You both would need to remain in your home kingdoms to rule properly. Living a continent apart? There will be no end to the troubles. One day you could discover he has mistresses, and perhaps they would just be rumors, but there is no way to truly know. The amount of scandals people would invent because they see it is easier to attack an individual instead of a united couple . . ."

Letting out a long breath, Fin failed to maintain his smile. "Leading a continent is a burdensome and trying life. You should ask the Troivackian king what it is like ruling without someone by your side."

Alina's eyes dropped to the table as she recalled how Brendan already expressed his view of her as a partner, and how a king shouldn't love his wife, but rather work together harmoniously.

"A political or a love marriage . . . a couple needs to be united in more ways than one. If you want to rule as the Daxarian queen, you will have my support. I'm sorry I can't share more with you about your brother," Fin interrupted her thoughts quietly, but his sincere apology somehow managed to incense her all over again.

"You swear to me he is alive, right?" Alina's sharp voice didn't succeed in moving the viscount.

With a sad grimace, he glanced at the assistant, who obviously shared Alina's displeasure over his secrecy, then Fin returned his shimmering gaze to the princess.

"The last I saw him, he was still breathing, talking, and walking about."

"Again with these riddles for answers," Mr. Howard muttered darkly.

The viscount didn't say anything as he slowly stood, and then bowed to Alina.

Without another word, he exited the council room, leaving behind an irate assistant, and an emotionally overtaxed princess.

Unfortunately, he hadn't even faced the storm that would await him in his own keep.

Tam continued jotting down his notes on one of the many pieces of parchment fanned across his desk, content with the solitude as doors slammed and shouts rang out everywhere else in his home.

His sister's return had been greeted with the expected whirlwind of lectures, fights, and the usual emotional chaos that followed his twin doggedly.

In a way, it was comforting.

It was a constant in their lives growing up, and a sign that everyone was accounted for and present.

If only I hadn't had to get involved in trying to help her . . . again . . . Tam thought to himself while outwardly cringing at the memory of his terrible proposal announcement to the king.

Glancing briefly over to the corner where the princess's birthday present already sat waiting, he hoped she would still like it when he'd give it to her in a month's time.

He had commissioned the lute to be made with several detailed features he had taken pains to ensure done. For one, the neck was smaller for her hands; for another, it bore fine inlays of mother-of-pearl and emeralds along the perimeter of the instrument's front and back. The emerald was the predominant gemstone in the Daxarian crowns, and the mother-of-pearl shining against the wood really brought attention to its fine-grain lines.

Sighing, Tam fiddled with the quill in his hands.

As possible wives went, Princess Alina Reyes was probably the woman who had enticed him the most into considering marriage . . . but he knew by the way she was instantly drawn to the Troivackians that she was seeking something more ambitious for her life.

Which, to Tam, was wildly unbecoming.

No, he just wanted to be left alone, in his chamber with his books and trinkets, and hope that one day . . . he would no longer feel his magic summoning him closer to its depths.

His chamber door suddenly burst open, startling him into dropping his quill and spilling his inkpot.

"Son of a— Kat?! What the—" Tam turned in his seat to stare at his sister's red face and wild glowing eyes.

"You *told* them where I was?!"

Closing his eyes slowly, Tam pushed himself up onto his feet to face his sister's wrath.

"They were about to send knights throughout Austice and the forest. I had to tell them to stop it getting bigger than—"

"Honestly—if you had just looked for the note in my room, none of this would have happened!" Kat snapped out angrily.

Tam crossed his arms across his chest with a frown. "Yes, it would've, Kat. She could've been hurt or in trouble. Stop being an idiot. She's a princess, not a maid you can run around doing whatever you like with."

"She's fine! Everyone keeps treating her like a bloody porcelain plate! She chose to stay with me!"

"Because you shoved her into it! You are always doing this! You make people do what you want, and if they don't like it, too bad, because you always have to have it your way! You're going to burn more than bridges with people you care about if you don't figure out how to bloody well control yourself!"

Kat stared at her brother, her chest heaving, and golden eyes sharp with her anger. Heat rolled off her body in waves as she turned and slammed his door behind herself without another word.

Tam stared at the closed door for a moment, his throat tight, and his hands locked into fists in his pockets before collapsing abruptly into his chair once more.

This might not resolve like it usually does . . .

Chapter 28

A STEP UP

Brendan was already in a foul mood as he sat outside in the cool night air of the east exit steps.

His meeting with the Daxarian king had not gone as he'd hoped.

He was perfectly fine with the violence; in fact, if anything, that helped him trust the Daxarian king a little more somehow. It indicated the man was capable of reactions that weren't calculated.

No . . . the part that had truly ruined the Troivackian king's mood was when his betrothal to the princess was put under fire.

Gods knew what she would say if she found out the details of the meeting . . . she may even want to break it off once learning of his provoking her father.

I'll have no proper defense for my words. Why did I have to get angry over the king's decision pertaining to the princess's friend? Sure, Lady Katarina would make an astounding soldier . . . but it was that the princess would be upset at losing her friend that made me angrier.

The sound of dainty footsteps coming down the castle steps made Brendan stiffen.

No one would dare approach him, particularly not a woman alone, in the middle of the idyllic summer's eve with its balmy breeze and chorus of crickets in the grass.

No . . . only one particular little princess would ever be so bold.

Seating herself beside him on the steps, Brendan could see the hem of her forest green dress in the corner of his eye; the faint aroma of jasmine wafted from her skin.

Why was his heart beating faster in her presence again? She wasn't a threat . . . there was no reason for it.

"I heard about what happened today."

Alina's voice was calm, but Brendan didn't bother turning to face her.

He could tell there was more she wanted to say, and he hated when women beat around the bush before getting to the point.

"Are you alright?"

His head snapped around to look at her, startled.

Her eyes in turn flew to the small wound he'd received near his hairline that the physician had insisted on stitching closed against his wishes.

She grimaced at the sight of it and gingerly reached her hand up to brush away part of his black hair to better see it. "Gods . . . I'm so sorry he did this."

Brendan's entire body was humming at her touch, and he was finding it strangely difficult not to kiss her.

Then her words reached him.

She was sorry?

Had she not heard what he'd said that put her father into a rampage?

"Even if you did bring up my brother, he shouldn't have done this. I can't apologize enough, Your Majesty." Alina's hand dropped to her lap as she let out a wearisome sigh and turned her face out to the night.

Brendan continued staring at her profile and found his mood gradually lifting as he studied the fine lines of her nose, and the way the corners of her lips curved down . . .

"I've had worse scrapes than this while training. Don't worry. Have you spoken with your father?" Despite his improved outlook, his voice still came out a growl.

The king's tone didn't bother the princess at all as she hunched over her knees and wrapped her arms around them. "No . . . and I snuck out of my chamber by lying to the guards about getting the Head of Housekeeping to find me some extra blankets, so I can't be out long."

Brendan frowned. "You've been lying quite often as of late."

"Well, I can't very well say, 'I want to go check on my betrothed in the middle of the night by myself,' can I?"

At this, a shadow of a smile touched the king's face. His stomach had leapt earnestly at hearing her still refer to him as her intended.

"I wanted to apologize and hear how you are," she explained with a note of defeat in her voice.

Brendan turned to face her more squarely. "Did something else happen today?"

Alina looked to him and tried to smile but didn't quite succeed.

He felt an unpleasant burr of emotion irritate his chest.

"I confronted the viscount about whether or not my brother was going to return and prepare to be king."

Brendan stilled.

"He evaded answering, and while he said he would support my desire to become Daxaria's queen, he expressed concern over my doing so while married to you."

I never liked that Godsdamn viscount, the king roared in his mind before grappling his anger back under control.

"He made valid points about the citizens feeling distrustful about you, and how they might resist my leadership with you as my husband out of fear of you controlling me."

When Alina glimpsed Brendan's murderous expression, she hurried on. "Lord Ashowan said he doesn't believe that personally, it was just what he could foresee happening."

Dropping her forehead to her hand for a moment, she tried to continue explaining.

"He also pointed out how difficult it'd be ruling our own nations, and being married . . . and I wanted to . . . to ask you something."

Brendan waited expectantly.

"Do you like . . . ruling alone? Is it easier not to have to fight with a husband or wife? Or to just worry about yourself at the end of the day?"

The Troivackian king grew somber as he processed her question, a strange emotion filling his eyes that was rather haunting.

"Princess, I have ruled alone since I was a child. It isn't something anyone can really understand unless they've faced it themselves."

He swallowed and a frown appeared over his brow as though debating whether or not to continue his reply. Yet despite his obvious uncertainty, he did.

"The expectations, the uncertainty, the thousands of decisions that affect more lives than you could possibly dream of. When faced with your failures, you are faced with people in a world of pain that you caused."

Alina felt her throat constrict as she saw Brendan's dark eyes grow distant.

"Some decision you made one day failed those people. It could have even been the right choice, but they still get hurt. No matter what you do, people will suffer. They will always want something of you thinking it'll fix their lives, and you *are* responsible for every part of their well-being. When my father"—Brendan's voice rasped and he hesitated in his response to clear it—"when my father met his end, it was because he led the charge up to this castle. He blindly ran into a wall of soldiers . . . alone. The endless abyss of our people's expectations chased him, and I think he ran to death, because he had long before grown tired. One day, I, too, will choose to let death take me so I can escape this fate . . . in fact, recently, I wanted it to be sometime soon."

Tears were rising in Alina's eyes as she recognized his sincere pain that he obviously struggled to share, but she didn't interrupt even though the weight of his words was making her chest ache.

"One day, I saw a peasant's wheat cart on the side of the road. The wheel had gotten stuck in the mud, and he couldn't get it out no matter how he pushed, sweat, and cursed. Then his wife jumped down from her seat and joined him. I had to hang myself out of the carriage window to see, but together, they managed to get it free."

Alina couldn't tear her eyes from Brendan's face even if she wanted to as she stared at the evidence of his burdens in his creased features.

"I realized then that if perhaps my mother had been able to help me . . . or even have been allowed to help my father more . . . things could be different. Better, and different."

Reaching out, Alina grasped his large coarse hands in her own.

"Your Majesty, when you say things like that, you make me worry . . . and you make me like you more than I should for a political marriage."

Brendan's heart flipped as he squeezed her hands in return. "All I've shown you are my shortcomings and weaknesses. I do so, not because it is easy, but because I think you should understand what awaits you as a queen."

Alina sniffed and took a steadying breath. "I just have one more question."

The Troivackian king nodded once to signal her to continue.

"Why didn't you or your guards stop to help the peasant on the road?"

Brendan didn't know why, but he suddenly felt a burst of laughter escape his chest.

Only the bleeding innocent heart of his betrothed would ask such a thing.

Instead of answering, he caved to the urge to pull her close and embrace her.

He felt her freeze in surprise in his arms, and he immediately began to worry that she would push him away.

Instead, once the initial shock wore off, he felt her shoulders gradually relax, as she rested her head against his chest and allowed his hand to cradle the back of her head and her upper back.

"We didn't stop because people have tried to murder me in the past using similar traps."

"O-Oh," was all Alina could manage.

She let out a slow breath, and she felt herself frown over how much the people of Troivack expected of their monarch and yet gave only pain in return.

"You're a good man, Your Majesty."

Brendan faltered for a moment, unsure of how to properly handle the emotions that surfaced upon hearing her kind words. Uncomfortable with expressing the elation he was feeling, Brendan contented himself with gazing out into the darkness and enjoying Alina's closeness.

After several warm moments in each other's company, their thoughts pleasantly muffled, and their beings consoled, Alina began to stir, prompting Brendan to drop a kiss onto her head as she pulled free of him.

"When did you start to mean something different to me, I wonder," the princess mused aloud, an enchanting smile on her face as her eyes searched his, making the king feel too many emotions than he cared to think about.

"As long as I am the only one you feel this kind of 'difference' with, I do not care."

Alina chuckled, but her expression faded into one far more serious yet again. "I suppose this presents a whole other bundle of trouble."

Brendan frowned in confusion.

"I can't be married to you and leave you to run a country alone, and I don't know that I want to do it on my own now, either . . . So that means I have to make sure my brother comes back, and that he is fit to take over as king." Alina sighed and let her head fall onto Brendan's shoulder, her hands folded in her lap.

"I'll speak with the viscount tomorrow," Brendan announced suddenly. His cheeks felt oddly warm.

The princess sat up, startled, and stared at him, with an undeniable spark of hope in her hazel eyes. "You will?"

"Yes. One way or another, I'm fulfilling my promise to you, and once we get the prince back in this castle, he better stay put." Brendan's foreboding tone didn't bother Alina at all as she instead felt a surge of gratitude over his help.

"Well, I wish you the best of luck. I want to hear all about it once you return from that meeting."

Standing swiftly, Alina turned to face Brendan with a bright smile on her face. "I should be getting back."

The king nodded thoughtfully and stood as well. "Before you go, Princess, there is one other matter I would like to discuss with you."

Smiling, and twisting her torso back and forth so that the skirts of her dress swished about her ankles, Alina stared up at him. She couldn't recall the last time she had felt so giddy and happy.

Brendan looked down at her mesmerized for a moment before giving his head a shake.

"Perhaps tomorrow we will discuss it. Go get some sleep, Princess. It has been a long day."

Alina smiled a little wider and dipped into a quick curtsy before skipping up the steps toward the door.

However, she abruptly turned back around and descended the steps until she stood only slightly taller than the Troivackian king.

Then, she leaned down and planted a quick kiss on his mouth.

Brendan felt his entire body burst into a strange ecstatic tingle as she pulled back, her cheeks pink and her smile intoxicating.

"Thank you for talking to me, I . . . I'm really glad I chose you."

She bound back up the steps and had just rested her hand on the door's handle, when the king called out to her.

"Ah, Princess, I hope you don't think in light of recent events that I've forgotten about our plans."

Alina looked down, perplexed at the king's out of character cheeky expression . . .

"We're going to make you stronger. Tomorrow we'll go for a walk through Austice once I return from the Ashowans, so I hope you pick out some comfortable footwear."

Alina's jaw opened and closed several times.

She had sincerely hoped he had forgotten about that!

Brendan did the unthinkable; he laughed for the second time that night as he slowly mounted the steps toward his adorably flustered betrothed.

Reaching for the door handle she was still holding, he opened it for her while maintaining eye contact.

Then, with a bow, he gestured her forward into the dark recesses of the castle.

"After you, Your Highness."

By the time Alina returned to her bedchamber, she found herself in a daze thinking about the time she had just shared with the Troivackian king.

She didn't even wish the guards good night as she always did when she touched the latch of her chamber door handle.

"Princess?"

One of the guards asked, his voice startling her out of her reverie.

"Y-Yes? What is it?"

"Where are the blankets you were going to retrieve?"

Alina blinked up at the man blankly before remembering how she had insisted on getting the linens herself.

"Oh . . . er . . . T-The walk all the way down to the Head of Housekeeping's chamber actually warmed me up considerably, so I . . . I decided I didn't need any extra blankets anyway!"

Before they could question her further, Alina slipped into her bedchamber and closed the door firmly behind herself.

Fanning her face and stepping farther into her room, she then realized she was once again smiling.

The expression of surprise mixed with uncertainty and gentleness in Brendan's eyes when she had pulled back from kissing him was burned in her memory, and she never wished it to fade.

Well, as first kisses go . . . I think that went pretty well.

Chapter 29

VISCOUNT'S VEXATIONS

B rendan stared at the closed doors of the viscount's estate grimly. Mr. Levin stood behind him and sniffed indignantly as the summer sun singed the back of their necks.

They continued to stand and wait; the only sound that reached them was that of the crashing waves far below, and the Troivackian king couldn't help but feel his ire grow.

Then, when he was just about to pound on the damn door yet again, it swung open and once the solid barrier had been removed, he could hear the cacophony of shrieks and door slamming from within the keep before the viscount himself slipped out and closed the door behind himself. Wearing only a cream tunic and pale brown trousers, it'd be easy to mistake him for a peasant.

"Good morning, Your Majesty," Fin greeted with a strained smile. "What brings you to our home?"

"Viscount, why does it sound like your entrance is a den of horrors?" Brendan asked slowly.

"Ah . . . my apologies. It is the reason our house steward couldn't invite you in. You see, erm, Duke Iones . . . well . . . he is staying with us while here in Austice, and his wife and children arrived late last night." Fin rubbed the back of his neck, his eyes lost to a traumatic memory.

It was then the Troivackian king noted the bags under the man's eyes.

"Why does that equate to . . . that." Brendan nodded toward the keep as Fin jammed his hands into his pockets and stepped farther out onto the stone landing.

"Well, Lady Iones wasn't originally supposed to come; however, she discovered an old notebook of the duke's that happened to contain sketches and sonnets regarding an old love of the duke's."

No sooner had the viscount said the words when the sound of shattering glass interrupted.

Brendan's hand was on the hilt of his sword immediately as his head and attention snapped to the broken window on his left side.

Fin didn't even bother batting an eye as he began descending the steps to the gravel drive.

"Would you perhaps like to see the stables, Your Majesty?" he asked pleasantly.

Brendan peered at the ground where what looked like a suit of armor's helmet lay amongst the shards before looking to Mr. Levin, who appeared every bit as stunned. Finlay Ashowan, however, had already begun striding toward the aforementioned stables. Were it not for his brisk pace, a casual observer would have thought he was unaffected by the chaos behind him.

Eventually returning to their senses, the Troivackians followed the viscount to the stables that had been carved into the cliffside along the side of the keep. The rock was damp from the sea mist, and yet also blissfully cool outside of the summer sun.

"So, what brings you by?" the viscount called over his shoulder while nodding a greeting to the stablehands who were walking away with empty feed buckets.

"I wanted to talk with you about a few things. The first is Prince Eric Reyes."

Fin stopped in his tracks, and slowly turned back around, his expression no longer at ease, but guarded.

He studied the Troivackian king for a long moment before his eyes moved to his assistant, Mr. Levin.

"If I could please have a private word with His Majesty."

The assistant's eyes displayed a brief flash of hostility, before he bowed and retreated back several steps.

Fin noted this reaction but returned his gaze to the king all the same.

"Does this have anything to do with the meeting I had with the princess yesterday?" the viscount queried diplomatically.

"Somewhat. There needs to be answers about the prince sooner or later, especially as it affects the princess's decision about her future."

One of Fin's eyebrows shot up as a faint smile began curling the corners of his mouth.

"You really want to marry her, don't you?"

Brendan couldn't imagine why the question made him self-conscious.

"Well . . . I must admit, Your Majesty," Fin went on, "so far, I have grown to really respect you for how you treat Her Highness. I worried when you first tried to *tell* her you would marry, but I can see now how special she has become to you."

"She is going to be an appropriate queen. Of course I should—"

"She's going to be your wife, Your Majesty. Someone who will love you completely, and someone you will have to love completely back."

"Love has nothing to do with ruling the country together." Brendan's throat became uncomfortably tight. "It is not the same in Troivack as it is in—"

"You said you wanted to change that, though. You said you didn't want women to be the same as they are in Troivack anymore," Fin pointed out while crossing his arms.

Brendan balked.

He had no idea what to say to that.

Was love really so necessary to Daxarian women?

As far as he understood things, arranged marriages still occurred in both kingdoms, so why was there such an expectation?

"I wouldn't worry too much about it, Your Majesty. From what I can see, it won't be an issue between you two." Fin's eyes glittered with good humor.

Once again, that strange discomfort made Brendan feel uncharacter-istically awkward.

Clearing his throat with a grunt, Brendan did his best to regain control of himself as he fixed the viscount with a firm stare.

"Viscount, who are you protecting by hiding the prince?"

This time Fin's smile didn't fully collapse at the mention of the missing royal.

"Would you believe me if I said I'm just trying to buy time?"

Brendan's eyes widened. "Buy time for what?"

Fin sighed, his chin dropping to his chest.

Brendan didn't know why, but he suddenly speculated that being more candid with the infamous house witch might help.

"I made the princess a vow on my pride and honor that I would bring her brother back for our wedding."

Fin's head snapped up, his astonishment clear before he closed his eyes in a grimace and raised his hand to his forehead in distress.

"He was going to miss her wedding?" Brendan demanded angrily. "Regardless of how it would harm his family?"

Fin kept rubbing his head for a moment before dropping his hand to his side and looking up tiredly at the king.

"Look, I don't know that he will be able to. You should not have promised something so wildly outside of your control."

"I will drag him if I need to," Brendan growled, not liking the chastising tone the viscount was taking with him.

Fin let out an aggravated noise before throwing his hands in the air. "When do you propose you get married, hm? I thought you would be returning to Troivack with the princess to be wedded and have her crowned soon. Finding the prince could take—"

"We're getting married in Daxaria. In a year."

Fin blinked in silence for a moment.

"I have heard nothing about these plans. In fact, last I heard, the king was adamantly trying to *end* your engagement."

"The princess needs time to learn how to run a country. A year should suffice to give her an understanding of the basics, as well as time to refine her knowledge on the Troivackian customs. We'll wed in Daxaria because I think it means more to her than it does to me. Though my vassals will expect her to be bearing the next king by the time we return . . ." Brendan trailed off as he realized his heart was beating faster at the thought of Alina facing down the long row of shrewd, traditional Troivackian nobles . . . and scrutinized in every way . . . her teasing smile fading away to nothing as she would be subjected to their sly methods. What of giving birth? Hadn't her father said her mother nearly perished? Would Alina die giving birth to their children in Troivack, alone and unhappy all because of him?

"—jesty! Your Majesty, are you alright?"

The viscount's voice broke through Brendan's spiraling thoughts.

"You've gone pretty pale, are you feeling well? I know that the notion of breaking a vow of honor can be—"

"Viscount, do you think the princess will be happy in Troivack?"

The king hadn't even realized the words had left his lips until he noticed the lord's stunned reaction.

"Well, if what she says about wanting to rule is true . . . then I imagine she would be, though it will most likely be hard, and lonely."

Brendan shifted as he recalled another important matter he had been meaning to discuss with the viscount.

"I want your daughter to join the princess in Troivack for a year."

The viscount's expression hardened. "I beg your pardon?"

"Your daughter needs discipline, and we can provide that for her. Not to mention the abilities her magic has given her would make her an exemplary—"

"No."

Fin's icy tone made the Troivackian king go still.

"Don't you wish to discuss it with the viscountess and your daughter before—"

"No."

The viscount didn't say another word as he strode purposefully by the king, his eyes gaining that magical glint, and in that situation, they looked more than a little menacing.

"I will not reveal your wife is a spy, and even let her keep *one* informant," Brendan called after him, his fist curled at his side.

Fin halted in his tracks and glanced over his shoulder, his facial features like marble, but he said nothing as he then continued on his way, passing by Mr. Levin, who had been waiting out of earshot.

When the Troivackian king rejoined his assistant, the man didn't have to ask to know that the discussion had not gone smoothly.

"Let's go," was all Brendan said as his assistant turned to the nearest stablehand and ordered their horses to be resaddled.

Besides gaining no new information about the prince, and the king's suggestion to take Katarina Ashowan with them to Troivack being shot down, the meeting with the viscount had brought something even more troubling to light.

Was ruling Troivack what the princess truly wanted? What if she grew to resent him? What if she couldn't even conceive a child and was subjected to having to choose Brendan's mistress in order for him to bear an heir by the other nobles . . .

The scenarios made the king's stomach roil.

Then the final question crossed his mind that made his mood blacken instantly.

Was Troivack really going to ever change enough to be worthy of her?

Annika leaned back into her chair in the solar, her brow knitted and her arms crossed. Fin had just finished recounting his conversation with the Troivackian king, and there was a good deal to think about.

"If he's bringing up bargaining about my spying, then that means he either isn't as certain as he thought he was about me, or . . . he has plans for Katarina in his army . . . perhaps he intends to turn her against me."

Fin's jaw was clenched as his gaze remained fixed on the floor. Despite the keep gaining quiet once again, he was not feeling peaceful in any way.

"Or the third option is him wanting to try and keep Alina happy. I think he is genuinely afraid of taking her to Troivack now that he is developing an attachment to her."

"Do you think he will try to break off the engagement to protect her?" Annika asked with an amused smile.

"He could if he ends up falling in love with her."

Annika laughed, drawing her husband's troubled eyes upward; seeing his wife in a good mood effectively lightened his own.

"You're making him sound like you."

Fin grinned. "What can I say, men become fools when they fall in love with pretty girls. All we want is the absolute best for them."

The viscountess smiled at her husband, her warm brown eyes still filled with nothing but love for him. "Well, we shall see. He is a duty-bound man. You were lacking a good deal of ambition before I came along."

Fin chuckled. "Yes, dear."

Annika looked to her lap, her expression becoming pensive as she studied the gold rings on her fingers.

"I think she should go with them."

The viscount's levity disappeared instantly. "You what?"

"I think Katarina should go to Troivack and be with Alina. Not for forever . . . just a year."

Rising to his feet, Fin's bright blue eyes regarded his wife in a way that made her stomach flip. "We are not sending her there. She could get hurt, or attacked, or—"

"—She needs the chance to grow up, Fin. I think that's why she has been struggling so much. She needs to be responsible for herself in a place that isn't going to cater to her impulses."

"Then we can send her to Sorlia with Harris, we do not need to—"

"Fin, you know they'll dote on her the same way we do. Doesn't it tell you something that both our children haven't found their familiars here? You were the one who told me that once a witch found where they were meant to be, their familiar would appear."

"It could also be a situation that draws out their familiar," Fin ground out irritably.

"They can't be our babies forever, and you know it. Give me one good reason we should let things continue on as they are," Annika demanded.

For a tense moment, neither of them spoke as they contemplated each other angrily.

"We will ask Kat and go from there. Can we agree on that much?" Fin demanded, a rasp entering his voice, which made Annika's heart ache when she heard it.

"Fine . . . we will talk to our daughter about this."

Putting his hands on his hips and his gaze moving to the windows, Fin tried to swallow past the lump forming in his throat, when he felt the familiar comforting embrace of his wife around his waist.

"One way or another, we're always a family, Fin. None of us are ever going to stop being a part of our home. I promise."

Chapter 30

TURNING THINGS AROUND

Alina stared at her father's haggard face and haunted gaze and struggled not to immediately run and embrace him.

Instead, she curtsied politely as Mr. Howard, Prince Henry, Captain Taylor, and Lord Fuks offered her their own greetings.

"Thank you for joining our meeting, Princess." Mr. Howard nodded respectfully as Alina strode over to the chair on her father's immediate right-hand side and seated herself.

"Of course, I understand there are many things to discuss this morning," she replied while worriedly eyeing her father.

The king didn't bat an eye at the exchange taking place as he continued sitting slumped back in his chair.

"Right . . . His Majesty would like to end the engagement between the Troivackian king and the princess," Mr. Howard began tentatively, giving the king a troubled glance before addressing everyone else present.

"We do not agree to this," Prince Henry interjected without even bothering to consider it.

The prince's expression for once was not friendly and smiling, making the nobles seated around the counsel room table shift uncomfortably at the sight.

"I don't wish for it to end either. Father, I know you and the Troivackian king got into an argument, but—"

"Where is King Brendan Devark?" Norman's harsh tone set everyone even closer to the edge of their seats as his hollowed gaze moved to the prince; there was no indication he had heard his daughter's words.

"My brother went to speak with Viscount Ashowan this morning." Henry's voice was calm, but his eyes were uncharacteristically sharp. It was a strange new side of him that Alina hadn't glimpsed at all during their courting times . . .

"What is it that he was going to speak with him about?" The king's unwavering demeanor was met with equal firmness by the Troivackian.

"I believe he wanted to discuss the possibility of Lady Katarina Ashowan joining the princess in Troivack for a year."

Alina's eyebrows shot up and she had opened her mouth to respond delightedly, when her father slammed his palm into the table.

"He was supposed to do that *with* the princess; furthermore, it is rather brazen of him to ignore my wishes with regard to ending this engagement." Norman straightened in his seat and continued to focus his attentions solely on the prince.

"The contracts have been signed, and we have not been in violation of any of the terms. If anything, Your Majesty, your assault of my brother could be grounds for renegotiating *several* points; however —"

"There is no renegotiation, this engagement will be ended or —"

"No, it won't!" Alina interrupted angrily, turning on her father, who still didn't move to face her despite her outburst. "We need more than an emotional reason to end this engagement."

At long last, Norman's attention snapped to his daughter, and the look in his eyes made her want to flinch.

"You want a good reason? I intend to have *you* take over Daxaria and you cannot do that while married off in Troivack."

Alina's jaw dropped, and the entire room fell into silence.

"I do not know if or when the prince will return to resume his duties and education, and with that uncertainty, I will not have my only other child who is capable of taking over the throne be married off," Norman continued while staring around the table, daring someone to disagree with him.

"Sire, where *is* the prince exactly? We know he is in Sorlia, but I also happen to know he is no longer living with Duke Iones's family," Captain Taylor asked hesitantly.

Norman regarded the military leader silently for a moment and tapped his finger on the armrest of his chair.

"Are you displeased that I have chosen Alina to be the next ruler of Daxaria, Captain?"

"No, Your Majesty. I just wish to know what prevents the prince from performing his duties. The Daxarian citizens will surely ask the same question when told of this new plan. It could lead to a divide amongst the people and even cause rebellions to form," Captain Taylor reasoned out carefully as though trying to soothe an aggressive animal.

"Then how about this . . . I will give the prince one year to return, and if at that time he does not, Alina's engagement will be nullified and she will be named as the official heir to the throne," Norman countered, looking once again over at Henry.

The Troivackian prince's jaw clenched, then his eyes shifted over to Alina, who was in too much shock to give him any indication of her feelings on the matter.

Finally, letting out a long sigh, Henry spoke, though it was clear he was not pleased with the way the meeting had gone. "I will explain this to my brother, and we will go from there."

Norman didn't say anything in response as his gaze moved around the table. "Are there any other matters you all wish to discuss?"

Clearing his throat awkwardly, Mr. Howard turned to face the king. "Sire, are we sending a letter to the prince with this information or—"

"I will send word with Duke Iones," Norman replied coolly.

Mr. Howard slowly pushed his chair away from the table, its legs scraping the stone floor loudly in the tense silence. "Right . . . well, I suppose I best begin drafting the revisions to the betrothal contract."

"And I best see that the men aren't slacking off from their morning training," Captain Taylor began while hesitantly standing with a bow toward the king.

"I best go find the original betrothal contract so that we can make the adjustments." Henry rose swiftly, his bad mood evident as he gave a quick bow to Norman and turned for the door without a word to Alina.

The princess swiveled in her seat to face her father as the men filed out, but Lord Fuks caught her eye.

"Princess, why don't you run along now. I would like to have a private word with the king, hm?" The elderly earl gave her a friendly smile and a wink that somehow managed to be comforting. Still . . . she needed to talk to her father . . . He was behaving far too erratically, and it was worrisome.

However, while giving her father one last fretful glance and seeing that he was not looking anywhere near her, Alina decided to perhaps let someone a little wiser, if ten times more insane, try to help.

Giving her father a small curtsy she bid him farewell, and left, already eager to see Brendan and hear what his advice would be.

Once alone with the king, Lord Fuks placed his maimed hands on the table with their few remaining digits and tapped the wood slowly.

"Have you gone fully mad?" the earl asked casually.

Norman's gaze cut to Lord Fuks sharply. "What was wrong with my suggestion?"

"The princess quite likes the Troivackian king from what I can tell, and he seems a good fit for her. Seems a steady sort and everyone is talking about the courtesies he has shown her."

"He is the exception not the rule to Troivackians. Besides, he dares to try and tell me how to be a father to my children? Going on about how I've lost a son and will lose Alina. Well, I won't lose her to him, that's for certain!" Norman barked while pounding his fist on the table.

Lord Fuks raised a wiry eyebrow. "So bring your son back. It isn't as though it is outside of your power to make it happen. Let Alina do what she thinks is best and —"

"She only wants to marry him to become a queen. Well, I'll give her the damn crown and then I don't have to send her off. Everyone can be happy then."

The earl blinked and leaned forward. "I've never seen you act so tyrannical in all the fifty-some odd years I've known you. You're making *me* be the sane one and I don't like it one bit!"

Norman was caught between a laugh and anger over Lord Dick Fuks's exasperation.

With a sigh, the earl shook his head and leaned back in his chair, his expression pensive. "After the prince and the princess, who is next in line for the throne? Isn't it technically one of the dukes? Which duke was it, though . . . Was it Iones? Or —"

"It'd be Duke Knowles of Xava, and he will not be setting foot in any throne room as long as I'm alive," Norman uttered darkly.

"Ah, that would be unfortunate. I pity his youngest daughter; she seems a decent sort." Giving his head a shake, Lord Fuks once again attempted to hold a sane conversation. "You could always adopt a child, I suppose."

The wry look Norman gave him dismissed the idea immediately.

"Right. Well, I can't seem to reason with you in the usual way. I suppose I'll have to do it my way." Lord Fuks stood, his old knees trembling as he rose.

The king didn't like the new direction the earl was taking the conversation . . .

Clucking his tongue, Lord Fuks gripped his cane and sighed somberly. "I intend on going to speak with Viscount Ashowan's cat, Kraken, and I will let him scheme something to fix this situation."

Norman's eyes grew wide. "Don't you dare bring that devil beast into this."

"Sorry, old friend, you've forced me to go over your head with this. I'm too old and too impatient to wait on you to come around, but I know for a fact the familiar will set things right one way or another."

"Did you just say you were going over my head by going to Kraken?"

"Your Majesty, it's just us two here. We both know if that cat wanted it to be so, he'd burn the castle to the ground with us inside and still be worshipped by all of Daxaria. Of course he's our superior."

Norman opened his mouth to argue, but the old man was already on his way out the door.

"Dick, don't you dare talk to that cat! I'm warning you!" Norman was on his feet as the unmistakable cackle of Lord Fuks echoed back to him from the corridor.

"DICK, I'M SERIOUS! DO NOT, UNDER ANY CIRCUMSTANCES, BRING THAT ASININE HAIRBALL INTO THIS CASTLE!"

Once again, Norman received no answer, and he felt his incredulousness as he dropped his head to his hand.

"What the hell has my life become?"

Alina all but skipped down to the front entranceway. She couldn't remember the last time she felt so excited to go for a walk.

She wondered what Austice was like, traveling on foot! Perhaps she could convince the Troivackian king to look for the ancient dragon bones with her! Or perhaps they'd have lunch in a tavern! She'd always wanted to try a local eatery but had never been allowed.

When she reached the entrance, she found that the Troivackian king had indeed arrived, but he was speaking quietly with his assistant and brother. Slowing her pace down and waving to her two handmaidens who were following to fall back a step, Alina stepped closer to the three men curiously. However, she failed to notice Lord Fuks and bumped into him.

"Ah, my apologies, my lord!" Alina curtsied hastily, then realized that the earl was holding the viscount's familiar, Kraken. "Oh! Hello, again!" She smiled beautifully down at the creature's bright green eyes and reached her hand out to let him give her a tentative sniff.

"What are you doing with Kraken, Lord Fuks?"

"Oh, this little beast has been hanging around the Troivackians for a while, and I needed to have a word with him."

Alina was in the process of stopping herself from laughing, when she remembered that this was the cat that Finlay Ashowan could talk to and understand. So instead of laughing or treating the outlandish claim seriously, she gratefully scratched Kraken's cheek and decided not worry about it. If she were honest, she had always been a little dubious about the story of Kraken taking down hundreds of soldiers and a dragon.

"How did the talk with my father go?" she asked while attempting to sound cavalier.

"Not well, I'm afraid, but do not worry. This beast will take matters firmly in paw and get them sorted," Lord Fuks assured the princess while joining in on giving Kraken cheek scratches that the cat closed his eyes to enjoy.

"If you say so, Lord Fuks, but thank you for trying." Alina sighed but did her best to smile gratefully.

Kraken's eyes suddenly flew open and he sat up alert in the earl's arms.

Both Alina and Lord Fuks turned to see what had caught his attention, and that was when they noticed Brendan had turned and taken a step toward them.

"Gods, thank you!" Alina looked back to the cat brightly. "He always startles the cheese from me because I can't hear him coming!"

Kraken responded by leaping down from the earl's arms and casually rubbing himself against the princess's skirts.

"Alright, Emperor Kraken, I will leave these grave matters to you. Good day, Princess." Lord Fuks first bowed to the familiar, then to Alina, making her once again almost laugh aloud.

Then, with impressive speed for his ninetysomething age, Lord Fuks hobbled away.

"Did that man just bow to a cat?" Brendan's voice was beside Alina as she stared after the earl, shaking her head.

"Yes, he was . . . Is everything alright, by the way?" she asked while glancing behind her betrothed to see if Mr. Levin or Prince Henry were anywhere to be seen.

"Ah, my brother was informing me of your father's new condition to our betrothal. I must say I'm relieved."

Alina looked up at him, her face already split into an excited smile.

"Really? You think it's good? Oh, please tell me why! I was so worried when he said that, and I—"

"You were worried?" Brendan asked with a frown.

"Yes! I mean I'd feel horribly guilty if I just left Daxaria without a good ruler, and—"

"You didn't even consider your father's offer? You could become queen of Daxaria and not have to leave home. Isn't that what you wanted?" Brendan's concern made him unconsciously draw closer to the princess.

Alina bit the inside of her cheek and lowered her gaze. "I-I already told you that . . . I don't want you to . . . I don't want you to have to rule alone anymore, and I . . . meant it," she finished awkwardly as she began to fidget.

Brendan didn't realize he was smiling yet again as he grew distracted by his charming fiancée.

As a result, he was oblivious to everyone around them who had become frozen in shock over seeing the Troivackian king look so happy and loving while gazing upon their very own dear princess.

Chapter 31

CREATIVE SOLUTIONS

Alina stared at the armed knights in front of her, then glanced to the Troivackian king at her side. Her eyes trailed down his torso to the sword clipped to his belt, then to the dagger in his boot.

I suppose I should be more grateful that he isn't wearing any armor, she thought to herself dejectedly.

"Are we all prepared?" Brendan asked, nodding to the four knights belonging to the Daxarian king.

"Erm . . . would it be possible if we weren't so . . . crowded and, uh, noticeable?" Alina interrupted just as her father's men began to nod to the Troivackian monarch.

"Princess, your safety is of the utmost importance. If something should happen while on your walk in Austice, His Majesty King Norman would never—" one of the younger knights began.

"Perhaps Sir Cas is right and we should also bring the Royal Physician," one of the knights with light brown hair, stubble on his face, and a small silver earring in his ear speculated suddenly, his brown eyes brightening.

"Ah, Princess, Sir Vohn makes an excellent point, perhaps we should bring the physician in the event that—"

"No," Alina interrupted the spiraling discussion amongst the knights vehemently. "Can we please just have a nice *simple* outing?"

Her weary expression and hunched shoulders irked Brendan. Even more troublesome was how he was overcome with the urge to try and bring back the effervescent smile the princess had worn earlier. Her new crestfallen features were making him feel restless . . .

The knight named Sir Vohn straightened to attention as he turned to face the royal. "We must protect you, Princess. It is of course expected that we have the adequate amount of guards to ensure—"

"Why not just go out in civilian clothes with concealed weapons and keep your distance?"

The voice that made them all stop and turn was none other than that of Lady Katarina Ashowan, who had appeared in the entryway behind the group with her mother and brother.

The viscountess was staring daggers at her daughter over her interruption, but Kat's defiant expression indicated she was unphased.

"What do you mean, Ka— Lady Katarina?" Alina asked eagerly, ignoring how everyone else had grown tense.

"Well, it makes sense that you have guards with you, but why not have them follow at a distance in civilian clothes so that you can enjoy the city? Plus, if the big lu—the Troivackian king—good day, Your Majesty." Katarina curtsied dutifully while Brendan's eyes narrowed at her near insult. "If the Troivackian king is present at your side, won't he be able to protect you from most threats? It isn't as though an army is out in the streets waiting to attack you, Princess."

Kat finished her explanation while her mother stood with her hands dutifully folded in front of her skirts and her eyes cast downward, but the rigidness in her shoulders indicated her displeasure over her daughter's interruption.

Alina smiled excitedly and turned to Brendan, who grew still at the sight of her shift in mood and made a strange objective growl in the back of his throat that made her excitement dwindle once more.

Seeing Alina become crestfallen all over again in light of his reaction, Brendan's features collapsed into one of resignation.

"Princess, if it means that much to you, we can try Lady Katarina's idea, *but*," Brendan added pointedly as the knights opened their mouths to object and Alina's previous hopefulness began to return, "we will double the knights accompanying us. We will meet back here in one hour to take our leave."

Everyone glanced at one another and slowly nodded in agreement at the compromise.

Kat shot a wink to her friend before her mother stepped in front of her and addressed the king.

"My apologies for asserting ourselves during your outing preparations; if you will excuse us, Your Majesty, we must be on our way." Dipping into a curtsy that for once Katarina mimicked perfectly, the trio of Ashowans' stepped around the entourage toward the grand staircase.

The knights bowed and disbanded as well to relay their new orders to Captain Taylor, leaving the couple alone in the entryway as servants drifted by, eyeing them interestedly.

Alina stared after Katarina and her family and wondered what had brought them back to the castle that day without the viscount, but she was pulled back from her thoughts by the Troivackian king.

"It will take some time before the knights change and return with more of their comrades. Did you have any other plans or duties for today, or would you care to have . . . tea . . . in the courtyard?" Brendan struggled with the word tea, as the mere thought of the wet leaf beverage made him want to gag.

Regardless, he didn't want to lose time with her. Even though he had a pile of work that had been sent by his council, and letters he needed to write, if he ended up doing nothing all day but drink a horrid beverage and go on a long walk? If it was with the princess? It felt as though he was accomplishing something even more worthwhile.

"How about you have some Troivackian moonshine while I have tea?" Alina grinned up at her betrothed knowingly, and he felt his features instantly relax.

"That's what I meant," Brendan replied while clearing his throat and a hint of a smile passing through his dark eyes.

Alina giggled. "I didn't know you even had a sense of humor. Shall we go to the courtyard? I'm certain we can flag down a maid and ask the kitchen to send some snacks."

Brendan gave a brief jerk of consent with his chin before offering his arm to her, his eyes fixed on their path ahead as he felt a peculiar heat in his cheeks.

He was beginning to wonder if he was coming down with a fever, when the princess's cool hands wrapped around his arm and his stomach somersaulted, while a baffling spark ran down his spine.

Clearing his throat and blinking several times to try and regain his composure, Brendan stepped forward tentatively, with Alina at his side.

He was unable to look at her despite being curious about what expression she was making. All because he knew that if he did happen to glance her way, he was not confident he would be able to withhold his honest expression from her at all . . .

And that alone was enough to make his insides quake.

* * *

Annika stood in front of the Daxarian king, who appeared to have aged another ten years since she had seen him the previous day. His complexion was pale, his eyes sunken, and his entire form seemed smaller.

He sat slumped on the library couch, his head propped up by three fingers on his right hand, which was resting upon the sofa's arm. He stared blindly at the floor ahead of himself, and for a brief, terrifying moment, the viscountess wondered if the man was even breathing.

"Your Majesty, I have brought my son and daughter with me so that we might discuss punishment for their actions regarding the princess's impromptu camping trip." Annika dipped into a curtsy, and rose once more, her face as calm and cool as ever.

Norman didn't move for several moments, and the tension in the quiet space grew until at long last he moved his head to regard the three members of nobility before him.

"Where is the viscount?"

Annika gave a small smile. "Duchess Iones surprised us with a visit at the keep late last night, and Lord Ashowan is currently attempting to . . . mediate . . . the situation."

The king blinked and then, like a dead man being given the breath of life, slowly stretched his back straight and turned his body with interest.

"What is happening with the Duchess Iones? I was unaware she had any plans on joining Lord Harris for this season at my court."

"Are you familiar with the duke's time prior to his marriage and rise to nobility?" Annika asked delicately.

Norman frowned, his thoughts gradually whirring back into action as he cast his memory back, perplexed by what the viscountess was referring to.

"Do you happen to recall . . . the matter of the duke's bacherlorhood during his first ten years as a noble?"

The king's hazel eyes widened.

"Do you mean to tell me Duchess Iones discovered the details of Lord Harris's . . . *interest* in a certain maid we know?"

"She happened upon the duke's old journal, as well as some letters, sketches, poetry . . ."

"Oh . . . Oh Gods . . ." The king's hand with his golden ring moved to cover his mouth. "Are you certain it is safe to leave Lord Ashowan to handle the situation?" he managed, his mind filled with premonitions of blood and chaos.

"He is preparing food for her while she accompanies him in the kitchen. Duke Iones is supervising their three boys out in the courtyard until it is safe to enter and the servants have handled the damages."

Norman winced. "Are they expensive damages?"

The viscountess's eyes shifted upward as she began to mentally tally the cost of fixing her home after the duchess's warpath.

"We may ask the duke to compensate for the fire damage in the dining hall. Replacing the decor in the entrance, the torn linens, and transportation of the cattle we have at the estate we will be able to handle."

"What did she do to the cattle?!" Norman couldn't help but burst out, his expression filled with trepidation.

"The beasts are unable to produce milk at this time due to the stress of the experience. Pardon me, sire, but the details are perhaps better left unsaid."

There was a weighty silence as everyone present allowed the horrors of the duchess's wrath to echo in their minds.

After several moments, Norman shook his head and stood.

"Are their children alright?"

"The viscount saw that they were kept in the solar with their governess with the doors locked and sound magically blocked in for the worst of it. Though admittedly they seem rather unphased even from the parts they did witness."

Norman couldn't help but notice haunted looks on the viscountess's children behind her.

"I . . . see." Letting out a long breath and wondering if the fallout between the duke and duchess would reach him, the king decided to speak with Mr. Howard later that day about the possible implications.

"Back to the matter at hand, I suppose . . ." Norman absentmindedly gestured to the couch across from himself.

The three Ashowans stepped forward, and while Katarina and her mother seated themselves on the offered furniture, Tam took the armchair. Despite his rigid posture, his hands were folded loosely in his lap and his brown eyes remained fixed on the low mahogany table between them all.

It was apparent he would've been happy to be nearly anywhere else. Save perhaps for his own home between a feuding couple.

"The viscount and I discussed the Troivackian king's request with Katarina, and we were rather surprised to learn that she had already told the princess she wished to join her in Troivack for a year."

Norman's eyebrows shot upward before turning to Katarina.

The young woman's golden eyes glinted from the light of the windows behind the king, and he could tell by the set of her jaw she was rather determined on the point.

After all, her father had the exact same expression when he had his mind made up.

"I see. Well, then . . . I suppose it is decided. You will be joining the princess in the event she does go to Troivack. However, given that those events may not come to pass, and they are also a year away, I have chosen a more imminent punishment," Norman began, and he watched as a flicker of uncertainty passed through the young woman's eyes.

"My daughter recently fired her most senior handmaiden and is in need of another who will be in charge of her schedule and managing the duties of her other attendees. This includes, but is not limited to, her meals, her sleep schedule, her health, her wardrobe, her lessons, and, now, ensuring she is fully prepared for official council meetings. You will be working closely with Mr. Howard, as well as the Royal Cook, the Head of Housekeeping, and multiple others."

Katarina's face had grown quite pale, and her brother was biting down on his lip caught between a laugh and a wary groan. The king wasn't finished.

"It is a massive responsibility, and you yourself will be attending all her lessons. During the year before she marries, you will be prohibited from courting, and your parents will not be permitted to enter any marriage negotiations on your behalf as your priority will be to serve the princess without distraction. While that is not a normal stipulation in the job, this *is* meant to be a punishment."

Annika, who had been rather pleased with the punishment at first, was incredibly uneasy by the end, though her facial features did not give any indication.

Katarina, on the other hand, sat speechless.

She was being faced with her own personal hell.

Her actual, horrific, nightmarish hell.

She knew if she tried to speak, she would betray that fact.

It was one of the rare times she wished her mother would speak on her behalf and save herself from having to respond appropriately.

"When . . ." she attempted to speak, but the words came out as a croak. She licked her lips and tried again while Norman waited expectantly.

Similar to her father, the young woman was easy to read.

He could see that he had indeed chosen the perfect punishment for her.

At long last, Katarina remembered how to form appropriate words that were not *I'd rather impale myself on a sharpened mage staff than take that job*.

"When am I expected to start . . . Your Majesty?"

Norman almost smiled. "I will give you two days to pack and organize yourself before coming to stay in the castle. I will have quarters prepared for you."

"I understand. Th-Thank y-you . . . Your Majesty."

The effort it was taking Katarina to not stand up and run away from the castle was making her eyes water.

"Now"—the king turned to Tam, and he watched the young man's left cheek twitch—"it is time to address your own punishment for lying to me, Lord Tamlin. After that, I will be discussing privately with the viscountess what the punishment will be for the adults involved in the deception."

Annika raised an eyebrow, but when the king looked to her she could tell that it was nothing to worry about.

After all, he already knew that ordering their daughter to leave the Ashowans' home was the greatest punishment to them.

Norman returned his attention to Tam, whose features had frozen thicker than any pond in winter.

"For you, my dear boy, I have something quite special in mind."

Norman's slow smile did little to comfort the future viscount, and as he waited for the monarch to reveal his fate, Tam swallowed down his apprehension best he could.

It wouldn't be too terrible . . .

Would it?

Chapter 32

PLAYING NICE

Alina happily strode beside Brendan as the summer sun soaked her skin and the flow of traffic brushed by them without a bow or curtsy in sight.

Thankfully, Alina had been able to procure clothes that hid any evidence of her nobility. She had managed to borrow a senior maid's beige dress with a white apron and white hair covering and, once she donned it, discovered that she looked just like any other serving wench.

It was wonderful!

The only thing that was dampening the day was the fact that Brendan was being shot all kinds of angry, hostile glares, and as a result he kept Alina close to himself and his expression guarded as though expecting someone to pick a fight at any moment.

"It might help if you smiled," Alina announced suddenly after Brendan frowned at a particular group of children who were gaping at his size and taunting him by sticking out their tongues.

"Why would I smile when they look at me like I am something vile?" the king asked gruffly.

"Meeting hostility with hostility means that is the only road the exchange can go down. However, if you greet it with a friendly smile, you open up three possible options. Hostility, a friendly change in demeanor, or . . . neutrality. You've increased the likelihood of a better outcome from zero to more than a third," Alina explained while holding up her fingers to count down the presented possibilities.

Brendan paused.

It was peculiar logic, but he had to admit it was a strategy he had never tried before.

His eyebrows and corners of his mouth grew tense as though already imagining trying to smile.

"If a situation escalates in hostility, I will have the upper hand in an altercation."

"It will only create *more* hostility though," Alina pointed out evenly.

"What if I let them win?" Brendan tried again, as he realized he was starting to lose his footing in the debate.

"Then you fought with them proving that you are what they assumed, and now they have no reservations about treating a Troivackian like that again, because they learned nothing. Only that violence confirmed their original thinking."

The Troivackian king let out a guttural grunt, indicating his displeasure over the idea.

Alina did her best to hide her smile.

Despite many people in the street shifting away from him as a result, to her she was beginning to find his reactions rather funny . . .

He was like a grumpy dog.

"Is there something you like to do for fun, Your Majesty?" Alina asked while clasping her hands behind her back.

She'd let the topic of smiling go for the time being and hoped that a shift in the conversation would help him lower his guard a little.

"Not particularly."

Alina blinked up at his stoic face. Was this just another facet of his personality he was used to keeping to himself?

"What about viewing plays? Do you like any of the popular performances circulating these days?"

"I've seen one or two plays at my court. They were mediocre at best."

"Which plays were they?" the princess managed to ask despite beginning to flounder on how to keep the conversation going.

"They were reenacted accounts from the soldiers present the day my father died."

Alina halted in her tracks, making several people along the side of the road exclaim in anger as they stepped around her to continue hauling bags of flour or baskets filled with flowers.

The Troivackian king didn't notice until he was several steps ahead of her, but when he turned back around, he was perplexed over her stunned, mortified expression.

He strode back to stand in front of the princess.

"Who . . . made you watch that?! That sounds horrible! Why would you use that as a point of reference?! Don't you know there are plays that aren't about tragedy, but are comedies? I've seen some that had me laughing until I cried!" Alina exclaimed passionately, while Brendan gave no reaction.

"Did . . . you . . . want to see a play today?" he asked hesitantly. He wasn't sure if that was what she was getting at.

"No! That isn't my— Well . . . maybe! I mean, I honestly can't believe that you have never seen a play that wasn't about your father's death!" She continued her rant while growing slightly breathless.

Brendan remained unmoved.

"Alright, that does it! We are going to find a matinee somewhere! Then we are having an early supper, and I don't want to hear any arguments!" Alina snapped, then set to seizing the Troivackian king's hand and tugging him along.

Brendan allowed his fiancée to pull him farther down the street, wondering what in the world had her so fired up, but her hand clasping his made him reluctant to question it further. Meanwhile, he failed to notice that a good number of people watching the terrifying mountain of a man be dragged by a woman who was less than half his size were suddenly more amused than fearful.

After all, any fellow that size who allowed his sweetheart to treat him thusly couldn't be all bad . . . Troivackian or not.

Brendan regretted caving to the princess the moment she had forced him into the shadowy seat of the rustic theater.

Rough wooden benches were placed before the stage in enough rows that it could comfortably seat a hundred people. The only saving grace of the situation was that because it was in the middle of the day, most people were at their jobs, and only about fifty people were present, including the knights and the royal couple.

Earlier when the princess had first hatched the idea of seeing a play, they had gone into the nearest tavern and she had demanded to know which performances in Austice were taking place. After an annoyingly lengthy discussion and a few copper coins, the tavernkeeper had finally referred them to a theater located on the dodgier side of Austice down by the docks.

"Apparently this play is so popular that they might have to run it for the rest of summer!" Alina whispered to him, her eyes dancing with excitement.

Noting her flushed face and breathy voice, Brendan heard himself let out a long sigh as resignation overtook him. At the very least her knights were seated directly behind them, though he wasn't entirely trusting that they wouldn't literally stab him in the back either. That being said, he sincerely doubted the king would subject his daughter to the gore of his death.

That was one thing that continued to be irrefutable about the man in Brendan's estimation . . .

The Daxarian king loved his children with everything he had.

The only problem was, the love for his children came before the love of his kingdom.

"I think I just saw one of the actors backstage!" Alina's hushed tones once again drew Brendan from his thoughts as he turned to face her with his arms remaining crossed.

"Is it possible, Princess, that you have seen a public play before? You seem oddly comfortable in this surrounding," the king observed quietly while his eyes had moved to the actors behind the dusty red curtains.

"Oh, well, you see, my mother and Viscountess Jenoure once snuck me into one."

Brendan's head snapped back to look at her.

"I was perhaps about nine years old, and we had gone to Sorlia to visit my brother. The Ashowans were there doing their routine inspection of the schools they've established, and my mother begged the viscountess to help us sneak off, and . . . well, we did. We went and saw the most marvelous play about a music teacher who—"

The princess's story was cut short as a performer strolled out onto the stage and a single beam of light was angled onto him from someone maneuvering a mirror above the benches.

The room fell silent, and Alina, without thinking, had reached over and gripped Brendan's sleeve in anticipation, her face bursting at the seams with joy.

The Troivackian king found himself incredibly grateful for the poor lighting of the room, as he felt his face relax into the beginning of a smile . . .

He stared at the small hand gripping his sleeve, completely ignoring the actor introducing the play, and when he had moved offstage, Alina released the king's sleeve to clap along with the rest of the attendees.

In a move that surprised even himself, Brendan's hand shot out and grasped the princess's, stopping her clapping immediately before pulling her hand awkwardly between them.

Once he had done that, aside from remaining alert to noises from the audience in case someone tried to attack, he barely registered anything happening on the stage. Even when a man pretending to be a woman with literal melons slung down the front of the costume pranced onto the stage, earning several rounds of laughs and catcalls from the audience.

At first, Alina was equally quiet, and in the dark Brendan couldn't make out her reaction to his gesture, but eventually the story onstage pulled her in and she was laughing with the rest of the audience easily—yet she never let go of his hand.

. . . Even when his palm began to sweat.

He wasn't sure if that was a normal phenomenon. His hands usually only sweat like that when he was training outdoors in the heat.

Eventually, Brendan recognized from the cadence of the actors that the story was nearing its finish, when all of a sudden, the actor who had been prattling on the most during the entire blasted production turned to the audience.

"Who amongst you can help us guide this poor, poor man." He gestured to a fellow actor who was on his knees before the bloke with the melons.

"We need one of you, a common man, to teach this poor soul what his lady needs to hear! You there!"

Brendan watched darkly as the actor pointed directly at his face.

"Won't you come tell our hero what he needs to say to his woman!"

"No."

The actor hesitated for a brief moment, his smile frozen on his face, but he recovered instantly.

"Come on there, chap! You have a beautiful lady friend at your side; does our hero not deserve the same?"

Brendan could hear the Daxarian knights behind Alina struggling to stop their laughter as he continued to stare stonily at the actor. He was about to repeat his original answer when Alina's hand left his, and her soft voice whispered to him, "Come on, they'll make you say three words then it'll end the play." Her tone was teasing, but Brendan turned to look at her sharply.

"Three words and we'll leave? You swear it?"

Alina giggled, and in the faint light from the stage, she looked more beautiful than ever . . .

That was when after a dazed moment, Brendan realized that he had stood up and was approaching the steps on the side of the stage as the entire audience burst into applause for him.

"Right, there's a good man! See everyone, some folks are just a bit shy and— Uh . . . oh." The actor had not realized precisely the size of the audience member he had summoned. Nor had he realized how terrifying he was.

He nervously reached out to grab Brendan's arm once he had stepped into the stage lights, but one flash from the inky eyes had the actor snapping his hand back and dancing farther away.

"C-Come over here! Er, sir! Come tell this poor . . . poor man . . . what his sweetheart needs to hear!" The actor nervously summoned Brendan over to the side of the stage so that the scene might continue to play out.

A small growl came from the king's throat and several other cast members shifted away from him as he strode over to the spot they'd hastily cleared for him.

"Say the words," the actor whispered nervously to Brendan as everyone remained frozen in a tableau.

It hadn't been at all how they'd rehearsed that scene, but they all were rather aware that the man standing in front of them was capable of single-handedly strangling them all quite easily, and quite quickly . . .

"What words?" Brendan countered quietly, his tone unimpressed.

"I am sorry!"

"You'll be forgiven when this waste of my time is concluded. What are the words I need to say?"

The actor's face grew pale and sweat began to drip down the side of his head for a number of reasons.

"Th-Those are the words you need to say. You need to tell him 'I am sorry.'"

Brendan stared at the actor attempting to direct him, then to the man on his knees, then to the man with the melons. He returned his attention to the fool who had summoned him onstage.

"I will say three words, walk off this stage, and you will end this immediately, are we clear?"

The actor genuinely could not tell if the giant was threatening or ordering him. Either way, he wasn't about to disobey and risk his life, so he gave a single nod of affirmation.

"S-So, chap! What is it our dear . . . sweet . . . good hero—whoprobably-hasafamilytotakecareof," the actor added under his breath with a weak wheeze. "W-What does he need to say to win the heart of his lady?!" The man's voice had grown louder, and the crowd cheered and whistled.

Brendan faced the melon-filled actor, who for some reason felt as though he should be bowing in response, and said the three words he had promised everyone.

"I'm always right."

"I-I-I'm a-always right," the actor on his knees repeated faintly as though he were about to wet himself.

The audience fell silent as Brendan's heavy boots then turned and clod off-stage; the creak of the bench could be heard as he resumed his seat beside Alina.

The actors remained petrified, until Brendan cleared his throat loudly.

The bloke with the melons broke free of his fearful state and slapped the male hero across the face in a moment of inspired improvisation.

"You're always right?! My sister was right about you after all! I suppose I-I-I SHALL TAKE A VOW OF LIFELONG CHAS*TITTY*! Yes, I can feel that while this heartbreak weighs heavily in my bosom." He hefted the melon and earned a rejuvenated wave of laughter from the audience. "Good day to you, sir!"

The audience clapped and whistled as the narrator of the play stepped forward and pointedly ignored Brendan's stare.

"A-And from that day on, our young . . . lovers . . . lived alone! Happy, but alone, and our hero would forever rue the day he failed to learn the words: *I am sorry!*"

The actor swept into a bow, and the audience rose to their feet cheering.

Satisfied to see the actors lining up to bow for the finale, Brendan then realized he hadn't had the courage to look at his fiancée to see how she had felt about his interference with the play she had been enjoying.

Feeling disappointed with himself, he chastised himself, and turned to face her.

Only to find that she was laughing so much that tears were running down her face, and her hand was covering her mouth in an attempt to silence herself.

At seeing Alina's reaction, her small body shaking as she snorted over and over and tears continued to stream down her cheeks, Brendan couldn't help but release his own boom of a laugh.

The entire cast and audience around them all jolted in surprise, but soon, everyone was smiling.

Perhaps not all plays were so terrible.

Chapter 33

NOBLE NEWS

As Brendan and Alina strolled back out into the sunny street, the two knights who had been seated behind them could still be heard howling from the depths of the theater. They, like their princess, had found Brendan's dalliance onstage to be a source of great entertainment.

Alina was still in the process of wiping tears of humor from her cheeks, while Brendan's face had resumed its usual scowl. He hadn't minded when it had been his betrothed's amusement, but the knights were a whole other matter.

Turning to stare up at the Troivackian king and noting his soured mood, Alina gently touched his arm, drawing his deadly attention down to her.

"Shall we have an early supper and return to the castle? I believe we passed a relatively clean tavern on our way here."

Brendan's features softened when, in the remaining light of the day, he saw her bright eyes fill with gladness.

"Very well, the more walking for you, the better, I suppose," he managed to say while looking forward and thinking he should perhaps talk to the Royal Physician about how erratic his pulse was becoming as of late.

Though he was distracted when, without prompting, he felt Alina's small cool hands wrap around his forearm and draw herself closer.

It became incredibly hard for Brendan to fight off a smile.

"Ah! Pardon me, you two there!"

Both Alina and Brendan stopped and turned toward the voice and found themselves staring at a man in his midforties, with deep green eyes, light brown hair with silver touching his temples, and a slightly mischievous grin on his face.

He was handsome for an older man . . .

"You two wouldn't happen to be a Troivackian king and our one and only Daxarian princess, would you?" he asked while stepping closer and dropping his voice so that only the three of them might hear.

"I believe there is only one Troivackian king as well," Brendan noted coolly.

Who was this person?

He didn't look like a fighter judging from his relatively thin appearance.

"Ah, yes, yes! I meant no offense, Your Majes—"

The ominous warning that crossed Brendan's face made the stranger instantly cease talking, and he was forced to reroute his choice of words.

"Apologies for interrupting your outing. I am Mr. Reese Flint. I will be meeting you officially, Princess, in the near future." The man winked at Alina while giving her a charismatic smile.

The princess's gentle features hardened, and the Troivackian king growled.

Reese had the good sense to no longer look so frivolous and gave a small bow.

"Apologies again, I meant no offense. I only meant my services have been acquired for the princess at a later date and I—"

"What kind of *services* are you supposed to be providing, and who has paid for them?" Brendan demanded, his tone threatening and his stare bloodthirsty.

"O-Oh, well, it was meant to be a surprise for the princess for her birthday, so I—"

Brendan bore down on the man named Reese Flint, who subsequently gave a rather unmanly squeak and moved back hastily. When the king didn't proceed with beating the handsome from his face, he cleared his throat and tried again.

"Viscount Ashowan has purchased vocal lessons for Her Highness for her birthday."

"He did?!"

Brendan's head snapped back to see Alina's face once more filled with excitement.

"Wait, Reese Flint . . . aren't you that infamous bard who has served two different courts?!" she asked, her hands pressed together earnestly.

The musician's previous wary expression gave way to pride. "It's good to see I am not completely forgotten. Yes, Your Highness. I am indeed that very bard. I was the musician who heralded your birth in court as well as the one who entertained your father during the dark months of war."

Brendan remained unimpressed.

"Why is it you are approaching the princess so boldly here today?" he asked while observing Alina's transformative attitude toward Reese Flint, and not liking it one bit.

"Ah, forgive my impudence; after seeing you onstage and then catching the princess's profile, I couldn't help but let my curiosity get the better of me. Your Highness"—Reese turned to Alina—"while not many of us commoners have received the privilege of glimpsing you in public, you and the crown prince carry an undeniable resemblance to each other."

Alina's expression grew taut for a moment before she remembered to mask her reaction and instead issue a polite courtly smile.

"That is kind of you to say, Mr. Flint."

"Yes, though I count our crossing paths early to be quite fortuitous! You see, Your Highness, I have been working on arranging a wide repertoire of music for you to learn during our lessons, but I would love to hear more of your preferences so that we might make the most of our time together." The bard gave a slight bow and a friendly smile.

Alina was opening her mouth to reply when the two knights who had been gradually composing themselves in the theater appeared behind Reese.

"Sir, please step away from the young woman." Sir Cas's voice was sharp, and the bard nearly leapt out of his skin (much to Brendan's secret amusement).

"Sir Cas, it is alright, this man is—"

"Reese Flint?!" Sir Vohn cut the princess off before he was able to stop himself. Realizing his error, however, he quickly bowed an apology to her. "Sorry, Your Highness, I was caught off guard by the bard's presence. I have not seen him since my childhood when I would train with the crown prince."

Alina's lips twitched for a moment, but she was quicker about covering up her surprise than she had been after initially hearing about her brother from Reese. Turning back to the bard, she felt a spark of curiosity ignite as the man grinned at the knight while studying his face closely.

"Let's see . . . you said your name was Sir Vohn? I believe I remember you as one of the children in His Highness's band of friends in Rollom, yes?"

The knight smiled and crossed his arms as Sir Cas and the princess looked equally stunned.

"Ah . . . yes . . . sorry again about the . . . the Winter Solstice incident. His Highness was rather down those days, but tormenting you seemed to be one of the few joys he got."

Reese sighed, though a laugh burbled in his throat as he did so while he shook his head at the memory.

"Yes, I'm afraid when the prince and I first met— Actually he and I had both met when Lord Ashowan was still known as Mr. Ashowan, the Royal Cook . . . anyway . . . I fear the viscount at that time had colored His Highness's opinion of me."

"My brother pulled pranks on you? Like what?" Alina asked, unable to hide her interest.

Reese's grin widened when he regarded the young royal's renewed curiosity. "Princess, the stories I could tell you about your brother, I believe would surprise you a great deal."

Brendan glanced down at Alina's attentive stare and felt another burst of irritation as a begrudging realization worked its way through his awareness.

"Mr. Flint . . ." the king began slowly, the words thick in his throat as his crossed arms flexed. "Would you care to join us for a meal to tell the princess these . . . stories."

The words pained him, and he wished he could take them back; that is, until Alina turned to look at him.

Her expression was nearly indescribable, and yet it made Brendan's mind cease to work.

There was appreciation, shock, hopefulness, and . . . perhaps something a little bit more that made him feel, moderately, or a great deal more than moderately . . . well . . . happy.

"It would be my absolute honor!" Reese replied delightedly, splaying his hands on his slim hips before turning back to Sir Vohn, who looked stunned at the Troivackian's invitation. "I must admit, I have wondered for quite some time, how is it you and His Highness managed to change the tuning of *all* the instruments *and* oil all the musicians' chairs when we only left the musicians' corner for at most the time it took for us to all have a drink of water that solstice?"

Alina's jaw dropped as she turned to one of her father's elite knights, who, aside from laughing hysterically at her betrothed, had always been a model knight.

Sir Vohn winced and fidgeted as he felt the weight of the two monarchs' presence when his former mischief was revealed. "W-Well . . . it was Eri— I mean the prince's planning that had us be so, er, efficient."

There was a moment of absolute silence as the knight appeared too embarrassed to find the right words.

Letting out a grunt and rolling his eyes to the sky, Brendan startled everyone into looking at him. They had forgotten he was listening to the entire conversation.

After briefly shutting his eyes as though forcing himself to remain relatively polite, the king then fixed Sir Vohn with an expression that could only be described as defeated.

"Let us go to the tavern. Even I would like to know the details of this story."

Alina sat shoulder to shoulder with Brendan and across from the bard, who was smiling at her despite Brendan's scowl. Sir Vohn sat beside Reese Flint while Sir Cas had pulled a chair up to the end of the table.

The tavern that Alina had chosen was called the Wet Whistle, and after seating themselves on the slightly sticky booths, Brendan's eyes finally adjusted to the dim light and he looked around. He was far from pleased with the kind of company that the establishment welcomed.

He didn't get a chance to suggest moving to somewhere safer, however, before the busty auburn-haired serving wench arrived, and the knights hastily ordered ales for everyone—the princess included.

Brendan had been about to interrupt and insist that she not partake, but once again he was not given a moment to do so.

"So, you're saying my brother . . . he organized you into two groups? One for putting the instruments out of tune, and another group for oiling the chairs," the princess began, leaning forward in her seat.

"Yes, Your Highness. The musicians promptly slipped out of their chairs onto the floor, and Mr. Flint here found himself singing more than one solo to accommodate his fellow performers becoming indisposed." Sir Vohn laughed, then quickly transitioned into a cough over the bard's wry gaze.

"I must confess, I don't remember you all that well, Sir Vohn. My brother and I are eight years apart in age after all." Alina unconsciously began to pick at her thumbnail.

"Ah, you wouldn't recognize me from court, Your Highness; I'm the youngest son of a former knight. I have inherited no land myself, but the crown prince was never one to discriminate his friendships based on status, you see."

Alina smiled. "I do remember that bit about him."

Encouraged by the princess's positive reaction, the knight leaned forward conspiratorially.

"Did you happen to hear about the time we got ourselves shipwrecked on the southern islands about a year and a half ago?"

Both the princess and Troivackian king stilled.

A year and a half ago . . . that meant that Sir Vohn had been with the prince more recently than anyone else they knew, save for Viscount Ashowan.

Sensing increased alertness from the rest of the table, even the talkative bard knew not to point this out to the man. .

"What happened?" Alina asked as she feigned lighthearted interest.

"Well, it was not yet spring, and it was bloody cold . . . we had taken a boat to try our hand navigating around the infamous rocks by the islands, only we didn't fare so well. It was the prince and myself along with perhaps three other friends, all piled into a fishing vessel . . . not our brightest idea of course, but His Highness was rather adamant about it."

"Why was he so adamant?"

Sir Vohn grinned then shook his head. "I fear that is a story I most likely can't share to the fullest. I apologize for bringing it up. I wondered if His Highness had told you, and if he had, I was going to share my take of it. I imagine the king—your father would not be exactly pleased to learn that I didn't stop the prince from doing something so foolhardy, so perhaps we don't mention this again if . . . if that's alright," the knight requested, looking a little sheepish, his light brown eyes dropping to the table in a subtle bow of apology as the bar wench came and passed around the ales.

"When is it you moved from Rollom to Austice?" Alina asked while taking a small sip from the tankard that required her to use two hands to lift; she hoped he wasn't going to force the entire subject to change.

Brendan watched her out of the corner of his eye.

He was willing to wager that a few mouthfuls of the drink in her hands would render her immobile.

"Oh, I transferred up last spring for my qualifying exam under Captain Taylor to see if I was fit to be an elite knight, with the crown prince's recommendation," Sir Vohn added, a hint of pride passing through his features.

Alina gave him a warm smile, but Brendan could see the pain in her eyes that she was working to hide.

"Last spring, you mean a few months ago?" Reese Flint asked offhandedly.

It was the first moment Brendan had been grateful the bard was present.

They needed the knight to keep talking before he realized he was revealing precious information.

"Ah, I wasn't clear. No, I came up just over a year ago." Sir Vohn nodded his head, but his good humor was dwindling as he glanced around the table at the attentive faces.

A small frown began to work its way across his brow. "Is something the matter?"

Sir Cas spoke up then.

"Er . . . I don't think I've met anyone in the past three years who has seen the prince and spoken about it." He was the newest addition to the elite rank of the knights. Though despite at least seven years of knighthood being a requirement, meaning he had to at the very least be in his late twenties, Sir Cas looked to be a similar age to the princess.

His short blond hair and round face were the primary culprits in giving him a boyish appearance.

Sir Vohn stared at his comrade's somber expression, then slowly turned to the princess, who looked like a rabbit caught in the carrot patch by the gardener.

"Well . . . I don't understand why that would be the case. His Highness is perfectly fine . . ." the knight began before trailing off as though a sudden thought were occurring to him.

He blinked several times, his hand curling around the handle of his tankard. Then he closed his eyes with a small cringe.

"Oh. I'd forgotten . . . what the viscount said . . . I'm so sorry, Princess. That was thoughtless of me. We were just talking about some of the mischief His Highness got into in his youth when he was upset about moving to Rollom, and I just happened to think of the most recent event . . . I'm sorry."

"What is it that Viscount Ashowan said to you?" Brendan demanded, as Sir Vohn began withdrawing from the conversation.

"Knowing our beloved house witch, it was probably something along the lines of 'do be a dear and keep quiet about having seen the prince as it might upset certain people,'" Reese Flint interrupted airily while taking a deeper drink from his ale.

Alina's eyes snapped to the bard, and it was then she noticed something . . .

Reese Flint had a knowingness in his eyes that he didn't bother to hide when he gazed calmly back at her.

"Mr. Flint, did *you* happen to see my brother recently?" She rounded on him, the sharpness in her tone taking everyone aback.

The bard opened his mouth to reply when a sudden burst of violence broke out in a booth by the bar.

A large man was being restrained by two smaller companions as he lunged for someone standing in his way. The bartender was ambling over wearily, clearly having experienced such occurrences more times than he could count, only he had not been prepared for the table of men where Alina sat to burst into motion the moment the fight broke out.

Springing into action, the knights stood and created a human shield as Brendan roughly hauled Alina up, and then ushered her past the bar to the back entrance.

How did he even know where this exit was?! Alina found herself thinking as the series of movements happened faster than she could properly process. The group burst out into the alley that was fortunately empty, but Sir Cas began leading them to the left toward a main road.

Sadly, in the chaos of her knights and betrothed whisking her away from the tavern to the back alley, Reese Flint had strode away quickly in the opposite direction without another word.

Before she could stop the bard, Sir Cas gave a single sharp whistle and a black carriage with no adornments pulled up at the opposite end to the alley that Reese Flint had taken.

There was nothing she could do, but at least all was not lost.

She had the name of, and private music lessons with, someone who may have seen her brother far more recently than anyone else.

And that was more hope than she'd had in years.

Chapter 34

ROOFTOP REVELATIONS

As soon as the carriage reached the castle steps, Brendan exited, and then helped Alina down. Sirs Vohn and Cas dismounted their steeds in front and behind the carriage, followed by the other knights who had followed at a greater distance.

Smiling thankfully up at Brendan, and not being hasty to release his hand, Alina then looked to the castle entrance and noticed her father standing there with Mr. Howard at his side.

The Daxarian king looked ready to kill someone.

Uncertainty and apprehension filled Alina's belly, until Brendan's grip around her hand tightened. Then, as though he had cast some kind of spell, a small swell of strength surged to the pit of her belly, allowing her legs to move, regardless of her worry, up the castle steps until she was face-to-face with her father.

"I was told you two were going for a walk," Norman began coldly. "It is now nearly dinnertime, and you have been gone since this morning— Did you two ride in the carriage without a chaperone?!"

Alina's eyes widened, and all reasonable thoughts left her head.

"Your Majesty, Sirs Vohn and Cas rode along each side of the carriage windows and had a full view of us the entire duration of our time together," Brendan interjected calmly.

Norman rounded on the Troivackian king, nearly making Brendan put his hand on the hilt of his dagger out of habit.

"Where were you all this time?"

"W-We went and saw a play—" Alina started nervously.

"A *PLAY*?! In the dark?" Norman roared, making Alina take a step back so that she was almost behind Brendan.

"Sirs Vohn and Cas sat directly behind us," Brendan clarified immediately.

Norman looked past Brendan where the two knights who had been the supposed chaperones stood at attention, their eyes cast downward dutifully.

"Is this true?"

"Yes, Your Majesty," both men answered in perfect unison.

"Nothing happened, I swear, Father. It was a perfectly innocent outing! I . . . I will go . . . change for dinner." Alina released Brendan's hand and slowly crept around her father, who seemed deaf to her as he continued glaring daggers at her future husband.

When she was at the doors, she mouthed a heartfelt apology to her betrothed, who didn't dare acknowledge her message—he was all too aware of the fact that he was a muscle twitch away from the Daxarian king taking the nearest weapon and killing him on the spot. Witnesses or not.

Alina resolved to grovel for Brendan's forgiveness over her cowardice at dinner should he still be intact by then . . .

Once safely behind the closed doors of the castle, she raised a hand to her chest, shut her eyes, and managed a shaky breath before taking a step forward and bumping into someone.

Stumbling back but catching herself against the front door, Alina managed to straighten herself and discover that she had walked into none other than Tamlin Ashowan.

The young man's eyes were lost to the present world. His face was pale, and there was a hopelessness about him that seemed to ward off the servants who filed past his peculiar location.

"Er . . . Tam?" Alina waved her hand in front of his face, trying to break him out of whatever trance he seemed to be stuck in.

When he still didn't respond, she reached out and pinched his arm.

He jolted back from the sharp pain and blinked several times.

"Ah, Princess, my apologies." He bowed.

"Not a problem, but . . . is everything alright?" she asked with a small frown

"I . . . wouldn't . . . say so, no," Tam replied vaguely before shuddering.

Alina waited, but his gaze was growing haunted again and she worried he'd drift away before telling her anything, so she gingerly poked his forehead and once again forced him back to reality.

"Tam! What's the matter?" she asked nervously. She had always known he was a tad aloof, but this was something else entirely.

"TAMLIN ASHOWAN! TAMLIN ASHOWN, WHERE HAVE YOU GONE? I TOLD YOU THAT I— Oh, hello, Princess!"

Alina leaned to the side to peer around Tam and found Royal Mage Keith Lee descending the grand staircase behind Tam with his usual broad smile.

"Mage Lee," she greeted with a small curtsy before turning her questioning gaze to the youngest Ashowan.

"Ah, pardon my interruption, Princess, but Lord Tam here is to assist me for the next month with my work, but he keeps disappearing and it is growing rather tiresome. Come along, Lord Tam! Just because it's nearly dinnertime doesn't mean we slack off! Now, I want us to conclude the chapter we began working on today as it is imperative that I may finish my autobiography before the end of the year."

The mage had turned back around and was already chattering to himself while once again mounting the stairs, unaware that Tam hadn't moved an inch or even acknowledged the chastisement.

Alina stared at the future viscount with a small smile.

"Tam . . . did my father—"

"It's my punishment. For an entire month."

At long last Tam looked at her, his features stressed as he tentatively reached out and gripped her shoulders.

"Please . . . never again ask me to help you. I can't ever do this again . . . I'm sorry."

"LORD TAMLIN!" Mage Keith Lee's voice roared down the stairs.

Giving Alina's shoulders one final squeeze, Tam turned, and like a man facing the executioner's block, trudged toward the stairs.

Alina waved to her friend's back, a pang of guilt making her wince.

"I'm so sorry, Tam. I swear, one day I will repay this debt!"

The future viscount weakly waved over his shoulder to indicate he had heard her, then continued his climb to his doom.

Katarina Ashowan was resting comfortably in one of her favorite places of her childhood home as the brilliant glowing sunset waved its dying rays against the orange sky.

Despite the beauty of the sunset, she had her back to the view.

In fact, she was sitting on the roof peak of her bedroom balcony, leaning against the fine stone spire with her legs dangling on either side of the masterfully crafted stone.

She was still wearing her emerald dress that she had worn to see the king earlier that day, but she had removed her jewelry and her long waving red hair fluttered freely in the breeze, as the waves of the Alcide Sea crashed against the cliff over and over.

She stared at the rock wall before her that led to another peak of her home built into the cliff. While the scenery behind her was always spectacular, sometimes she needed less stimulating sights to wade through her thoughts.

"Rough day?"

Kat resisted jumping at the familiar voice.

Looking up, she regarded Likon, the boy her parents had taken in thirteen years prior, peering at her from over his own balcony ledge.

She didn't bother answering as he skillfully descended from the balcony until he could comfortably seat himself across from her. His light brown eyes studied her patiently.

"When did you get back?" Kat asked while folding her arms across her middle.

"A little while ago," he answered vaguely.

"Let me guess, work for my parents you can't talk about?"

Likon's weary smile and brief nod made Kat roll her eyes.

"I don't understand why they trust you more than their own children. Honestly, it feels like my mother is trying to get you to take over the viscount title," the young lady muttered bitterly before watching Likon grow tense.

"Wait, is that what's going on?! Are they finally going to admit my brother is doing shit all to prepare to take over?" Kat's golden eyes sparkled, and Likon for a moment was humbled by their magic.

After a breath of stillness, he dropped his chin down, his white tunic hanging loosely across his chest as his freshly washed dark brown hair fell forward.

"Come on, you can tell me that much!" Kat goaded, feeling a devilish smile take over her mouth.

Releasing a long sigh, Likon raised his gaze to her once more. "You seem oddly happy about the idea," he observed ambiguously.

Letting out a snort, Kat slumped back even more against the spiral, her smile faded, and in its place was anger.

"I'm tired of being the devil to his perfect witch."

Likon had heard her make the same rant thousands of times, but he waited to listen yet again without any attempt to interrupt her.

"You know how the first witch always is praised as being the perfect bridge between nature and the Gods, while Satan is the one who failed his family and tries to destroy everything good? That's Tam and I. He wasn't extraordinary in his studies, he learned how to wield daggers better than me, I'll admit, but . . . just because he doesn't get in trouble doesn't mean he's perfect! It just means he does nothing! It's like all he wants to *be* is nothing, because he is so scared of whatever it is that happened when we were children."

Kat shook her head irritably. "He won't tell anyone what happened! So he's going to shrivel up and die alone because he can't be bothered to try and be better. Meanwhile, I try all the time and all I get is punished."

"Kitty Kat?" Likon asked quietly.

"Don't call me that. You know I made Da stop calling me that years ago. Only Hannah still refers to me that way now."

"I know, but you'll let me because I'm your favorite person in the whole wide world," Likon teased with a smile.

She laughed but didn't contradict him.

"Kat, that thing you told me about years ago . . . is it still . . . is it getting worse?"

The young noblewoman's face froze, then melted into a look of open pain and fear.

She swallowed with great difficulty.

"Yes. It . . . It isn't getting better like I was hoping."

"How are you controlling it?" Likon asked, his hands gripping the roof as he tried not to convey the full extent of his worry.

"I just try to keep moving. Though lately it's been harder. I know I'm doing stupid things . . . mindless things, and I know it's my fault, but . . . they don't understand. They don't know how hard it is to . . . to . . ."

"Think clearly?" Likon supplied quietly.

"Yeah." Kat reached up and wiped away the tears from her eyes hastily before they could fall.

Sliding forward so that they sat toe-to-toe, Likon reached out, and gently touched her cheek, drawing her eyes back to him.

"Don't tell me to tell my father! He'll just get scared, or summon another teacher, or . . . worry. I don't want them to know," Kat burst out, her voice frustrated but her face saddened.

Likon gently tugged a lock of her hair. "Hey. I'm not telling them anything. It has to come from you. You know you're my real master."

Kat's chest ached as she stared at his softened gaze and familiar face.

He'd been there for her for almost as far back as she could remember.

"I don't know what'll happen if one day it gets the best of me," Kat croaked, suddenly unable to hold his gaze. "I have to become the princess's handmaiden, and . . . I have to be still for most of what we do and I don't know if I can do it."

Likon reached up with his other hand and forced her to face him directly, her eyes once again meeting his. Somehow her tears made her seem even more untouchable.

"You're an Ashowan. You just need to find a way to handle this, and you will. Keep looking for an answer, and you know if you ever need my help, I'm there."

Kat couldn't speak past the lump in her throat, only nodded as she allowed unbidden tears to fall.

Likon didn't release her face as he continued to gently rub his thumb against her cheek, waiting for her to calm down.

"Why couldn't *you* have been my brother?" Kat asked with a watery chuckle.

"Because the Gods assumed I had enough problems," Likon replied quietly, only half teasing.

Kat felt a new wave of grief flood her being as she stared into his eyes.

"I'm sorry you're in love with me."

Her words hung in the air, and she watched the familiar, horrible sight of pain filling Likon's face before he managed to conceal it again.

"Don't be. It isn't your fault. I didn't have a chance when you made my Winter Solstice wish come true all those years ago." He then leaned his forehead to hers, the touch causing the heady rush to fill his being. "You still feel the same about me as before, I take it?"

Kat reached up between them and wiped away the fluids leaking from her nose.

"Given that you aren't self-conscious about doing something as gross as that, I will take it as a yes." Likon sighed, but he managed a smile.

With great hesitancy, he leaned forward and kissed her forehead before finally releasing her and leaning back, his hands falling to the peak and his shoulders hunching.

"If you want me to avoid you or not bare my soul to you, I—"

Likon held up his hand, stopping her. "Your mother sends me all over the continent and to foreign lands on a regular basis. One of these days, I'm going to find myself a fine woman, with breasts that could make a man weep, and you will be left regretting turning me down as I shower her in riches and attention."

Kat laughed while wiping away the last of her tears. "I will call her sister and welcome her into the family with open arms. I will also thank her for helping you see that I would be the worst wife in the world as I am too outspoken, unrefined, and impulsive to give anyone a peaceful life."

Another moment of forced joviality and sadness passed between them, which made Kat regret her words. Knowing that any further discussion on the matter would only result in more heartache, she tried with renewed vigor to change the subject.

"Are you going to be in Austice for long this time?"

Likon gave a partial shrug. "I haven't a clue. I just got back . . . Though I think your mother wants me to stay until the end of summer at least."

"That's good . . . I think by the fall I'll be rather sick of you." Kat playfully tapped her toe against his shin.

Gently, Likon returned the kick, his smile genuine this time. "I heard about your brother's punishment. I think I already saw your father and him breaking into the Troivackian moonshine."

Kat cackled. "I have to admit, hearing his punishment was by far the best part of my day. The look on his face . . . I know I'm an awful sister to admit this—"

"—At least you know you're an awful sister," Likon added sagely.

Glaring, Kat continued her train of thought. "It was nice to not be the only one having to face some consequences."

"Keep in mind he is only in trouble because he was trying to help you, Kitty Kat. Your brother . . . Your brother might be feeling something similar to you, you know. We all know he has some kind of magic. Maybe it's doing to him what it's doing to you," Likon reasoned slowly, knowing that the topic of Kat's sibling could be met with a variety of strong emotions.

Surprisingly, however, she refolded her arms across her middle and raised a lazy eyebrow at him.

"Can't I just gloat for a day before feeling terrible again?"

Likon laughed. "The sun has set. Your day is officially over."

Kat grinned in response and turned her face up to the pale sky where two stars had already begun to twinkle happily.

"So it has."

Likon studied her face for several extra moments before he too turned to look upward.

"By the way, they're sending me to Troivack with the princess," Kat announced matter-of-factly.

As Likon's head jerked back down and he stared wide-eyed at her, his heart tripped over itself and his stomach lurched unpleasantly.

Kat gave him a small apologetic glance before her already glowing eyes fell down toward his chest.

"Not for forever, but a year . . . I leave after they're married. So maybe

while I'm gone you can finally find that busty wench you're already so fond
of—"

Likon reached for her and pulled her into himself, hugging her tightly,
his heart pounding. He didn't dare let her look at him and risk his control
weakening to the point of stealing a kiss that he had no right owning.

Even though it would not have been the first time he had done so with
her, he didn't wish to add another burden onto her shoulders.

So he held on to her as long as she would allow. Already fearful of how
she seemed to be slipping further and further away from him . . . with no
hope of him ever closing the distance again.

Chapter 35

A PRINCESS'S PREMIER

A lina smiled happily as she glanced around the table of nobles, who all had looked moderately uncomfortable over her presence during their meetings that morning.

Though none of them could come close to the awkwardness of the princess's new handmaiden.

Lady Katarina Ashowan looked pale, and even slightly sweaty, as she gripped the arms of her chair. Her eyes were wide, staring blankly at the table in front of her. Though what was even more disconcerting to the poor young baron across from Kat was that she hadn't appeared to have blinked in an hour.

Meanwhile, Viscount Ashowan sat closer to the king at the opposite end of the table and was deep in conversation with Lord Fuks.

"The first hour was a bit dry, but by the end of the third I must admit I'm really excited for the discussion that we will get to be a part of after lunch!" Alina whispered to her friend as she pretended to be oblivious to the murmurs going around the table along with the disparaging side-eyes directed at them.

The Daxarian king had stepped out to relieve himself, and they all needed to wait for him to return and tell them the next topic of their meeting. Presumably it would be about Zinfera as rumors had been circulating about the aging emperor.

"Alina, after lunch are there . . . *more* discussions?" Kat asked as she forced her expression to remain as blank as possible—which only made her look all the more deranged.

"Well, after lunch there will be the fiscal review of the kingdom's finances as well as a discussion on the allotted budget for my wedding . . ."

Kat's head dropped back against her chair roughly, as though she had been hoping the force of it would render her unconscious.

"Honestly, are these meetings really so bad?" Alina giggled before noticing how unhinged her friend's gaze had become. "Goodness, you really don't do well sitting still . . . how did you study when you were growing up?"

"I was given frequent breaks. At least once an hour."

Alina's eyebrows shot upward. "That . . . is surprising. Was your brother as bad?"

Kat shook her head. "No. He preferred sitting and working for hours on end. If he could, I'm certain he'd stay glued to his desk."

Alina thought back to the day Tam had fought with Brendan in the ring, recalling that he had appeared to be quite skilled with a sword as well. Perhaps he had always been the studious type while his sister . . .

Despite recalling the glee Katarina had taken in teasing Alina in the woods on their camping escapade, the princess couldn't help but feel a pang of sympathy for her friend's distress as it appeared far more uncomfortable.

However, she was unable to ask Katarina more about her issues with sitting still as her father, the king, had returned.

"I thank everyone for waiting. Today, we are going to discuss the issue of the Zinferan emperor's declining health, as it pertains to his concubines."

Many of the more elderly lords perked up.

"As he grows more frail, some of the concubines are growing more unruly and daring in their activities. Normally the empress would be the one responsible for managing the women's behavior; however, Emperor Taejo never chose an empress. Instead, he has a harem of several women from powerful families, and not all of them are adhering to ethical practices. In fact, some of the princes and princesses are going missing. It is suspected that the third concubine is trying to strong-arm the emperor into putting her in charge of the harem," Norman explained calmly.

"Your Majesty, are you suggesting that the concubines are murdering the possible heirs of the empire?" a marquis spoke up, leaning forward with a frown.

"Didn't you say that they are missing? Should we not suspend assumptions they are being murdered until we have more information?" Alina jumped in, making every eye turn to her, causing her to blush.

"No ransom has been requested, so it is a fair assumption that they are deceased," Norman pointed out evenly.

Alina felt her face flame even brighter.

"It's possible they could have smuggled in assassins with the new waves of slaves they have been bringing in. Apparently entire starving villages have been pressured into signing away their lives to some of the concubine's families," Captain Taylor informed everyone sternly.

"Precisely. Which brings me to the topic of our discussion today." Norman straightened in his seat and cast his gaze around the table. "Should we intervene, and if so, to what degree?"

"If we storm the emperor's palace with our military, it would undoubtedly force a war to break out," an earl who was one of the younger members of nobility present volunteered.

"If we send only a handful of diplomats, they could still respond poorly and our relationship with them could turn sour regardless," Lord Fuks's son, Les, reasoned. "They shouldn't be trading slaves to begin with; they know our stance on this. We could always approach the matter indirectly and reduce our trading with them until they agree to our terms. It could be the wake-up call their officials need to get things in order."

"That'd be too indirect," Finlay Ashowan countered. "Such a subtle move would only give the impression that without the emperor's leadership we aren't willing to work with them. What might be within our purview according to Lord Ryu is that we try and encourage the emperor to at long last select an heir who could begin to take over the duties."

"The emperor has made it well known that the selected heir will be revealed at the time of his death. This is most likely why the concubines may be trying to eliminate some of the children who seemed the most likely to take over," Lord Richard Fuks reminded everyone wisely.

"He might be willing to change his mind about naming the next heir if we suggest these problems could be handled by whoever he chooses as his successor." Fin turned to Norman, who was frowning but nodding along with the flow of the discussion.

"Couldn't a bigger issue be how these heinous acts are being perceived by the general public or the emperor's closest allies? The murder and slave trading must be conducted with some powerful figures involved, but how many and how far reaching their influence is could make the matter of another heir pointless. It sounds like we need more information," Alina spoke out, once again making every eye fly to her. This time she gripped her hands more tightly in her lap and tried to appear confident.

"We have the invaluable insight of Lord Ryu, who has been a longtime diplomat for the —" The same marquis who had spoken before had begun taking a less than friendly tone with her, but Alina was quick to cut him off.

"One informant can't give us all the information. That would be like asking you, Marquis Fassi, the well-being of your own home and only hearing your answer. When there are your stewards, your Head of Housekeeping, your maids, and of course, Lady Fassi. They may have more to say on that matter."

The room fell into silence.

Everyone knew Marquis Fassi was in the midst of attempting to placate his wife, who had found out about not one, not two, not three, but four mistresses.

"Her Highness makes a fair point; however, learning more can be dangerous as well as it could be seen as illegally gathering information for potentially harmful reasons from Zinfera," Lord Richard Fuks commented, his eyes twinkling at the princess while Marquis Fassi gritted his teeth from across the table.

"True, but surely getting to know more Zinferan nobles and their thoughts on the state of their court via a diplomatic envoy we send would give more clarity to the situation. Not only that, but it could also give a better idea of what angle to approach the emperor with regarding both his succession and the slave trading," Alina countered back to the elder Lord Fuks, who gave her a wink of approval.

Marquis Fassi was opening his mouth again, when Norman held up his hand silencing everyone.

"I believe that the way this dialogue has moved indicates that we are all of the belief that military intervention is still too aggressive at this time. However, a diplomatic envoy who could gather information and also persuade the emperor may be beneficial. For this task I personally believe Viscount Ashowan would be best suited. Would anyone else like to object or volunteer their services?"

Everyone glanced back and forth at one another uncertainly.

It was rare for the king to send away their greatest source of protection; however, no one could refute that Finlay Ashowan had a long history of resolving situations amicably, and usually with minimal violence. It also helped that one of the emperor's advisers was none other than Lord Jiho Ryu, a close friend of the viscount's.

"Good. Then it is settled. Lord Ashowan, I will arrange a ship for you and your personally selected attendants to leave before the end of summer, does this sound agreeable?"

The viscount bowed his chin to the king. "Yes, Your Majesty."

"Excellent. Now then, shall we all retire for the luncheon hour?"

Alina leaned back in her chair with a grin on her face.

Her heart was hammering, her palms were sweaty, but . . .

She had loved being a part of the discussions, and she was more than a little pleased that there only seemed to be one person who was taking an outward exception to her presence.

Katarina on the other hand looked like she needed a bath as her knee bounced mercilessly under the table, and her forehead perspired heavily.

"Good Gods, are you unwell?" Alina asked as the nobles began to stand and file out of the council room. She turned to search for the viscount to alert him of his daughter's state, when Kat pressed her burning hand to Alina's arm, drawing her attention back.

"Princess, would you mind if I went for a walk? I think some fresh air might clear my head."

"Of course I won't mind," Alina replied, her worry increasing.

"Also, please don't mention this to my da. It's fine, I promise. I just need to get used to this is all." Kat managed a brief smile before giving her friend's arm an appreciative squeeze.

Slowly, the young royal nodded her consent, and with a quiet breath of relief, Kat launched herself from her seat and fled the council room without another glance back.

"Ah, Princess, did Kat already head down for lunch?"

Alina nearly leapt out of her skin when Viscount Finlay Ashowan's voice sounded just behind her right shoulder.

"Ah, y-yes, or rather, I believe she said she was going for a walk," the princess replied while giving a strained smile that was meant to be reassuring.

Fin's brows furrowed, but as he opened his mouth to ask another question, the king joined them.

"Well done, Alina! You handled that well today," Norman proudly complimented his daughter.

His good mood was a breath of fresh air for the nobility who witnessed the exchange, as everyone had grown rather wary of their leader in light of his recent feud with the Troivackian king.

"Thank you." Alina curtsied, her face bright with gladness. "Viscount, I'm sorry to hear you will be leaving us for a while; I've been enjoying getting to know you and your family."

Fin smiled warmly down at her. "I will be sad to leave as well, Your Highness. However, I will do my best to return as quickly as possible . . . Ideally, I'll manage to make it back before the Winter Solstice." He sighed while earning an appreciative nod from Norman.

"I know how you dislike leaving the viscountess for so long, but this could be an excellent chance for your son, Tam, to start practicing for taking over given that you have been discussing—" Norman began.

Fin's expression shifted as he quickly shook his head ever so slightly, making the king fall silent.

Alina turned stiffly to face the viscount.

"Do you mean to tell me you have even *more* secrets? Honestly, Lord Ashowan, I had heard rumors you were terrible at hiding your nonsense! Now I'm thinking those rumors were started as a joke!" she snapped before she could stop herself.

Both Fin and her father looked greatly surprised by her outburst, and for a moment she considered apologizing, but when both men remained silent, decided against it. Instead she folded her arms and waited.

After another beat of silence and the last of nobility had cleared the room leaving only the trio and Mr. Howard behind, Fin addressed Alina more directly, his expression apologetic. However, she had seen and heard enough apologies from him already.

"I'm guessing Tam taking over the duties has something to do about you relinquishing the viscount title for him? Why should that be such a big secret?"

"Princess, that is because people are already concerned about Tam taking over. There are several other factors that at this time are of a confidential nature. I apologize that the king and I must keep things from you, but—"

Alina waved his next words off angrily as she began to turn to the door to leave.

"Alina, the viscount is entitled to privacy in his family matters," Norman interrupted her departure gently.

"Then why does he get to know more about our own damn family matters than the *actual* family members?"

Without giving her father or Finlay time to stop her, Alina stormed from the room.

As time goes on, I'm beginning to see why the Troivackian king is so suspicious of the viscount.

Once her thoughts had turned to Brendan, however, Alina felt her mood pick up, and she found herself suddenly incredibly grateful that she was on her way to eat lunch at his side. Perhaps he may have some insight on how to handle the situation . . . or perhaps she would find something new to tease him about.

Either way, she was beginning to walk a little bit faster toward the banquet hall to see him.

Chapter 36

FLYING SPARKS

"Then I asked why the viscount got to know about all our family nonsense, but we couldn't know his!" Alina had just finished recounting her confrontation earlier that day to Brendan, who had been unable to join her for lunch but made sure to make it to their nightly walk around the castle grounds.

Katarina followed behind them at a distance with three maids. The daughter of the house witch had not been informed of the princess's spat with her father, as when she had returned from her "walk," she had reappeared in a different dress and her hair sopping wet just in time for the last meeting of the day. Alina had decided she would discuss the details with her friend when she seemed less . . . stressed.

"You are right to be angry about the viscount's private knowledge of your brother. However, the viscount relinquishing his title for his son is information that people in Troivack are killed over. I understand it being a private matter," Brendan replied evenly as they rounded the front of the castle to begin their second lap.

"Well, people don't usually get killed in Daxaria over a legitimate son inheriting a title," Alina pointed out, only slightly irked that Brendan was siding with her father on the matter.

"The viscount isn't just a viscount, however. He is the hero of Daxaria. To what extent is he stepping down? This could send the message that he is no longer going to protect Daxaria in times of war. Not only that, but he is a diplomat for the Coven of Wittica. Does Lord Tamlin also take on that title? Is he capable of assuming all these responsibilities when, as far as everyone is aware, he is nowhere near as powerful as his father?"

Alina found her frustration melt into defeat as she realized the truth to his words.

"Furthermore, Princess, you should exercise more caution when telling others these things. It could cause rumors that would then make more problems."

Feeling herself grow more than slightly embarrassed at the small lecture, Alina's grip on Brendan's arm tightened. "I didn't tell other people, I just . . . am telling you . . . because I believe spouses should tell each other these things and it will be safe. I mean, when we are in Troivack together we can't have secrets. I believe spouses, especially rulers, should be transparent and—"

Brendan's look of apprehension made Alina's stomach flip.

"*Are* we going to have secrets?" Alina felt her throat begin to close. Why was she becoming upset so quickly? Perhaps because she had been so excited to see him, and he seemed somber for some reason that evening.

"There are some things my vassals will confide in me, and it is not my business to share with you. Not all matters that I handle will be communicated with you."

The princess stopped then turned Brendan to face her directly.

"For personal matters I understand need to be kept between friends, but . . . pertaining to ourselves and the kingdom, shouldn't I know everything you do if we are to rule together?"

Brendan stared down perplexed at her. She seemed upset, but surely she knew that a king and queen were privy to very different information, surely her own parents . . .

A light went on in the Troivackian king's mind.

"Princess, do you mean to tell me that your parents shared *all* information with each other?" he asked slowly.

"Yes! The courtiers all understood that my parents were ruling jointly. My mother was a princess and my father was a baron's son, it only made sense that they conferred together on— Why are you staring at me like that? You said you wanted Troivack to evolve and bring women onto more equal footing!"

"More, yes. However, it will not be exactly like here, Princess. Troivack will always be different from Daxaria. There will be things I will not share with you. You will be tasked with keeping the court women in line and maintaining positive relationships with them to further strengthen our position with regard to including them in discussions and changing laws pertaining to inheritance." As he spoke, Brendan was beginning to grow more concerned by the tears he saw rising in Alina's eyes.

"So we will have secrets from each other, and . . . and rule completely separate areas? Will I even get final say on what I decide with my own duties?"

Brendan's answer was no, but he was starting to suspect she wanted him to say yes . . . He was saved responding, however, when she continued her questioning.

"If as a woman I am not privy to secrets, then I don't understand why you are so angry on my behalf that my father isn't telling me about my brother!" Alina's tone was rising, and the Troivackian king felt his face turning stony.

"I am angry because your brother is supposed to be taking over to rule Daxaria. Your father has left his kingdom's future uncertain, which in turn affects my own kingdom as it is unclear whether or not you will be Daxaria's queen."

"So because of the political implications, you were bothered?" Alina's voice rasped as she attempted to lower her voice when two guards near the castle entrance turned their attention toward them.

"I didn't like you being sad, either. I've . . . I've come to grow quite fond of you, and if I am honest I do not quite understand why you are becoming so upset." Brendan spoke evenly, as though he were trying to manage her, and that alone only made Alina want to scream at him all the more.

"I thought you said you were always truthful," she snapped as she recognized the angry tears were once again coming to her eyes.

"I am. I am telling you now that there are things I will not be sharing with you because they are private dealings as a king."

"Will I be afforded the same privacy without your intervention in my rulings should I deem it necessary?" Alina's eyes flashed as she repeated her earlier question, and Brendan had fought enough people to recognize a warning.

Even so. He would not lie.

"No. I am Troivack's leader, I need to—"

"Aren't I supposed to be one of Troivack's leaders?" she interrupted. By then she was nearly shouting.

The guards by the castle doors were beginning to take tentative steps forward as the princess's voice carried over to them.

"In a way. But your knowledge and understanding of my kingdom will not be to the same degree as my own. Should you not know something or commit an error I need to be able to—"

"So I'm on a leash? For how long? How long before I am trusted to make changes? You indicated you wanted help ruling, but you are now saying that you merely want someone to handle the women just like your predecessors. Tell me, what is it you want to be different exactly?"

Brendan was becoming annoyed over her constant interruption.

"You will be minded until your knowledge is sufficient to work without close observation," he started, his voice coming out a growl and his dark eyes sharp. "I intend for you to be apprised of decisions prior to official public announcements, and in the event of my death, you will rule with the help of my advisers until an heir takes over. The most significant hurdle we will need to work jointly on will be allowing women to hold titles and to freely make decisions regarding their estates."

Alina took another step back away from Brendan as her face grew pale.

"As your wife, would my opinion regarding your decisions and announcements have any effect?"

Brendan felt his will begin to fortify against her wrath.

"No. You would merely be aware of what was happening."

Not trusting herself to speak, Alina gathered her wits as quickly as possible; her heart began to race as another subtle thing he had said nagged at her . . .

"You said *an* heir. Not . . . *our* heir. Or *our* son." She wasn't sure why that particular ambiguous wording had stuck out to her, but as the rest of the world had faded away, all she saw was the object of her fury.

Especially when she saw the slightest flinch in the corner of Brendan's eyes.

No one else would have been able to see it, but she had learned the meaning of the tiniest movements in his face.

"Do you already have children, Your Majesty?"

The guards who had been drawing nearer to the couple halted in their tracks and slowly backed up several steps.

Brendan continued to stare down coldly at her.

"I do not."

Alina folded her arms across her middle, her gaze intense despite the occasional tear falling. "Then why did you word it like that?"

Brendan's palms were beginning to sweat . . .

He had faced far more savage and bloodthirsty opponents, yet he hadn't felt so . . . off balance since the first year following his coronation.

"Your Majesty?" Alina's sharp tone brought him back to the present, and perhaps it was because she had jarred him from his thoughts that he spoke before considering his words more carefully.

"It is a well-known fact that your mother had significant troubles carrying children. For your safety it has been discussed that other possible heirs may be required."

"Are you . . . telling me . . ." Alina took a full, careful breath as she felt the threat of an attack drawing nearer. "That you intend to take a mistress . . . or that you never intend for us to have children?"

Brendan felt sick. A fear unlike anything he had ever known was making an unseemly tremor run through his hands, making him ball them into fists . . . all because of the ragged hurt in her voice.

"My vassals were the ones to make the suggestions," he managed to say after a moment of quiet passed between them.

"You . . . are such a coward. You're considering it and don't want to own up to it." Alina's voice had quieted, and that made her words cut Brendan all the more deeply.

"There is no reason to address this with you as a decision has not been made," he replied, though it was becoming harder to keep his voice level. There was a rattling in his chest that told him he was nearing an end of his patience. It would be wise for him to leave the situation to calm down soon.

"Oh no, a decision has most definitely been made. This is like us getting married all over again. You decide things about *my* Godsdamn life without making me a part of the discussion. I thought you had moved past this, but I suppose I was wrong."

"I am not going to ignore the concerns of my supporters and your potential death. I am considering which outcomes would be best for everyone involved," Brendan replied as he noted Alina's toes turning away from him.

"Well, let me tell you why you're wasting your time thinking about such things, Your Majesty." Alina's gaze was angry, and pained, and it made the king's shoulders slump as the twist in his gut worsened.

"I will never stay with a man who is willing to take a mistress while married, doesn't consult with me about matters that affect *our* married life, or won't be willing to give me children. I believe in light of this discussion w-we should end the engagement here. I-I will inform my father." Alina moved away from him, and instinctively Brendan reached for her, but instead of the advancement of the guards forcing him to stop, it was the burning touch of a woman's hand as Katarina Ashowan raised her angry golden eyes to him.

When had she moved closer?

"You will leave her alone, or you will be on the next boat to Troivack." Katarina Ashowan's tone was deadly, and despite her being a mere daughter of a viscount, Brendan could tell that she intended to have her way—or at the very least become a rather large annoyance in his life should he disobey.

So he stared at Alina's retreating back, his thoughts jarring and broken in panic, then turned back to Katarina, who had removed her hand but was watching him closely.

"Good evening, Your Majesty." The redhead then executed a flawless curtsy and left him alone outside the castle as the last of Alina's maids followed her.

Brendan's hand moved to the hilt of his sword before he turned and began taking long strides back down the way they had come.

He needed to calm down. Fast. Sparring. Yes. That always helped . . .

The Troivackian king had hoped taking the long way to the barracks meant he'd burn a small fraction of the ire or work off the throbbing that wracked his heart and stomach. Otherwise, there was a greater chance of accidentally killing whomever he sparred with.

By the time he reached the ring, however, he knew he was far from being calm. If anything, the movement had fanned the flames of whatever it was he was feeling. To make matters significantly worse, standing just outside the entrance of the ring was none other than Lord Finlay Ashowan.

The viscount was shaking hands with one of the king's elite knights, who then bowed to Fin and proceeded back toward the castle—most likely for an ale with his comrades—without noticing Brendan.

When the viscount turned around, he appeared perfectly at ease and unaware of the looming threat.

"Ah, Your Majesty. How was your walk with the princess this evening?" Fin asked pleasantly.

Brendan didn't answer; instead he continued striding straight to the viscount, then he grabbed the tall slender man by the front of his tunic, making his eyes widen in surprise just before the Troivackian threw him into the sparring ring.

A small burst of wind softened Fin's fall as he landed squarely on his feet, though his knees buckled and his blue eyes began to glow as the sun touched the horizon and set the sky ablaze in bright red.

"Your Majesty, what in the world are you doing?" Fin's voice was annoyingly breezy, despite Brendan slamming the gate closed behind himself. He drew his sword and continued moving purposefully closer to the viscount.

Fin blinked in confusion.

"Spar with me, witch. I want to see what kind of great power it is that Daxarians have such unwavering faith in."

The king swung his sword halfheartedly at Fin, more as a warning, only for the viscount to duck easily and sidestep the monarch, his eyes narrowing.

"Your Majesty, if you would like to discuss whatever it is that has—" Fin leapt back as another slash of the king's sword swept near his middle, ripping his tunic.

"Now see, my wife just purchased that for me and she might take exception to it already being ruined," the viscount informed the king while stepping backward again as though they were having a casual discussion.

"Your son fought me the same way. Letting me think I had the upper hand until I gave him no choice," Brendan observed bitingly as he shifted the hilt of his sword into his other hand. "Show me your power, house witch."

Fin held up his hand to stop the king drawing closer yet again, a frown slowly lowering his brow as he took proper stock of the murderous intent in the king's eyes.

After a brief moment of consideration, Fin let out a small breath and shook his head in resolution.

"Right. I can see you're rather upset about something, and you are quite literally asking for this . . ." Fin began wryly as the king stepped closer, his body ready for violence.

"You're bloody well right I am."

"I suppose this was a long time coming. One final thing before you cool down then." Fin's mouth curved into a small humorless smile that dissolved any notion Brendan had of trying to hold back.

"Can you swim?"

The king opened his mouth to demand why the viscount would ask such a question, when Fin's hand shot out and grasped the front of Brendan's tunic, drawing him closer. Brendan was about to cut the viscount down where he stood, when a strange force overtook him, holding him still.

The witch's blue glowing eyes began shining brighter, and brighter, and lightning began crackling down around them, scorching the packed earth beneath their feet. Brendan could taste the electricity in the air, he could feel the earth trembling and . . . there was . . . *something* that was beginning to push him.

The king had never felt anything in his life like it before; it was as though the earth itself was rejecting him from its ground.

Then there was an explosion of power that sent Brendan high into the sky; his sword lay forgotten far below—he hadn't even been aware of the moment he'd dropped it. He sailed over the rooftops of Austice, saw the castle shrinking away . . . and then . . . he realized he was over the Alcide Sea, and it was rushing up to greet him until at long last he plunged beneath the inky waves that were already cast in the city's shadow.

The moment the foam of his crash began to clear, he flailed against the bitter chill of darkness and water around him. He kicked against its weight as it pulled at his heavy boots. He looked around as he struggled and saw only blackness . . . and nothing.

The abyss was calling him like in his nightmares . . . dragging him into its depths.

His heart pounding and his panic rising, he wondered why the sky wasn't growing closer?

Then, in a moment of sudden clarity . . .

Brendan realized that he had stopped swimming.

At some point, he had stopped kicking and thrashing and was simply adrift underwater. He turned his face upward, his lungs beginning to burn.

Above him was more trouble, more problems he would have to face, and Alina was leaving him.

In the abyss . . . it was all over. There was nothing. No pain. The voices of his people's cries and demands silenced.

Henry would take over the Troivackian throne, and knowing him, his brother would marry for love. He would struggle at first, but he was far better equipped than Brendan had first been.

Troivack would mourn the king's death for a month, but then he, too, would fade from people's hearts and minds.

It didn't matter that Brendan had sacrificed every promise of warmth or happiness for his citizens . . . his sacrifice merely prevented his people's hunger from igniting toward one another.

He began to sink farther into the cold depths.

Peace could be his in a matter of minutes.

All his anger was gone here. Nothing . . . nothing was precisely what he had always feared wanting.

He closed his eyes.

Instead of even more of the darkness he desired, though, all he saw was . . .

Alina smiling at him the day at the theater.

Then, the time she had told him she didn't want him to be alone, her golden hair glowing in the firelight behind her.

The day she had told him she was glad she had chosen him.

The day she had kissed him . . .

When she had said she would end their engagement . . . the anguish and disappointment in her teary eyes.

Slowly, Brendan began to kick toward the surface; his eyes opened and felt as though they were burning.

At the very least . . . if she is going to end things . . . I need to tell her that I'm sorry.

Chapter 37

ADDRESSING AN ALTERNATIVE

Alina continued dashing tears from her cheeks as she strode into the castle, and she did her best to ignore the whispers of concern that fluttered around her.

Picking up her skirt with one hand, she began to climb the stairs to the second floor to speak with her father about ending her engagement. She knew he most likely was in the council room with Mr. Howard summarizing his notes, and so, even though the thought was churning her stomach violently, she set her course.

When she reached the door, her face completely tearstained, and her nose starting to run, the guards glanced at each other uneasily.

"Erm . . . everythin' alright, Your Highness?" the one on the left asked worriedly.

"F-Fine," Alina choked out the word. "P-Please tell my father that I need to speak with him now. It is of an urgent nature."

Both guards turned hurriedly at the same time to deliver her message and nearly crashed into each other as a result. Once they sorted themselves, the man on the right slipped into the room and returned almost immediately.

"His Majesty says to enter."

Alina nodded, then burst into the room unceremoniously.

Norman sat at the head of the table with Mr. Howard seated at his left. Between them were stacks of books and documents, and the king's navy blue tunic was rolled to his elbows to reveal smears of ink on his hands and the occasional smudges across his arms.

It was clear they were in the midst of some serious work, but after seeing Alina's face, the two men rose to their feet.

"Princess, whatever is the—" Mr. Howard began, his frown matching Norman's.

"I want to break off the engagement," Alina declared before wiping away the fresh tears that began to fall from her eyes at having to speak aloud the purpose of her visit.

"What did that Troivackian do?" Norman said in a deadly tone as he rounded the table toward his daughter.

"He . . . He said I would only be in charge of the women in Troivack. Th-That a king couldn't always share everything with his wife," she began. Her throat was beginning to ache fiercely.

Norman glanced at Mr. Howard, his dark expression easing away. "Alina, love, that isn't . . . given his time ruling his kingdom on his own . . . and you would take a long time to become established with your own power, it makes sense that—"

"—He said he doesn't want us to have children of our own. He said that he'd have to name someone else as his heir or, or . . . or even consider mistresses."

At first Alina thought her father would begin to agree with Brendan yet again, but all she heard was silence. After a moment she risked raising her flushed face to see Norman's reaction and found herself watching Mr. Howard handing him his sword. Both looked eerily calm and serious . . . though both had a coldness in their eyes Alina had never seen before that made it all the more disconcerting.

The two men moved toward the door. "I'm going for a walk, love. Go to your chamber, and don't fret. Your engagement will be dissolved. I swe—"

A sudden commotion interrupted the king before he could finish what he was saying.

There was plenty of shouting, a few shrieks . . .

"Stay here," Norman ordered, tension springing to his features as he stepped around his daughter and threw open the door.

"What is the meaning of this?" he demanded as his guards stared transfixed down the end of the hall where a herd of people raced toward the stairs.

"U-Uuuh, Your Majesty, I cannot say for certain, but it sounds as though . . ."

"GOOD GODS!" Mage Keith Lee bolted past them from the opposite end of the hall with Tam Ashowan close behind.

"KEITH! WHAT IS GOING ON?" Norman roared, making the mage skid to a halt, which forced Tam to leap to the side to stop from crashing into him. Despite the near collision, Tam's eyes were fixed on the floor, but they were wide . . . he had clearly just seen something very troubling.

"The house witch just blasted the Troivackian king into the Alcide Sea!" the mage explained breathlessly before turning and once again running toward the stairs without any further explanation.

This time, however, Tam did not follow suit; instead he stayed behind and nervously raised his eyes to the monarch to see what his reaction was about the news regarding his father.

He was surprised by the expression that greeted him.

Norman Reyes was smiling and appeared incredibly happy before allowing the tip of his sword to tap the stone floor, his grip relaxing as he looked to the ceiling.

"I knew you sent that witch here for a good reason."

Then, Norman casually raised his sword and rested the flat of the blade against his shoulder and strode toward the chaos, only his pace was far more leisurely.

Mr. Howard followed behind him grumbling. "I know it saves you from getting violent, but this probably won't go over well in the contract dissolvement negotiations . . ."

Alina stared after them, her worry for Brendan momentarily consuming her thoughts before she remembered the house witch would never do any real harm with his magic.

She slowly redirected her path and moved farther down the hall with the intention of taking the servants' staircase to go to her room. It seemed they had all flocked to the source of the excitement, and therefore that route was most likely her best bet on returning to her chamber unnoticed.

"Alina? Are you alright?" Tam's quiet voice behind her halted her labored step, and she turned to face him knowing she looked a fright.

"Not right this moment," she managed before giving him a small weak smile.

Tam stepped closer, his hands opening and closing at his sides. "Would you like to talk about it?"

Clasping her hands gently together in front of her skirts, Alina felt her tears rejuvenate once more.

"Not really, but thank you. I'm sure you're curious about why your father blasted a foreign king into the Alcide Sea . . . you should go find out."

As she turned around again to leave Tam, Alina was startled to find he had reached out and gently clasped her shoulders, stopping her and adjusting her to once more see his face.

"I understand you don't want to talk right now, but just know, if you are ever in need, the Ashowans will protect and help you. It's what we do, so don't—"

"There you are! My Gods! Did you hear what my da did?! I just finished convincing the guards not to arrest that big lug and— Oh . . . hi, Tam." Katarina Ashowan's exuberant greeting cut off her brother as she appeared striding down the hallway, having somehow freed herself from Alina's maids.

Kat's greeting to her brother momentarily piqued the princess's curiosity. She remembered hearing they'd been fighting back at the ball where she'd sung with Prince Henry, but were they still fighting?

"I'm going back to my room. Excuse me." Alina curtsied and at last succeeded in extracting herself from further conversation, leaving the siblings alone as she resisted the need to outwardly sob.

She also didn't want to risk a breathing attack while out where people could see her.

Once the princess had disappeared around the corner and stepped foot on the servants' staircase, Katarina faced her brother, her golden eyes bright and her expression grim.

"What were you saying to her?"

Tam regarded his twin calmly. "I was just reminding her that no matter what, the Ashowans will do or be whatever she needs."

Kat nodded briefly. "Godsdamn right."

"Do you know why Da blasted King Brendan Devark?" Tam asked idly as his sister stepped to follow the princess.

"His Majesty made Alina cry, and she indicated she wanted to break off the engagement. My bet is the Troivackian goon tried to pick a fight with Da to let off steam."

"Da wouldn't rise to the bait so easily though, unless . . ." Tam closed his eyes as he pieced together the final mystery of the event. "Unless the Troivackian king literally asked him to do it."

Kat snorted. "Well, I suppose we have nothing to worry about then."

Tam shook his head. "This matter won't just be waved off. The king's entourage and brother will most likely take great offense . . . it has the potential to brew very bad blood."

"Well then, it's a good thing our father can be charming when he feels like it. Now, if you'll excuse me, brother, I would like to attend to the princess." Kat once again began moving away from her kin, only for him to once again speak out and stop her.

"Kat, can we . . . can we really not make up now?"

Glancing over her shoulder, her eyes flashing angrily, Kat stared at her brother for a wordless moment. Then, as she continued studying him, and he met her gaze unwaveringly, she finally sighed and turned around to face him.

"I . . . know . . . you had some decent points, but you're stupid and annoying to concede to because you never admit when I'm right about you needing to try and step up! Otherwise Likon is going to take over for Da, and what will you do, hm? Hide forever?"

"Kat, it isn't . . . it isn't that simple for me to just . . ." Tam trailed off, his pained expression worsening.

"Well, it sure as hell isn't easy for me to sit through Godsdamn meetings without moving a muscle and speaking politely to every person there! Do you know how many asshats are in this castle?! Way too many! It's terrible! I hate it! But . . ." Kat stopped and closed her eyes while trying to get her emotions back under control. "I do it because it's the right thing to do."

"I thought you did it because it was your punishment for going camping?" Tam mused mildly.

Kat's irritated snort as her golden eyes snapped open had the same level of ferocity as a bull's, and it was directed at her brother's person.

"See? This is why I'm not ready to make up with you!" Turning on her heel and storming off, she was resolute in not letting him distract her further.

"Likon is going with Da to Zinfera."

Tam's shout succeeded in making Kat freeze for a breath, but she held fast to her resolve and continued on to the servants' stairwell.

Her brother remained in the corridor, completely alone.

As he let out a long stream of air, he leaned against the castle wall while reaching up and rubbing the back of his neck.

Sorry, Kat. I just don't know how to tell you that I have enough I'm worried about . . . I really don't think I should ever be viscount.

Kat paced the princess's room while Alina lay curled on her side hugging a pillow on her bed, her tears falling more slowly. At least the threat of a breathing attack wasn't imminent.

"So you're a free woman again! Isn't this good? You could just become the queen of Daxaria, and you can stay here with your father!" Kat theorized energetically.

"I-I wanted to . . . feel . . . I wanted to feel stronger, and he . . . he always made me feel like I was," Alina murmured brokenly.

"Well, you *are* strong! You don't need some king with the manners of a dog and the facial expressions of an ale barrel!"

"Kat . . ." Alina began while sitting up, her wavy blond hair mussed.

"The ale barrel is more expressive, you're right . . . I think even a rock is more telling than that Troivackian's face is."

"No, Kat, that isn't right! He does show his thoughts and feelings, it's just . . . more subtle. I mean, what would you expect? He's had people try to take advantage of him and hurt him since he was a child!" Alina bit out vehemently.

"Well, why's he such a grumpy dolt about my family?" Kat tried again, throwing her hands in the air while continuing to pace.

"From an outsider's perspective, your family could appear very suspicious, and I'll be honest, I am not at all in agreeance with your father when it comes to my brother. I'm the prince's sister, and I deserve to know where Eric is and what he's doing more than the house witch!" Alina was on her feet, and her voice was beginning to grow stronger as she spoke.

"Well . . . I, too, think you have the right to know about your brother. I mean, I'm pretty sure my mother doesn't even know anything, and she normally knows more than my da!"

A thought suddenly occurred to Alina then, a wild yet . . . enticing thought. "Kat, remember how I told you I ran into that bard your family hired for my birthday gift?"

Kat finally ceased her harried movements, confused by the princess's sudden shift in attention.

"Yes? He should be coming to the castle next week."

"Well, I think he knows something about my brother! Maybe while he was traveling he saw him."

"Then you need to talk to him!" Kat grabbed Alina's hands excitedly.

"I know, but if I wait until he comes to the castle, I'll never get a chance to talk with him alone," the princess reasoned. "The viscount or my father may make sure the servants in the room don't ever let him talk about anything other than music."

"Well, we can go one of these days to Austice and—"

"I'll be too busy dealing with the fallout from my canceled engagement! No, I need to go tonight!" Alina's eyes shone with urgency as she peered up pleadingly at her friend.

"Er . . . tonight? With . . . with guards, right? Do you even know where he lives?" Kat asked while trying to take a step back from the princess's keen determination.

"No guards. One of them might try to stop me, and as for where he lives . . . I don't know. But you do." The princess's wry smile brightened her still teary face, and Kat winced as she had an ominous sense of where this discussion was going.

"I do, but, Alina, I really am not sure this is the best—"

"Please! I know I can't do this without you, and aren't you and your brother the ones saying how the Ashowans will always help me?!" The princess was clasping Kat's hands tightly and pulling them closer to her chest as she appeared on the verge of begging.

After a tense moment of silence and Kat studying her friend's desperate face, she let out a whoosh of air and allowed her shoulders to slump forward in defeat.

"Alright, but we go dressed as boys, and take no risks. For the record, I don't believe this is the only chance you'll get for questioning him, but you're going through a bad time and I think a little adventure might help, so . . . what the hell?"

Alina's brilliant smile illuminated her features as she began professing her deep love for her friend and the other Ashowan family members.

Kat chuckled while listening to the litany of compliments, trying to brush off the bad feeling she got in her gut.

It'll probably be fine . . . I mean . . . at the very worst we find out something terrible like the prince is secretly dead or something.

Chapter 38

UNTIMELY DEPARTURES

Slipping out of the castle was easy thanks to the commotion surrounding the Troivackian king's airborne departure.

There was plenty of shouting, some swords were drawn, and all the while the house witch stood back, leaning against the castle wall of the front hall, his arms folded as he waited tiredly for . . . something.

No one seemed to think to ask whatever it was.

Though Prince Henry looked ready to slaughter the redhead on behalf of his brother as he shouted at Norman.

No one noticed the two servant boys in hooded cloaks sneaking out of the castle, or them darting through the darkness toward Austice.

"We can't hire a carriage until after we speak to the bard or else we'll be seen," Katarina murmured to the princess as they strolled down the streets of Austice. Surprisingly, the foot traffic was still high despite night having settled over the city, as taverngoers and nefarious figures emerged from their dwellings for a night of revelry, mischief, or trouble.

The night populace of Austice noted the two hooded figures passing by them but shrugged off their shabby cloaks as unworthy of their time . . . at least not when the night was so young with plumper prey lurking about the streets.

Katarina set a grueling pace, but thanks to Alina's more recent bouts of exercise with the Troivackian king, she didn't struggle nearly as much as she normally would have.

"Remember, we need to make this quick. I told your maids you went to bed early, but this is still risky," Kat murmured under her hood while narrowly dodging a drunkard who stumbled in her path.

"Of course," Alina huffed as they walked, then caught herself from nearly tripping over a small tabby cat that was sent darting off to the alley beside them.

It took them longer to reach the bard's residence than Kat had hoped, thanks to the uncoordinated citizens they were constantly dodging, but given the fact that they hadn't run into any troubles, they still counted themselves lucky.

The two-story boardinghouse was built in three sections with an open railing running around the walks to all the rooms. A pretty fountain burbled in its center, and a well-kept flower bed at its base added an extra note of cheer.

It was definitely one of the nicer boardinghouses in the city, and this alone helped both Alina and Kat feel more at ease.

"His room should be on the second floor, the back left there," Kat said, nodding from under her hood before turning to the stairs.

"I must admit, I was bluffing a tiny bit that you knew where he was staying . . . how *did* you know about this?" Alina felt her heart race as the promise of answers about her brother hung before her.

Kat's golden eyes shot to the princess, and she didn't bother masking her exasperation over her confession.

"I eavesdropped on my parents. They talked about it after an argument about . . . other things . . . and happened to mention it . . ." Kat trailed off. She didn't particularly want to relive the exact heated discussion her parents had been having about her reckless behavior when the bard's residence had been revealed.

As the two women finally reached the back corner of the building, Kat wasted no time in rapping her knuckles across the door.

"Remember, he might already be out at the taverns, and if that is the case then we are turning around and—"

Kat was interrupted by the door opening and a swath of warm light pouring over them.

The bard Reese Flint stood in a loose white tunic and trousers in his bare feet. A towel was around his neck and his hair was damp from having just been washed.

His dark green eyes squinted at the hoods, and it was then Kat took it upon herself to wordlessly lift her chin and reveal her identity to him.

"Oh! My lady! Whatever brings you to—"

Alina stepped forward, her chin lifted.

The sight of the princess rendered the man speechless as he quickly craned his neck outside the doorframe and looked to see if knights were accompanying them.

"Please . . . please come in," the bard ushered them in urgently as he continued glancing around the outside worriedly.

The man seemed rather flummoxed by their appearance, which only spoke well of his mental faculties in Alina's estimation.

Why in the world would she, a princess, and a noblewoman be out without any kind of protection?

"Mr. Reese, you have my apologies for seeking you out in this manner," Alina began formally. "I am afraid the nature of my visit forced me to resort to this measure."

Kat said nothing as she leaned her back against the closed door.

The room they stood in was a respectable size, and though not lavish, it was of decent quality and comfort. A fire crackled happily, and two worn armchairs whose fabric may have at some point been red sat before the hearth. A single window overlooked the street behind the boardinghouse, the four-poster bed sat unmade, and a tub was still filled with water. There was a small round table with two chairs in front of the window, and a chest of drawers with a pitcher atop.

"Whatever could I do to be of service, Your Highness?" Reese asked quietly while gesturing toward the round table and chairs.

Alina stepped forward gracefully and seated herself across from him. When she had settled herself down, she lowered her hood and stared calmly at the bard's expectant face.

"I am here for clear answers, and don't worry about protecting my innocent mind should it come to that," Alina said, waving her hand dismissively. But her eyes never left him.

Reese glanced warily at Kat, then back to the princess. "I . . . will do my best, Your Highness."

"Good." Alina nodded. "Now, where did you see my brother? And if you happen to know why he has more or less disappeared, tell me now."

The bard stilled.

His face drained of color, and it was clear he was mentally trying to calculate what to say.

"Stop figuring out how to get out of telling me the truth. I need to know." Alina's face took on an edge no one could've guessed she was capable of.

Reese Flint responded with a grimace before leaning forward, his hands folded loosely in his lap. "I don't know . . . as much as you might be hoping, Princess. I spotted him a little less than a year ago, but I've heard more about him—rumors if you will—from the odd souls I've crossed paths with."

"Where was he when you spotted him?"

"He was in a small town outside of Rollom . . . he was traveling with a few other mercenaries at the time that he seemed to know well."

"Mercenaries? Not knights?" Kat interrupted with a furrowed brow.

"Correct. I'm given to understand your brother would . . . drift in and out of similar groups since the queen's passing." Reese's answers were coming slowly and Alina was growing impatient.

"*Why* was he traveling outside of Rollom?"

Reese half smiled, half winced as he reached up and idly rubbed his thumb against his lip, the silver ring he wore catching in the light. "Who knows? Adventure? Money? Love? He and the men he was with talked about jobs they had taken, though no one seemed to know His Highness's true identity. He mentioned Viscount Ashowan a good amount . . . and they weren't kind words I'm sorry to say . . ." He nodded apologetically toward Kat.

"Why would he need money? Even if he was hiding the fact he was a prince, he was under the protection of Duke Iones—or should have been! My father would send money for his care . . ."

"Princess, I can't know the secrets of your father, or the duke for that matter."

"Why is my brother not coming back to where he should be? What was his dispute with the viscount?" Alina demanded while trying not to let her emotions bubble to the surface.

A look of apology passed through his eyes, and Alina knew right then that he would lie to her if pushed any further.

"If you attempt to deceive me right now, not only will I refuse lessons from you, but I will make sure you never work again."

Reese Flint froze.

After a moment, he swallowed with great difficulty.

"Princess, it is for your brother to tell you, please . . . understand my position. What I *can* tell you . . . is that it was well known how much the prince adored you. He would tell anyone who would listen about his little sister. How kind and talented you are. How he had spent months picking out the perfect lute for you and how you loved it so much that you named it Beau, because it was the most beautiful gift you had ever received."

Alina suddenly found it difficult to talk, and a warmth behind her eyes had her looking elsewhere for a moment as she regained her composure.

"As much as I want to be sympathetic to your position, Mr. Flint, I cannot. If my brother were present, rest assured I would take my questions to him, but given that he is not, the onus falls to you." Standing, Alina stared down at the bard, who looked more than a little saddened by her obvious heartbreak.

"Princess, if I weren't protecting my own brood I'd be swayed by your woe in a heartbeat, but I've had to become a changed man. Please know that while I hold you in the highest regard, I know for a fact Viscount Ashowan has the resources and motivation to make good on his warnings. A feat I do not believe you can manage at this time."

Alina felt her hands curl into fists. She wanted to shout at him and swear that she could bring tenfold the consequences on the bard, but didn't want her upset to cloud her judgment in the moment.

"Come on, Kat, we better get back."

Rounding toward the exit, Alina waited for her friend to open the door.

So far the entire day had gone into the dung pile.

Despite having grown perhaps a little in love with the Troivackian king, he had proven that he would give her nothing but pain and regret.

Then, she had almost found out about her brother, only to gather more useless information.

The princess was tired and angry, and she wanted to scream into her pillow before sleeping for an entire year at most.

When Alina stepped outside into the cool night, she took a deep fortifying breath and began to turn to the stairs when a flutter of movement caught her eye, but before she could react, a cloth with a stinging scent was pressed to her face.

She struggled for a few moments, while hearing the sounds of Kat shouting and scuffling alongside Reese Flint, before darkness claimed her, her body falling limp before she could even get a proper look at their attackers.

The only thought she managed to work out as she felt fear grip her stomach in her final moments was: *Gods, we're in real trouble now, aren't we? I hope . . . Father doesn't . . . hurt the Troivackian king . . . too much.*

The shouts and fighting in the castle entrance were finally beginning to settle down when a very wet Brendan Devark stepped through the doors, his face pale and somber.

"Brother! Thank the Gods you are alright! We cannot let this attack rest, how could they—" Henry exclaimed, rushing over to his brother and clasping his shoulders while checking him over head to toe.

"Henry. It's fine. I asked Viscount Ashowan to do what he did."

The room fell into stunned silence.

Brendan's gaze swept over the many heads of his entourage, then the Daxarian nobility, and finally landed on Finlay Ashowan, who continued leaning against the wall of the castle, though his blue eyes were bright and shimmering.

"Viscount, did you retrieve my sword?" Brendan asked calmly while waving off a trembling maid who had come forward with a towel for him.

"I returned it to your brother, though he did try to stab me with it afterward, which I can't say I was fond of." Fin straightened then strolled over to Brendan.

It was clear to the witch that there was something different in Brendan's eyes. The fire of anger wasn't there hiding his pain like it had been when they'd fought.

Instead, there was sadness and remorse that transformed him into a humbled man.

Fin bowed his head. "I'd prefer to not have to blast you off like that again, Your Majesty."

Brendan barely registered his words before turning to Norman, who stood watching him stonily with his assistant at his side.

"I will go along with whatever the princess wishes and end the engagement if she so desires. I only ask that I be allowed to apologize to her before I board the next ship out to Troivack."

There was an explosion of whispers amongst the nobility.

Everyone knew, Troivackians didn't apologize.

Especially their king.

He had indeed committed a grave sin if he needed to apologize.

Norman's jaw flexed as he stared at the young man before him whose tone left no room of doubt with regard to his sincerity.

"You may. Ruby, please go fetch the princess. We can send His Majesty out tomorrow morning if he so chooses. This way Alina will not need to be woken before dawn." The Daxarian king's voice was cold as the Head of Housekeeping debated telling him that the princess was already asleep in bed, but she decided she'd rather face the princess's slight upset over the Daxarian king's wrath. She nodded to the nearest maids, who took off in a near sprint up the stairs.

"Your Majesty, why are you apologizing? What happened between you and the princess that warrants us being chased out?" Prince Henry demanded while addressing his brother and eyeing the nobles who were hanging around simply to enjoy the drama.

"That is a matter between the princess and me. No blame is to be placed on her, and please let it be known that she has conducted her time with me with the respect and bearing of a future queen. It is simply our irreconcilable differences that have us believing she would be better appreciated here in Daxaria." Brendan's voice boomed effortlessly, and it was apparent to everyone in the room that he was ensuring no one had any scandalous ideas or cannon fodder for rumors pertaining to her virtue.

"Brother . . ." Henry dropped his voice down to a whisper as the Daxarian guards finally began herding the onlookers out of the way. "What in the world happened? You asked to be shot off land into the sea? And now you're apologizing?!"

Brendan fixed Henry with his eerie stare once more, making his brother back up a step. The Troivackian king no longer looked impenetrable. Rather, something in him looked . . . defeated.

"I will tell you about everything once we—"

Several shouts of alarm interrupted Brendan that drew everyone's eyes up and over to where the two maids Ruby had sent reappeared with a slew of guards.

"The princess isn't in her room! No one has seen her since she went to bed!" one of the younger maids burst out fearfully while wringing her hands.

"Lady Ashowan is missing as well!" another maid who had lagged behind gasped out as she began rushing down the stairs alongside her coworker.

Norman's head swiveled instantly to Finlay, who looked equally concerned by the news.

Brendan felt a heavy dread fill his stomach. His gut instinct was screaming at him . . . it wasn't at all like the time the two women had disappeared to go camping.

Alina had been angry and upset . . . Katarina knew how to sneak around . . . but . . .

Something in the air felt off.

Norman glanced at Brendan as though he were thinking the very same thing.

"Everyone fan out and search every inch of this castle. Viscount, send word to your estate and see if they went there. I want them found before dawn, am I clear?" the monarch ordered as all guards and knights within earshot snapped to attention.

Fin strode toward the doors past Brendan and his entourage without another glance back, his anxiety clear as day as his eyes began to shine even more brightly; his magic rushing to life.

"How can we help?" Brendan asked loudly, his eyes hardening and his fists curling at his sides.

Norman regarded him for a brief moment before wearily shaking his head and turning to the stairwell. "Nothing. This is not your concern anymore, Your Majesty."

Then he left, and Brendan could feel the cold hand of helplessness seize his heart as his gut continued to bellow that things were far from alright . . . and he began to fear that he may never get to see Alina again.

Chapter 39

IRRITATING INTRODUCTIONS

Alina's head felt like it was filled with wool, and her entire body felt heavy . . . sleepy. But why was there a draft?

Her eyes snapped open.

She had been taken!

Someone had grabbed her, and she couldn't remember who!

Peering around the room she found herself in, her mind immediately leapt to her father's teachings about what she should do if such a situation ever happened.

Leave as many clues as possible so that she could be found.

Remain calm, speak slowly, but clearly.

Don't agitate the kidnappers.

The princess couldn't see any rooms aside from the one she currently sat in. There were white plaster walls, a pile of hay behind her, and worn unsanded floors. No chairs were in sight, but a fireplace was burning to her left, lighting the room, and a door was straight across from her.

A door that three men were huddled in front of.

The tallest and beefiest of them had a clean-shaven face, and medium-length brown hair. He looked to be in his midforties, with a slight gut and a broad nose, but he was not unfortunate looking like the other two.

The smallest of them was perhaps only as tall as Alina. He was even thinner than she was, and his whiskers had not been shaved in several days; when he whispered, he whistled a little bit as though he were missing several teeth.

The other man was undoubtedly a mercenary. He had a deep straight scar in the middle of his forehead and looked as though he were in his sixties. His eyes were dark, and his silvery hair long and partially tied back.

What indicated his profession was the telltale sword hanging at his side, and knives in his boots that most commoners wouldn't have . . . and none of them could be knights . . . there wasn't any coat of arms anywhere on them.

"Oh, good. You're awake."

Katarina Ashowan's cheerful voice made Alina jump, and as a result, she realized her hands and ankles were tightly bound.

When she turned and saw her friend's usual lively face, Alina felt more than a little stunned, especially when she realized Reese Flint was on the other side of her still unconscious.

The three men turned to stare at them.

Alina shrank back and did her best to mask her fear.

Katarina Ashowan, on the other hand, took a very different approach.

"Ah, hello there! I think we need to do a quick introduction here before this gets out of hand."

The men wordlessly strode over to them, their heavy boots thudding loudly in the small room.

Then they stood in front of them, their arms all folded save for the small wiry man, who was grinning maniacally; Alina realized she had been right about his teeth. He had two small silver hoops in each of his ears, and his bright green eyes bulged out of his head making him look even more deranged.

"Ah, yes, it probably is easier to hear me if you're closer," Kat began, completely nonplussed. "So . . . given that it's been only you three who caught us, carried us, and have been whispering about releasing us once Reesey here tells you what you want to know, I feel like you should know that your plans have a couple of unforeseen issues."

The men looked collectively startled. "You . . . You were awake for all that? How—"

"I'll get to that after the introduction. This lovely lady beside me is actually the princess of Daxaria, Alina Reyes. Beloved daughter of our king and sister to the crown prince."

The men snorted in disbelief.

Alina, on the other hand, became confused.

They hadn't kidnapped them because she was the princess? Then why . . . ?

"I realize it's a tough thing to believe given our current dress"—Kat nodded down at the trousers and tunic she wore—"but once you're discovered it'll be properly verified."

The ringleader of the men laughed coldly again and slowly crouched down in front of Kat, his dark blue eyes wide and unblinking as his face was cast in the shadows of the fire.

"Your lies won't save you and your friend."

Kat failed to be moved by his ominous warning.

"Again, not a lie, and you aren't allowed later to declare that you had no idea who she was when the king sentences you to death. Now, I suppose we should move along with the introductions. My name is Lady Katarina Ashowan of the Viscount House Jenoure. Daughter of the house witch Finlay Ashowan."

The man didn't laugh at that; instead, he continued to stare with a curling lip. "Oh sure. I just happen to kidnap a princess and the daughter of our kingdom's hero at that bard's place. More like you two are the whores he hired for the night."

"What kind of whores dress in men's britches?" Kat asked flatly.

The man paused, a small twitch in his eyebrows appearing before the wiry man spoke.

"Maybe he has a fetish for the boys!" the wiry man interjected.

"Exactly," the ringleader agreed, his confidence swiftly returning.

"When . . . ow . . ." Reese Flint sat up with a wince as he recognized his bound hands and stared groggily at the men around them. "When have I ever hid my exploits? Hi there, Roscoe."

The ringleader's gaze turned murderous when he turned to the bard.

"Furthermore," Katarina jumped in loudly, once again drawing attention back to herself. "Check our hands. Do our hands look like we've ever spent a day with a broom or rag in them? Do we really look like prostitutes? We aren't even wearing makeup."

At this the leader named Roscoe roughly grabbed and wrenched her hands forward, making Kat wince before saying, "Easy there, you're in enough trouble as is."

Roscoe ignored her as he checked her palms and noted the softness save for the pads of her fingers on her right hand, where there were calluses earned from being an archer.

The flicker of uncertainty that passed over his features had Kat letting out a world-weary sigh.

"Yes, yes. There you go. Now, send us on our way and I'll forget about this as will Alina for all of . . . a day? A day's head start seems fair." Kat's patronizing tone resulted in a backhanded slap across her right cheek from the man named Roscoe.

Alina squeaked, tears in her eyes.

"Hey, Roscoe, your problem is with me, not these two ladies. Let them go," Reese jumped in, his voice only warbling slightly.

"I'll let them go once you tell me where my wife an' daughter are." The man's deadly tone directed at the bard made Reese swallow hesitantly.

"I-I-I don't know! I sent them to friends of mine; who knows if they are still—"

Roscoe grabbed the bard and punched his stomach, instantly winding the man.

"You'll tell me where you stowed my wife an' her daughter, or the three of you are in for a world of suffering."

"Mister . . . Roscoe, was it?" Katarina's unfailing chipper voice interrupted yet again, and a muscle in the man's jaw jerked. "Yeah, hi, me again . . . so what is your long-term plan here? Are we going to move locations if the bard doesn't talk? The longer you all stay here, the riskier it gets, you know."

Roscoe turned to face her, and this time he didn't stop at the backhanded slap; this time he grabbed her by the top of her mussed red ponytail and yanked her face up, earning a flinch from Kat as the bruise on her cheek deepened in color.

"STOP IT!" Alina's voice rang out in the small cabin, making everyone freeze for a moment. They had forgotten she was there, and that was when she realized that had been exactly what Kat had been trying to do . . . she'd been trying to protect her by consuming the men's attentions.

However, princess with weak lungs or not, she couldn't let them hurt her friend without doing anything.

"That's right. You should get the bard to tell Roscoe what he wants to know or we'll keep hurting this chatty woman here." The wiry man bent down in front of Alina, who was already beginning to breathe heavily.

"I'll do nothing of the sort." Alina's voice was calm, and low. How she was managing it despite the familiar rattling in her lungs that started to worsen, she wasn't sure.

"Do you see Roscoe there, little girl?" The wiry man smirked as he gestured with his head to the large ringleader. "He's going to make you and your friend scream."

"Alina's not really ticklish. I don't think so, anyway . . . ?" Kat mused, her tone impressively casual as though she were having a mildly dull conversation while her golden eyes slid sideways to her friend despite Roscoe still clutching her hair.

Alina glanced at Kat worriedly without giving any indication aside from a small sharp intake of breath as she fought off another attack.

"Oh right, your breathing thing. You might die if tickled . . . makes sense . . ." Kat reasoned out with an understanding sigh.

Roscoe gave her a rough shake.

"Tickling the blonde will kill her?" The cold interest in his eyes made Alina's stomach churn.

"I mean . . . possibly? Though I did hear the mercenary mention you did not pay him to keep quiet about murder, so I don't recommend trying," Kat pointed out exasperatedly.

Releasing Kat's hair with a snarl, Roscoe instead grabbed the front of her tunic and drew her close to himself. "You don't want to see what I'm like when I'm angry."

The redhead did the unthinkable and laughed in his face. "Gods, man, I've pissed off a Troivackian king, and you think you're scarier than that oaf?! Alina, tell him! That giant dumbass of an ex-fiancé of yours is what . . . twice his size? At least in muscle . . ."

"Oh, I'd definitely say about that," Reese Flint volunteered with a pensive nod before the princess could say anything.

Alina was too terrified for her friend to say anything.

How could she make Kat stop trying to protect her in such a way without making things worse?!

Fortunately for the two noblewomen, Reese's interruption had once again drawn Roscoe's attention, but before the man could take another swing at the bard, the mercenary with a scar in the middle of his forehead interrupted.

"How did you stay awake?" His question was directed at Kat, who grinned wolfishly in response.

"It's part of my being a mutated witch. I'm a tad tough to drug. Not to mention it makes getting drunk more than a little challenging—though I had wild success on my sixteenth birthday! I mean, who hasn't heard about me and the donkey."

The mercenary's lips twitched as though warding off a laugh. The donkey story involving Katarina Ashowan was indeed a famous one across the kingdom. Then he realized he was becoming distracted, and his expression once again turned hostile.

"Ros . . . I want to check about these two. What if . . . what if they're telling the truth?" the mercenary pondered slowly.

"Dexter! Look at you! Being the voice of reason for this ragtag group is not easy, I can tell." Kat winked at the man, who scowled at her condescending, gleeful tone. It didn't help matters that she called him by name, which meant without a doubt she had been awake the entire time that she'd been kidnapped.

A look of realization and curiosity sparked on Dexter's face.

"Wait . . . if you weren't drugged, why did you let us take you?"

Kat leaned back leisurely against the hay pile and smiled up at the kidnappers despite the bruise on her cheek looking painful.

"Well . . . it's what Ashowans do. We protect people."

For some reason that admission disturbed them all more than her outright introduction.

"Everyone outside," Dexter growled, making Roscoe shoot him an icy glare over his shoulder, and the wiry man roll his eyes and let out a small whine.

Yet they all rose and strode out of the room, though only opening the door a crack, which blocked the three prisoners from being seen.

Once the door had slammed firmly shut, Alina rounded on the bard.

"Who are they? What is it this 'Roscoe' is talking about?" The anger in her voice made the bard wince while smiling apologetically.

"Ah, well . . . bit of a story, but as you can imagine he is a rather poor excuse for a husband, and his wife happened to be a former . . . *friend* of mine and her daughter is . . . well . . ."

"Yours?" Kat asked with a sardonic raise of her eyebrows.

Reese cleared his throat awkwardly in confirmation.

"Why does he want them back so badly?" Alina frowned as Kat wrapped her bound arms around her knees.

"Well, he is the prideful sort. So learning his wife was once mine and our daughter is from our . . . time together . . . it was rather embarrassing for him to say the least. Plus he wasn't able to touch the money I contributed to her dowry. Then I added insult to injury and hid them. My daughter, I imagine he had some sort of profitable marriage arranged for her to try and claim some of the money. Not too sure. Lorelai and my girl didn't want to give too many details." Reese shrugged, and it was clear while his expression remained complacent, there was genuine worry behind his eyes. "They're with a friend of mine, and, and I'm sorry, but I'm not throwing them both in front of death's carriage."

Alina let out an aggravated yet resolute breath before turning to her friend.

"Kat, how is your cheek? Are you alright?"

"Oh, I'm peachy. Though I am most definitely enjoying the idea of him having to face off against the cavalry that'll come for us." She grinned then was jolted by the pain in her face.

Alina raised her bound hands and reached out to gently cup Kat's face.

"I know you're trying to distract them from me, but I'm worried they may try to assault us. Don't provoke them like that." Her hazel eyes stared directly into Kat's golden ones, making the lady shift uncomfortably.

"I can take care of myself; don't worry. Besides, assault? Pfft." She chuckled. "That's a little dark. It won't happen when it'd directly affect the house witch. That sort of thing seems to somehow avoid my family . . . it's the hair, I think." Kat tossed her red gleaming ponytail over her shoulder dramatically, and despite not wanting to, Alina couldn't help but smile as she bit back a laugh.

"What about your brother? Something happened to him," she finally managed when she was certain she wasn't going to giggle.

"He has black hair! Try and keep up! It's like *you* were the one that got hit . . ." Kat trailed off shaking her head in mock exasperation.

Alina couldn't help it, she laughed.

As she studied Kat's good-humored, albeit bruised, face, she couldn't help but feel a swell of gratitude in her chest.

She counted herself the luckiest woman in the world to have a friend like Katarina Ashowan.

Even if she was too careless about her own well-being, Alina could tell that without a doubt the reckless redhead was the best woman to have by her side during a time as frightful as the present.

Chapter 40

SEARCHING FOR SOLUTIONS

Norman's deadened stare regarded the sea of armed knights and common foot soldiers surrounding him, along with any and every man or woman available. Everyone was convening in the castle entrance to be assigned new districts to search and team leaders who would gather the report of the patrols before once again heading out to search for the two missing noblewomen.

Alina and Katarina had been missing for a day and a half, and no one had the slightest idea where they had gone . . . as though they'd vanished into thin air.

If it weren't for Finlay Ashowan burning his magic throughout Austice looking for any hint, and Annika's round-the-clock work of contacting every source in her underground network, the king would've suspected them of once again covering for a new escapade their daughter had crafted and dragged Alina into.

In a way, Norman wished it were Katarina Ashowan's free spirit that was responsible for his daughter's absence. Perhaps she had sympathized so strongly with the princess's heartbreak over the Troivackian king that she had suggested a long, fun journey to Sorlia.

However, the heart-wrenching terror in Fin's eyes told him otherwise.

"She isn't frightened."

The house witch would whisper that phrase over and over to himself as the smallest thread of comfort.

According to Fin, if Katarina had felt truly afraid he would have seen *something*, but Norman couldn't help but remember how he had once said when Tam's traumatic incident had occurred that the house witch hadn't seen or heard a thing . . .

Norman had no doubt, though, that if Katarina Ashowan were dead, her father would be the first to know. The king simply didn't know if that indicated whether his own daughter was safe or not.

Neither Norman nor Finlay had slept or eaten since the previous day, but it never occurred to either of them that this was an issue. The world felt bleak and hellish without their daughters home where they should be . . .

The king hadn't experienced such darkness since Ainsley had died . . . but this time it was different.

Alina could still be saved from wherever she was.

One annoying detail that did nothing to help his frayed nerves was that Brendan Devark remained in the castle.

He didn't walk about or even demand any information. He simply sat in his chamber with his brother, the prince, and waited.

Norman wanted to be angry. Wanted to shout at the man for being a burden during an already stressful time, but he was also begrudgingly appreciative that the king was so obviously distressed by Alina's disappearance.

Not that he was forgiven for considering a mistress while married to Alina, but at least he appeared to care. The loud clack of someone entering the castle drew Norman's attention upward and his thoughts back to the present.

Finlay Ashowan was striding through the great doors. He looked more like the cook he used to be; he wore worn brown trousers and a casual cream tunic made of poorer quality. His hands were settled in his pockets, and alongside him trotted his familiar, Kraken, who would chirp occasionally and Fin would answer.

Once Fin reached the king, his facial features sharp and tense, he shared with the ruler the contents of their dialogue.

"There is a cat in Austice who believes they saw Alina and Kat dressed as boys heading down the hill. They were amongst the taverns, but the feline witness doesn't believe they went into any of them for a drink. Meaning they were there for something else."

"This isn't for certain, though?" Norman asked thoughtfully while absent-mindedly stroking his beard.

"No, but it's a possible lead where we have none."

Norman nodded in agreement, and as he opened his mouth to issue an order, he found himself interrupted.

One of the elite knights had approached the viscount and himself, the knight's light brown hair brushing his shoulders and several days' worth of stubble shadowing his high cheekbones.

"Your Majesty, might I . . . make an impertinent suggestion that I believe could be helpful in our search?"

Turning to face the man, both the king and viscount regarded him with an intensity that had him visibly sweating.

"What is your name?" Norman asked, his voice ringing sharply as soldiers and maids faded away from them nervously.

"Sir Gabriel Vohn, Your Majesty. I was one of the escorts to the princess the day she visited Austice." The knight had his hands clasped behind his back and his feet braced wide apart.

Norman and Finlay shared a glance before looking back to the knight.

"What is this suggestion, Sir Vohn?" the king asked, the edge in his voice intimidating.

"Ask the Troivackian king where he thinks they would have gone."

The room fell into complete silence.

Sir Vohn to his credit kept his eyes downcast, and despite the lump in his throat bobbing from a gulp, he remained firm.

"Why do you suggest that?" Fin was deceptively calm.

"As of late, the Troivackian king has spent the most time with the princess aside from Lady Katarina, and he might have valuable insight." The knight had spoken a little too loudly, which indicated his apprehensiveness, but his expression remained neutral.

"You trust that His Majesty Brendan Devark had nothing to do with the princess and Lady Katarina's disappearance?" Norman's voice withheld most of his emotions, but his face was a slab of ice and his eyes deadly.

"Yes, I do. I am suggesting this as the king might have noticed someone suspicious or know where Her Highness may have wished to go because he would be aware of where her interests lie more recently," Sir Vohn explained carefully.

Fin glanced at Norman.

It was a good idea . . . the question was whether or not Norman would be receptive to it given his dislike for the Troivackian king.

For a moment, the Daxarian king said nothing, and Fin began to wonder if he went behind his back and asked Brendan Devark himself, would it be perceived as "treason."

"We will ask him. Thank you for the suggestion, Sir Vohn. It is a good idea. You are dismissed."

The knight bowed and left the viscount and king to return to his unit to continue searching the outskirts of Austice.

Norman and Fin shared a brief moment of eye contact and a complete understanding.

As much as Norman didn't like Brendan Devark at the moment, he wasn't about to let such a petty matter interfere with finding their daughters.

The two men mounted the grand stairs and strode purposefully to the Troivackian's chambers.

When they knocked, Prince Henry was the one to open the door, his glare indicative of his displeasure over recent events pertaining to his brother.

"Prince Henry, we need to ask the Troivackian king some questions that could be helpful in finding the princess and Lady Katarina," Norman greeted stiffly.

Henry gripped the door handle a little more tightly.

It was interesting to see the dual nature of the previously smiling and charming young man the prince had first appeared to be upon arriving. He was clearly very protective of his brother.

"I was told there was nothing we could do to help. The Troivackian king hasn't requested information, yet he also hasn't been given the courtesy of—"

A large hand that could only belong to one person in the world interrupted the prince's refusal and silenced him by resting on his shoulder.

Brendan Devark stepped forward, dark bags under his eyes, and his face unshaven, but aside from that, he looked every bit as controlled as ever.

"How can I be of assistance?"

Norman stared at the man, his thoughts unclear, but after a moment he let out a humbling sigh.

"I would like to share with you our findings and see if you can make sense of them."

Brendan didn't say a word before he stepped outside his chamber, closing the door behind him.

"Where would you like to discuss this?"

Grateful for his lack of attitude, Norman gestured toward the stairs. "The council room on the second floor, if you don't mind."

Brendan nodded.

The three men made their way back down the stairs to the council room, and once seated at the table, Norman folded his hands atop the table and fixed the younger man with a level stare.

"We have two options on what has happened. One being that Lady Katarina and Alina were in her chamber and abducted directly from the castle."

Brendan shook his head. "Lady Katarina would not leave quietly. No matter what, she'd find a way to draw attention if they were being abducted. The only reason she could have for being quiet would be if someone had a knife to the princess's throat. Which is possible, but again, I sense this to be unlikely."

Fin appreciated the truth of the man's words. He, too, had had similar reservations.

"The second option comes from a potential eyewitness who believes they saw the princess and lady in Austice dressed as boys," Norman continued briskly.

Brendan nodded. "They were dressed as boys when they were camping."

"They were seen amongst the taverns yet didn't enter any of them. What could have drawn them to Austice? No tavernkeepers or brothels have heard anything."

Brendan didn't answer immediately.

Instead his brows drew together, and he stared at the table thoughtfully in silence.

Then, his head snapped up and his dark eyes locked with Finlay Ashowan's.

"She went to see the bard."

Fin blinked, his eyes widening from surprise, then after a beat he turned to the king.

"Roscoe Vonousch," the two men said together.

Brendan sat up straighter. "No, I'm certain the bard's name was Reese Flaun or something to that effect."

Norman shook his head, but he and the viscount were already rising back to their feet.

"His name is Reese Flint, and there is someone with a deep grudge against him," Fin explained while he and the king strode purposefully to the door.

"Your Majesty," Brendan called out, stopping Norman in his tracks. "Include me in the search."

The Daxarian king stared at the younger man, studying him scrupulously.

After two breaths following the request, he finally gave a small nod of his chin.

Brendan needed no further invitation.

He was on his feet and out of the room in long strides with both the viscount and Daxarian king joining his sides as they moved.

Kat continued her bored observation of their guard of the hour, Dexter.

Alina would occasionally drift off into a restless sleep, and Reese, who had been beaten black and blue, lay with labored breathing on his side.

Not Kat, though.

No, she hadn't slept for a minute since they'd been taken, and somehow she showed no signs of fatigue. This alone was making the men grow even more guarded around her as she would alternate between chattering aimlessly and staring at them hungrily.

"So . . . is the plan to kill him? I thought that wasn't what you were paid enough to do?" Kat asked with a long sigh while glancing at the bard on the floor beside her.

It would seem she was going to chatter.

Reese let out a garbled moan from the floor.

"It's okay. Luckily for you, my father knows a deficient witch who can regrow bones and teeth. Real handy woman to know. I actually already lost my two front teeth thanks to Harold the donkey, but in fairness, I deserved it. Anyhow, she regrew them for me! Mighty painful, but absolutely worth it."

"Shut. Up." Dexter enunciated the words with great difficulty as he reshuffled the worn cards in his hands to redeal himself in his solitaire game.

"Why? Am I growing on you? Are you feeling guilty and wanting to send us home?" the redhead asked brightly.

"If I could have stabbed you every time you opened your mouth, I would have," Dexter growled as he began tossing down the cards onto an overturned crate.

"You seem moderately good at your job to have lived this long. You must know that we shouldn't stay in one location. Even if we were just the daughters of wealthy merchants and not, say, the princess and daughter of a hero . . ." Kat noted idly while rolling her eyes to the ceiling.

Alina had noticed that despite Kat always sounding calm and in control, her temperature had steadily risen since they'd been captured. She could feel it through their clothes as they sat practically pressed together on the small pile of hay. However, Alina hadn't had a moment of privacy from their captors since their first night to ask Kat if that was a normal thing for her as a mutated witch.

"I don't make the calls, I just make suggestions," Dexter said irritably.

"Even if it's your life on the line? Gods, man!" Kat guffawed.

Dexter stood up swiftly and glowered down at her.

Instead of looking startled or fearful as Alina did, Kat merely smiled in satisfaction.

"I'm beginning to think you like being hit," Dexter speculated while eyeing the bruises around Kat's throat where Roscoe had strangled her when she had told him he had the personality of a midget horse.

"Not really. I just know the worse I look, the harsher your punishment will be, and you've pissed me right off. So I want you all to know what a horrible mistake you've made . . . The vision of Roscoe being electrocuted by my father and screaming like a little girl brings me great pleasure." Kat laughed joyfully.

One would have thought her on a delightful outing with friends. Her composure was sparkling, her disposition sunny . . .

It was disturbing.

Alina had begun ignoring the oddness of it as of that morning.

She was tired, and she constantly worried about inducing a breathing attack if she didn't remain in charge of her emotions.

Reese Flint had been equally as cheerful as the redhead until the third round of "questioning" he had received.

While he lay beaten and bloodied, he had not given a single word of information, and the longer it went on, the more Alina and Katarina respected the man for it.

"Why . . . can't . . . the viscount . . . find . . . you?" Reese's weakened blood-filled voice burbled from the floor, interrupting Kat's conversation with the mercenary.

"Ah. That'd be because at no point in this venture have I felt afraid."

Alina's head snapped to attention. "What is he talking about?"

"Ah . . . well, my father can see pictures of a place if someone who lives in his home or family is in danger. However, I am not in danger, and I have known this the whole time," Kat explained with a shrug.

The irony was she had a split lip in two different places, and a cheek to match. Despite Roscoe having threatened to hurt Alina multiple times, he must have wanted to err ever so slightly on the side of caution . . . just in case they weren't lying.

The only reason Kat was the exception was she took every chance she could to annoy them, and right then, Alina was more than a little irritated with her friend as well.

"We have been kidnapped, and you two have been beaten for two days, you don't think we're in danger?!"

Kat chuckled. "Which is a problem, I admit! Though, even if you lived with us at the estate, my father couldn't sense you being in danger because we aren't on the grounds of the estate. No . . . at great distances he can only sense if my mum, my brother, or I am afraid, and like I said . . . I'm not."

"You honestly don't think these men are an inch away from *really* hurting us?! *Why?!*" Alina burst out vehemently.

"Dexter isn't paid enough for that nonsense. Roscoe's friend there . . . Patrick, was it? He may want to, but he won't unless Roscoe tells him to. Yeah. We're fine." Kat's sigh sounded bored, and it only incited a deeper rage from the princess.

"Our definitions of '*fine*' are not the damn same, you crazy wench!"

"Aww! I love you too!"

"Reese is suffering, I am terrified, why in the name of the Gods do you not care?!" Alina demanded, as tears rose in her eyes and her bound hands tightened into fists.

Dexter, who had witnessed the entire exchange was frowning, and a swell of panic was rising in his brown eyes. He was growing more and more convinced that the insane redhead had been telling the truth.

"Oh, I do care. I can't help that I'm not afraid, Alina. I'm sorry. I really am, it . . . it has to do with . . ." Kat faltered then, her good-natured expression fading.

"What does it have to do with?" Dexter growled.

"YOU STAY OUT OF THIS!" Alina barked, her fear momentarily forgotten and her tone so imperial the man unconsciously straightened his shoulders for a moment.

Kat pressed her lips together.

Maybe Alina would understand, and maybe she wouldn't . . . Kat's guilt over knowing her inability to feel fear was far more than she let on, but all she could do was continue to keep the mood cheerful and distract the men from hurting her friend.

"I just . . . I'm sorry. I guess because I know how powerful my father is, and I know he'll find us, I just can't make myself feel fear."

Alina knew that, if she spoke, she would curse and become even angrier over her friend's strange emotional processes, and so she turned her face away, her teeth clenched together and her throat burning.

What she didn't know was that her friend had lied, and Katarina Ashowan had to silently confess to herself that in some ways . . . she did feel fear . . . just not the kind that could get them help.

After all, she wasn't sure anyone would be able to look at her the same if they knew the truth.

Chapter 41

HELPLESS AND HOPELESS

Tam sat on the stairs of his home in Austice, staring at the doors as servants quietly crept around him.

He had barely eaten, slept, or even moved since his sister had disappeared three days ago.

His mother had left that morning with his father to interrogate some of the local mercenaries they knew in the city who could potentially know of someone being hired for a kidnapping job.

Since learning the most likely culprit of the abduction was a man named Roscoe, who had been looking for Reese Flint, they discovered a new problem. The men Roscoe had hired were most likely from Rollom or Sorlia, and, unfortunately, there wasn't any organization of the groups to track who it was. The only vein of information available to them, aside from talking to any mercenaries they could, were the brothels that reported to Annika Ashowan as she happened to own the majority shares of nearly ninety percent of the brothels in Daxaria.

The king had sent messages to the magistrates of the cities to round up any and all mercenaries who could have taken the job, but he knew it'd take time to see that done.

In the meantime, knights scoured Austice and the roads leading to and from the city. After they had contacted Roscoe's estranged wife, Lorelai, they learned that he did not have the money to purchase a boat ticket. Even so, all trading ships were thoroughly checked before being given the clear to leave the port.

Suffice it to say, word about the two missing women was well known in Austice, and it was beginning to trickle down through the rest of Daxaria's cities.

The king had not yet set a reward for their return or information in order to avoid a flood of false claims from the general public, as some may become greedy for a quick copper.

Day in, and day out, everyone worked to find them . . . everyone except Tam.

He sat on the steps, his fingers locked, and his teeth clenched.

His dark eyes fixed on the doors, but he didn't breathe a word.

Servants tried to ply him with water and food, but he barely ate or drank any of what they offered.

At long last, Raymond, their cook, was summoned. His beard more snowy than black, and what remained atop his head trimmed short, Raymond listened to the maids' concerned whispers and found himself standing before the future viscount, drying his hands on a tea towel, his apron caked in flour.

Tam had always worried everyone, but the large cook believed wholeheartedly in him. It didn't matter that Tam didn't like to be in big spaces or crowds. As a child, he would even wedge himself between the storage shelves in the kitchen and read for hours. He often retreated there to hide from Kat when she would refuse to let him read in peace.

Admittedly, Raymond was embarrassed to say he favored the lad. Tam was quiet, and didn't talk much, which was far more a Troivackian tendency than a Daxarian one. More than that, however, despite everyone always being critical of Tam, the old cook believed that the son of his masters was actually far stronger than anyone knew, only *something* in Tam required everything he had to hold back.

There was a fear in Tam, but it felt different from fear in men who had seen violence, or death. It was . . . something far harder to understand.

Slowly, Raymond lowered himself onto the step beside Tam; the tea towel was lightly flipped onto his shoulder as he then mimicked the young man's posture of leaning his beefy forearms on his thighs.

"You don't need to tell me to eat or sleep. The maids do that plenty."

Raymond cast a sidelong glance at Tam, appraising him before he let out a long sigh.

"Not everything's about you, Tam. I just came out here to pass gas. I figured since you've become a statue you wouldn't mind."

When the young man still didn't respond, Raymond turned his head to face him.

"Why are you sitting here like a pup waiting for its master to come home?"

There was a brief flutter in Tam's eyes before he blinked and momentarily dropped his gaze.

"Funny that that's what you call me, because that is exactly what I feel like right now."

Raymond continued to stare at Tam . . . and waited. He knew there was more festering in the lad's heart.

"Kat always . . . always says how useless I am because I don't try. It's never bothered me, but now . . . now I can see why . . . why I should maybe . . ." Tam let out a grunt and dropped his face to his hands and began rubbing his eyes wearily.

"What exactly is it you think you should be able to do right now?" Raymond asked quietly.

"At the very least? I should be able to do what Likon is doing by looking for them, checking with contacts and powerful friends. But I've never made contacts anywhere. For anything. I've made myself alone, and I've not started taking over any of Da's work and even that . . . Well, if I could take on his duties a little bit right now, maybe he wouldn't have so much on his plate as he burns his magic day and night trying to find them. But I've always refused to learn." His chin fell to his chest, and Tam felt an ache in his throat and moisture behind his eyes. He knew his next words would not come easily.

"Kat was right. I'm running away from it all, and I can't protect or help anyone. Worse than being useless . . . I'm a burden."

"Why have you refused to learn everything or to make connections, do you suppose?" Raymond managed to sound easygoing, but everyone knew it was the mystery worth a gold pile to discover the answer to.

"I'm scared," Tam replied bluntly. "Kat isn't scared of anything—even though I know she should be." He shook his head before continuing, "I'm scared of what my magic *does*."

Raymond waited with his breath held. This was more information than *anyone* had received from him. He watched as, in a move entirely like the lad's father, Tam reached up and rubbed the back of his neck.

"Something happens to me when . . . when I use it, and I don't know how to control it, or what exactly happens, but it is terrifying. It's shameful how scared I am of ever using my magic again, but I can't . . . I can't do it again."

"So that's why you refused explaining anything to everyone? You were worried that they'd make you try to use it again to help you understand or control it?"

Tam nodded, his eyes suspiciously wet, and once again fixed on the doors.

"What is it about big rooms and crowds that make you so uncomfortable with your magic? Is it that you're scared you'll hurt people?" Raymond could feel his mind putting together the information rapidly, but there were many puzzle pieces missing.

"No. I'm not." Tam chuckled bitterly. "Nothing as good or noble as that. The absolute truth? I'm scared of what it does to *me*." A look of utter self-loathing filled every crease in the young man's haggard face. "Isn't that pathetic? Making everyone cater to all my fears . . . making myself cumbersome."

He shook his head and his folded hands gripped together more tightly.

"I don't want to live like this anymore. I can't . . . I can't fail to even try." Tam swallowed with difficulty. "The best thing about me right now is my last name, but I've never really deserved it."

Raymond opened his mouth to disagree vehemently, but the future viscount wasn't finished.

"I'm going to start learning with Da. I'm going to start going out with Likon when Mum sends him on her errands to the brothels. Just because I never want to use my magic again doesn't mean I shouldn't try my hardest to live like a regular human."

Raymond felt a small flame of pride burst in his chest as he watched the young man's face suddenly seem a bit livelier, resolve burning in his eyes.

Wordlessly, he reached out his large hand and clapped it down on Tam's shoulder, nearly knocking the lad down the steps face-first. Raymond's hand tightened its hold and stopped Tam from pitching forward, allowing a small, tired smile to lift the corners of the young man's mouth.

"Now we just have to find Kat and Alina, and hope they're alright."

"With your sister involved, I'm more inclined to be worried about the kidnappers," Raymond announced with a small shrug before dropping his hand away from Tam's shoulder.

Tam shot the cook a flat glance. "Raymond, this is serious. They could be hurt."

"Your sister would've gotten scared then and your da woulda found them," the cook countered defensively. "Besides, if they do touch our Kitty Kat . . ." Raymond's eyes darkened, and Tam saw the man's mind turn to a place that he didn't visit often since becoming a cook in Daxaria.

It was hard to believe at first glance, but Raymond *had* been a Troivackian squadron leader at one point . . .

"If they hurt a hair on her head, I will squeeze their heads in my hands until they explode like melons."

Despite Raymond's voice being quiet, the threat was completely sincere. Tam nodded in approval.

After a moment of silence between the two, Raymond stood, shaking the murderous and gory thoughts from his head with a grunt as he rose. Then he turned to face Tam with his eyes once again kind.

"You'll be alright, Tam. Just take a deep breath and think logically like your mum and I taught you."

Tam gave a half smile of appreciation and another bob of his head as Raymond turned and began walking away, a sudden smile on his face brightening his normally stern features.

Confused for all of three beats, the most rancid stench Tam had ever smelled stung his nostrils, sending his hand flying to his nose to try and block out the odor and a yelp of distress yanking free of his mouth before he could stop it.

Raymond's cackle rang out in the great hall as the giant gasbag of a man left behind his latest victim.

Alina awoke to the sound of the cabin door banging open and their three captors flooding in, all wearing grim expressions.

Without a word, the men stepped forward producing three blindfolds, making Alina shrink back nervously, and Katarina, in her typical fashion, grin wryly.

"Oh good, you're finally listening to Dexter's advice. Alina, don't be scared, they are just moving us to a new location because they're noticing the knights becoming more active."

Alina didn't bother looking at Kat and instead looked at the three men to see their reactions. Dexter's face remained stony, Roscoe's was already stormy, and Patrick was rolling his eyes irritably at Kat.

"So you've most likely heard by now who we are. Why not let us go before you make things worse?" Alina queried while forcing her voice to remain calm.

"Then have you two tell them everything? I don't think so," Roscoe snapped while roughly tugging the blindfold over Alina's eyes, though his hands had a noticeable tremor.

"So what's the new plan?" Kat asked delightedly as Patrick tied her blindfold while yanking her hair roughly.

Reese Flint said nothing as anything he said seemed to agitate Roscoe further.

"We're moving you. That's all yous need to know." Patrick gave Kat's head a shove as he stood back up.

"That's going to be tough with knights patrolling the roads. Do you have a good plan to move three blindfolded and bound captives unnoticed?" Kat wondered aloud enthusiastically. It was as though she were proud that her captors were planning something she'd been advising them to do.

"That's for us to know an' you to deal with," Roscoe informed her while straightening and turning to the door once more. "As bratty as you're being, I see you sweating like a pig," he observed smugly.

Alina had noticed her friend's affliction as well, but even more concerning was the fact that Katarina, as far as she was aware, had not slept at all in over three and a half days. Somehow, she appeared as alert and normal as ever save for the rapid increase of her body heat. The princess knew her friend, while technically a mutated witch, still had her powers aligned more with fire, and so took it as a sign of stress, but even so . . . it was worrisome.

"Finding a place to stash us so quickly means it's a place you know well. They'll have knights there," Kat called out, ignoring Roscoe's observation of her damp appearance.

Roscoe didn't bother answering as he stepped outside leaving Patrick and Dexter alone in the room with them.

"Kat . . . isn't this bad?" Alina whispered anxiously to her friend.

The redhead let out a long sigh. "Not really. Chances are we'll have to be out in the open at some point. We're near some woods right now, and unless they want us walking to the next spot, which would be another absolutely terrible idea because that means more chance for evidence and tracks to be left, we have to get into a cart most likely. Seeing as it's nighttime they're hoping to go off the road undetected."

"How do you know all this?" Alina couldn't help but be slightly awed by her friend's in-depth deduction of the logic of their captors.

"I was awake when they brought us here, and when you two sleep, I have a lot of time to think. It's really annoying, but it does make me admit my mother was right." Kat let out a long-suffering sigh. "If I use my head, great things can happen. Though understanding the half-assed plan of these dimwits I'd hardly call great."

A surge of movement could be heard by the door and Kat grinned.

"Aww, Patrick. Did I strike a nerve? Good reflexes, Dexter."

The redhead had accurately guessed that the bloodthirsty Patrick had attempted to step forward and strike her, only to be stopped by the mercenary.

"I was just going to gag her," Patrick muttered, though his bulging eyes said otherwise.

"A gag! Gods! I've been waiting for one of you to think of it! Twenty points to Patrick!" Kat cheered. "You all started with fifty points, but each day I annoyed you and none of you thought of it, I took off another ten points. I was worried we'd hit the negatives if I'm honest."

Patrick threw Dexter's hand off his chest and lunged forward, only for the mercenary's fist to catch him in the gut.

"We know who they are. Don't do any more damage," Dexter hissed.

"I think you're forgetting *you* work for *us*," Patrick snarled after regaining his breath from being winded before shoving the mercenary away.

"Which also means I can quit," Dexter responded evenly while taking a menacing step forward.

"Hit him again! Don't be shy on our account, Dex!" Kat called out happily.

"SHUT UP!" Dexter roared, making Alina and Reese wince.

The door opened again. "Grab them, and for the Goddess's sake, be quiet! You want the whole kingdom to hear you?" Roscoe's panicked but dangerous tone broke the tension of the room. Dexter and Patrick shared one final look of disgust at each other, then began moving over to their captives.

Patrick roughly shoved a rag in Kat's mouth and then hauled her up to her feet with great difficulty—she was taller than him, after all.

Alina could tell Dexter was the one helping her up as his touch was far gentler than Roscoe's, and while she was grateful for the small mercy, she was becoming even more desperate to go home. As she tried once more to think of a way to escape, she couldn't help but feel disheartened, and even worse . . . utterly powerless. She couldn't even run without having a breathing attack . . . and so . . . her hopes sinking, Alina resigned herself to her fate of being half dragged across the cabin floor to the outdoors where a cart and horse sat waiting.

Chapter 42

A RISKY RUN

All Alina could see was blackness.

She felt the edge of the knife at her throat, and she knew that Kat had fallen silent, meaning that her friend's blindfold had been removed.

"Gods, would you look at her eyes? Theys ain't right. Like an animal's," Patrick exclaimed mockingly.

"If we needed any proof that she was the house witch's daughter, I suppose we have it," Dexter grumbled from the back of the cart.

"I never noticed because of the fire always being lit, but I can see now it isn't just her mind that's unnatural." Roscoe's voice sounded from the driver's seat.

Alina could feel the jostle of the cart beneath her and the cool night breeze brushing her cheeks and tousling her hair.

Her insides kept clenching over and over . . .

She was scared.

She was tired.

Her wrists and ankles were bruised and bleeding.

Kat had been hurt multiple times protecting her, though, admittedly, she seemed to be enjoying a little too much the freedom of speaking whatever crossed her mind.

Alina let out a soft breath through her nose.

She wondered what her mother would have done. Ainsley Reyes.

Probably negotiated a release with the captors calmly . . . but Alina didn't want to negotiate with them. She wanted to kick their shins and sensitive manly bits until all three of them were crumpled on the ground.

She wanted them apologizing and groveling at not only her own feet, but Reese's, Katarina's, and Lorelai's and her daughter's feet.

Then the princess wanted them to be tossed in a cell for decades until they were withered old men.

Imagining herself sentencing them in such a way seemed almost like a dream from the perspective of another woman.

Alina imagined her dress . . . green and gold . . . could feel her crown on her head, and . . . could feel Brendan's silent strength behind her. Supporting her, protecting her.

She missed him. Missed his unwavering steadiness, his controlled reasoning . . . the way his eyes became gentle when he saw her. How she knew every slight shift of his face and what he was feeling. It had become comforting in a way that she didn't realize until she was scared and alone.

Then, as her mind turned to her father, thinking of him slumped in his throne, surrounded by nothing but dust and silence, remembering how his wife and children used to all convene and happily read or talk during better days, Alina could feel her throat begin to ache.

She wanted to go home. She missed her mom. She missed her father, and she missed her brother, and she wanted everything about her present to be an absolutely terrible dream.

These men . . . these horrid men . . . for the sake of coin and pride hurt people. If she hadn't been a princess, or Kat a lady, they would've done worse, and that alone made Alina's stomach roil.

A strange unfamiliar feeling began to spread through Alina's chest, one that she hadn't felt so potently ever before.

She knew she'd been angry before, but she had never felt . . . enraged.

The cart rolled over quiet grass for the rest of the night, and the princess could make out the faint light of day from the seams of her blindfold.

"We're here. No one makes a sound or the princess's life will end today," Roscoe ordered them before snatching the blindfold from Alina's face so that she was faced with the trees her captor spoke of. They were in front of a new forest . . . one that was not familiar to her. There were fewer pines, and similar needled trees, meaning they had traveled farther south.

It took two of the men to haul Reese off the cart in his battered state, and so for a brief moment it was only Alina and Katarina seated in the cart while Patrick sat on the end.

"Kat, you can get away, can't you?" Alina asked quietly. She was taking an educated guess after seeing her friend's handling of a bow and arrow and hoped she wasn't wrong.

Slowly, Kat nodded, eyeing her friend suspiciously, the gag still firmly placed in her mouth.

"You heard Dexter. They know now I'm the princess, and they aren't taking risks. They're threatening me, but odds are they won't risk their necks over it. Get out of here, and get help. Unless you've been bluffing this whole time about being alright, in which case I'd like to take this opportunity to tell you, you are the most annoying creature to walk the face of the earth, and I'd like you to sweat away from me from now on."

Kat's eyebrow quirked upward, indicating she found Alina's words humorous, before her eyes darted to the men who were still struggling to get Reese to stand on his own.

"Reese and I will be fine, Kat. I know you want to protect me, but we can't do this forever. Just get help. Please. I don't want to wait for the cavalry. We just need to go ho—"

Alina's words were cut short as Dexter strode over to the end of the cart and gestured them toward himself. "Move along. We have to walk through the woods, and I don't want any tricks or you'll sleep outside."

Alina sighed, then began awkwardly scooting herself closer to her captors. When she reached the end of the cart, she glanced back at Katarina expecting to see the same mirth and grating calm confidence that she had plagued everyone with for days.

Instead, Alina caught a look of hesitancy . . . of dread. She saw the trickle of sweat down Kat's temple and frowned. Yet when Kat lifted her face and they locked eyes, her gaze morphed from uncertainty to tentative resolve.

Kat gave her friend a barely perceptible nod, then Alina turned her head in time for Dexter to gingerly clasp her bound wrists and shoulder to set her on the ground.

"We're going to cut the ties from your ankles so that you can walk through those trees, but I am tying the three of you on a line together, so don't even think of trying to run," Roscoe informed them while eyeing Kat in particular, who was shifting forward carefully on the cart.

The large man frowned as he watched the redhead draw closer to him.

Was it because he had driven the cart all night that he thought she looked to be glowing orange and gold?

Blinking and shaking his head, he waited for the redhead's feet to dangle over the edge of the cart before he began cutting the rope from her ankles.

He made sure to keep a firm grip around her slim calves to stop her from trying to kick him in the face—an idea she had definitely thought of at least five times on their journey there.

Alina, meanwhile, was already being tied onto the line connecting her to Reese.

The rope fell away from Kat's ankles onto the grass, and Roscoe raised his face to stare at the golden eyes that had taunted him for days.

Only . . . those golden eyes weren't just gleaming like they had the previous night.

They were shining like two brilliant suns, and the strange aura he thought he had seen before was now undeniable, flickering around her like flames.

Startled, Roscoe took a step back as Kat spit the gag out of her mouth.

"I'd like to say sorry, but I'm not a liar."

Then, before Roscoe could seize her again, Kat's boot shot upward and collided with his groin.

As he doubled over, she headbutted him, and that was it. She took off at a sprint, her long legs easily carrying her across the green grass, leaving behind her companions, despite her hands still being bound.

"GODSDAMNIT! *GET HER BACK HERE!*" Roscoe roared from the ground, forcing Patrick to scurry after the redhead and abandoning the bard, who slowly collapsed back onto his knees.

"Unhitch the horse and get after her! Send Patrick back here to help me with these two!" Dexter ordered Roscoe before grabbing Alina by the back of her shirt and holding her firmly. "She can't go far; she hasn't slept for days and has barely eaten."

"DID THAT WENCH LOOK HUMAN TO YOU JUST NOW?! WHO KNOWS WHAT MAGIC SHE IS CAPABLE OF!" Roscoe shouted while finally managing to stand again and limp to the front of the cart where he hastily unhitched the horse and mounted it bareback, only for his bruised balls to protest painfully, making him double over yet again.

"Oh for the— Get down, I'll go after her myself!" Dexter snapped, catching the horse's reins as Roscoe slid meekly from the steed.

Quickly, Dexter mounted the horse and took off after Katarina, who had already grown significantly smaller in the distance. Patrick had failed to even come near her . . .

Alina watched, her heart racing as she hoped with all her might that her friend would make it.

"If that witch doesn't get back here, we are moving you to a different location. She won't be able to find you." Roscoe's breath tickled Alina's ear and made her stomach burn with her fury.

"I should be your favorite person in the world right now for giving you some peace and quiet, and that's how you thank me? Gods. My father always did say citizens could, at times, be ungrateful."

Alina turned her chin slightly over her shoulder, her eyes sharp when they met with Roscoe's, and she took pride in seeing him flinch.

"You realize you will most likely not survive the consequences of this." Alina knew her hands were trembling, but her voice was steady.

"Which is why plans have changed," Roscoe informed her gruffly.

Alina raised an eyebrow. "Change your plans all you like; this will not end well for you."

This time the brute didn't respond, and instead he pulled on the rope linking her to Reese and tightened the knot around her wrist until it bit deeper into her skin.

Roscoe glanced at her briefly as he worked. "I guess that remains to be seen."

Alina snorted and smiled coldly at him.

"Roscoe, if you live to see the day of your trial, I want you to remember this moment when the three of you are brought to your knees in front of me. If at that time you open your mouth to plead for your life? You should know that *I* don't change my plans once I've made them."

Fin stood with Norman and the Troivackian king on the castle steps leading up to the front doors while receiving the latest report from Captain Taylor, when Mr. Howard exploded out of the doors, tripping over his feet as he ran with a small piece of paper clutched in his hands.

"LADY KATARINA ESCAPED! SHE SENT A MISSIVE!" The assistant stumbled to a halt before the three men, brandishing the note to Norman, who immediately snatched the paper from him.

He read the page swiftly before thrusting it toward Fin.

After he, too, read the note at record speed, he faced Brendan. "Kat escaped and ran until she reached a village where some of our knights have been posted. They sent a bird as soon as she reached them."

"Where is the princess?" Brendan demanded, moving closer.

"The village Kat made it to is between Austice and Xava. She ran straight through the woods, so my guess is there is a cottage, or hut, the princess and the bard are being kept in on the outskirts of Xava," Fin explained while Norman was already moving down the steps with Mr. Howard at his side.

The monarch was already commanding that orders be sent to the knights residing in Xava, and to any of the local coven members who might be able to hasten the investigation. He then ordered horses be prepared for himself and Finlay.

The house witch was descending the steps with Brendan at his side, but something was peculiar in the witch's eyes. There was a strange milky light slowly filling them . . .

"Viscount, is that all the missive said?" Brendan asked, a little louder than he normally would as the chaos of the men around them grew.

Fin turned to face him, his blue eyes nearly invisible behind the strange glowing white light.

"They said that there were signs that Kat had been abused, and . . ." Fin trailed off for a brief moment as everyone around him slowly began to notice the magic filling his eyes.

Brendan's stomach churned at the thought of anyone laying a hand on Alina, and instantly he felt uncontrollable wrath unlike any he had ever known before.

"My daughter . . . is . . . terrified."

That was all the viscount managed to say before he fell to his knees.

He did not fully collapse, however, as the light in his eyes shone brighter, and Norman stepped forward, his expression grave.

"What is happening?" Brendan asked while instinctively reaching for his sword.

Norman placed a hand on his forearm stopping him, his face grim. "Fin can see images and sometimes hear sounds of his children or wife when they are extremely afraid, or in pain, or in danger . . . Katarina has been none of those things, until now."

After another moment, the light faded from the viscount's eyes, and as he momentarily swayed, Brendan stepped forward to catch the man's shoulder, only a small, gloved hand appeared on the viscount's shoulder before he could.

Brendan's eyes snapped up in time to see Viscountess Annika Ashowan standing before him.

Fin was slowly pushing himself to his feet, his face pale, but when he spoke, his voice was hoarse with ire. "Kat isn't scared for herself, she's terrified that she had to leave Alina, but, Gods, . . . I saw her face, Annika. They hit our girl multiple times . . . they *hurt* OUR girl."

The viscountess's face was drawn and weary, and she wore britches instead of a dress, but her eyes . . .

Oh . . . her eyes.

They thirsted for blood, and when her gaze locked with Brendan, in a single moment the two understood each other completely.

They would see justice dealt, and it would be carried out the Troivackian way.

Chapter 43

TRYING TALES

"I am going with you whether you like it or not— Get away from me! I am not the type to be shy about kicking you in the face! Shove off!"

"M-My lady! Please! T-The viscount will—"

"Well, the *king* will have more than a few choice words for *you* if you butcher rescuing his daughter!"

Katarina Ashowan sat upon a saddled mare, her long hair tied back and the bruises on her face and throat prominent as she scowled down at the two knights and three villagers who surrounded her and her steed trying to make her wait for the king's rescue team to arrive and whisk her away back to Austice.

"I'm the only one who knows where they were, and I can look for signs of where they've gone!" Kat shouted while forcing the speckled white-and-gray horse to dance away from one of the knights who nearly succeeded in grabbing the reins.

"My lady, His Majesty would have already summoned the Xava knights; you don't need to—"

"I came from the other side of the woods! You know as well as I do that while it is Xava territory, it is on the farthest border. It'll take the Xava knights at least three days to get there if they ride hard. Austice is technically closer!" Kat countered while trying to calm the horse that was growing more than a little antsy at having so many people lunging for her rider.

"My lady, please think of your own safety, I'm sure your recent trauma—"

"Where did she get a horse?" One of the knights stopped his frantic swaying with his arms out and straightened with a frown.

"Sir Finkle, I will have you know that I merely *borrowed* this fine animal and—"

"Oy! That's my horse!" Another villager, a man in his midthirties, came barreling down the dirt road, his brown vest fluttering in the wind and his cap clutched in his hand as he waved down the group of people on the road leading away from the small village called Hickleson.

Both of the knights turned to stare at Katarina flatly, while she in turn deigned to look shocked.

"Sir, this comes as a grave surprise! I found this horse, minding her own business, grazing on grass over in a field that way." Kat rested her hand on her chest in a show of sincerity that was not being bought by anyone.

"Nay, that's my mare under yer arse . . . m'lady." The farmer only mumbled the "m'lady" after a sharp look from one of the knights.

"Sir, I will without a doubt return this beautiful horse to you, but right now, I have great need of it as the kingdom's beloved princess is in grave danger." Kat changed her tactic, her tone becoming noble.

The farmer eyed her warily, then the knights, who made no move to contradict her words.

". . . Not like I can object to a noblewoman anyway," the farmer said resignedly, giving his head a small shake.

However, his words had an entirely different effect than he had anticipated.

There was a brief pause where no one moved or said a word, and then, he heard a rustling of movement before two boots appeared in his vision.

Looking up slowly, the farmer found himself staring into the inhuman golden eyes belonging to the redhead, who was as tall as he was—and he was not short by any means.

"You can tell me no. Nobility or not, this is your horse. Don't ever think your voice doesn't matter. I'm sorry that I presumed you didn't need the mare." Katarina's serious expression and remorseful tone surprised not only the farmer but the knights and other villagers present as well.

"Why'd you try to steal it then?!" the knight named Sir Finkle exploded behind her while grabbing the reins.

"Because I had honestly thought she wouldn't be missed if I took her for a day or three . . ." Kat looked abashed for a moment before turning to face the group of people who had been blocking her path.

"With or without a horse, I'm joining you. You'll have to tie me down if you think I'm not going, so make up your minds with how we are going to get along with one another." The redhead's tone had turned combative, and it made the knights glance at each other with great unease.

"My lady, the viscount will surely—"

"He knows what I'm like and won't blame you. Now, shall we go?"

"O-One of us was going to stay with you while we waited for the viscount to arrive with . . ." the younger knight trailed off uncertainly while looking to Sir Finkle and visibly fidgeting.

"Both of you come with me. That'll be better anyway." Kat then turned to the farmer, who stiffened at the shift in her tone. "What is your name?"

"Name's Melvin Newhart." The farmer bobbed his head, and while his face still looked drawn, there was a change in his tone when he addressed Kat. He sounded slightly more respectful, and less exasperated.

"Could you please inform Viscount Ashowan when he arrives that Sir Finkle and— I'm sorry, what was your name?"

The younger knight, who was watching the exchange apprehensively, bowed deeply. "My name is Sir Gary Mistiv, my lady!"

The farmer who had come stilled and was frowning at the two knights, then at the lady still standing before him, her hands resting on her hips as she acknowledged the knight's bow with a regal nod.

"Yer . . . tugging my cap, aren't yous?"

Kat turned back around with her serious expression still intact, only this time, when Melvin Newhart laid eyes on her, his attention flew to her bruised cheek and temple, then her cut lip, and at long last her golden eyes and flaming hair.

"Yer not serious that the . . . the hero of Daxaria is . . . coming *here* . . . for . . ."

"Mr. Newhart, my name is Lady Katarina Ashowan. I apologize for not introducing myself sooner; however, we must go *now*."

The urgency in her voice snapped the man out of his astonishment, though his eyes with their deep bags widened as he stood at attention.

"O-Of course, my lady! Wh-When I heard that a noblewoman was found, I-I-I'm sorry, I thought yous was one of the ones that, that ran here to s-seduce Finkle a-a-a-an—"

Kat blinked in confusion before turning to stare at Sir Finkle. She raised a quizzical eyebrow. While she knew that the knights had been notified of her and Alina's kidnapping, she supposed not every commoner would be privy to the same information.

Were noblewomen throwing themselves at Sir Finkle regularly? She tried not to laugh when she noticed the man's evident discomfiture.

"My lady, if you are coming with us, we are going now, and we are not going to stop to rest until nightfall. Are you certain that—" Sir Finkle interrupted while clearing his throat uncomfortably and dropping his bright green eyes to the ground.

"Don't worry about me, I can see in the dark, now, let's move!" Kat began to head toward the village past the knights, her strides long and her back straight. If she was tired after running the entire night, she didn't show it. Sirs Finkle and Mistiv glanced at each other and each took off in her wake to catch up.

"M-My lady!"

Kat and the knights turned back around to face Melvin Newhart, who stood wringing his cap between his two hands.

"I-It'd be my honor if ye'd take my mare."

Kat grinned at the man and then broke the spell of her commanding mature aura by skipping like a child excitedly over to the horse, mounting it in one quick motion, and setting it off at a trot.

"Thaaaanks, Melviiiiiin!"

Alina stared at the small grimy window of the hunting blind she had been thrust into beside Reese, who was doing significantly better after a day where he had not been beaten by Roscoe. He even managed to sit up, drink, and eat. Once dusk had fallen and their three abductors were outside huddling around a fire whispering amongst themselves, the bard leaned over to Alina, though he winced as he did so. He definitely had more than one broken rib.

"Princess, I'm worried that they might be trying to find a way to . . . unload us."

Alina looked at the bard abruptly, her stomach jolting unpleasantly. "How do you mean?"

"They could try to sell us, or . . . you, rather, in an effort to . . . get rid of cumbersome baggage and the pressure of every armed man in Daxaria looking for you," Reese began carefully.

"W-What, like to a brothel o-or—"

"I'm afraid I heard them whispering about Zinferan slave traders when they presumed me unconscious. I don't mean to make you even more frightened—"

"Too bad, you would've been congratulating yourself right now if you were," Alina croaked, as her nails dug into her palms.

"I'm sorry. I only meant to keep you informed. Just in case."

Alina could feel her nose starting to run as she fought off her tears.

She suddenly was missing Kat's endless chattering a great deal.

"I-I understand that you mean to be considerate. Thank you."

"Your Highness, they may not let me live long if they decide they'd like to wash their hands of us, and so . . . would you mind if I tell you my story?"

Alina looked to Reese, tears rising in her eyes as she stared at his battered and weakened form, his voice soft and his dark green eyes bright in the moonlight.

"I was born to a mistress of a knight. She was said to be the beauty of her town . . . it's a town near Rollom actually. It's called Ovin. There isn't much to see there . . . a shrine to the Goddess, houses and farms, and of course, the knight's keep, my father's." A smile lightened Reese's features as he thought of the town, his mind stretching back to days long gone.

"As beautiful as she was, my mother was vain, and wildly unpredictable with her moods. The life and light of any room or party, and then bedridden for days. She loved me, but when a broken person loves you, it isn't a whole expression, and it brings with it its own pains."

Alina reached out and gingerly covered Reese's hand with her own as she listened, offering quiet comfort.

"I began to enjoy singing because it could take my mind off my worries for my mother, and eventually I found friends who enjoyed it the same way I did. The more we practiced and fun we had together, the better we became, and next thing I knew, I . . . I was in love. I fell in love with music and I fell in love with the lifestyle it brought. Making people feel special, or frivolous, for a window of time . . ."

Reese closed his eyes and leaned his head back on the rough wooden walls, his gaze floating to the ceiling as his smile widened, revealing one of his missing eyeteeth.

"I've met the Zinferan emperor and spent many nights drinking and carousing with him. I've seen every nook and cranny of Daxaria. I've seen a cook who was self-righteous and fearless . . . except when it came to risking the happiness of a woman he loved. I've seen war and peace, and music has guided me through it all. The happy songs, the sad, the fierce . . . I have lived a good life, and I even recently discovered that the journey music has led me on has gifted me thirty-two beautiful children."

"I beg your pardon?" Alina sat up, startled. "Did I hear correctly? *Thirty-two* children?"

"Yes, I had . . . *quite* a marvelous journey thanks to music. I have produced enough offspring to make a settlement, and Princess? They are all just so darn wonderful."

"Did the viscount know about this when he hired you?" The flat note in Alina's voice was not lost on the bard.

"Oh, he did, and believe me, you are taking it swimmingly by comparison, Your Highness. Truly!"

Alina's mouth was suspended open as she blinked in dumbfounded shock.

"Why in the world . . . did the viscount think you would be appropriate as my teacher?!"

"Oh, it was Katarina Ashowan's idea to hire me, and the viscount owed me a rather large debt."

"Of course it was Kat's idea." Alina couldn't help but give a small laugh before registering the latter half of Reese's reply. "What did you mean that the viscount owed you? Was it a large sum of money?!"

Alina began to wonder if she were about to find out Finlay Ashowan had even *more* secrets.

"Oh no, nothing as insignificant as that. No, he owes me because without *my* sparkling performance on a particular birthday party for your brother, Lady Katarina and Lord Tamlin Ashowan would not exist."

"What in the world do you mean?" Alina demanded, her alarm making her voice sharp.

"Ah . . . it was something your brother, Prince Eric, told me actually. Your father and mother were laughing about it after sharing some drinks of Troivackian moonshine. He relayed the story to me when we crossed paths last time."

"I still don't understand—"

"Perhaps ask . . . maybe not your father. Hm. Tell me, do you have any kindly old womenfolk around you who might explain to you the facts of life—"

"Oh Gods, please stop talking." Alina didn't like the direction the discussion was taking, and she immediately began thinking how she really didn't need to know her best friend's conception story.

"Right. Well, I suppose that brings us to the end of my tale, though I had been hoping for a bit more of a poetic finish there . . . it's your turn."

"My turn to what?" Alina asked wearily while pulling her knees closer so that she could rest her forehead upon them.

"It is your turn to tell me your story. Your interpretation of your life thus far because who knows what meaning or theme it could take from here on; sometimes it is good to have perspective."

Alina didn't answer right away.

Instead she looked back up out the window and felt an odd sense of peace that brought with it new clarity.

"Right . . . my . . . my story."

It dawned on Alina that not once had she ever honestly told her whole story.

She had been surrounded by people who loved her and would have listened with all their hearts, but somehow that made it harder to share.

Yet, sitting in a cold blind with a man who was little more than a stranger (and a lot more promiscuous than she could've imagined), she felt as though it was the perfect time.

So, taking a slow fortifying breath, Alina allowed herself to speak and for once not think about how her words would be heard or received; she only focused on giving them her truth.

Chapter 44

HONEST HOURS

"When I was a little girl, my breathing affliction never seemed as frightening as it does now. Back then, my mother would be the first to help me feel less afraid when I couldn't breathe. She'd act as though I just needed to go a little slower for a moment. She would rub my back, and speak quietly, but . . . better yet, she . . . she always looked at me calmly and lovingly. Like there wasn't a bone in her body that believed there was a reason to be scared." Alina let out a long shaky breath and gripped her interlaced fingers more tightly.

"It made me feel like it was just something that occasionally happens and I shouldn't worry." Alina felt her voice rasp as she recalled the familiar soft hands of her mother working soothing gentle lines on her back. The warmth in her gaze, the beautiful smile on her face . . .

"It wasn't until I was eight that I noticed that father always needed to leave the room when it happened, and it was then I learned that he couldn't see me like that without getting frightened, and he couldn't hide it. Sometimes he would cry and beg the Gods to stop making me suffer outside the room while I'd have an attack. It apparently was even worse when I happened to catch a cold. When I found out, it taught me to be scared because, well, *he* was scared. A king. My father . . . My father, who was always in control and kind. I wondered if it meant I was secretly dying."

Reese Flint stared at the princess, his bruised face turning sorrowful.

"I told my brother about it, when he came to visit from Sorlia—it was during his first year training under Duke Iones, and . . . he told me that *both* he and my father would be terrified out of their minds together when it happened, and that it was just because he and Father loved me too much to ever see me struggle for a moment of my life."

Reese gave a small smile.

"My brother was the one who gave me my first lute when I had told him I wanted to learn, and my father hadn't wanted me to because he was worried I'd have more attacks as a result. My brother, though, he . . . he said he was still frightened for me, but he believed I should be able to live as I wished."

Reese nodded, a glint of gladness in his eyes as he beheld the princess, whose eyes had yet to move from the window.

"Then, when my . . . when she . . . when my brother and mother got sick . . . he got better, and she didn't, and I wasn't . . . I wasn't allowed to say goodbye to her because . . . because my father didn't want me to get sick, too. He begged me to understand, and he said how sorry he was, and I realized how helpless I am. How weak I am. The best I can do is not worry others and be alright for them. Especially when my brother left." A darker look passed through Alina's face that seemed foreign to the normally kind and innocent princess.

"Father was always tired, always sad. Even if we got a letter from my brother, it made things worse, and I didn't want to add to that. I wanted to be as fine as I could be, so that things could maybe get better someday. But then he . . . my brother . . . he stopped writing, and no one has seen him. Now being alone with my father feels like . . ."

"You aren't allowed to be strong, nor are you allowed to be weak," Reese finished softly.

Alina nodded as tears dripped off her cheeks. "If I can't be strong enough to be there for my father, who is growing weaker as he gets older, and my brother is nowhere to be found, I think my family is going to crumble to nothing."

"So this is why you wanted to marry the Troivackian king. He was strong enough," Reese speculated slowly.

"Yes. His Majesty wanted me to be strong, and he believed I could become so with time and practice. He didn't get frightened when I had my breathing episode, and he instead gave me control even when I felt at my weakest. I thought . . . and felt like . . . he was someone who could help me become what I always wished I could be. He believed I had the potential to be strong enough to be queen of Troivack, and it made me feel powerful, and capable for the first time in my life, and it was intoxicating." Alina felt her heart flutter at the memory of facing the room of courtiers as she told them of her engagement, or the times when Brendan wouldn't move out of a room without her nod of permission.

"So why did you break off your engagement with him? Our dear Katarina mentioned that he was now an ex of yours?" Reese asked curiously.

"He . . . He revealed that he didn't think I'd be able to rule beside him as a partner. Instead, I'd be in charge of managing the Troivackian noblewomen, but again under supervision, and I'd only be able to change things to a point. It once again felt like I was being treated as weak, or pointless, and . . . and he . . ." Alina swallowed. She almost felt too embarrassed to say the next part aloud, but she couldn't taint her story with any half-truths.

"He revealed that he had been discussing with his court, and he himself had been considering . . . us not having children given my constitution. The suggestion of him taking a mistress came up and he didn't refute it immediately." Cheeks burning, Alina bit her tongue to stop herself from growing any more emotional.

There wasn't a single sound aside from the crickets outside for several long moments.

"That poor . . . beefcake of a man . . . oh . . . oh no . . ." Reese gasped, caught between a moan and a laugh. "Gods, did your father maim him himself?"

"I'm glad this is so amusing to you," Alina remarked glibly as her throat tightened. "No, my father didn't hurt him. Viscount Ashowan magically blasted him off Daxarian soil."

Reese let out a loud laugh that had him gasping in pain then clutching his side and groaning.

"Ahh . . . I always knew that redhead was going to be a great wealth of material for my ballads," he managed through gritted teeth before righting himself against the wall again.

"So . . . that's my story." Alina decided to finish her monologue then and there with a long sigh. For some reason telling Reese everything had completely dulled her emotions.

"Hm, well, might I offer you a bit of my worldly insight?"

Resisting the urge to refute the bard and instead try to go to sleep after feeling more than a little offended by his reaction to her pain, Alina turned to face him expectantly.

"Name a single woman who could have taught Brendan Devark, a king of Troivack, a man who was crowned at the age of seven, with his mother bowing before him and excluded from his education from that time on . . . who could have taught him what the other side of marriage outside of politics would be?"

"He has made it perfectly clear he believes love has no place in the marriage of a king."

"Yes, and who taught him that?"

"His . . . advisers, and . . . tradition. I'm sure his parents must have—"

"Assuming for a moment that his advisers were politically uncorrupted, what would their biggest concern be for their king?"

"That he make wise decisions and ensure the stability of Troivack."

"Right. So him not having an heir and opening up a war for the throne would be . . . ?"

"A problem," Alina admitted though she was narrowing her eyes as she did so. "Then why not have children with me? Why does it have to be a mistress? Do I really matter so little to him that—"

"He loves you so much that he is terrified of you dying," Reese interrupted with a gentle chuckle.

"If he loved me, then talk of a mistress wouldn't be on the table!" Alina snapped furiously, her ire over the situation reigniting anew.

"His advisers have guided him to safety as an adult, and they've clearly been loyal through something I don't think anyone can really understand, Princess. A boy leading a kingdom. He is not going to dismiss them immediately, even if he wanted to deep down."

"What makes you an expert on nobility, hm?" Alina demanded hotly, her restraint on her frustration dwindling dangerously low.

"Your Highness, I have served two different noble courts and seen far more of the world than you ever will. I have seen true depravity and evil, and I have seen true nobility and good. As fun as it is to act as foolish as I please, it doesn't mean that is all that I am. The reason my songs ring true is because I can see people's true nature. The peace my music has brought my soul gives me this gift." Reese eyed Alina steadily then, his face serious, and his voice unwavering.

"That man loves you far, far more than you love him, and I could tell that the first day I laid eyes on you two. You are the light in his abyss of darkness. He loves you the absolute best way he knows how, just as your father does, by protecting you."

Reese's words shook Alina to her core as Brendan's description of the abyss that hounded him echoed in her ears.

She could feel the power of the bard's words, and she knew he was right.

"Princess, he has known you and been your betrothed for a few weeks, but he's been a king for nearly twenty years. One of those roles is going to be a little more natural to him, and you can't expect to rule as his equal as you are. You need to be patient with yourself, with him, and with the situation. That is, if you want to try and reunite with him."

Alina stared at Reese in silence, the lump in her throat growing.

"Though, I'll be honest with you, Princess, if you decide to pass on him, I may try to take a run at climbing that tree of a *man*—honestly . . . he looks absolutely delic—"

"Reese, for the love of the Gods, please stop talking," Alina interrupted the bard's lusty musings while turning away from him so that she could lie on the floor with her back turned to him.

He had given her a lot to think about, but . . . there was a chance none of that would matter because right at that moment, Brendan was somewhere far away, and the possibility was growing that she would never see him again.

Letting out a quiet, trembling breath, the princess closed her eyes and prayed that at the very least, Katarina had made it somewhere safe.

Alina awoke the next morning feeling a rattle in her lungs that instantly ignited a cough.

Wincing and noticing how warm her face felt, she slowly sat up and glanced outside where the fire had been successfully snuffed out. She could see Dexter sitting on the ground with his back against a tree, his arms crossed in front of his chest.

It was clear that he was still alert, though, as his face remained tense, but still.

Alina coughed again.

She hated waking up feeling dewy, but worst of all, she hated having to shout that she needed to relieve herself.

"Excu—" Her voice was cut off by a far more aggressive coughing fit that didn't end after a few gulps of air . . . instead, after her third breath, she found it being inexplicably cut off.

Leaving her gasping.

She pitched herself forward, her eyes watering; she couldn't breathe, couldn't make a sound.

"What's going on with you? Hey! Hey! Stop that! We aren't going to fall for whatever plot you think you have figured out." The rustling from the ground just outside the blind signaled that Dexter had risen to his feet.

"She has a breathing affliction, she isn't pretending," Reese called out as he struggled to sit up to try and help her.

Dexter scoffed as Alina continued to fight for a clear breath on the floor, completely oblivious to their discussion. "Like I'll believe anything you say, you—"

Alina went limp.

Both Dexter and Reese stared at her startled.

"GOOD GODS, YOU DAFT IDIOT!" Reese winced as the effort of shouting hurt him. "MAKE SURE SHE'S BREATHING!" he hollered while trying to move closer to the princess despite the pain in his ribs becoming blinding.

"Alright! Alright, you just stay still," Dexter ordered while trying to remain in control of the situation despite his face betraying his concern.

Slowly, the mercenary reached his hand down near Alina's nose, extending his fingers out to feel for breath.

After a moment, his brows relaxed. "She's breathing again."

Reese let his own body go limp as he thanked the Gods he didn't have to bear partial responsibility for the princess's death.

"She's running hot, though." Dexter frowned as he noticed the red in Alina's cheeks and gently turned her onto her side while placing his palm against her forehead.

After a moment of quiet thought Dexter dropped his chin to his chest. "Godsdamnit, why does this bloody job just get more, and more . . ." He trailed off unable to finish what he was murmuring as he shook his head, exasperated.

"Probably because it's a job that involved kidnapping," Reese wheezed with a grimaced smile.

"You know it's your own fault you crossed Roscoe. And that you abandoned your daughter in the first place," Dexter fumed back while glaring at the bard's battered form.

With great difficulty, Reese managed to shift his head so that he could raise his eyes to meet the mercenary's, and with a breathy laugh replied with, "And it's your fault for not releasing the princess and the daughter of Finlay Ashowan. While my consequences have been grave, and to a point, deserved, I'd take them ten times over before facing what awaits you, Mr. Dexter."

Chapter 45

THE CAVALRY'S CHORUS

Alina stood with her hands bound in front of herself, her face burning, her eyes glazed, but at least she was conscious. The kidnappers had separated her and Reese once she had awoken, and currently Roscoe and Dexter were standing fidgeting on the edge of the forest. A hundred feet away was the cliffside that overlooked the Alcide Sea, which shone brilliantly in the summer sun.

The princess's groggy mind told her that she was most likely near the farthest reaches of Xava's border, though all she recalled being in that area were farmlands and forests as far as the eyes could see. There was no dwelling or settlement for anyone to hide, let alone a harbor or inlet.

"You'll not say a word," Roscoe warned, though the man looked more than a little skittish with his eyes bloodshot from lack of sleep and his entire being tense. "Sooner I'm rid of you, the better."

Alina didn't bother asking him who exactly he was pawning her off to. She knew it had something to do with the Zinferan traders, but her energy was depleted and her throat hurt brutally. She had a horrid cold and was focusing on remaining upright and breathing slowly so that she could avoid another attack.

It felt like an hour that Alina stood swaying on the spot waiting for Gods knew what, but then, she could hear distant voices.

She wondered for a moment if she were going mad thanks to her sickness, but the antsy shift in Roscoe's footing told her he heard them too.

After another few moments, five heads appeared over the cliffside edge, making Alina guess that there was a hidden path that led down to the water.

The five men were all Zinferan, and all wore faded loose pants tied with sashes at their waist. All were armed with curved swords at their hips, and all looked appropriately rough with their dirty tunics varying from white to black. Most of them wore their hair long, though not all of them looked particularly well kept.

The man who appeared to be their leader wore a tricorn hat that had seen better days a decade ago, and he had an impressive full set of white teeth.

"I hear we're providing passage for a young lady?" the leader called out as his men behind him either smiled or craned their necks to catch a glimpse of Alina.

"Yeah, we got ourselves a noble. Worth a decent amount, but we'll give her cheap if you take her now, no questions." Dexter stepped forward and blocked Alina from view while also keeping his hand resting casually on the hilt of his sword.

"Why the hurry?" the Zinferan asked with a slow blink of his slanted eyes. He could sense their impatience and was enjoying having the upper hand.

"We have other matters to attend to, and I said no questions," Dexter answered shortly.

"I see . . . and this wouldn't have anything to do with a certain missing *princess*, would it?" The Zinferan trader grinned knowingly.

Dexter's hand slowly curled around the hilt of his sword, and the Zinferan men behind their leader immediately drew their weapons. Roscoe took a halting step backward, though Alina stayed put.

She was so tired . . . but she knew she should be panicking.

"You'll get the girl and we'll be on our way. I'd say eight gold is more than a fair price, and if you want to try and pawn her as the missing Daxarian princess for more money, that's your neck to risk. Just keep me out of it." Dexter's voice was steady and confident, but while the Zinferan leader hesitated in his movements, he didn't stop smiling.

"Considering that the missing princess has made moving my . . . *product* in and out of Austice near impossible with all the checks the guards are doing, I'd say I should be *receiving* gold rather than paying it. Not to mention even the Dragon is getting involved now because of it."

Dexter grew stiff. "The Dragon? I thought they were lying low; why would they—"

"Perhaps you should consider retirement. To be involved in kidnapping nobles you should know at the very least that the Dragon still has eyes and ears everywhere." The Zinferan drew a circle in the air as he drew closer with a mad glint in his eye to match his smile. "The Dragon has just become powerful enough to become a ghost. Let me tell you . . . if even the Dragon is angered by this, you're in a *world* of trouble, old man."

"So make this girl disappear. You took Zinferan princes and princesses and made it happen." Dexter sneered, darkly.

"No one cared about them. Do you know how many Zinferan princes and princesses there are? Some of them aren't even blood related but were adopted because of the emperor's whim." The Zinferan laughed while still staring intently at Dexter. "Daxaria only has *one* beloved princess." His eyes darted to Alina for a moment before his smile turned hungry. "One princess, who, a little bird told me, just so happens to also be the next queen of Troivack. The way I see it, she's worth almost as much as my own beloved emperor."

"So do you want her or not?" Dexter demanded irritably as the Zinferan then stepped around the mercenary, his hands clasped leisurely behind his back as he moved closer to Alina, who didn't bother looking up.

"She's sick. You said she was in prime condition. I'll come back in three days, and if she's recovered, I might take her." The Zinferan strutted back to his men jauntily.

"That was not the deal!" Roscoe shouted hoarsely.

"You aren't in a position to negotiate, my friend. If you survive the three days and she's well, I'll consider it fate. Best wishes to you." The Zinferan slave trader didn't bother turning around fully as he glanced over his shoulder and touched the tip of his hat in farewell, his smile still smug.

Once the men had disappeared over the edge, their swords still drawn as they warily watched Dexter, whose gaze looked rather deadly, the mercenary rounded on Roscoe, his jaw set and his face pale.

"We bury her, and we split up. Take your bard, and never contact me again. Understand?"

At last, Alina raised her eyes to Dexter's strained profile.

Was this the end?

Was she going to see her mother in the Forest of the Afterlife . . . or . . . was there still a chance for a bloody miracle?

"What is this?" Brendan asked, eyeing the cart with what looked like a sail attached to it.

"It's a recent invention that can move faster than any horse if an air witch is at the back pushing us forward like a ship on water," Fin replied while leaping nimbly up onto the cart's driver's seat.

Norman, Captain Taylor, and Annika were already in the back.

Brendan followed suit and settled down beside Annika, who was pinning back her dark hair more firmly before reaching for the crossbow at her feet and tucking it into her lap.

"It's quite telling, you realize, that you are a part of the rescue team," Brendan murmured to the viscountess while looking at the squadrons of elite knights boarding another cart with four members of the Coven of Wittica moving toward each vehicle.

Annika shifted her eyes forward, too, while replying just as softly. "I know what you suspect me of, and if this becomes a war between us, then so be it. Today, however, we work for the same goal." While quiet, her voice was cold.

Brendan held her gaze unflinchingly. "Agreed."

"Straight Troivackian justice, or the jigsaw?" she asked while gripping her weapon more firmly.

Brendan shot her a sidelong glance and couldn't help but feel a corner of his mouth lift in dark appreciation.

"I like that the Troivackian jigsaw method is on your mind. We will see if there is time."

"Once we find them, we have all the time in the world—my husband will make sure of it," Annika replied while ignoring Norman's frown as he began to eavesdrop on their exchange.

"If Alina is . . . if she . . ." Brendan began, his voice becoming tight.

"If they've done worse to Alina than they have my daughter, the king will not permit you to carry out . . . *that* method. Though I can arrange it for you to see it done regardless," Annika managed ambiguously.

Brendan nodded in understanding.

Captain Taylor had managed to hear the exchange while sitting across from the two Troivackians and resisted the urge to shudder. The former kitchen knight turned captain had learned of the viscountess's secret work and identity shortly after he had been promoted from his station as elite knight. While he knew his perception of his friend's wife shouldn't change so drastically, he had seen and learned some things in his time that made it impossible not to.

"We're off!" Fin called over his shoulder.

Whatever Brendan had been expecting, it most certainly wasn't the wild ride that nearly rattled his teeth free of his head, or the mind-blowing speed that he had never experienced in his life.

In fact, it was so quick, his stomach was beginning to churn as the scenery began to blur.

Gods . . . let us . . . make it in time.

* * *

"I'm not paying you more money to kill her!" Roscoe shouted, his spittle flying as they moved deeper back into the forest nearer where Patrick and Reese waited.

"I know. I'm not staying with you after it's done, and we conclude our business once it is complete. I recommend once things settle down, to get out of Daxaria as soon as possible." Dexter continued walking, while guiding Alina along, her gait slow thanks to her weakened state.

"Alright, then l-let's just do it here!" Roscoe rounded on him, his eyes flashing, and his cheeks flushed.

Dexter hesitated then looked at the young woman, who was very clearly fevered.

"We will not breathe a word about this after today," Dexter started while slowly drawing his sword out.

Alina's gaze flew to Dexter's, and when he gave a small guilty wince, she straightened her shoulders to address him again. She couldn't let it end without another word, without another try . . .

"You have not listened when we've given you sound reasoning, or threats, and I will not beg you to spare my life," she began, her voice faint, but her stare steady. "I just hope that you know this is your last chance to walk away from this situation morally and physically safe. Don't kill me. Leave me here in the woods and run." Alina's eerie calm was disconcerting to both the men. Though she wasn't entirely certain she knew where her strength was coming from, if she were being honest with herself, she suspected it had more to do with her compromised health dulling her senses.

Both Roscoe and Dexter stared at each other, both obviously torn about the decision.

"RUN! THAT CRAZY BITCH IS BACK!" Patrick's sudden roar had the two men snapping to attention as their third accomplice bolted toward them from where he and Reese had waited.

The bard had been left behind on the ground, and when Dexter squinted to stare beyond Patrick into the trees, at first he saw nothing. Then, the unmistakable galloping hooves reached his ears, and not long after, the beast and its rider appeared. The faint orange-golden glow told them that it was indeed their former captive returning.

As Patrick wove between the trees in frantic zigzags, Roscoe was about to ask what the hell he was doing, when an arrow whistled through the air and winged Dexter, making him instinctively drop his sword.

Roscoe hastily grabbed Alina and pressed a dagger to her throat as he backed away.

Patrick, on the other hand, seized the dropped sword as soon as he reached his accomplices and swung with all his might from behind a tree at the horse's breast as it bore down on them.

The beast bucked its rider with a shriek and crashed to the ground, but the force of the blow had Patrick dropping the sword with a yelp.

Roscoe continued backing away while glancing periodically over his shoulder to make sure he wasn't running into any trees.

Kat was on her feet, a dagger in her hand and the glow around her burning brighter as her eyes gleamed magically, making her look even more beastly.

"Two knights are behind me, let her go," she panted while sidestepping the horse and eyeing Roscoe, who kept the blade pressed to Alina's throat until it began to bite into her skin.

Patrick was slowly lifting the sword back up as he faced Kat, who was already bending down and picking up the bow she had borrowed from the knights.

"Roscoe, you make me any more nervous and it'll summon my father here a little faster, and believe me, for now, I'm the lesser evil," Kat called out while raising the bow alongside a knife she had pulled free from her boot. Patrick hastily brandished the sword at her as Dexter backed away with a single hand in the air.

Roscoe didn't have time to respond before Patrick lunged at her, making Kat dodge and instead whack his forearms hard enough with her bow that the sword once again fell from his grip. When he moved to pick it back up, Kat kneed him in the face, then shoved him to the ground.

"S-STOP!" Roscoe roared, the knife against Alina's throat breaking through the skin.

It was at the sight of her friend's blood beading along the blade that something strange happened to Kat . . .

Her eyes suddenly filled with golden light, and the magical aura around her burned higher, and brighter, as though she were ablaze.

"I've held off as long . . . as I can," she ground out before she flipped the knife in her hand, and Alina then realized that Kat was aiming for Roscoe's face.

Her arm wound back to throw.

"N-No!" Alina's shout was interrupted when blue lightning exploded around them, launching Roscoe and her apart.

Katarina, however, despite the earth beginning to heave in waves beneath them, landed on a knee, her free fist punching the ground to steady her as her glowing eyes remained fixed on Roscoe as though nothing of great consequence had happened.

Finlay Ashowan emerged through the trees in the distance where Kat had originated from, as several other elite knights surged forward, with Brendan Devark at the front, all running straight toward them.

The cavalry had arrived.

Chapter 46

A FRIEND'S FOLLIES

Alina lay on the ground, disoriented, as the shouts of men rang out and flashes of lightning kept crackling around her. She felt her fever threaten to drag her into unconsciousness, her body already overtaxed . . . that is, until she laid eyes on Kat.

Her friend shone brighter than ever before, her eyes filled with nothing but the fierce magical light that was slowly turning white.

Yes, Katarina Ashowan looked like a divine being sent from the Goddess for the purpose of wrath and revenge as she clambered over waves of magically churning earth like an animal. Her attention fixated on Roscoe, who was on his arse, scrambling just beyond the waves of dirt and forest debris.

Despite her prey growing farther from her, this did little to deter Kat . . .

She didn't seem bothered by the new obstacle as she crawled and leapt with inhuman accuracy toward Roscoe, who was beginning to become more frantic as he watched the woman who looked to be an unnatural mix of beast, pure magic, and human draw closer. Unbeknownst to Roscoe, a lightning dome surrounded the scene, so when his head bumped into it, he issued a startled yelp, though the shield had done him no harm.

Even so, he couldn't move any farther away from Katarina as she rapidly closed the distance between them without slowing or hesitating for a single moment, her expression blank, but her aura growing.

Then at long last, a wave of earth rose up beneath her feet, and that was when Kat leapt an impossible distance over a chasm separating her from Roscoe and landed with her knees on either side of him.

Alina's panic tripled. Something was wrong . . .

Kat began to pummel Roscoe, only her punches looked stronger than what they should be given her size and stature, and the more she hit him, and the more blood that came from him, the bigger her glowing aura became.

Alina knew her consciousness was fading as she watched the gory scene, her breath rattling her lungs and her fever burning away the wisps of energy she had left, but she couldn't look away as Kat continued to raise her fists up and slam them back down into Roscoe's face mercilessly.

Alina noticed Roscoe weakly fumble with the discarded dagger he had been wielding at her throat and swipe upward. Alina opened her mouth to shout a warning to her friend, but it appeared as though Kat was unharmed as she continued her savage beating of the man.

A new fear bloomed in the princess's chest.

"Don't . . . kill . . . him." Alina raised her hand and began to sit up, but she found that the encroaching darkness she had been staving off had grown unavoidable.

As the colored spots danced before her, stopping her from witnessing Kat about to murder Roscoe, a set of strong arms lifted her off the ground, jerking her face up.

Through the haze and dwindling consciousness, Alina found herself gazing into the worried dark eyes she had doubted she would see again.

"Brendan, hello." Alina smiled weakly as she lifted her hand to touch his cheek with his unshaven whiskers tickling her palm. A swell of happiness rose in her chest, along with a slew of things she wanted to tell him, but her energy had finally reached its limits, and so she floated away into the nothingness that she'd been battling for too long.

Brendan stared at her still face, his breath coming out ragged as a powerful emotion surged through his chest, ripping his heart to shreds as he lifted his hand to check her throat for a pulse.

He could feel her fever beneath his touch and ground his teeth in fury, but he waited until, sure enough . . . he felt her heartbeat. Strong, and steady.

She was alive.

Momentarily calmed, Brendan then glanced down at her bound wrists that were blistered and bleeding, and his vision filled with red.

He gathered her closer to his chest as the mayhem prevailed around him. Getting her to safety was the most important thing in the world.

Lightning was all around them, men were shouting at two grimy-looking commoners on their knees with their hands behind their heads, while the earth rolled over and over to Brendan's left . . .

The power of the house witch was something remarkable indeed, but that was when he laid eyes on the glowing woman astride the man he guessed to be Roscoe, who had had a knife to Alina's throat. Brendan watched Katarina Ashowan as she continued beating her captor, her aura bright and emitting a heat that he could feel from where he watched at a distance . . . Her knuckles were red with blood, and her blows didn't slow.

Brendan stood and turned his back to the violence behind him.

Justice was being dealt.

He didn't need to interfere.

Fin strode past the two men who had surrendered without a second look back.

He passed Brendan, who cradled Alina preciously against his body, and he didn't spare the pair another look, even when he heard Norman's panicked holler behind him.

No, Fin's eyes were fixed on Katarina, his stomach gripped in horror.

Her face . . . the blood that splattered her cheeks as she continued her endless strikes. Her eyes were entirely aglow, but the aura around her was . . . turning white.

Fin moved faster, and the earth stopped waving like an angry sea around her.

She was burning her life instead of just her magic.

"KAT!" Fin shouted, his heart pounding in his chest as he began to run, his eyes fixed on his daughter's blood-splattered features.

Annika sprinted past him, and as a result, she reached her daughter before anyone else and immediately began whispering in her daughter's ears, her arms wrapping around Katarina's waist.

Fin watched his daughter turn on her mother, and for a terrifying moment, Fin had a nightmarish premonition that Kat couldn't *recognize* her mother. Then, Annika said something . . . and suddenly the magical aura faded.

It dwindled down further and further until at long last, Kat crumpled into her mother's arms.

Annika's gaze cut to Fin, and the two shared a nod of understanding, though a far greater emotion passed between the two of them that bordered along great unease and fear.

"A physician! We need to get to a physician!" Norman called out over everyone, making Fin turn back to his king and rake his hand through his hair. He was surprised to feel the sweat along his hairline as his terror had made everything seem rather cold.

Giving his head a shake, Fin acquiesced that there would be a better time and place to address the power his daughter had just shown.

"Your Majesty, there is a physician waiting back at—" Fin's words were cut off.

"Kat? Kat? Oh, Gods— KAT!"

Everyone turned back around to see the young woman collapsed like a broken doll against her mother.

Fin bolted back over to his wife with Norman close on his heels.

"HER SIDE!" Annika shouted, as her hands trembled, clutching her daughter to her.

Dropping to his knees, Fin checked Kat over, and sure enough, once his eyes fell to her side, noticed the blooming crimson stain that was steadily growing.

"Oh, Gods." Fin's voice turned hoarse as he wasted no time in ripping Annika's cloak and pressing it to the wound. Stripping off his coat, he then took his daughter into his arm, and stood. Annika covered Kat with the discarded coat while brushing her snarled red hair away from her pale face.

Fin all but ran with his daughter in his arms, his panic unlike anything he had known before. He barely had the presence of mind to direct himself toward the group where Captain Taylor waited with emergency bandages and the physician.

Annika remained by Roscoe, her insides quaking as she noticed her daughter's blood on her tunic. She then saw Norman standing over the man Kat had been brutalizing moments before. The bloody dagger was still in his hand.

"Is he—"

"Yes," Norman confirmed gravely.

Annika stared at the corpse coldly before turning her back on him to return to her daughter's side. "It was too swift a death for him."

Alina could hear the birds singing outside, and she could feel the balmy summer breeze wafting through the window.

She groaned and turned over in her bed, not quite ready to cast off the heavy cloak of sleep.

That is, until she realized that she was *in* a bed.

Her bed in Austice in fact.

Sitting bolt upright, Alina's wide eyes surveyed her surroundings frantically. Her wrists were stinging but they were wrapped neatly with clean snowy white bandages.

How had she returned?

Her mind strained to recall her final moments before passing out, and after a great deal of brow furrowing, she remembered Kat attacking Roscoe, and then seeing Brendan . . .

Turning to swing her legs over the edge of her bed, Alina halted when she found herself locking eyes with her father, who sat in a chair beside her, his eyes bloodshot and sunken.

"There's my girl," Norman greeted, his voice coming out a croak. He wore a cream tunic and black pants, but it was clear he hadn't changed in days.

"F-Father? What happened? How did we get back? Is everyone alright?!" Alina asked all in a single breath, but then she had to stop as she felt her lungs rattle ominously. She coughed a few times but could tell someone had already rubbed the minty-smelling salve on her chest, and it was helping her keep her breaths long and smooth in between.

"Easy, easy . . ." Norman soothed as he reached out and brushed his daughter's soft wavy blond hair from her face and gently clasped her hand. "We rescued you two, and after you rested in a small town for a day, we moved back to Austice. Gods, Alina, when I saw you unconscious in *his* arms . . ." Norman couldn't finish the sentence as he visibly shuddered.

"I'm safe." Alina reached out and clasped her father's other hand. "We're back, and . . . is Reese Flint okay?"

Norman went still for a moment and Alina began to fear the worst, until he finally nodded slowly.

"Reese will make a full recovery. The Ashowans have asked a witch capable of regrowing bones and teeth to help him grow back the ones he lost."

"Oh, thank the Gods . . . I know he is a bit unorthodox, but he didn't once tell those nasty men where Lorelai and her daughter were. He was rather brave in my opinion."

Norman rested his elbows on his knees as he stared up at his daughter pleadingly.

"Why . . . Why in the world did you go to see him that night?"

Alina shifted back away from her father.

Strangely, when she had been kidnapped, she never had imagined her father ever being able to ask her about why she had been out that night. Now it all seemed so long ago.

"I . . . was upset. Kat . . ." Norman winced, and Alina frowned. "What's wrong? Father, don't tell me you punished Kat! She tried to stop me! I begged her, and—and, no! It wouldn't be fair if she—"

"Lina," Norman interrupted his daughter, his eyes falling to the bed and his grip around his daughter's hands tightening.

Alina froze.

Since their mother had died he rarely, if ever, had called her by that nickname . . .

"Lina, love . . . Katarina . . . you know Katarina is a witch, right?"

"Y-Yes . . . ? Father, you're scaring me."

"Well, when witches use a lot of their magic they . . . sometimes they use too much. Not to mention when she was stabbed—"

"She was stabbed?!" Alina cried out fearfully, grasping her father's arm as she braced herself for more information.

"Yes, though those injuries, thankfully, weren't fatal. She will take a long time to recover, but Katarina has been unconscious for as long as you have; we aren't sure how much longer it will be. Fin says the first time he had experienced burning too much magic was when he was a lad and he slept for a week. It's been . . . not quite a week since you both returned. Your fever only broke last night, and . . . you must've been so tired . . ." Norman's expression was pained as his mind brought back the image of his precious daughter lying with deathlike stillness in her bed for days and nights on end.

"Kat will wake up, though, once she recovers, right?"

Norman hesitated, then grimaced.

"We believe so, but . . . the Ashowans are all rightfully distraught right now."

"Oh, Gods . . . it's all my fault," she whispered, her eyes flooding with tears and her features twisted in anguish. "Kat hadn't slept in days and barely ate and, and then I made her run to get help and—"

"Alina, it is not your fault that those terrible men took you. Nor is it your fault that she chose to follow you that night. Though I will say thank the Gods she did. If not for her, we would not have found you nearly as quickly."

Alina shook her head, unconvinced, before dropping her forehead to her hand.

"Don't you blame yourself for this, Alina. While you should not have snuck out, you did not deserve to have such terrors forced upon you." Norman stood and kissed the top of his daughter's head.

"Get some more sleep, I'll have a meal and bath sent up."

Norman slowly made his way to the door to leave his daughter to gather her thoughts in peace.

He could at the very least leave her side knowing that she had awoken.

Alina watched her father go, the guilt in her heart feeling like a slab of granite as it weighed her down into a place of deep regret.

When the door opened, her father stepped out, and Alina glanced back up, about to say farewell . . . when she caught a glimpse of a large, unshaven Troivackian king slouched against the stone wall staring at her door.

A familiar sense of warmth and relief spread in her chest, and just as Brendan's eyes were about to meet hers, the door once again closed.

With her gaze still fixed in the exact direction she had just seen the Troivackian king's face, Alina leaned back into her pillows. She couldn't deny the exhaustion she still felt in her bones, or the pain in her muscles, lungs, and wrists, but . . . seeing that Brendan was still there, even though she knew things were far from right with Kat still being unconscious, something in her knew that there was still time to fix things.

For now, though . . . she needed to rest.

Chapter 47

FOR SANITY'S SALVATION

When Alina awoke again, the sun had drifted across the hazy blue sky, passing its high point for the day; however, she felt far more wakeful than she had that morning—albeit a little bit sticky with sweat. No longer having a fever and experiencing chills meant that sleeping under blankets in the midst of summer was similar to being stifled in a blacksmith's shop.

Rising from her bed slowly, and nearly passing out at the sudden exertion, Alina grabbed one of the four posts of her bed to stop herself from completely crumpling to the floor.

Days lying down had not done wonders for her stamina.

"E-Excuse me?" Alina called out while clearing her throat.

She didn't want to risk crossing over to the door, even though she knew that the odds there were maids standing right outside her room were—

The door flew open, and in charged Paula with several other maids behind her, who all looked as though they had been weeping.

"Princess! We were so worried! Those horrible men! How could they?!" Paula, completely forgetting any sense of decorum, threw her arms around Alina, her tears starting to run anew.

Alina gingerly wrapped an arm around the young maid, as she felt sheepish for only being able to vaguely recall her name.

"There, there, I'm home safe, and . . . a bit hungry." Alina felt her cheeks turn pink at having to bring to attention the fact that while their concern was heartwarming, she hadn't had a proper meal since before her abduction.

"O-Of course, Your Highness! We will go fetch your meal straightaway! We'll also tell the kitchen staff to start warming the water for your bath." Paula released Alina hastily with a sniffle as all the maids dipped into curtsies.

"Thank you, I truly appreciate it." Alina managed to resume her mask of nobility as she smiled politely and bowed her head.

Her maids filed out, and when the door was open, Alina found herself craning her neck in an effort to see if Brendan was still waiting outside.

Unfortunately, the cluster of maids blocked the hall from view, and so she couldn't help but feel disappointed.

No. I should be relieved . . . I need to sort out my own feelings and thoughts about him first.

Alina gave her head a small shake, which proved to be a poor idea as a wave of dizziness overtook her, making her once again have to seize her bedpost.

After a moment, she managed to take another deep breath and do what she always did when faced with tangled thoughts and emotions.

She paced.

Though at a far slower speed than usual.

I still haven't forgiven him for considering bringing in a mistress to bear his children, and no matter how well-intentioned he is, if he tries to tell me that we won't have our own children, then we really will have to end the betrothal.

Alina felt her hands grip her sleep shift nervously.

My own mistake in the situation was underrating the amount of preparation I need to be a queen. Though once I'm more familiar with the Troivackian customs, perhaps I could try suggesting to him that he share more about his work and prove myself to him with any insights I get. Then, perhaps he'd let me join discussions with some of his closer advisers. Prince Henry would most likely help me. Though I doubt he has a high standing in court, I think I can count on him to be honest about the state of their political dealings.

Alina sighed. Much of her conversation with Brendan Devark relied on how he would respond.

The fact that he remained in Daxaria despite everything was promising.

Alina froze in her tracks then as her wrists began to sting. Casting her eyes down to her bandages with a frown, she discovered . . . she was trembling.

The sound of her three kidnappers shouting at Kat and Reese . . . the images of Katarina being struck across the face . . . Reese returning from outside more battered and bruised each and every time . . . the memories flashed in Alina's mind and suddenly she was huddled on the floor as the shaking weakened her knees.

She remembered Dexter reaching for his sword as they discussed leaving her buried in the woods.

The maids burst through the door carrying Alina's meal and an empty tub.

"Your Highness, we—! Oh, there you are!" Paula observed Alina's hunched position on the floor with a relieved smile after realizing the royal was not in her bed. Though the expression faded when Alina didn't rise.

"Princess, is everything alright?"

"Is something wrong?" Brendan Devark's voice from the corridor made all the maids jump and turn to curtsy as he stood behind them, his dark eyes searching the chamber for Alina, but unable to spot her as she remained crouched.

"O-Oh, Y-Your Majesty, the princess is, uh . . ." Paula trailed off, unable to finish the sentence as she stared at Alina's back. She had yet to lift her head.

Brendan strode forward past the guards and maids.

Stepping around the bed, he regarded Alina's still form, his jaw clenching powerfully for a moment before he squatted down in front of her.

"Princess, you aren't there anymore," Brendan murmured as he recognized her unsteadiness and her eyes staring blindly at the floor. "You're home."

Alina's shaking grew worse as she lifted her pale face to stare at Brendan. It was clear, though, that she was barely able to register his presence through the haze in her mind.

"Princess, you are home with your father. You and Lady Katarina are safe," Brendan repeated, his voice even.

"What've I done?" Alina breathed weakly. "Kat is . . . she's . . ."

Words no longer came out as Alina felt a cold sweat spread across her skin.

"It is not your fault. You will come out of this, and when you do, you will feel very tired," Brendan explained, his voice soothing and gentle.

"They were going to kill me," Alina managed, her throat restricting as she stared at Brendan desperately. "They were going to . . . bury me in the woods. They tried to sell me. Kat could . . . she might . . . die. I—"

"Lady Katarina is not dead. They did not kill you, you will not be sold. You are home. You are safe," Brendan counseled, making sure to repeat his words firmly despite a bloodthirsty rage filling him as she recounted what she had been through.

"What is—" The sound of Norman's voice had Brendan's eyes flitting to the king for a moment, but despite seeing the Daxarian king's agitated expression, he remained where he was and dropped his gaze back to Alina.

"Princess, your father is here. Now, can you tell us the words to your favorite ballad?"

"W-Why?" Alina asked, her eyes beginning to drift down to the floor.

"I'm curious what your favorite song is." Brendan managed to remain casual despite Norman's frown.

Alina blinked vacantly. She didn't speak, and Brendan began to worry she was slipping into a place farther than his words could reach, when she spoke once more.

"To the port of my home
To the land of my father
I bring tales of woe
Tales of love, storms, and fun
I bring flowers for my mother . . ."

Brendan nodded along as Alina recanted the lyrics, the tension in her shoulders gradually easing as she spoke.

Meanwhile, Norman became uncertain as he watched the exchange.

Behind him the guards and maids shared bewildered stares.

When Alina had finished the song lyrics, she felt her body grow heavy with weariness . . .

"How about you have a meal with your father, a bath, and a good sleep." Brendan gave Alina a tender smile while offering his hand to her.

Alina stared at Brendan then, her mind still not entirely clear, but the details of his face becoming sharper nonetheless. He hadn't shaved in ages, his eyes were encircled in shadowy bags, and his hair was disheveled. He wore a simple black tunic and pants, but they were rumpled after days of wear.

Alina blinked.

"I'm sorry," she whispered quietly.

Brendan's features stiffened, a look of pain passing briefly through his eyes.

"You don't have anything to be sorry for. Come, have something to eat. You must be hungry," he prompted again while inching his hand closer to hers.

Slowly, Alina reached out and clasped Brendan's hand.

She hadn't realized how cool or clammy her palms had become, and she wasn't entirely sure what had just happened to her either. Perhaps the stress of the abduction and sickness was making her a little mad.

Once standing, Brendan guided Alina over to her father, who was all too grateful to take his daughter's hands into his own.

"Come, my dear. Let's eat, and then I will leave you to wash and rest in peace."

Alina nodded, though she couldn't deny she was already struggling to keep her eyes open as half the maids sprang back into action, setting food on the small round table for her while the other half moved and set the tub down by the hearth.

Everyone kept casting pitying, sympathetic looks in Alina's direction, however, to the point where she hunched her shoulders and avoided their stares. She wished they'd stop and leave already.

As her father moved her over to her chair, Alina glanced over her shoulder and noted Brendan's back as he left the chamber, his shoulders as straight and broad as ever.

Her gut twisted, and she had to bite down on her tongue not to call out to him. It wasn't time to talk to him yet.

Taking a careful, fortifying breath, Alina regarded the steaming plate before her.

Perhaps tomorrow she would have recovered enough to regain some of her strength again . . . and with any luck, maybe Kat would wake up by then as well.

Fin sat beside his wife, his forearms braced against his knees, his hair oily and unkempt. His face was unshaven, and his clothes were unchanged from the day they had first rescued Alina and Kat.

Annika sat beside her husband, cleaner but no less haggard.

Neither of them said a word as they sat at their daughter's bedside.

Katarina had been permitted to stay in the castle so that not only the Royal Court Physician could attend to her, but also members from the Coven of Wittica.

More mutated witches had been permitted into the inner council of the coven throughout the years thanks to Fin's influence, one of whom could put people to sleep for hours at a time, which was incredibly useful to the physician she aided . . .

However, despite every resource being available, the simple fact was that there wasn't anything they could do but wait and see if Katarina Ashowan would wake up.

Tam sat on the opposite side of his sister's bed across from his parents, lost in thoughts about the threat of possible death his sister slept under, and how the world would become a little colder as a result if she did board death's carriage.

"She . . . she killed a man," Fin's quiet voice broke the heavy silence.

"A man who kidnapped and beat her. A man who threatened Alina's life—" Annika countered passionately, though her voice was still hushed.

"I know. I understand everything, but, Annika, she didn't even seem like herself. It was like her magic overtook her and she just kept hitting him; she won't ever be the same even if she does awaken." Fin eyed his daughter's bruised and battered knuckles, his stomach churning at the sight.

For a moment, the silence returned.

"She won't be the same if you treat her like that," Tam interjected, his breaths quickening. "She's the same as ever until she shows us otherwise. We can't go treating her differently right away."

"Tam's right," Annika agreed. "We can't presume anything about how she is or how she'll be . . . Fin, is it that you feel differently about her after what you saw?"

The viscount didn't respond at first, as his blue eyes stared off blankly, his brows furrowed.

"I think I'm worried what exactly it is her magic does. Her tutors did say that her abilities may reveal themselves more as time goes on. I also know Kat has a heart of gold, and I'm worried how she'll feel about what's happened. I guess the root of my concern . . .is that she wasn't entirely in control when she killed Roscoe."

Both Annika and Tam pondered Fin's words. Both shared similar worries but were unable to say anything.

As he watched Kat's sleeping face, her long red hair fanned out on the crisp white pillow and bed beneath her, Tam felt his anguish surge.

"I never got to tell her she was right. That . . . that I need to do more to prepare for the future . . . that I shouldn't just be an observer . . ." He trailed off, unable to finish the sentence as his parents stared at him, both with matching expressions of sad tenderness.

Annika and Fin shared a glance with each other, a wordless communication passing between them before Fin squeezed his wife's hand and stood.

Slowly, the viscount rounded his daughter's sickbed and moved to kneel before his son.

"You will tell her. Right now, she is just recovering her magic. The physician said everything else was healing remarkably well. I myself was unconscious for a week the first time I started burning away my life energy instead of magic," Fin reminded his son with a faint smile. "Your sister is strong. She'll come out of this, I'm sure of it."

Tam remained morose; the knowledge didn't help him feel any better.

A black plume swished by Fin and Tam that drew their attention.

"Hi, Kraken," Tam greeted as the feline gave a small chirp in response and leapt up onto Katarina's bed.

Fin raised himself up from the floor then lowered himself back down onto the edge of the bed as he watched Kraken stroll over carefully to Kat and sniff her face, then turn back and seat himself in front of the viscount.

"Witch, what is the status here?" Kraken raised his wide green eyes to Fin.

"We're just waiting for Kat to wake up. No telling how long it'll be."

Kraken glanced back over his shoulder at Katarina's sleeping face, then returned his attention to Fin and began kneading the wool blanket beneath his paws.

"Ah. That explains it. I was wondering why everyone was still like this. I see you haven't realized our eldest kitten is awake and pretending to sleep."

Fin's eyes shot up to his daughter's face. His look of shock and alarm startled both Tam and Annika.

"Kat?! Kraken says you're awake, and I swear to the Gods, young lady, it is not funny if you are!"

Katarina didn't move, but had there been a slight tremor in her shoulders just then?

Kraken let out a short huff followed by another chirp and proceeded to stroll right back up to her face. Everyone watched as Kraken unceremoniously bumped his head against Kat's forehead repeatedly and pressed his wet nose into her mouth while Fin rose from the edge of the bed back to his feet, his gaze never leaving his daughter's face.

When Katarina still didn't stir, Kraken turned around and proceeded to sit his fluffy arse right on her face.

There was a beat of silence before her hands slowly rose up and hoisted the large fluffy black cat off her face, her golden eyes glaring at her father's familiar.

"You know for a cat, Kraken, you can be a pretty crappy rat."

"Katarina!" Annika burst out, jumping to her feet, her voice a mixture of chastising and relief.

Fin let out a long breath mixed with a groan of irritation and happiness while Tam's face broke into a smile before he started laughing, his hand covering his eyes in relief.

Kraken squirmed in Katarina's grip until she released him, and as he sauntered toward the foot of the bed where he resumed kneading the blankets to begin making a perfect nap spot, he looked up at his witch.

"*Once again, I have saved the day. I will accept my reward of grilled mackerel by dinnertime.*"

Fin didn't bother with replying as he, Annika, and Tam all descended on Kat, hugging and kissing her as she squawked under the barrage of affection.

At long last, things were beginning to turn right again with the world.

Even though dark days were ahead, and more work needed to be done . . . at the very least, the Ashowans were together again, and in that moment, it was enough for them all to know they could take on any hardships to come.

Chapter 48

BRACING OF A BACKBONE

Alina stared out her chamber window lost in thought. It was the day after she had awoken and succumbed to a distressing attack of nerves. She didn't fully understand what had happened, but she decided of all her pressing issues, dealing with her betrothal to the Troivackian king needed to be the most carefully considered.

Especially now that Katarina was awake and, according to the maids the princess had spoken to, was as energetic and talkative as always. Alina smiled to herself; at least that was one weight off her chest.

Glancing to her right, Alina regarded Paula, who sat embroidering the sleeves of one her dresses. At first Alina worried the maid would insist she stay in bed all day, but Paula had even offered to go bring her sheet music from the library to practice her lute. While Alina had thought she might try playing later in the day, she found that her wrists were still smarting. Unfortunately, the physician had informed her that the wounds from being tied would most likely leave some scarring . . . but Alina was too grateful to be home to mind it much.

A knock on her chamber door drew both Alina's and Paula's attention away from the tranquil moment. Rising swiftly and striding over to the door to see who it was, the maid was greeted by a quiet voice.

The young maid squeaked, and it was that alone that informed Alina who was at her chamber door.

Her heart was already pounding and her expression hopeful when Paula turned to face her.

"Y-Your Highness, His Majesty King Brendan Devark has requested your presence in the rose maze for the luncheon hour."

Alina smiled and nodded her assent.

She was grateful that there wasn't a lot of time to prepare for the meal, as she knew she would've worked herself up to an even greater level of stress if given the time.

Paula tried to summon more maids but Alina managed to dissuade her relatively easily, saying that the commotion would be tiring.

With her dirty blond waves brushed to shining, and a fresh pale green dress covering her bandaged wrists, Alina headed down to the maze with Paula as her chaperone.

As she walked the castle corridors, she noticed the serving staff and several courtiers stopping to bow and curtsy quietly to her. None of them dared to whisper in her presence or speak to her.

No one really knew what to say . . .

In truth, Alina was relieved that she wasn't expected to make small talk or discuss her time away just yet, and she decided instead to enjoy the rare peace that followed her, even if it was a peace that was filled with worry and apprehension.

By the time Alina reached the second floor of the castle she found she was quite winded, and she had to rest for a few moments before she could once again begin her journey to the garden.

While she was feeling markedly better than she had the previous day, she still was regaining her strength in small doses.

As a result, the princess was a little late to the luncheon, but she had the feeling that the Troivackian king would be in a forgiving mood.

When she finally appeared at the entrance to the center of the maze under the brilliant blue summer sky, Alina noted Brendan's broad back to her as he sat before a table laden with their lunch under the shade of the gazebo. The Troivackian king was talking to his assistant, Mr. Levin, who was nodding along seriously and jotting something down in a leather-bound notebook before the assistant himself noticed Alina and must have said as much to the Troivackian king. Brendan then stood and strode over to the princess purposefully, while the assistant bowed and backed away.

Looking better rested than he had the previous day, Brendan had even shaved his stubble. He wore a clean set of black clothes—as was his usual attire—but despite all those changes, there was still a somber look in his eyes that made Alina wary.

"Princess Alina, thank you for joining me. I know it is not the ideal time as you are currently recovering from your sickness." Brendan bowed, and his stiff tone reaffirmed her worries.

"I was grateful for the invitation; I was hoping we might talk . . ." she returned the greeting as he offered her his arm to escort her to the table.

Once they'd reached the gazebo, Brendan helped her into her chair, and he then proceeded to alarm her even more so by kneeling down in front of her.

"Your Majesty, what in the world are you doing?" Alina felt panic rise in her chest. What was happening?!

Brendan's black eyes met with hers, but he waited until her breaths slowed once again before speaking.

"Princess Alina Reyes of Daxaria, for hurting you and suggesting a betrayal of loyalty, I offer my sincerest apologies."

Her jaw dropped.

"I am sorry for not being a better affianced to you, as you have done nothing but shown kindness and respect to me during our time together. I hope in the future, as our kingdoms continue to improve their relationships, that you will be able to see that my shortcomings when it comes to personal bonds will bear no burden on my efficiency as a ruler. I say this with the hope that you will not condemn my court because of my own weaknesses as a man."

Alina blinked rapidly as her mouth opened and closed several times. She was trying desperately to form words, but she was struggling grossly as the leader of Troivack, the country of men who did not apologize, did so on his knees before her.

"Additionally, I gave you my vow to see your brother attend our wedding. Given that our wedding is no longer going to take place, I ask that we alter the vow so that I may bring your brother to you when you choose a better man to be your groom. I do not assume that I will be invited to your wedding, I only ask that I may hold on to my honor and pride and see that my vow is upheld."

Brendan waited for Alina to say something for several prolonged moments.

It wasn't until she had worked through a deep breath that she dared to answer.

"Why did you consider a mistress in the first place?" she finally managed, her eyes searching his features desperately.

Pain filled Brendan's face.

"I never wanted to, but . . . I don't want you to die."

"What if I want to take that risk? You're losing me now, anyway, so why—"

"You'd still be alive."

"You think if I end up marrying someone else I won't want children with them?" The glib tone in Alina's voice when she asked the question made Brendan pause.

"Perhaps, but at least it wouldn't be because I allowed it to—"

"Stop being a coward, Brendan Devark. If you love me that much, then take responsibility for it."

Silence fell between them for a long moment as Brendan's face drained of color.

"Please get off your knees," Alina requested more gently as she tried not to show her apprehension and instead tried to be a little more like the man before her . . .

Blunt to a fault.

"I was rash in assuming I could have a voice or say in the Troivackian court in a short amount of time. You've been king for the majority of your life, and it was ignorant and wrong of me to assume I could appear and share the work-load. However . . . I'd like to discuss the possibility that, after a few years, you let me take more on. Or at least try. Be open-minded to it. If you can promise me that, on a political level, I think we can figure something out."

Brendan slowly shifted up from his knees back into the chair across from her. His eyes studied her carefully, but they no longer looked quite so . . . broken.

No, there was something else beginning to stir in him.

"Now, on to personal matters . . . A mistress is off the table, and I want children. I may die, I may not, but do you think another man is going to take care of me the way you will? Will another man humble himself and remain as strong as you did today for my sake?"

Brendan frowned.

Alina waited to see if she needed to keep ranting logic at him, or if he would finally snap out of his silence.

Straightening his shoulders after a few more moments of Alina staring back at him unabashedly, Brendan folded his hands in his lap.

"I don't think it is a good idea for us to wed." His voice was quiet, but the sting in Alina's heart made it feel as though he had shouted the words.

"Why?" Alina tilted her head over her left shoulder. She didn't hide her look of anger, or the tears in her eyes.

"If something happens to you, I don't know that I will be strong enough."

"Strong enough for what?" she fired back breathily.

"Strong enough to be a king." Brendan focused on the table between them. "I was supposed to be on a boat back to Troivack almost a week ago. I was supposed to review countless documents and write correspondence to the advisers I'd left in charge. Instead, I stayed up every night trying to find you. I thought as long as I knew where you were, then I could return, but then you were sick, and all I could do was sit in the corridor and wait outside your door."

Alina felt her tears start to fall, but she didn't move a muscle.

"Then when you slipped into the soldier's spell and told me what you'd gone through, instead of going back to work, I started negotiating with certain people to break several laws and torture your captors in ways that are far from humane."

Alina nearly flinched at the murderous expression that crossed his face, but instead she latched on to what he had said earlier.

"What's a soldier's spell?" she asked, briefly dashing her tears and finding that they had thankfully stopped for the time being.

Brendan shifted in his seat. A sure sign that he too was growing emotional.

"A soldier's spell is when a soldier has lived horrors and they continue to haunt his mind. That is what was afflicting you yesterday in your chamber."

"Ah," was all Alina managed to say as the sincerity of Brendan's confession sank in.

"I apologize again, Princess. For everything. I will be boarding a vessel to Troivack tonight, so you will never have to see me again." Without another moment's hesitation, the Troivackian king rose and began to step around the table to take his leave.

Only Alina wasn't quite finished with him.

"Tell me, does your position still hold firm regardless of a factor you've foolishly missed?" she asked, stopping Brendan in his tracks.

"Nothing will change my mind, Princess," he replied, though Alina could see the flicker of devastation in his eyes as he did so.

"Really? So the fact that I love you back doesn't matter. Hm. I suppose the bard was wrong."

Brendan went rigid, and his eyes widened.

In the distance, outside of earshot, Mr. Levin grew alarmed at what could've warranted such an emotional outburst from his king.

Alina feigned disinterest in his reaction and slowly stood.

"The bard I was taken with told me you loved me more than I loved you. He said I was the light to your abyss . . ."

Brendan's eyes were transfixed on Alina's face, his lips parting in surprise and his face filled with feeling.

"However, the way I see it . . . I'm willing to risk death just to have your Troivackian heirs, and when I'm in danger, whether it be kidnapped in the middle of some woods or under some sort of soldier's spell as you called it, you're the only one I trust enough to hold on to. You're the only one I want to turn to to become stronger."

Squaring her body to fully face him, Alina gave up her final shred of pride and dignity, knowing if she didn't give that moment her all, she'd feel weak and pathetic the rest of her life.

"Brendan Devark, we all have things we get scared about. I'm scared of not being enough to convince you that you should be my husband, but that only makes me want to be even better. If all I make you is scared and I inspire no desire in you to overcome that, then I guess I'm not the right woman for you, and you're not the man I thought you were."

With a final imperial look that she was faking down to every bitty bone in her body as her insides quivered and she wanted to break down sobbing, Alina forced herself to turn away from Brendan.

Her posture flawless and her eyes fixed straight ahead, she made it all of three steps before she felt a strong arm swing her around, and suddenly Brendan Devark was kissing her with everything he had.

His arm wrapped around her waist, and his other hand rose to cup the back of her head tenderly.

All Alina felt was an explosion of fireworks in her mind, heart, and belly.

Pure euphoria unlike anything she had felt before sang in her blood, and she never wanted the moment to end.

When Brendan did finally pull back, his dark eyes searched hers worriedly, clearly checking to gauge her reaction. She smiled.

"I take it . . . you'd like us to be betrothed again?" Alina asked faintly, as a blush bloomed in her cheeks.

Brendan didn't outwardly say anything, but he did manage to growl in approval.

"Good." Her smile widened, but just as Brendan's head swept down to kiss her in that wonderful way again, Alina's hand gently drifted up to his cheek and stopped him.

"On one condition." A playful twinkle entered her eyes.

Brendan frowned for a moment, concerned that there was something else unresolved that would need to be discussed and therefore get in the way of the more important act of kissing her senseless.

"I need you to say three little words for me." Alina's innocent smile grew mischievous, and Brendan felt himself become awkward.

"I love you," he managed quietly.

It wasn't that he minded saying it, it was more that he was aware Mr.

Levin and Alina's maid were both making a silent commotion several feet away as they watched the entire scene unfold.

"I love you, too, but those aren't the three words I was looking for." Alina leaned in closer until the tip of her nose touched Brendan's.

"What do I need to say?" he demanded as his eyes dipped down to her mouth once more.

Alina couldn't help it, it was too perfect. So she decided to finally tell him exactly what she needed to hear from him. "You see . . . I need you to say . . . I'm always right."

Brendan's dark eyes snapped back up to hers, and after a beat of silence, he threw his head back and roared with laughter.

Chapter 49

ROLLING ONWARD

Kat sat against the mountain of pillows while happily consuming her fourth bowl of soup, and what must have been a loaf and a half of bread with half a wheel of cheese. Though this was only a light snack following a breakfast of an entire leg of ham and two bowls of fruit.

"This might be a record for you," Tam observed mildly as he looked up from his book, his legs stretched out casually from his chair beside his sister's bed.

Setting down the empty bowl with a clatter, Katarina leaned back with a sigh. "Would you believe me if I said I was still hungry?"

"Yes, I would. Do you want me to send for more?" Tam slowly began to close his book.

"Maybe in a few minutes. I might want a roast . . . or pie. I could eat a pie . . ." Kat pondered aloud wistfully.

"I know that the more you use your magic, the more food you consume, but you do realize you haven't stopped eating since breakfast, right? You're going to bankrupt the king," Tam pointed out with a wry grin.

Kat rolled her eyes at her brother's gibe before her expression grew more somber.

"So . . . when do you suppose Da and Mum will get around to my lecture about the whole ordeal?"

Tam's good-humored smile faded from his face before he eased himself forward in his seat to rest his forearms against his legs.

"Maybe by the Winter Solstice. Though I'm happy to try and make that happen a little sooner. I wanted to point out for them that it was a stupid thing for you to do to go back to the kidnappers anyway. You should have waited until Da and the elite knights took care of things."

"Mum was there, too, which is odd. I know she's good with knives, but why would the king allow her to come along?" Kat mused, a small frown wedging itself between her brows.

Tam tensed, but his sister was too deep in thought to notice. "Don't change the subject. Kat, I heard that Alina was the one responsible for making you go see the bard in the first place, but you hadn't slept or eaten properly in days. Why the hell did you go back to save her?"

Katarina raised an eyebrow at her brother. "I took a risk, and while I know it could have gone better . . . I'd like to think it says something about my character."

Tam shot her a flat look. "That you're reckless?"

"That I'm someone who is brave!" Kat fired back with dramatic indignation.

"Bravely stupid? In the face of the consequences to your stupid decisions?" Tam taunted with a smirk.

"Bravely willing to strangle the next person to insult my honor while I lie in bed recovering . . . *from a Godsdamn knife wound!*" Kat said indignantly as she pointed at the aforementioned wound.

"See, this is why Mum and Da aren't going to lecture you for a long time. You're going to use that excuse to get away with everything from now on, aren't you?"

"I'm sorry, are you saying I have no right to a little sympathy for being stabbed?!" Kat slapped her hand over her chest.

"If you were a normal human woman, sure. I'd pull out all the stops for a normal human woman who got stabbed, but you're you, and I know you better."

Kat crossed her arms across her chair while openly pouting. "I should've known you wouldn't care."

Tam rolled his eyes and stood, his book in hand. "What kind of pie do you want?"

Kat's face lit up with a reinvigorated smile. "A peach pie would be the best thing in the world, I think!"

Tam chuckled. He wasn't surprised. Peach was her favorite, particularly if it was made with rum or brandy.

As he moved to the door, and Kat stared at her brother's back, her levity melted away as a new thought crossed her mind . . .

"Did you mean it when you said I was right?"

Halting in his tracks, Tam only turned his head instead of his entire body to address his sister's question.

"I did. I've already started working with Mum and Likon. Once Da isn't slaving away in the kitchen trying to cook for your every whim, I'll be splitting my time between them. You were right that . . . it isn't enough to simply be present. I need to be able to protect people, too."

The shadow across her brother's face made Kat's gut twist with worry.

How was it that, after waiting what felt like her whole life to be told she was right, it only made her feel guilty?

"Will you . . . will you be okay?" she asked tentatively.

For a moment Tam didn't say anything, and he turned his face back toward the door.

"Not sure, but I'm going to have to try."

Then, he was gone, leaving Katarina feeling too many emotions for her to properly understand a single one. She knew that both she and her brother were pretending that things were normal between them, but the truth was that she didn't feel normal anymore, and something was different about him, too.

Casting her eyes down to the emerald green coverlet pensively, Kat debated throwing the thing off as her body temperature began to resume its normal high, when a slight breeze had her casually glance at the window.

She was startled to the point of giving a small start when she saw Likon climbing down from the window ledge, then winced against her stitches that protested her sudden movement.

"How the hell did you— Never mind. What are you doing here?!" Kat demanded as Likon walked over to her bedside and seated himself, his light brown eyes slightly bloodshot as he peered quietly at the bruises along her temple and cheek.

"I'm fine, I swear it hurt more when Mum taught me self-defense." Kat snorted and waved her hand dismissively.

Likon still stared, and it was the look he would give her whenever he was able to see straight through whatever façade she was putting on, and . . . right then, right there, it made her throat begin to close.

"It finally happened, didn't it?" Likon asked, his soft voice cresting the quiet in a way that made Kat's heart skip a beat.

"What do you mean?" Kat attempted to laugh, but when she finally risked meeting Likon's eyes, maintaining any act grew too painful.

He didn't have to say anything. He had known the answer before he'd even asked.

"You killed someone. Just like you were always worried you would."

Tears rose in Kat's golden eyes, and for some reason she couldn't speak.

"So has it changed that feeling at all? That feeling that you could go off and—"

"I don't know," Kat interrupted while looking away.

At first, Likon didn't say anything as he waited for the woman he loved to regain control of her emotions.

"If you need anything, you know you just have to ask." His soft voice nearly broke the redhead's tentative grasp on her composure, and sensing this, Likon stood from the bed once more and began walking back to the window.

"Is my brother really going with you when my mum sends you to check on her businesses?" Kat asked while clearing her throat in an effort to loosen the tightness that had gripped it moments before.

"He has come on an outing already, yes." Likon turned back to face Kat, a small smile on his face. "When you were gone he was . . . lost, and since then he's at least trying to find his way."

"So you think it's a good thing? Didn't you want to be viscount?" Kat asked with a hint of teasing in her voice.

"Gods no. Most nobles I'd have to deal with would be very annoying, and you know it. Of course I'm relieved Tam's starting to step up. Besides, if for whatever reason I did happen to need a title, I'm sure I could purchase a barony. Especially with your parents sponsoring me." Likon winked before climbing back out the window, leaving Kat grinning at his back.

Once the young man had disappeared yet again, Kat felt a small knot in her chest loosen.

At the very least, Likon hadn't changed his view of her despite knowing the truth.

Kat's brief lift in mood immediately crashed down, though, as she couldn't help but think, *Even if I don't see myself the same way at all.*

Alina stood in the hallway outside of Kat's room nervously fiddling with her thumbnails, as Brendan shot her a sidelong glance with an arched eyebrow.

"Why are you nervous to see your friend?" he asked slowly.

"Well . . . I . . . she came to save me, and because of that she . . . she . . ."

"She killed the man who made you both suffer. His life was hers to take. Or yours, but you weren't in the condition to." Brendan shrugged.

Alina began to chew on her lip. "I wanted them to have a fair trial, and—"

"You are too generous—"

"—I wanted Roscoe more than the others to be the one begging at my feet," Alina cut Brendan off, and earned his startled reaction, followed by an impressed nod.

"It's true I don't have the stomach for violence, but even I'm not a good enough person to want him to get off without any revenge," Alina admitted, her normally soft, friendly features firm and serious.

"Are we going to stand here and wait for her to rise from her sickbed then?" Brendan pondered aloud while turning his gaze to Katarina's door and folding his arms.

Alina could tell that he was being completely serious in the question. Though if she hadn't seen him waiting by her door while she had been recovering, she would've thought him jesting.

Hesitantly, the princess raised her hand to knock, when the door swung inward all on its own, to reveal Katarina in a strange contraption. It looked like a chair with wheels attached on the bottom, and her brother, Tam, stood behind her, his hands wrapped around handles attached to the back.

"Alina!" Kat burst out with a stunned reaction.

The princess stood frozen, her hazel eyes wide and her hand still suspended in the air prepared to knock.

Kat's gaze flitted to the Troivackian king, and her excited expression faded, her shoulders drooping. "Oh . . . hi . . . Your Majesty."

Brendan couldn't help but scowl for a brief moment before he took a deep breath and let out a long sigh. "Lady Katarina, you really will need to fix that poor habit of yours of displaying your dislike of me before journeying to Troivack. Otherwise my kinsmen will place us both in an uncomfortable position."

"Wait— Troivack? That means you two are . . . ?" Kat trailed off, her eyes darting between the king and the princess as her finger pointed at her friend then back to Brendan.

Brendan frowned at the gesture, but Kat was too flustered to care.

Tam was the one to gingerly reach out and flick the back of his sister's head to snap her senses back into place.

"Oww— Ah, right then. I . . . will . . . work on hiding my true feelings better," Kat managed once she had returned from her daze.

Alina fought off a smile as Brendan let out a soft agitated growl only loud enough for her to hear.

It really did speak wonders of the man that he was willing to suffer her friend, who annoyed him horribly, for the sake of her happiness.

"What is that you are sitting in?" Alina asked, changing the subject quickly, and smiling brightly down at her friend.

"Ah, this is something that an inventor in Austice came up with in the past few months. Tam tracked it down when he realized I'd be a raging bitc— I'd be *unpleasant* . . . if I were bedbound for another while." Kat caught herself, batting her eyes prettily up to her friend, who couldn't resist a laugh.

It was good to see her friend act every bit like herself as always.

"Princess, would you perhaps like to try pushing the chair? I have a mission to discuss with His Majesty from my father," Tam interjected suddenly while bowing his head.

Everyone's attention jumped to the future viscount, whose gaze remained downcast as usual.

Even Kat tried to twist around to look at her brother, only to cringe in pain from the wound in her side.

"O-Of course, Tam!" Alina stepped forward after overcoming her momentary surprise.

"The princess is still herself recovering from her sickness, so perhaps—" Brendan began gruffly, only for Alina to wave him off.

"We'll just do one lap of this floor. I'll take a rest if I need to. I need to start building my strength, don't I?" she asked, shooting Brendan a knowing smile that softened the man's features.

"I suppose. Don't push yourself, and you . . . "—Brendan turned his narrowed gaze to Kat—"don't make her take any unnecessary risks, such as shoving the chair to see how far it'll take you."

Kat's jaw dropped. "Your Majesty! I never— How could you have thought of . . . Well, now that you mention it, that does sound rather fun." Kat's grin turned wolfish as she looked to her friend, who was already laughing and grabbing the handles that Tam had released.

The king let out another guttural snarl in the back of his throat, but neither of the women paid it any mind as Alina slowly began pushing the chair out of the chamber, leaving Tam and Brendan alone. The two young women chattered away happily to each other, as though nothing had happened and they were simply meeting for an afternoon stroll.

Brendan faced Tam, who was in the process of exiting the chamber and closing the door behind him.

"His Majesty has allowed us use of his council room." Tam gestured down the corridor toward the stairs while inclining himself respectfully.

After studying the future viscount carefully, Brendan began the journey down to the second floor, where he wondered what in the world the Ashowan family wanted from him. Especially since news of his and the princess's engagement being renewed was still not publicly known. The main reason for that was because he still had to find time to speak with the Daxarian king, who was making arrangements for the official court hearing of the kidnappers.

As Brendan moved, it then occurred to him that he couldn't hear Tam's footsteps behind him, and so he stopped and turned to see if the young man had fallen behind. Instead, he found that Tam was nearly standing beside him, his face blank as he halted at the king's side.

Brendan hadn't sensed him at all, and it gave him a small surprise. Which was strange; in the past whenever Tam had lurked nearby, Brendan had always been able to sense him.

Had that been because Tam had consciously *chosen* to be noticeable back then?

A small frown formed between Brendan's eyebrows as he resumed walking.

The princess was right, someone silently appearing can definitely be disconcerting.

Chapter 50

OVERCOMING OBSTACLES

B rendan sat across from Tam and waited.

The council room was quiet aside from the sounds of birds tweeting outside in the beautiful summer afternoon, and the occasional voices of serving staff passing outside in the corridor.

"The missive, Your Majesty," Tam reached inside his thin black coat and procured two pages of folded parchment with the seal of House Jenoure keeping them closed.

Stretching his arm across the table, Brendan took the papers gingerly as he continued to try and glean an emotion from the future viscount.

After a moment more of scrutiny, he acknowledged he wasn't getting far, and so he set to reading what the young man's parents had decided to say.

Brendan's eyes flew across the pages, a strange half smile curling his lips.

Once he had finished with the contents, he raised his dark eyes once more to Tam, only this time, the future viscount was watching *him*.

"Are you aware of the contents of this missive?" Brendan asked, leaning back in his chair and locking eyes with Tam calmly.

"I am."

"Why is it I find myself seated across from you and not your mother or father?"

"That is because I am set to take over as viscount for my father in the coming years, and therefore the relationship between House Jenoure and Your Majesty will be carried on mostly between ourselves," Tam replied, his tone even, but the slight twitch of his shoulders indicating he was nervous.

Brendan nodded.

"So your parents wish to know if we are going to have a shadow war between ourselves. I find it interesting that they ask this so directly, as they tend to be more . . . understated in most of their dealings."

Tam said nothing, only held his silence.

Brendan almost smiled at him. The young lord wasn't being overeager and was waiting to see his opponent's reaction before pushing the matter and revealing more of his hand.

Despite it being a first negotiation for Tamlin Ashowan, he was handling it better than most would.

"I find the last part of this . . ." Brendan pointed to the second page. "Interesting."

Still, Tam said nothing.

"Your father says he will personally bring the prince to the castle grounds where the princess is to be wed, and he will allow me to escort the prince the rest of the way to Her Highness in order to uphold my vow. The viscount wishes to keep the prince's location a secret to the very end. I must admit his ability to keep such an important figure hidden is rather impressive."

"Your Majesty, will you agree to the terms that the viscount and viscountess have outlined? It was your proposal after all," Tam asked, tilting his head and forcing his posture to remain still.

Brendan tilted his head thoughtfully, his hands resting on the armrests as he once again pensively regarded Tam.

"I never could determine what your intentions were with the princess. You became close with her quickly, hovered around her and me, and yet never seemed to seek out anything more of a relationship with her. You hide a great deal about yourself."

Tam sat upright in his seat and leaned his forearms on the table.

"I've not had any designs to wed the princess. It is the duty of an Ashowan to protect those who are good—and need protecting. I believe if you choose to look at my family in that light as opposed to one with sinister intentions, you might find our actions making far more sense."

Brendan gave a small, humorless smile. "So I've been told time and time again. Regardless, I cannot ever be free of skepticism. So this is my counteroffer to your parents. I will allow your mother to keep her spies in my court as I have nothing to hide. That is, unless she tries to meddle in my affairs; should that ever happen, I will not hesitate to seek Troivackian justice. However, it has come to my attention that your mother is now a majority owner of nearly all the brothels in Troivack."

Tam froze.

"Did you think I wouldn't have my own ears out amongst my people?" Brendan's smile sharpened. "My refined proposal to keep 'the Dragon's' true identity hidden is that she shares with me any and all information regarding rebellious groups gathering. I'm well aware with my brother being alive, and my marriage to the Daxarian princess, that some will oppose the direction I am taking Troivack."

Tam raised an eyebrow but continued to listen.

"If your family truly is in the business of protecting people they are loyal to, I am guessing Princess Alina is one of them. It would be in their best interest that I remain informed to keep her safe. Wouldn't you agree, Lord Tam?"

For a moment, the future viscount didn't say anything, and then a cool smile of his own climbed up his face.

"I think my parents may be amenable to those conditions, though I have one I myself would like to add as well."

It was Brendan's turn to wait in silence.

"With my sister joining Her Highness in Troivack for a year, it is expected that Mr. Levin's wife, Lady Carolina Levin, formerly known as Lady Carolina Piereva, will cease her meddling with my family in her ill-guided sense of revenge for her dead father. My uncle Charles Piereva."

Brendan's eyebrows flew upward, and then after a moment, he allowed his impressed expression to show.

"How long has it been that your mother figured out who outed her secret identity to me?"

"I figured it out after gathering some information of my own," Tam replied, keeping his expression and voice neutral.

"My compliments to you, Lord Tamlin. I thought we had the information hidden quite well." Brendan's face gradually shifted back to its impenetrable mask before speaking once more.

"If I fail to stop Lady Carolina's ploy to seek revenge, what recourse will your family take?"

Tam's smile turned rather impish then, and it was such a foreign expression on his usually blank face that the king was mildly taken aback.

"We won't need to do anything. Your soon-to-be wife would be the one to suffer along with my sister should Katarina, Alina's close friend, be met with any sort of malice. Don't you think?"

Brendan's countenance turned murderous. "You dare threaten the princess?"

Tam grew serious once more as he locked eyes with the king.

"I would never threaten the princess. I just think you should know that their fates are tied in the future. If you allow my sister to experience malice and hostility in Troivack, this will affect your future wife as well. My trust in your willingness to protect the princess is what leaves me to believe you will also see to it her beloved friend, who has risked her life several times for Her Highness, will also fall under your sincere care. Am I wrong? Or are you a man who does not respect and honor my sister's recent actions?"

Brendan wasn't forthcoming with his response. Instead, he regarded Tam with renewed interest.

"You know, Lord Ashowan . . . I don't care for you. Or your parents, but I think we have come to an understanding. You are right that your sister has earned my respect, appreciation, and even a debt from me that I cannot foresee being repaid easily. Your observation of my nature and the situation is commendable, and I do not offer praise easily."

"I do not seek praise, though I thank you for it. Do we have an agreement?" Tam's stare was direct, and the king held it easily.

Slowly standing, Brendan offered his hand.

"We have an agreement, and you have my word I will protect your sister and monitor Lady Carolina."

Tam shook the king's hand, but before he could release it and pull away, Brendan gripped his palm more tightly.

"Don't think I'm not aware that you are hiding some kind of darkness in you. I will continue to be wary of your house and your nature, but should you ever master whatever it is that lurks beneath this façade of yours, I would enjoy a proper duel with you."

Tam's stricken reaction was all the king needed to release the man's hand and exit the throne room satisfied that at least he had one headache resolved before his next greatest hurdle . . .

Facing the father of the woman he loved.

Daxaria's king, Norman Reyes.

Norman sat brooding over his folded hands.

The Troivackian king and his daughter had just left after sharing the news that they had reconciled after Brendan's apology.

Mr. Howard didn't dare say a word as he sensed that his king was in a rather foreboding mood.

After a few more moments of stifling silence, the assistant wondered if he should perhaps leave the room, when the king suddenly turned to him, his hazel eyes ablaze.

"He will continue to hurt Alina, and in Troivack with no one to hold him accountable to common decency, he could become even worse! I cannot condone this. What if they wed and he changes his mind about taking a mistress? Alina would be trapped!"

Clearing his throat delicately, Mr. Howard dared to point out, "His Majesty King Brendan did say he would be happy to include the clause of it being prohibited in their marriage agreement. We could seek just recourse to the extent of annulment, and any offspring they may have would be then considered nobility of Daxaria."

"As if he wouldn't be able to hide an affair," Norman seethed, his fingers gripping his armrests.

Mr. Howard was beginning to grow worried that the Daxarian king might not be in the right mindset to hear his own counterarguments for the match, and he was debating bringing in the inner council to perhaps help the man see things more practically, when a repetitive brushing sound at the door interrupted his thoughts.

The assistant turned puzzled at the sound, whereas Norman stood up abruptly.

"Gods, no. Dick Fuks should have known better than to bring *him* into this."

Mr. Howard blinked in confusion until Norman stormed over to the door and opened it to reveal none other than Finlay Ashowan's familiar, Kraken.

The fluffy black feline peered up at Norman and let out a breathy "Meeooww," before beginning to saunter into the room.

"What is it you want, you little—" Norman was starting to grumble before Kraken circled back around and began brushing himself against the king's legs and striding forward again with another chirp.

"It looks like he wants you to follow him," Mr. Howard observed as he, too, slowly rose curiously.

"I'm not going to follow the whims of a stupid— Ouch!" Norman jumped as a small bite around his ankle had him stepping out the door.

The guards on either side of the doors had their lips pursed and their eyes bulging as they worked diligently not to laugh as the fluffy cat continued to amble forward before turning back and meowing at the king.

"If I follow you, will you leave the castle and give me some peace?" Norman demanded while glowering down at Kraken's bright green eyes.

The familiar chirped again, then turned and continued padding away.

Letting out a final disgruntled groan, Norman began to follow the beast.

He moved past servants who bowed, and nobility whom he barely acknowledged, as Kraken wove effortlessly through the many legs that flowed past him.

It wasn't until they stood before a chamber door that Kraken finally stopped.

Norman halted and said bluntly, "What now? These are guest chambers."

Kraken gave him a languid stare before he proceeded to reach up and paw repeatedly at the door.

"What in the world are you—"

The chamber door opened to reveal Prince Henry, who looked down at the familiar as though he had been expecting him.

"Kraken! It's been a while, have you come for a— Oh. Good afternoon, Your Majesty." The prince bowed once he realized Norman was standing off to the side. Ever since his brother had been magically catapulted into the Alcide Sea, the prince's former friendly persona was replaced with a hardness whenever it came to the Daxarian king.

"What is it that brings you to my brother's chamber?" Henry asked tonelessly as he met Norman's gaze unabashedly.

"I'm following that thing so it will leave me alone. Why are you in the Troivackian king's chambers?"

Henry blinked down at Kraken, who meowed, then strolled into the room before addressing Norman's question.

"I was helping my brother catch up on his correspondence with the Troivackian court so that he has more time to spend with the princess."

Norman gritted his teeth and didn't say a word for a moment, until a rustling sound drew both Henry's and his gaze within the chamber.

Kraken was perched atop the Troivackian king's rather messy desk and was sniffing various piles of parchment.

"Oh, Kraken, perhaps don't, I just started—" Henry stepped forward.

The cat proceeded to topple over a rather large pile of paper that sent the pages fluttering in every which way across the floor.

"Godsdamnit," Henry muttered while hastily rushing over to the desk and plucking up Kraken and dropping him onto the floor.

Norman watched as the cat then proceeded to sit and stare at him while letting out a particularly long, "Meooooooooowwwwwww," in front of a particular group of papers.

Henry frowned when Norman took a step into the chamber uninvited, until he realized what had caught the king's attention. All at once, Henry's hostile expression shifted to a knowing smile.

"Ah. I heard rumors of the great Kraken's intelligence. I suppose I can't refute it now." He chuckled before Norman raised a questioning gaze to the prince, as Mr. Howard moved in behind the king, his own eyes roaming over several pages that were scattered near them.

"Feel free to read those, Your Majesty." Henry nodded while folding his arms, no longer in a hurry to pick up the mess.

Both Norman and Mr. Howard plucked up pages and pages of letters, and notes . . .

All about Alina.

"The king . . . began messaging the physicians in Troivack the day he arrived . . ." Mr. Howard announced dumbly.

"Yes. When my brother learned of the princess's breathing difficulties he sought out the most renowned physicians in Troivack to see if our climate would be safe for her. Apparently our dry heat and winters may actually be beneficial to Her Highness," Henry informed them, his eyes twinkling.

"Then this . . ." Norman looked briefly at the pages he held before staring at the prince with growing wonder and shock.

"Those are the notes my brother made every time the princess got upset with him. He recorded what he discovered she liked, as well as her improvement on their walks."

Dumbstruck, Norman peered at the papers once more.

The parchment at the top of the stack read:

Don't make conversation an interrogation.

Likes folk music.

Doesn't always cry because sad.

Wants to be queen.

Misses her brother.

Enjoys theater performances.

Likes raspberry tarts.

Snorts when she laughs uncontrollably.

Norman's grip on the pages tightened as he read.

"I kept trying to tell everyone my brother means well. He just is a little slower to learn. He makes up for it by trying over and over until he gets it right."

Speechless, Norman felt emotion seize his throat as he stared at the list once more and remembered that he hadn't heard his daughter truly laugh since before Ainsley's death.

He realized then why she hadn't.

She laughed like her mother.

With crashing clarity, Norman understood how much his daughter had been trying to care for him . . . and how it was preventing her from being truly happy.

"Of course, I ask that you not tell my brother I let you look at his private correspondence, but I hope this helps clear the air a little."

Tears rising in his eyes, for a moment, Norman refused to look up.

"I will keep this exchange between us." The king hastily handed the notes to the prince, then turned and swept out of the room with Mr. Howard following close on his heels.

Another small chirp drew Henry's eyes down to the fluffy feline that had taken to lying across the desk while licking his paw leisurely.

"I guess I now know who is really in charge around here, don't I?"

Kraken stared up at Henry and responded with a slow blink.

His answer was perfectly clear.

Chapter 51

WHAT GOES AROUND

Norman sat in his office, blindly staring at the cold hearth, the dining hour drawing near as he listened to the corridor growing busier with nobles hurrying down to the banquet hall for their meal.

The trial for his daughter's kidnappers was to take place the very next day, and the energy in the air was rising steadily.

A knock on the door reached through the king's daze slowly, until with a clearing of his throat he finally managed to call out, "Enter."

He tried to straighten himself in his chair, but he decided he wasn't quite up to the task yet as he locked eyes with Brendan Devark.

The Troivackian king, who wore a simple tunic tight around his chest and biceps and loose at his middle, slowly rounded the sofa and seated himself across from Norman. The look of wary concern on Brendan's face at the mere sight of the Daxarian king's pale expression was almost touching.

"Your Majesty, you asked to see me?" Brendan asked while loosely clasping his fingers.

Norman's eyes drifted back to the empty hearth for a moment, listening to the sound of the evening once more as he tried to sift through his thoughts for what he needed to say.

When he once again turned his attention back to Brendan, he could see the younger man watching him carefully.

"As a father, I've always been of the mindset that you love your children the best you can, and the rest will fall into place. At least that's what my father told me before I was married to my Ainsley," Norman began with a small melancholy smile. "It was . . . difficult for us, as I know you've heard, for us to successfully have both our children. Something that I am already fearful of when it comes time for Alina to have her own family."

Brendan stiffened.

"I want you to know something, Brendan Devark, and that is . . . I think my daughter takes far more after her mother than she realizes, and she is sadly completely unaware of that because I have lacked as a parent the past three years. A fact I am far from proud of."

Norman met Brendan's hard gaze, the Troivackian allowing his elder to finish his speech. "The reason I tell you of this, and my shortcomings, is I think you and I may have similar stories to share one day, and so I wanted to tell you the worst of mine so that you might better understand the kind of woman Alina's mother was, and to help you avoid repeating my own errors."

Frowning, Brendan wondered why there was an ominous note in the Daxarian king's voice.

"When Ainsley was in labor with Alina . . . there came a time when Mrs. Katelyn Ashowan told me she may not be able to save them both." Norman's eyes drifted down to the carpet as the pain of that day echoed in his entire being. "Do you know what my wife said to me?"

Brendan felt his heart quicken—he had a hunch—and just as Alina's father had predicted, it was because he somehow knew exactly what Alina would do in that situation as well.

"'Save her. No matter what, you choose our daughter, you hear me?'"

The thought of Alina saying those words to him made Brendan's gut twist and his face pale . . . a reaction that only a short while ago was impossible for even the goriest of scenes to yield from him.

"I tell you this story not to frighten you, but to prepare you for the kind of woman who will bring you to your knees in ways you didn't see imaginable. I tell you this so that you know . . . to treat her strength with the respect it deserves. I am not as strong as my wife was, and my children are the ones who are paying for that. It is a burden I will take with me to my grave. Which brings me to the final reason I tell you all this." Norman's grief and pain passed over his wizened features slowly, but eventually a look of resolution settled between his brows.

"Should the worst befall the two of you . . . Don't let whatever joy that remains in the wake of loss to forever live in its shadow."

Brendan found himself unable to look away from the Daxarian king, who looked . . . defeated.

"I give you and Alina my blessing." Norman's voice was quiet, but when he met Brendan's eyes once more, his sincerity shone through.

Awash in a strange tingling of emotion that touched him from mind to heart to toes, Brendan bowed his head to Norman. Gratitude and respect burgeoned in his chest with every breath he drew.

"If you ever bring up the possibility of a mistress again, I will ensure the rest of your life is spent in terror."

Brendan's head snapped up as he grimaced guiltily. "It will never happen again."

Norman didn't react other than to nod and raise a stern eyebrow in response.

"I entrust you with my daughter's happiness and well-being; please keep that in mind for the rest of your days."

Brendan bobbed his head in agreement once more.

"Good. Now, shall we go to dinner and see what the viscount has decided to serve in celebration of his daughter's return to the conscious world?" Norman began to rise from his seat, when Brendan suddenly remembered one other detail.

"Pardon me, but there is something that I promised to Lord Fuks that I don't quite understand."

Norman's lax posture straightened immediately. "Oh, good Gods, what did that man make you promise? I thought we had warned you sufficiently about him."

Brendan gave the king a quizzical look. "The earl stopped me this afternoon during my walk with the princess and made me promise that if you gave your blessing for Alina and me once more, and it was due to the cat named Emperor Kraken, I was to request an inner council night similar to the night of the ten fountains."

Norman's face froze as he shifted his gaze from Brendan to the wall then to the door. He seemed to be at a complete loss as to what to do, until after another moment of silence he dropped his chin to his chest and let out a long breath.

"That bloody cat, I swear to the Gods, it might be the death of me," Norman muttered under his breath before raising an irritable yet resigned face to Brendan.

"Alright, Your Majesty, please meet the inner council and me in the council room after dinner and . . . perhaps don't plan on getting any official work done first thing in the morning."

Then without another word, Norman swept out of his study to join the dinner crowd moving to the banquet hall, leaving Brendan wholly confused about what in the world he had promised Earl Fuks. He had assumed the elder was relatively harmless, if a touch mad with a poor sense of humor, so . . . whatever was this all about?

Staring around the table at the inner council, Brendan congratulated his forethought in inviting his brother along as an ally. He wasn't sure he was fond of whatever was brewing in the air.

The council themselves, however, seemed pleased about the whole arrangement, and even Lord Harris, the duke of Iones, who hadn't been present the first time, had joined. The men all wore casual clothes that made them look like civilians, and all appeared rather excited . . .

Brendan was just about to ask what in the world was supposed to happen, when the council door opened yet again, with Finlay Ashowan carrying a crate filled with bottles that he hefted onto the table.

Behind him floated in platters of meats, cheese, and fruits that drifted over and down the entire table. The viscount kicked the door closed behind himself casually with the heel of his boot.

"Alright, gentleman, we have Troivackian moonshine." Fin pulled out five bottles of the clear liquid, making Henry and Brendan perk up in their seats. "Also four bottles of wine— Kevin, no breaking into the castle's cache to steal more like last time. You're too old to act like that."

The king's assistant openly glowered, but his eyes remained fixed on the bottles of wine.

"Two bottles of absinthe—compliments of Peter and his husband, Karter Dawson—and last but not least, a bottle of rum that our Zinferan merchants have brought for us." Fin set the empty crate on the floor beneath the long wooden table and stood with his hands on his hips before the rest of the seated group.

Brendan squinted at the viscount expectantly. Was it a tasting event? What did this have to do with the fountains?

"Finlay, my boy, perhaps you can explain to the newcomers what this is about!" Lord Fuks raised his cup with a grin.

"Your Majesty, I thought you already told your future son-in-law about this?" Fin quirked an eyebrow in question to the king, who was leaning forward on his forearms in the most relaxed position the Troivackians had ever seen him in.

"Oh, no. This was entirely the fault of Lord Fuks and your Godsdamn cat."

"My *Godsdamn* cat?" Fin squinted at the king, his expression odd . . .

Norman let out a long sigh before resting his elbow on the table and pressing his face into his hand.

"I'm sorry, Fin, but I am too old to keep up this pretense. I acknowledge your cat is responsible for saving thousands of lives and has a special bond to you and your soul, but . . . he annoys the hell out of me."

Norman shook his head in apology and mild shame before he realized Fin was looking at Mr. Howard with a growing smile.

"You didn't tell him?" the viscount asked Mr. Howard as both Captain Taylor and Duke Iones were fighting off the urge to snort the drinks they had hastily poured and were beginning to sip.

"Tell me what?" Norman stared back and forth between Fin's bemused smile and Mr. Howard's reddening cheeks.

"Your Majesty . . . every time you drink a little too much you've . . . you've written me a letter from wherever you are, and you write a very detailed list of why you hate my cat. It's been happening at least biannually for . . . I want to say almost twenty years. I kept the letters if you don't believe me," Fin finished as Captain Taylor and Lord Harris succumbed to laughter.

Norman's jaw dropped as he looked to Mr. Howard for verification and found the man pointedly avoiding his gaze.

"Why did no one tell me?!"

"Honestly, they were the highlight of our Winter Solstices. It's family tradition that I read it aloud when it arrives every year," Fin reminisced fondly.

"Wait . . . did Ainsley know?!" the king demanded while his incredulousness toward his assistant rose steadily.

When Mr. Howard still refused to answer, Norman dropped his forehead to his hands.

"If it makes you feel any better, Kraken isn't exactly fond of you, either. I've stopped him pooping and . . . other things . . . all over your belongings for years whenever we would visit for official meetings." Fin chortled while grabbing a goblet and pouring himself a cup of Troivackian moonshine.

Prince Henry watched the entire exchange in confusion before glancing at his brother, who was waiting patiently.

"So what does this have to do with the fountains?" Brendan asked, bringing everyone's attention back to the matter at hand.

"Ah, well . . . the fountain incident was sort of what bonded us all in a more informal way on a deeper level. It was the cause of the ten fountain mystery, as well as the long-running one-sided love story between Mr. Howard and myself," Fin began after taking a hearty gulp of his drink.

"I swear to the Gods, Ashowan, if you bring that up again . . ." Mr. Howard grumbled over the brim of his goblet.

Fin smiled handsomely while swirling the contents of his own glass and plunking himself down on the other side of Captain Taylor.

"So more or less, powerful figures of the continent drink like young foot soldiers and cause a ruckus?" Brendan asked, his stern expression making everyone present stiffen.

"That is precisely what it is, only because it's us, the ruckus becomes the stuff of legends," Lord Harris grinned at the Troivackian king boldly. "After all, I met my beloved wife the first night I drank with the inner council. We also usually dispose of formalities and insult one another in good fun."

"I had just been hired as the Royal Court Mage," Keith Lee interjected with a fond smile. "I wound up naked on the roof of the glass tower . . . Mr. Kasim Jelani, our Royal Botanist, has never quite forgiven me for that one. I'm also unclear whether it was my own doing or Lord Ashowan's . . ."

"It was a team effort." Fin, with a warm twinkle in his eye, gave a small bow to Keith.

Henry turned to look at his brother, worried that Brendan would excuse himself as he would deem it too compromising a position to be placed in.

However the Troivackian king didn't acknowledge his brother and instead fixed his attention on the viscount, his dark eyes unreadable as ever. "There is a grave problem with this."

"Yes, Your Majesty?" Fin asked, his smile dimming slightly. "The trial for tomorrow has to be postponed to the afternoon already, so don't worry about this being a ploy to have you sleep all morning. Mr. Howard needed more time to revise your engagement contract in order for you to be present at the princess's side during the trial—"

"There isn't nearly enough moonshine for me to become as inebriated as you expect me to be."

After a single beat where everyone absorbed what had been said, the entire table of men broke out in whoops and whistles as Fin had a bottle of Troivackian moonshine float over to Brendan's and Henry's goblets and fill themselves.

"Don't worry, Your Majesty, I have more supplies in the kitchen. Congratulations on your engagement by the way!" Fin raised his goblet in a toast earning another round of good-hearted cheers from the men.

Brendan proceeded to drain the goblet in one mouthful and met the viscount's eyes levelly as though challenging him.

Fin grinned and shrugged before once again having the bottle float over and refill the king's cup.

"Say, lads, you know what we haven't played in a dog's age? Honesty or Guts," Lord Harris pointed out, the duke's smile a little too mischievous.

After glancing at each other, Henry and Brendan looked to the duke seriously.

"So," Prince Henry began. "How do we win?"

"Alina . . . why . . . do I have to be up at the crack of dawn?" Kat yawned as she continued to wipe her eyes while being wheeled out of her chamber by the princess, who was a little too chipper that morning.

"Remember how you told me of our fathers having their 'inner council meetings,' which really were just drinking escapades?" Alina asked sunnily as she pushed her friend down the corridor.

"Yeah?" Kat's unenthused response only made the princess all the more gleeful.

"Well, it just so happens, my very own beloved fiancé and his brother joined such a meeting last night, and to be quite honest, I'm a little upset that we ladies don't get to have such a rousing good time. So I figured we'd do the next best thing."

Kat slowly turned her head to look over her shoulder and noticed her friend's devious smile.

"Alina . . . does this have something to do with the lute you have strapped onto your back?"

"It does. It's the lute your brother got me for my birthday and, you know, I haven't had the time to tune it. Tell me, do you know how to play the lute, Kat?"

Her beautiful wolfish smile began lighting Kat's face. "I can't say I do."

"Good. You play, and I'll sing. I'm feeling a little pitchy this morning so don't be shy about playing loudly."

Alina dropped the lute into her friend's lap, Kat already cackling merrily as Alina wheeled her around the corner.

"You know, my dear princess, I'm beginning to like how bold that fiancé of yours is making you. Or can I take some of the credit?" Kat wondered as she prepared to give the worst performance imaginable for the hungover inner council members, who most likely had only gone to bed an hour or two earlier.

Alina smiled. "It's thanks to you both. Now, should I count us in?"

Kat shot her friend one final delighted glance over her shoulder.

"Where's the fun in that?"

Chapter 52

TRIALS AND TRIBUTES

Sitting beside her father, her crown resting atop her braided hair and her velour emerald mantle around her shoulders, Alina waited, her chin raised regally for her kidnappers to be escorted in. Her lips were painted a bright red that had at first earned many skeptical glances from the matronly crowd. It had, after all, been Kat's idea . . . she believed it would make a bold statement, and at first Alina had merely felt like a painted trollop when she'd gazed at herself in her mirror still wearing her chemise. Once dressed, however, she agreed . . .

It made her feel a little fierce.

Alina's father sat at her side wearing his official finery—his crown, his ring with the royal seal on his finger, his own emerald mantle—and his beard was trimmed to the perfect point it had always been.

"Bring in the prisoners." Norman's voice rang out imperiously as he sat with his arms casually draped over the arms of his throne. The only contradiction to the rest of his body was the cold murderous intent in his eyes.

The doors opened, and in were pulled Patrick and Dexter, both looking gaunt and dirty from their time in the castle dungeon.

While Dexter kept his dark eyes downcast and his jaw clenched shut as he strode stiffly past the whispering nobles, Patrick visibly winced and rounded his shoulders over his bony form.

"Presenting Patrick Ludoff of Ovin, and Dexter Cremon, mercenary of Rollom." Mr. Howard's tone was disdainful as he eyed the two dirty men who were being forced to their knees before their king.

"You are being charged with kidnapping, assault and battery, and plotting the murders of Her Highness, Princess Alina Reyes, Lady Katarina

Ashowan, and Mr. Reese Flint. How do you plead on these charges?" Norman's sharp, regal voice succeeded in even making Dexter recoil.

Patrick folded himself in half in a bow. "S-Sire, w-we had no idea s-she was the princess, o-or rest a-assured, we would have never—"

"Ohhh, I don't know about that. I introduced who we were that first night. Don't you remember, Patrick? I was very specific in saying you couldn't claim to not have known at a moment such as this."

Every eye in the room flew to where Lady Katarina Ashowan was being pushed by her father the viscount through the crowd of nobles in the strange contraption called a "wheelchair." The infamous house witch was typically perceived as a man incapable of looking threatening by most who had encountered him, that is, until they saw the way he regarded the two prisoners before the king.

Kat sat in the chair, her long brilliant red hair falling about her in elegant waves, while she wore a burgundy dress with a golden belt. She had her elbow leaned on the armrest of the chair, and her bright golden eyes trained on the two men with a disconcerting glint in her eyes.

"Y-Y-You made it sound like a joke!" Patrick attempted to refute, his eyes darting back and forth from the king to the young noblewoman.

"Really? Even after you realized knights were positioned at every road looking for the missing princess? Why wouldn't you verify? Or better yet, why is kidnapping people fine if they aren't nobility?" A magical glimmering streak pulsed through Katarina's eyes that made more than a few nobles around her flinch.

"Your Majesty," Dexter interrupted without sparing Katarina a glance. "Should this not be a matter discussed and decided amongst these young women's guardians? These two have no place in these talks."

There was a beat of silence in the room.

Then, Norman leaned forward in his throne, his aura deadly, when his daughter's pale hand reached out and touched his own, stopping him.

Her hazel eyes were fixed on Dexter, who still hadn't raised his gaze.

The princess stood and made her way to the edge of the dais, staring down at the men before her the entire time. No one dared to breathe.

"Dexter, you dare to insult the person who will decide your fate?"

Both men's eyes leapt up to see Alina standing before them, her blond hair alight from the sunlight pouring in from the windows, casting her in a warm glow.

"Your Highness, you are a fragile—" Dexter began. His tone was not so much chiding as it was weary, as though addressing a bratty child.

"—*I* am the one you have wronged and the one you should fear. Attempting to call me fragile won't change that. The only thing fragile about me currently is my patience for you." Alina contemplated the man emotionlessly.

Katarina smirked from her chair.

"I will speak to you directly to avoid being misunderstood," Alina continued, her voice quiet yet even. "As it pertains to myself, Reese Flint, and Lady Katarina Ashowan, I am your judge. My father is here only to bear witness to my decision after I ask clarifying questions for my fellow nobility to understand your crimes. If this concept eludes you, then there is no point to this trial."

Dexter shot her a hostile glare. Alina raised her own eyebrow at the sight, before she then turned and nodded to Brendan Devark, who stood to the right of the stairs to the throne.

The Troivackian who had formerly been a mere statue, strode forward, and plucked the mercenary up by the neck as though he weighed nothing, until his knees lifted from the floor, forcing his eyes to the princess.

"Show me such an insolent look again, and I will sanction Troivackian justice prior to your death," she informed him, her voice filled with a cutting steeliness.

There were a few women present who gasped, but their husbands quickly gripped their hands, quieting them as they, too, watched the scene transfixed.

Brendan released the man to gasp on the floor while Alina continued to look upon him without an ounce of concern.

Only Brendan, her father, and Kat knew the princess's knees had buckled the moment Dexter and Patrick had entered the room.

"If I'm already sentenced to die, why bother with this farce of a trial?" Dexter spat despite his voice rasping and the Troivackian king's presence looming nearby, as though he were prepared to hand the man into death's carriage himself.

"If you showed remorse, or apologized, asked for forgiveness . . . many reasons. You seemed a mildly intelligent man before, surely you could see multiple options. Otherwise, your earlier prediction would be correct. This is a waste of everyone's valuable time."

Patrick immediately lowered his forehead to the carpet. "I'm sorry, Your Highness! I'm sorry! Will never do it again! I swear it!"

Alina's eyes cut to him, her disapproving frown deepening

"Now you only grovel for the selfish reason of saving yourself. Not out of guilt of hurting anyone."

Taking a slow breath in, Alina looked to the back of the throne room, over the heads of the nobles watching the dramatics completely captivated.

She felt the burden then. The burden of being a fair ruler, but wanting revenge. Of wanting to keep the blood of others from her consciousness, but knowing if she did not show decisive bold judgments she could leave herself and others vulnerable.

Her gaze was drawn to Brendan.

His dark eyes locked with hers, and a deep understanding passed between the royals.

He knew exactly how she felt.

It was the reality of ruling.

The balance of being a great ruler, and also human . . .

"For the sake of transparency, you will recount to these witnesses your plans and reveal how your crimes came to be. Following that, we will hear from the primary target of your illegal actions, Reese Flint, before finally deciding the extent of your sentence."

Alina turned and strode back to her throne.

Dexter rolled his eyes until he noticed not only Brendan Devark's foreboding stare from the corner, but his brother, Prince Henry, who proceeded to crack his knuckles.

Stiffening, Dexter turned his face down toward the carpet, which happened to be just in time for Alina to have settled in her chair.

"So, Mr. Dexter Cremon? Patrick Ludoff? We are waiting to hear how this all transpired from your end," she called out imperiously.

Neither man said anything, until at long last Patrick, trembling down to the smallest hair of his head, spoke.

"R-Roscoe, he . . . he had a mar-marriage lined u-up between Lorelai's girl and the local butcher. The deal was . . . they'd split the dowry . . . th-that the bard left for her . . . and sh-she would have to keep tending Roscoe's house w-with her mother."

Alina's left hand gripped her armrest a little tighter as she resisted the urge to pick at her nails.

"T-The bard stole Lorelai and her girl . . . a-an' we couldn't find them s-so we . . . hired Dex-Dexter. H-He found out . . . that the bard had c-come to Austice. An' after we found him . . . were gonna grab him, only . . . the day we found him . . . th-there was a crowd with him at the tavern. R-Roscoe still wanted to try and fight to get him, but we stopped him—"

"The brawl." Alina's eyes widened as she spoke without managing to stop herself. She remembered the day she had first met Reese and gone to the Wet Whistle, and how they'd all fled because of the scuffle.

"Y-Yes. W-We assumed you were a commoner student of his 'cause of how you were dressed . . . S-So when we saw you with the other girl . . ."

Alina closed her eyes.

So that was why they wouldn't believe it when they kept insisting she was a princess. They had seen her looking like a commoner twice and in similar company. It made sense that given they'd first seen her at a lowly tavern, and when they kidnapped her wearing similar clothes once again, there was no reason to think she was royalty.

"Well then," Alina began, then stopped herself to swallow past a lump in her throat. She didn't want to think about what had come next.

When her eyes opened and she saw Dexter's smug expression, she didn't even need to signal to Brendan.

He had moved in a blur, grabbed the man by the back of his neck, and slammed his head forward to the ground.

Alina rose, stopping Brendan from drawing back Dexter's head to bang it a few more times for good measure.

She strode forward and slowly descended the steps until the toes of her shoes were mere inches from Dexter's face on the ground.

"You've become tiresome. In light of Patrick's testimony and your silence, you will await your sentence in the dungeon. I've given you your chance." Brendan wrenched Dexter upward once more so that he had to stare into Alina's cold gaze.

Indeed . . .

There was nothing fragile about the woman with lips as red as blood peering at him.

His eyes widened a fraction before he was hauled out of the throne room, yet he found himself unable to look away from Alina as he was dragged from her presence. Alina watched his removal without a flicker of softness, and a few nobles found themselves growing moderately wary of this new side of their princess.

Once the doors had closed behind Dexter's departure, Alina finally looked to Brendan, who bowed to her before returning to his place at his brother's side.

"We will now hear the testimony from Mr. Reese Flint," Alina announced loudly, though instantly regretted it as her lungs began to rattle.

Her eyes closed for just a moment as she took a steadying breath, then she mounted the stairs once more to return to her father's side.

Once settled in her seat, she took yet another fortifying inhale then glanced to her father, who gave her a questioning look.

She nodded to confirm she was well and turned her attention back to the doors.

Only when they opened, Reese Flint didn't sail in and start a theatrical retelling as many had come to expect. Despite the fact that he, too, had been gifted a wheelchair during his recovery, to say he entered with his usual flair would've been inaccurate.

His actual entrance surpassed everyone's expectations . . . as was his way.

When Reese Flint rolled in, his face still battered and bruised, but raised proudly, behind him was . . .

A parade.

A parade of attractive young men, women, children, a few infants, and their mothers.

At first, no one understood who they were until certain physical characteristics matching Reese's began registering amongst the crowd.

"Mr. Flint, what is . . ." Norman's voice was faint.

"Your Majesty," Reese began, bowing his head as everyone behind him proceeded to bow or curtsy, "my . . . family members wished to be here to offer support."

Norman glanced to Finlay Ashowan, whose mouth already hung open, while the viscountess, who stood in the shadows, couldn't hide her widened eyes.

"I . . . see." Glancing once more at his daughter, who looked equally as stunned, Norman cleared his throat. "Well, shall we try to wrap up this ordeal so that some introductions might be made?"

Reese grinned. "Of course, Your Majesty. I shan't leave out a single wrinkle or freckle of a detail."

He then winked at the nearest noblewoman, making the older, pretty auburn-haired woman behind him pushing his wheelchair smack his head firmly.

"Right. Certain habits are hard to change."

Unable to help herself, Alina snuck a peek at Kat, and both were unable to hide quivering smiles as the court hearing then took on a very different tone for the rest of the afternoon.

* * *

Slumped in her throne, alone in the throne room at long last, Alina gazed outside briefly at the glow of the evening sun.

It had been a long trial, though Reese Flint's dramatic retelling had definitely made things more tolerable for the final two hours . . .

Sighing, Alina closed her eyes before forcing herself to try and stand, when the doors opened once more.

Prince Henry strode in, his warm smile greeting her as she allowed herself to relax once more into her seat.

"Your Highness, dinner will be starting soon; are you not going to your chamber to rest?" he asked as he moved down the plush red aisle toward the dais.

"My maids are waiting there for me . . . and they've been a little . . . excitable since I've returned. I'm merely enjoying the quiet while I can," Alina replied before slowly straightening herself in the throne.

Henry's smile widened as he stopped before the dais then scuffed his boot on the carpet in quiet understanding.

As she stared down at the man whom she had once considered marrying, Alina felt her newfound confidence suddenly making her less nervous to study the Troivackian more closely.

"Prince Henry, do you act the way you do to protect your brother, or yourself?"

Henry's smile faded as he regarded Alina in silence for a moment. After he continued watching her face as though waiting for some other accusation, he let out a long breath, his shoulders slumping forward.

"Neither. My brother protects me as I am because he is a good man. Affability and cheer is my natural disposition, and he . . . wanted me to have the freedom to keep it. I think because he knew he never could have anything like it. I believe allowing me to remain unharmed, and in place in court at Troivack, is . . . an indulgence of his." Henry shrugged casually after his insight.

"You have no designs for power yourself?" Alina asked calmly, though her eyes remained fixed on his face, alert to any sign of a possible lie.

Henry's smile grew strained yet understanding. "No. I truly don't. I was not jesting when I once said to you I was considering seeing how I might fit here in Daxaria."

Then, shaking his head, he allowed his posture to relax. "The only thing holding me back was I didn't want to leave Brendan before making sure there was someone else by his side . . . someone to keep him human as well as a king. Trust me, I count you a blessing from the Gods. I think everything is far better like this."

His grin turned warm once again, making Alina blush.

"Did you . . ." The princess cleared her throat uncomfortably while fighting the urge to drop her gaze or pick at her nails. "Did you ever have any interest in my hand?"

Henry winced, then his expression turned apologetic. "I'm afraid not. I greatly enjoyed your company and your singing . . . but I lost my heart to someone else not long ago and it has yet to stumble on home to me. Yet another reason for me to perhaps have a change of scenery."

Nodding with a sympathetic smile of her own, Alina wearily rose from her throne and descended the steps until she stood in front of Henry, her hands clasped in front of her skirts.

"I enjoyed singing with you, too."

Henry bowed in thanks.

"I promise I will take good care of your brother. I love him quite a bit," she admitted shyly, her earlier strength and iciness long gone, making Henry regard his future sister-in-law fondly.

"I know you do. I also know you are everything to him, which may be a more challenging role to have than you realize just yet, but . . . . next year when you two marry, you'll see. Especially once in Troivack."

Alina's sweetness melted away as she stared more somberly at Henry.

"I hope that I can count on your help at least for a little while in the beginning of my time in the Troivackian court. Something tells me my trial days are only just beginning."

Henry bowed once more. "I will do my utmost."

Nodding her sincere thanks in the quiet, Alina then opened her mouth to suggest they perhaps leave to prepare for dinner, when the throne room doors opened once again. Brendan appeared and halted at the sight before him.

He surveyed his brother's and fiancée's faces coolly. Then, striding forward, he seized Alina's hand and gently pulled her away from Henry without a single word.

"Oh, uh, I will see you at dinner, Your Highness!" Alina called over her shoulder as Brendan only slowed his pace fractionally for her.

Chuckling, Henry waved after her. "You will indeed! Oh, and, Princess?"

Brendan finally stopped so that Alina could turn for Henry's final message, though he let out a small irritable grunt as he did so.

"I recommend you ask my brother about his night with your father's inner council. There is a certain story about dragon bones I think you will find *most* interesting!" Henry's eyes shone with mischief and as Alina turned to face Brendan to ask him whatever that meant, she found her fiancé looking pale and perhaps . . . a little bit green.

She smiled.

She loved getting to see all Brendan's different facial expressions.

Chapter 53

BREATH OF RELIEF

"Slowly . . . Slowly . . . Yes. Now, exhale."

Alina let out a long breath through her pursed lips; however, an unseen wisp of pollen twinged a small warning tremor from her lungs.

"Again."

She cracked an eye open and openly scowled up into her fiancé's face.

"We've done this five times. Can't we take a break?"

Brendan raised a lone black eyebrow as his obsidian eyes regarded Alina seriously.

"I want your lung capacity that of a maid's before our wedding." His gaze shifted to the forest's foliage as his calm emotionless mask recounted his expectations.

Alina grumbled irritably. "My breathing has already improved significantly with a month of my lessons from Mr. Flint. Truly, he is a gifted musician unlike any other I've seen or met before."

Brendan grunted.

"Yes, I know you don't like him, but personality aside, we can't deny his talent."

The king's grunt shifted to a low growl.

"Of course I'm careful. I always have at least two other people in the room with me during his lessons."

A snort mixed with a sharp breath left Brendan's mouth, and Alina smiled knowing she had understood him completely and soothed his worries. After a moment of Alina quietly enjoying their unique methods of communication, Brendan lowered his gaze down to his fiancée's, and once he noticed the smile, his stoic face filled with warmth.

Smiling a little brighter, Alina then leaned against the tree behind them before tilting her head to rest on Brendan's shoulder.

"I can't believe you have to leave for Troivack tomorrow." Her voice had turned wistful as the thought of saying goodbye to Brendan dampened her previous good mood.

"I'll write to you," the king reminded sternly.

"You better. You also better not write your letters like a report. Write real letters. Telling me how much you miss me and love me." Alina turned her face upward to stare into Brendan's strained features.

After a beat of him looking as though he were being strangled, Alina acquiesced that despite his best efforts, he may not be able to express himself to quite those extents.

"Alright, how about this . . . you sign each letter saying 'Love, Brendan,' and you ask me one personal question per letter. You can say you miss me whenever you work up the strength."

Brendan's shoulders and face sagged in relief as he took several gulps of air. "I believe I can manage that."

After witnessing Brendan's blatant distress, Alina couldn't help it, she broke out laughing.

"Gods . . . I cannot say enough how much I enjoy you showing your feelings around me these days."

Brendan smiled for a brief moment before once again becoming serious.

"When we are in Troivack, I will not be like this," he began cautiously.

"Except when we're alone," Alina reminded sharply. She was not going to let his newfound emotional liberation vanish that easily.

Brendan managed a twitch of his lips in confirmation, before continuing on.

"In Troivack, your expressiveness may alienate you," he said bluntly. "I know your tutors will cover this, but—"

"It's alright, I'll have Kat with me, and something tells me she'll make me look rather . . . mild by comparison." Alina was grinning again as she recalled her friend that morning cackling merrily as she and Reese Flint raced each other in their wheelchairs. Much to Annika Ashowan and the maids' chagrins . . .

It was abundantly clear to everyone that Katarina Ashowan had recovered from her wound from the previous month, but her recreational use of the wheelchair had not yet been brought up in good company.

"I worry the most about Lady Katarina's presence," Brendan announced flatly.

Alina's smile faded as his words sank in. The king worried if he had perhaps spoken too candidly, but when his beloved fiancée reached for his hand and squeezed it tenderly, he couldn't help but forget his concern.

"I believe with all my heart that Kat . . . can do absolutely anything. So as much as I, too, am uncertain about how she will fare in Troivack, I know that, one way or another, things will turn out alright."

Brendan said nothing in response as he succumbed to the gentle seduction of contentment. He could smell jasmine and lilies from the top of Alina's head, and her small hand was wrapped safely in his own . . . two elite knights and two maids waited off in the brush of the king's forest at a respectable distance to give the couple a bit of privacy.

It was a rare moment of peace, and Brendan didn't want to be the ungrateful fool who would let the time pass unappreciated.

After a long, amiable silence, Brendan lifted his cheek from the top of Alina's head, which in turn made her lean back to stare into his eyes wordlessly once more.

They knew it was time to head back into the castle.

Alina slowly began to stand with a resigned smile, when Brendan's grip on her hand tightened, stopping her from moving any farther. Pulling her into his lap, he couldn't resist brushing a chaste kiss along her lips before pressing his forehead against hers.

"Will you truly be alright leaving your father alone here in Daxaria?"

It was a question Brendan had been procrastinating asking, but it had been weighing on him for a few weeks.

Alina's eyes gradually filled with pain, and Brendan felt his chest ache.

"I'm going to miss him more than anything," she began, her voice becoming soft. "I . . . I will also worry about him like he will worry for me, but I can't wait forever for my brother."

Alina's gaze dropped and an angry flush rose in her cheeks, before she gave her head a shake, clearly choosing to move on from whatever unpleasant thought had just plagued her.

"If anything goes wrong, you know I'll be heading back here immediately to help, right?" Alina's frown and the firm line of her mouth conveyed that, while she had made her declaration a question, it most definitely was not.

Brendan nodded.

He could never ask her to completely forsake her father and original kingdom, nor would he ever want her to. He didn't want her being any other way than how she was.

"Good." Alina jerked her chin down sternly, before she once again began to try and stand, only this time Brendan stopped her with a kiss that had one of the knights clearing his throat loudly.

When they finally pulled apart, Alina couldn't help but blush as she laughed.

"I'm looking forward to not needing nannies," she whispered with a devious smile.

Brendan couldn't help it, he grinned back and lowered his own baritone voice. "Yes, I also look forward to you telling me more about what you claim your mother taught you about bedding your husband . . ."

Alina's rosiness turned into a raging scarlet at recalling the time she had teased him, making Brendan release his boom of a laugh as his fiancée dropped her burning face to her hands.

Funnily enough, the maids and knights had all stopped jumping at the sound of his laughter a while ago . . .

After all, it had grown to be rather a normal thing to hear.

One Year Later

". . . After that one slave trader got away, they're being a lot more thorough in their searches. Then he went on to say how his mother has already begun ordering dresses for me." Alina read off the last letter she had received from Brendan, as servants bustled around her carrying vases of fresh cut flowers, and garments that were being packed for her to take to Troivack.

Kat stood behind her friend, brushing her long wavy dirty blond hair and assessing the king's letter over Alina's shoulder with a raised eyebrow.

"It sounds like his mother is more excited than he is about you arriving there," Kat remarked while doing her best to keep the disapproval from her voice.

Alina gave Kat a dry glance over her shoulder indicating she had heard her friend's tone behind the comment before turning back to her letter and flipping over the parchment to read through it again—even though she had easily read it more than twenty times already.

"I'll be taking a small group of knights to stay with me permanently, as well as a few maids . . . then you, of course, but you are supposed to return after a year." Alina rose from her seat, her white silk robe rippling down her figure as she did so.

"Yes, though who knows . . . maybe I'll be a smashing success and stay there my whole life! Your Troivackian brats will need a godmother who actually has a sense of fun after all," Kat mused while plunking herself gracelessly down on Alina's bed.

"I'm relatively certain the Troivackian king will have you gagged, bound, and returned to Daxaria the moment you try to mentor one of our children." Alina grinned at her friend as she finally allowed the letter to fall to her side.

"By the way, why is it your betrothed landed in Xava? Why has he not sent word to you?" Kat asked as the seamstress let out a small yelp from the corner of the room where she was working on the finishing touches of Alina's wedding dress.

When Alina and Kat realized that it had just been Kraken who had startled the poor woman by suddenly appearing under the skirts, they returned their attentions to their conversation.

"He said he needed to help your father with something, actually . . . how long has the viscount been gone did you say?" Alina wondered with a frown.

Kat let out a long breath as she squinted toward the ceiling.

"Let me see . . . Tam and Likon have been gone since Beltane, but returned to the estate in Austice last night, allegedly. Da left about a month after their original departure? He said he was going to . . . Rollom. Or was it Sorlia? Maybe he went to both!" Kat shrugged. "All I am excited for is there finally being an end to my lessons on Troivackian etiquette and nobles; my mother has been driving me mad!" She flopped back onto the bed, her long red hair rumpling beneath her.

"I thought your mother's lessons were wonderful. She was so informative and insightful . . . she made it sound all so interesting!" Alina smiled at her friend's scowling expression knowing that she was intentionally annoying her ever so slightly.

"I thought it was a pain studying with Tam, then you had to come along! Always on time, always clean, always attentive—"

"Never halfway through a turkey leg with the grease covering my face and wearing men's britches . . ." Alina added casually, earning her friend's well-worn mischievous smirk as she once again sat up.

"Was there any more information about the rebellion in the letter?" Kat asked before leaning against the bedpost.

Alina cast a hasty glance around them to make sure none of her maids had overheard her friend's question.

"No. Remember, we're trying not to alarm too many people. Otherwise, there might be some nobles who try to make me stay here." The princess dropped her voice and moved closer to the redhead while feigning a casual expression.

"Right . . ." Kat sighed. "Well, at least that'll give me something to look forward to . . . watching the Troivackians train for battles. I'm curious how different they are from the Daxarian soldiers!"

Alina giggled. "You just want to find a husband of your own, admit it!"

Kat snorted. "Now that Tam is actually working to take over as viscount, all I need to do is make sure I don't annoy him too much so that he agrees to taking care of me for the rest of my life. That way I can keep doing whatever I like!"

Alina's mouth twisted with worry. "Don't you ever wish that—"

"Your Highness! His Majesty, the king of Troivack, has arrived!" Paula, the maid, burst into Alina's room; she was utterly breathless as she doubled over—she had clearly run the entire way.

Without a second glance at Kat, Alina tossed the letter on her bed and flew out of her chamber, her silk robe clutched up in her hands to stop her from tripping.

"Your Highness! You shouldn't run out only wearing— Ah!'" Paula was cut off as a painful stitch in her side made her double over once again.

Kat stood leisurely, crossed the room, and patted the girl's back while staring after her friend with a knowing grin.

"Don't worry, she's wearing a shift underneath . . . I think . . . if not, a little fresh air on the breasts is probably rather invigorating."

Paula whimpered, and Kat proceeded to stroll out of the room merrily, her arms swinging as she slowly followed her friend.

It was going to be a wedding to remember, there was no doubt in her mind.

Alina darted past servants carrying linens for the guest rooms, stewards carrying trunks, and maids hauling buckets of water for baths, finally skidding to a halt at the top of the grand stairs leading down to the entrance hall.

There, standing with his back to her, his black hair curling near the nape of his neck, stood her fiancé as he spoke with two other men she couldn't see past his giant figure.

"Brend— Your Majesty!" Alina called out, her breath hitching in her throat. Her lips split into a smile when Brendan turned around and stared up at her, revealing a short trimmed beard he hadn't had last she'd seen him.

For a moment he looked utterly awestruck, as though he were seeing the Goddess herself.

Though the warmth of the midafternoon sun setting her hair aglow and her incandescent smile was successful in stilling more than just the Troivackian king as everyone present in the castle entrance hall gawked at the princess's loveliness.

Then, Brendan's face broke out into a smile and Alina picked up the hem of her robe once more as she began trotting down the stairs, gradually picking up speed as he strode toward her at the same time.

By the time Alina had reached the final three steps she launched herself into his arms, one of her slippers falling to the floor as she buried her face in his broad shoulder and he held her tightly, kissing the side of her head.

When she leaned back, he had already picked her up so that her head was above his, which gave her the perfect opportunity to kiss him soundly.

After a rather lengthy moment that no one bothered to interrupt, Brendan set Alina back down, his eyes filled with warmth and happiness.

Reaching up to caress his bearded cheek, Alina smiled up at him. "Hello."

As he took her hand from his cheek and kissed her fingertips, Brendan bent his forehead forward, prompting her to do the same until they were pressed against each other. "Hello. Did you happen to run here?"

Alina felt as though her face would break from her smile, unable to contain her joy a second longer. "I'm as fit as a maid now."

"It seems you have become a princess of potential in my absence," Brendan growled before kissing her, the note of pride not lost on Alina.

"I'm so happy you're here," she whispered excitedly, her eyes sparkling up at him without a care in the world.

"I brought you a wedding present," Brendan murmured quietly as though in a daze that he didn't quite want to break free of.

Alina looked at her betrothed with a laugh. "You managed to say you missed me twice over the span of a year, and now you mean to tell me you even thought to bring me a present? Was it Henry's idea?"

Brendan cleared his throat, and opened his mouth to respond, when he was interrupted.

"Glad to see you're doing well, baby sister."

Alina's face froze, then slowly paled as her eyes widened while continuing to stare at Brendan. She'd become unable to move as she searched her fiancé's face as though waiting to see if she had imagined the familiar voice that had just called out to her . . .

Her heart pounded violently in her chest.

Then Brendan straightened and turned to look at the man who had spoken.

There, with his long wavy dirty blond hair tied back from his weathered, unshaven face, in peasant clothes, with eyes the same as her own . . .

Alina stepped forward on trembling legs.

"Eric."

Epilogue 1

THE HOUSE WITCH
CHRISTMAS CHRONICLE

M *any years ago . . .*
     Likon sat huddled in the corner as the evening patrons began to trickle in.

He did his best to be as small as possible, hoping that he remained unnoticed until night settled over the housetops of Austice. The chilly eve before the Winter Solstice had been a sunny one . . . there wasn't a cloud in the sky, and the sunset was especially radiant with bright purples and pinks over the white caked roofs.

He comes tonight . . . and tonight . . . I'm going to ask him . . . A particularly bawdy laugh pulled Likon from his determined thoughts, making him grip his paper-thin pants in his hand as he reminded himself to not let his light brown eyes wander where they shouldn't.

Dena will be down soon, the lad thought to himself. *By then, the room will be half full, and I can hide by the empty crates.*

A small flush of excitement started in the pit of his belly. There was the taste of magic in the air, and it took every fiber of his willpower not to fidget with giddiness.

An hour passed, and there was nowhere near the normal amount of business on the floor.

Likon frowned as his anxiety deepened.

Normally the room was so packed with noise and perfume that one's senses were impaired without having imbibed a single beverage from the well-stocked bar.

At least Dena isn't here yet . . . he lamented while trying to stave off the sinking feeling that his plans would all fall to waste.

He was just beginning to bolster his hopes up again, when the few patrons who had come in began to leave . . .

"What's happening?!" Likon's pained whisper brought tears to his eyes as the room cleared out, and he felt himself shrink even farther back into the corner, his bottom aching from being cooped up on the hard floor for so long.

Then . . . the clatter of heels sounded above his head.

Closing his eyes tight, Likon listened with utter defeat as the women filed down the stairs he leaned against.

He didn't want to look into their faces.

Some were beautiful, some merely painted beautiful.

Yet painted or real, their features always arranged into looks of pity, annoyance, or exasperation whenever they saw him.

He didn't want to see that.

Not tonight.

Not when he had been about to ask the jolly elf that came on the eve of Winter Solstice to deliver a magic favor. Sometimes the spirit elf bestowed someone good luck, or a well-knitted pair of mittens . . . or perhaps a year of good health.

However, Likon had wanted to ask the Winter Solstice spirit named Osik for a very special magical gift. Even if he never received another gift as long as he lived.

The ladies were all talking and laughing amongst themselves, leaving Likon completely unnoticed on the floor in his corner.

He was sure Dena was there with them, and that meant he shouldn't move no matter what unless he wanted to get the scolding of a lifetime, and landing himself in trouble on Solstice's eve on top of failing to meet Osik was more than he could handle.

A swish of colorful muslin passed his vision, but instead of opening his eyes he made himself even smaller. He knew staring often drew attention, so it was best to look away and be as small and forgettable as possible.

Besides, if no one wanted to see him, he was easier to overlook anyway.

"Why're you here alone?"

Likon tensed, and he gripped his pants even tighter, his heart beating wildly in his chest.

Until he realized . . . the voice asking the question didn't sound like one of the women; it sounded like another child.

Slowly lifting his teary gaze, unsure of whether or not he should trust what he heard in the din, the small boy risked glancing at the one who had spoken to him.

He found himself staring into a round face with two golden eyes staring back at him. An expensive white cloak with fur around the sleeves, hood, and two pom-poms hanging from the cloak's clasp covered a festive burgundy dress. Despite the hood, he could see most of the girl's fiery red hair had been left down, while two chunks had been wound into buns atop her head.

"Hi! Why are you crying? It's Winter Solstice! Or almost . . ."

The girl looked to be two or three years younger than Likon, but he was too startled by her unnatural eyes to mention that to her.

"Hellooo? Hiiii? Are you okaaaay?" the little girl asked, tilting her head curiously at the boy before her.

"I-It's none of your business!" Likon burst out while feeling a fresh wave of tears threaten to fall down his cheeks.

"Okay! Did you wanna play? My brother is at home and it's kinda boring here alone." The small child let out a huff of irritated air before straightening and looking around herself displeased.

"Y-Your brother?" Likon managed while wiping his nose with his sleeve.

"Yeah . . . this year he got weird . . . we used to get to do all kinds of fun things together, but he's scared all the time now." The girl shook her head in a way that made Likon think she was imitating someone.

"H-How old are you?" he asked while trying to sit upright, only to wince in pain. He had been sitting crouched for some time.

"I'm five! How about you?" the girl answered happily while holding up her hand with all digits extended.

"S-Seven." Likon peered around the room nervously. Surely she was the daughter of someone important—she would draw unnecessary attention to him if he wasn't careful—but . . . what was she doing there?!

"Ah, you don't look that old, but then again you're on the floor. Here, I'll help you up! I'm told I'm tall for my age!" The young girl offered her hand with a cheeky grin.

Likon accepted her help gingerly. If she kept talking to him, there was no way he wasn't going to be discovered, and it was better if he started figuring out a way to head back upstairs anyway.

"My name's Kat, what's yours?"

Likon hastily wiped the residual moisture from his face when he faced the girl again, though he was surprised she was quite short despite thinking she was tall . . .

"I'm Likon. C-Call me Lin."

"Lin! Sounds like a girl's name . . . you're pretty for a boy!"

Likon gritted his teeth and blushed. "I *am* a boy though."

"Yeah? So? Boys can be pretty. My da's pretty. At least that's what all the castle maids say." The little girl named Kat recited this with a shrug.

Desperate to change the topic, Likon crossed his arms over his chest. "You're pretty short."

"An' you're scrawny! Whose son are you? I thought you all had apartments upstairs?" The little girl was unbothered by the boy's earlier observation as she pointed toward the ceiling with a red eyebrow raised.

"I-I do, I just . . . I-I wanted to . . ." Clenching his fists at his side, he knew he couldn't say it. Knew he couldn't admit to the childish hope he had clung to deep inside his heart.

"Are you hoping to see Osik too?!"

Likon took in a sharp breath as his eyes opened wide. He opened his mouth to exclaim his agreement, but he bit his lip and furrowed his brow instead.

"N-No!"

"I really want to meet him! Do you think he grants wishes? I know he gives magic gifts, but what about magic wishes?! I want to ask for something special." The girl named Kat looked around nervously before leaning forward conspiratorially, her hand cupped around her mouth. "I want to heal my brother. I don't think he's right in the head, but I feel mean saying it."

Likon felt any residual tension in his body fade.

Something about Kat's earnest confession dissolved an invisible barrier within himself.

"I . . . I wanted to . . . to ask to work for him."

Kat blinked her brilliant glittering eyes that were prettier than any tinsel in all of Austice up at him.

"You want a job for your magic Winter Solstice gift?"

"I want to be useful, and . . . I-I want to be . . . wa-wan-wanted." Likon burst out into tears. He hadn't meant to. He didn't want to hear the women exclaiming how childish he was being, or how crying boys were weak. Or see their looks of disgust, or their backs as they ran away.

Didn't want to hear Dena apologizing for him.

"Well, *I* want you to play with me, does that count?"

The small tug on his sleeve made Likon raise his tearstained face to the same blazing eyes that were slowly consuming his awareness.

"If you want, I can ask my da and mum to give you work! They always say yes. If my mum says no, I'll ask my da again later. Either way, it's okay!"

The small girl threw her hands in the air happily. She'd found a solution to all his plights, so why wouldn't she feel celebratory?

"Who . . . How . . . What kind of work do your parents do?"

Kat pondered the question for a while, but eventually she shrugged, which coincidentally made her white hood fall off her hair.

"No idea! I just know we see a lot of people an' try to make them happy!"

Likon frowned. "Pimps?"

"What's a 'pimp'?" Kat blinked in confusion and genuine interest.

Likon slapped his hand to his face and began to laugh. "Do they protect women in exchange for money?"

Kat thought hard again, her cherub face growing serious. "I don't know that they take money, but they protect everybody."

Likon stilled. "Even male prostitutes?"

"Prosti-whats?" Kat looked up at him in open bewilderment.

A strange tweak of fear entered Likon's mind as he once again surveyed the girl's clothing.

It was incomparable to any material he had ever seen come in through Madam Mathilda's doors, and she appeared completely innocent, well fed, and even her smell was refined . . .

"Kat! I told you that you shouldn't run off like that— Oh, hello!"

Likon cowered away from the adult voice above him.

"Mum! This is . . . shit! I forgot already! What was your name again?"

"Katarina! Where did you learn that word?!"

"Raymie said it this morning in the kitchen!" Kat answered the adult fearlessly, her voice as cheery as before.

An irritated sigh left the woman's mouth, and there was the dreadful pause that Likon knew all too well. The gap of time when someone was sizing him up and deciding whether or not they had to bother to be kind or not.

"What is your name?" The woman's voice had softened considerably when she turned from the redheaded child.

The boy felt his trembling intensify as the room around him began to fall quiet.

"L-Likon, ma'am."

"I see. Likon, where is your mother? Is she down here? Were you looking for her?"

The boy flinched as his hands curled into fists at his sides and his trembling began to intensify under the watchful gazes of those around him. He wished the floor could open up and swallow him whole, but then, it got worse.

"LIKON! WHAT IN THE— My lady, I am so terribly sorry!"

Face burning, Likon nervously looked up into the bright green eyes of his sister. Wincing at her fearful, yet angry stare, he swiftly looked back at the floor, retreating into himself even more.

Wait, did she just say "my lady"?!

"What is your name?" There was an edge in the noblewoman's voice that hadn't been there when she'd been speaking to Likon, but hearing it directed at his sister made his blood run cold.

"I-I'm Dena, my lady. I apologize, my brother was supposed to be upstairs. He must've snuck out to come see me, but he knows better. I-I can't apologize enough! Please don't—"

"What is going on?!"

Likon's stomach roiled when he noticed Dena's pale purple skirts pooling on the ground. The loud male voice had brought her to her knees, which meant . . .

The lad stole a glance up and saw the tall imposing redhead, his clothes making his nobility apparent.

The redheaded girl named Kat threw up her arms excitedly upon the man's arrival. "Da! This is Likon! He wants a job! What's a pimp?"

The silence that followed was heavy.

Too heavy.

Likon wondered if silence was capable of killing.

"That . . . is a question for when you're older. Now, Likon, was it?"

The boy couldn't look up. He couldn't face the disparaging glare the noble had to have. He wished with all his might he had stayed up in his room.

A pair of golden eyes filled his vision yet again.

"Hey, don't be scared! My da and mum are nice! Even when I accidentally eat all the cookies my da made this morning he still—"

"That was you?! I have to apologize to Raymond! Kat, you should have said someth—" The lord's voice was cut short when his daughter grabbed the boy's hand and yanked him forward.

"Da! Likon!" Kat repeated while completely ignoring the earlier trouble she had revealed to have caused.

A knee clad in fine black material entered the boy's line of sight through his tears.

"Hey, we aren't upset or going to hurt you."

Likon felt his cheeks burn in embarrassment and his lips quiver, and he couldn't hold back the sob that then escaped from his mouth as he shrank away from the adults.

A pair of firm, warm arms wrapped around him then as he wept. The feeling of being safe and comforted crept into his bones, and for some reason that made him cry all the harder.

"It's alright," the soft male voice soothed before picking the boy up and slowly moving away from the curious stares.

Likon registered that he was being carried up the stairs toward the rooms he was banned from, but something in him couldn't be bothered to care.

"Please, my lord! Have mercy on my brother! He-he hasn't been quite right since we lost our parents two winters ago!" Dena called out frantically.

The nobleman who Likon still hadn't glimpsed the face of stopped halfway up the stairs.

"I just want to allow him to calm down privately; he will not be punished, I promise."

Likon then became all too aware of how he felt big and awkward being carried. Everyone had seen him be treated like a baby!

"Sir, please set me down. I-I'm fine now."

The lad felt wood under his shoes, and finally, he lifted his gaze up . . . and it was then he met the bright blue gaze of a man who looked far too delicate to be dangerous. His red hair also confirmed that the little girl named Kat was his own flesh and blood.

"Likon, mind telling me what has you so upset?" the nobleman asked while crouching down.

The pattering of small feet rushing up the stairs interrupted the boy's response as he turned and saw the redheaded girl from before.

"Da! He needs a job!"

"Yes, I heard you, Kitty Kat. What I need is to listen to him right now." The lord's voice was firm, but kind, yet his shimmering eyes seemed strange to Likon.

Fin waited patiently for a few moments, but when the boy remained silent and awkward, the redhead glanced at their audience of his wife, daughter, and a sea of prostitutes.

"Let's head to the office, shall we?"

The little boy shook his head, his eyes growing round. "M-Ms. Nonata doesn't like interruptions at this time."

The lord smiled ruefully. "Oh, don't worry, she won't mind if I ask."

The redhead gestured up the stairs, and aware that he couldn't argue with a noble, Likon ascended the rest of the staircase and headed toward the office. His heart hammering in his chest, he hoped he wouldn't get flogged too badly for causing such a disturbance.

The lord didn't seem the cruel kind, but then again, some people weren't cruel when you'd first meet them.

I'll just make something up and apologize to Dena later, Likon reasoned to himself as the lord knocked softly on Ms. Nonata's door.

"I said I'd be down in a moment!"

The redheaded man chuckled then cast a wink down at Likon, who had retreated three steps and clutched his hands in front of himself nervously.

Opening the door, the lord stepped into the office and held up a single finger to the boy to indicate it wouldn't be long.

"Don't worry!"

Likon nearly jumped out of his skin when he heard the little girl at his side yet again, only this time her mother was right behind her.

When Likon peered up into the noblewoman's dark eyes, he was momentarily stunned by how beautiful she was . . . and then frightened by the cool depths behind her gaze. He knew eyes like those were dangerous.

Except . . . the lady smiled and, even though Likon could tell she was a dangerous person, he also could tell that she didn't want him to be afraid of her.

"My mum says she'll make sure we find you a job, as long as your sister says it's okay!"

"Wh-What kind of job?" Likon asked nervously as he hesitantly looked back at the little girl named Kat.

"She says I need someone to keep me out of trouble— I promise it isn't that often." The way the little girl suddenly avoided his gaze made Likon suspect it was even more often than one could imagine.

"Or you could keep my brother company, or both! We'll make sure you get to eat, learn, and play! The learning part can be boring, but Da says I'll be happy about it later."

Staring dumbfounded back up at the noblewoman's smile, Likon felt himself dare to ask an impertinent question in the face of such a generous offer.

"W-Why? You must get th-thousands of k-kids like me who want those jobs."

The lady's face softened, which helped Likon feel a little more at ease.

"It's you because Kat likes you, and sometimes the Gods arrange fate for us for a reason. We just have to accept such blessings. At least my husband says so."

The door beside Likon opened and out stepped the tall lord, his kind gaze smiling down at him. Likon then looked back to the noblewoman, then the brilliant gaze of their daughter, and . . . he suddenly felt like the most special person in the world.

"Wh-Who are you people?"

The tall redheaded man squatted down so that he was eye level with Likon.

"My name is Fin, and we are a family who would love to have you join us, if that is something you really would want."

"B-But—"

"It's okay!" Kat burst out, stepping forward happily and grabbing Likon's hand, making the poor boy blush. "We're the Ashowans! I told you, we help people!"

Likon's jaw dropped as he beheld one of the most famous families in all Daxaria.

They were all smiling at him, and as a strange sense of magic and wonder rose in his chest, he felt the corners of his quivering mouth begin to turn upward, right before he burst out into tears from sheer joy.

"Th-This is the best Solstice of my life!"

Then, three pairs of arms encircled him, making him feel happier than he ever had before.

Epilogue 2

CULMINATING CIRCUMSTANCES

Duke Sebastian Icarus of Troivack surveyed the vineyard imperially, his posture casual, but his instincts sharp. He glared through the small round spectacles perched on the end of his long nose, barely daring to breathe so as to remain as inconspicuous as possible.

"I see you're early, as usual."

Sebastian did his best not to react, though he was cursing horribly in his mind.

He hated how that wretched commoner always managed to sneak up on him from behind.

Turning slowly, he faced the half-blooded Troivackian with a disdainful lift of his eyebrow. "Of course. My time is precious. What news have you, Mr. Zephin?"

Leochra Zephin had chestnut brown hair that looked auburn in the summer, and his face was pale instead of olive . . . the only indicator his father was a Troivackian was his dark eyes.

"I have three noble families willing to help our cause." Leo smiled coldly. "The Troivackian prince is too well known as a fool. The scandal of his love affair with that gypsy has dissuaded most nobility from wanting him as king, even if it means he is more susceptible to their . . . suggestions."

Sebastian waited expectantly; he did not like the slow build to the more important information.

"However, the idea of murdering the Daxarian princess before she reaches the palace in Vessa for her coronation was incredibly well received. Our king would have no choice but to choose a Troivackian queen more fit for ruling our people. Perhaps even a daughter of one of our esteemed dukes . . ." Leo gestured his hand in the air.

Sebastian glowered in response.

"I do not wish to force one of my idiot daughters on His Majesty. Our king was the perfect leader until the legendary Daxarian foolishness rubbed off on him. I've heard rumors that he has even been known to laugh when the princess of Daxaria is present. Such weakness in our great leader must be eradicated early on."

Leo's hands dropped to his side as he tilted his head over his right shoulder, an amused glint in his dark eyes. "It's said our king truly loves Her Highness. Are you certain that your plan is a wise one?"

The duke rolled his eyes before making a "tsking" sound.

"An error in judgment. Our king has been perfect for much of his life, he is allowed one mistake. Once he is free of the Daxarian princess's spell, I'm sure he will return to his senses, and if not . . ."

"We could see about one of Princess Nora's sons becoming king, though they, too, were raised in Daxaria—as fishermen no less," Leo suggested while casually laying his hand on the hilt of his sword.

"A fact we could hide assuming they aren't grinning simpletons . . . a good idea. See if you might find some of the former princess's offspring. Though I still prefer the idea that we try to make Prince Henry king and have him as a puppet. It would make matters much easier to manage."

Sebastian touched his gloved hand to his temple as he felt the threat of a stress headache draw nearer.

"What about waiting to see if the princess of Daxaria even survives birthing her first child? It would negate much of the threat, and the offspring would be raised here in Troivack. Should we need a puppet, we could always have King Brendan Devark killed and place a toddler on the throne while more *seasoned* nobility manage the kingdom."

Sebastian was unable to mask his surprise. A compelling argument, given how well known it was that the last Daxarian queen barely managed to survive the births of her children.

That type of thinking was one of the reasons he had agreed to stoop so low as to partner with a commoner in his wish to gain better control over the Troivackian court.

Leochra Zephin had a broad scope of the world, and he often saw situations and opportunities others wouldn't even dare to entertain.

Not to mention he had organized multiple mercenary groups to operate under him, bringing to the table several hundred seasoned warriors who were uninvolved with the Troivackian court unless paid to be otherwise.

"I'd prefer a pure-blooded Troivackian on the throne. We will try to kill the princess shortly after she arrives," Sebastian announced finally after giving his options another few moments of serious thought.

Leo bowed.

"As you wish. By the way, Your Grace, what shall I do with the most recent delivery of Zinferan slaves? If we attempt to sell so many of them at once, it'd raise suspicions now that the Troivackian king has begun to focus his attention on eradicating the trades."

Sebastian began striding toward his horse on the edge of the vineyard, though he didn't particularly like turning his back on the mercenary leader.

"Try to sell them at a discounted price in groups to nobility in the south. It won't seem as strange down there as opposed to the north." The duke pulled his gloves on more snugly as he reached for his horse's reins.

"What of *the* slave?"

At this, Sebastian hesitated.

He knew it was a bad idea to keep any evidence of his involvement in his house, but . . . that particular one . . . that boy . . . he was something special.

"Bring him to my keep. I shall hide him until I go on a lengthy journey. I will claim him as a bastard of mine I've brought back to serve under my house," Sebastian explained, though it was more to himself than for the sake of the mercenary leader, who watched as the duke mounted his horse with a swish of his black cape.

"Very well," Leo replied pleasantly.

The duke kicked his heels into his horse's sides, but the animal failed to begin its trot as four men wielding swords emerged from the vineyard. Their deadened stares and silent footfalls made Sebastian recoil.

"Your Grace, I believe you forgot that this month was when my payment was due."

Leo's easygoing tone only made the duke feel even more disturbed as he reached with fumbling fingers for the gold sack attached to his saddle.

"An oversight. Here." He thrust the sack in Leo's direction, never taking his eyes off the men closing in on him.

Sebastian of course had his own guards nearby, but the question was how quickly they could get to him before any serious damage was done.

Leo plucked the gold from the Duke's hand then bowed.

"Until next time, Your Grace."

Sebastian gave an indignant sniff before once again pressing his heels into his horse's sides, urging the beast forward, and this time, his path was clear.

Leo smiled at the duke's back as he heated the gold in his hand and nodded to his men, his dark eyes shifting unnaturally in the moonlight.

"It looks like we need to arrange a proper welcome party for the Daxarian princess, men!"

Tam stared blankly at the desk heaped with books and letters before him.

He didn't even dare to breathe out of genuine concern that one of the piles might fall in an avalanche.

A strong hand reached up and clasped his shoulder. "Sorry to say with both your da, and you gone, things got piled up," Likon noted lightly.

"How . . . urgent is it that this all gets dealt with?" Tam asked slowly.

"Oh . . . definitely before the next full moon."

"In three days?"

"That's the one. Time does fly when you travel." Likon patted Tam's shoulder twice before strolling toward the door a little too spritely.

"I'm supposed to get through this *and* attend the princess's wedding tomorrow?" The future viscount's voice rose along with his eyes—a sure sign he was more than a little distressed.

Likon swung around wearing a bright half grin. "Aren't you glad you decided to start taking on more duties to prepare for becoming a viscount?"

Tam looked back at the desk, swallowed, then turned back to Likon. "You know, I've always thought of you like a brother . . ."

"Not a chance, my lord." Likon bowed dramatically. "The pleasure is all yours. How could a mere peasant like myself even *dream* of handling what the most sacred class known as nobility can?"

"Why don't you ask my husband? You know. The one who used to be a cook."

Likon nearly leapt out of his skin at the sound of Annika's voice behind him.

Tam grinned and waved to his mother.

The viscountess wore her usual Troivackian style dress that was cooler during the summer months. A navy blue flowing chiffon that made her dark eyes all the more striking.

Annika smiled and nodded to her son. "Hi, my love; I am glad you two made it back safely."

"Hi, Mum, has Da returned yet?" Tam greeted while stepping farther away from the nightmare of work on the desk of his father's study.

"I received word that he has just arrived at the castle with King Brendan Devark."

"That's good." Tam put his hands into his pockets and lowered his gaze comfortably to the floor again.

"Where do you think you're going?" Annika's sharp voice made Tam realize that Likon had silently made his way over to the window and was in the process of climbing out.

Likon froze and slowly turned his head until he could make eye contact with his mistress, a strained smile stretching his features.

"I . . . was . . . going to . . . write my report for you, Lady Ashowan," he managed to say despite sounding strangled.

Annika shared a wry look with her son before gracefully folding her arms across her middle and gliding forward.

"You are aware that if you are set on becoming my son's *assistant* with a pay raise, paperwork is part of the job, correct?"

Tam grinned triumphantly behind his mother, making Likon narrow his gaze for a brief moment before removing his foot from the window ledge and turning back around dejectedly.

"I thought I was *your* protégé," he muttered as he returned to the mother and son.

"You are, but that is not a long-term trade befitting a man of your talents," Annika began while staring at Likon with a knowing glint in her eyes.

"I would happily apply to be Lady Katarina's bodyguard then." Likon bowed hastily and hoped that his mistress failed to see any hint of emotion on his face.

Unfortunately for him, she did.

Annika's brows grew tense before she shared a knowing look with her son, who gave a small shrug of his shoulders and shook his head.

"Likon, my daughter is going to Troivack for a year. We can't have you being isolated in one location while I am still trying to settle all the brothels here in Daxaria and Lord Ashowan inspects the schools. The viscount may even choose to accept the title of duke at long last if our plans go accordingly." Annika's tone had taken on a firmness that left no room for debate.

Likon raised himself back up, his expression composed . . . but entirely too composed. It was obvious he was hiding his true emotions on the matter.

"Go have a bath and a hot meal, then return to help Tam with the viscount's work." Annika's voice softened as she reached out and gently touched Likon's arm, her dark eyes warm as she tried to soften herself for the sake of a boy she considered her adopted son.

Likon swallowed the words everyone knew he wished to say.

Once again pivoting toward the window, he strode forward and proceeded to climb out, as was his preferred method of getting to his room on the other side of the estate.

Once it was certain that he was no longer within earshot, Annika faced her son, her expression sorrowful. "So he has yet to let go of his feelings for Kat?"

Tam nodded. "I know Kat has told him several times that nothing has changed, and despite his best efforts, nothing has changed for him, either."

Annika let out a long sigh before raising her hand to her mouth and gingerly biting her thumbnail.

"Perhaps Kat being gone in Troivack will help matters, though I do still worry about how she will fare over there . . ."

Tam reached out and patted his mother's shoulder. "I'd be more worried for the Troivackian courtiers than Kat."

Annika dropped her forehead to her hand before letting out a short chuckle.

"I'm not so sure of that, Tam. As much as I've tried to impress upon you both what Troivack is like, I worry you think I am exaggerating things. I'd like Kat to learn to curb her more reckless impulses, but should things get out of hand I may even acquiesce to sending Likon there to handle things."

Removing his hand from her shoulder, Tam stepped so that he stood in front of his mother. "Let's try and have a bit of faith in my sister. As difficult as it is to believe she won't find any source of trouble . . . at the very least we have the king's word, and we know Alina adores her."

Annika nodded before looking to the ceiling, as though silently asking the Goddess for a miracle on her daughter's behalf that she stay out of trouble for once.

"Well . . . I suppose we've done all we can to prepare her. Now . . . shall we go get ready for the rehearsal dinner? I imagine it wouldn't be a bad idea for us to go and lend a hand given how chaotic the castle must be right now."

Tam let out a long breath.

Weddings sounded horribly tiring, time consuming, and worst of all, crowded.

He had avoided attending nearly all such events, but this one he knew he couldn't miss . . . not when Alina was his friend and his sister's best friend.

"I'm sure our presence won't help the wedding preparations go any faster," Tam called out to his mother as she opened the chamber door. He was hoping he could convince her to wait until the very last minute to depart in order to minimize the time he was expected to socialize.

"I'm surprised at you, love. I would have thought given that Alina is see-ing her brother for the first time in years that—"

"What?" Tam's eyes shot up to his mother's face, shocked.

Glancing over her shoulder, Annika's composed expression shifted to a grim smile.

"Ah . . . I see you and Likon haven't heard. You both need to work on staying informed no matter where you are."

Tam frowned and opened his mouth to retort, but he never got the chance.

"The crown prince of Daxaria has returned as of this afternoon, Tam. Your father and the Troivackian king brought him, and you better believe there is going to be more than a little excitement about that."

THE END
(FIN)

He just wanted a decent book to read ...

Not too much to ask, is it? It was in 1935 when Allen Lane, Managing Director of Bodley Head Publishers, stood on a platform at Exeter railway station looking for something good to read on his journey back to London. His choice was limited to popular magazines and poor-quality paperbacks – the same choice faced every day by the vast majority of readers, few of whom could afford hardbacks. Lane's disappointment and subsequent anger at the range of books generally available led him to found a company – and change the world.

'We believed in the existence in this country of a vast reading public for intelligent books at a low price, and staked everything on it'
Sir Allen Lane, 1902–1970, founder of Penguin Books

The quality paperback had arrived – and not just in bookshops. Lane was adamant that his Penguins should appear in chain stores and tobacconists, and should cost no more than a packet of cigarettes.

Reading habits (and cigarette prices) have changed since 1935, but Penguin still believes in publishing the best books for everybody to enjoy. We still believe that good design costs no more than bad design, and we still believe that quality books published passionately and responsibly make the world a better place.

So wherever you see the little bird – whether it's on a piece of prize-winning literary fiction or a celebrity autobiography, political tour de force or historical masterpiece, a serial-killer thriller, reference book, world classic or a piece of pure escapism – you can bet that it represents the very best that the genre has to offer.

Whatever you like to read – trust Penguin.